PLAGUE ARCANIST

FRITH CHRONICLES #4

SHAMI STOVALL

PLAGUE ARCANIST

FRITH CHRONICLES #4

Published by
CS BOOKS, LLC

This is a work of fiction. Names, characters, places, and incidents either are the product of author imagination or are used fictitiously, and any resemblance to actual persons, living or dead, business establishments, events, or locales, is entirely fictional.

Cover Design: Darko Paganus

IF YOU WANT TO BE NOTIFIED WHEN SHAMI STOVALL'S NEXT BOOK RELEASES, PLEASE VISIT HER WEBSITE OR CONTACT HER DIRECTLY ATs.adelle.s@gmail.com

ISBN: 978-1-7334428-2-4

Created with Vellum

To John, who never stopped believing.
To Beka, for her unflinching loyalty.
To Gail and Big John, for the family.
To Ann, for playing Volke's matchmaker.
To Brian Wiggins, for giving a voice to the characters.
To Tiffany, Mary, & Dana, for all the input.
To my Facebook group, for naming the khepera 'Akhet.'
And finally, to everyone unnamed, thank you for everything.

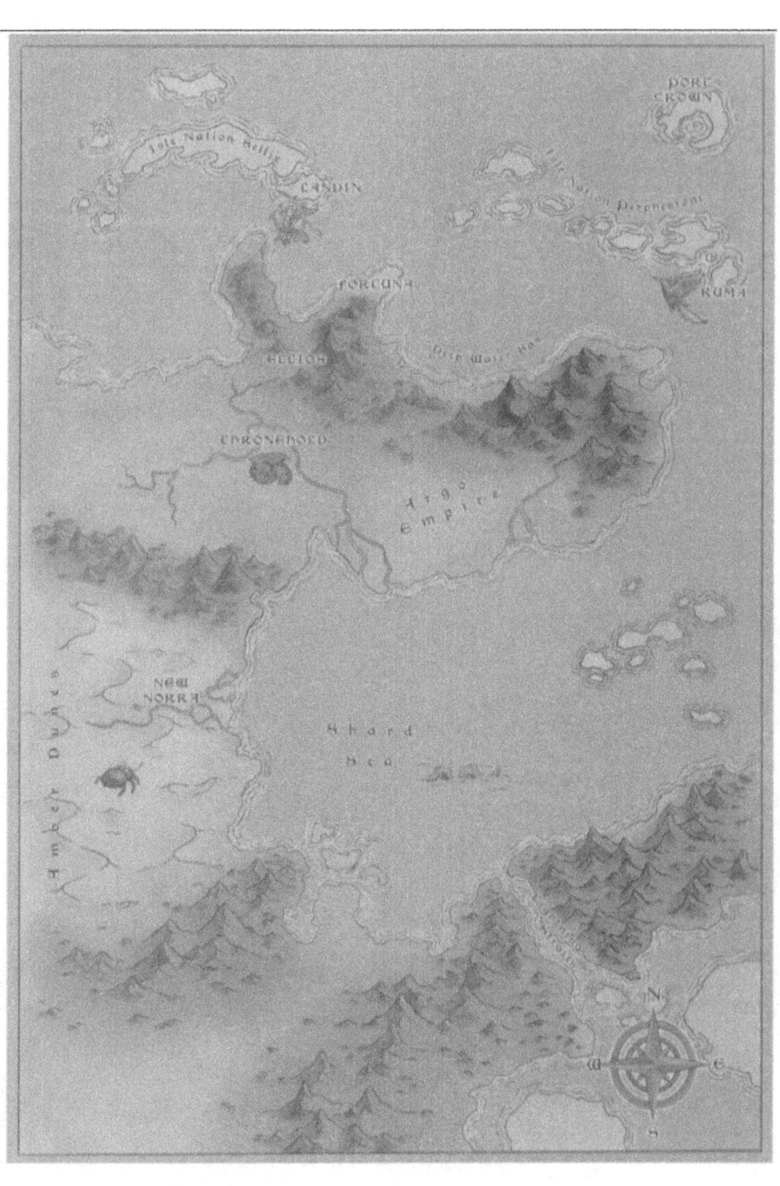

DORE
CROWN
Isle Nation Kellix
LANDIN
Isle Nation Perphistani
FORCUNA
RUMA
GEDIOH
Deep Water Way
STRONGHOLD
Argo
Empire
Amber Dunes
NEW
NORRA
Shard
Sea
N
W
E
S

THE ARCANE PLAGUE

I had never seen an airship up close before.

Even in the dying darkness of dawn, this airship—the *Sun Chaser*—was everything I had imagined and more. It had the appearance of a sailing ship, specifically a *brig*. Brig ships prioritized maneuverability, and while they were large, they were also long and sleek. Typically, brigs had two square masts to hold the sails, but this ship was different. Sixteen sails were positioned on the sides of the ship, jutting out like fins.

Winds whipped through the woodland trees, rustling the leaves.

The *Sun Chaser* flew at a slow pace, descending lower and lower, arriving with the first light of day. The oak wood used in the airship's construction shone with an amber brown. While sailing ships were often damaged by shipworms—sea water parasites—the *Sun Chaser* had no rot or damage. It was more beautiful up close than from afar.

I waited for the *Sun Chaser* at the edge of the royal hunting grounds, just outside of the Thronehold castle. Chaos still reigned supreme inside the city as everyone scrambled to deal with the aftermath of the queen's assassination.

The Frith Guild would help with the fallout. Master Zelfree, Hexa, Zaxis, Atty, Gillie, Guildmaster Eventide—even my adopted sister, Illia—they would all do what needed to be done, no doubt in my mind.

After a deep breath to calm myself, I removed my guild pendant and dropped it in the grass. I wasn't one of them anymore.

I had been infected.

Not with something mundane or manageable, but with the *arcane plague*—a blood disease that affected only the magical. It drove mystical creatures insane within days and slowly corrupted arcanists over the course of months. Each beat of the infected person's heart betrayed them, spreading the disease throughout their body.

Those infected turned to mayhem and evil. Their madness made even cruel suggestions seem reasonable. It warped every inch of them, and there was no known cure—at least, not yet. Once someone contracted the illness...

The legendary swashbuckler, Gregory Ruma, had thought he could bring back his dead wife with the deaths of countless others. Rylin, the griffin, had tried to consume his own son. The plague-ridden gargoyle I had fought on Calisto's ship had tried to rip apart all life he'd come into contact with.

I carried the same disease they did.

I rubbed at my arms as goosebumps formed. If I dwelled on the situation, I'd never have the strength to solve the problem. I had to focus on the immediate—on the new day awaiting me.

"Volke, are you okay?" Fain asked.

I nodded. "As much as I can be."

He stood close, his dark eyes narrowed in concern.

When I had first met Fain, he had been a pirate aboard the infamous *Third Abyss*. It amused me, that of all the people willing to stand by my side, he was one of them. He was immune to the arcane plague, however, which was the primary reason I hadn't insisted he abandon me.

All arcanists had a mark on their forehead—a star with the picture of their bonded mystical creature, their eldrin, wrapped around the seven points. Fain's arcanist mark had a wolf woven throughout. Well, not a *wolf*, but a *wendigo*, a mystical creature with a wolf-like body, a skull mask over its face, and large antlers. They were beasts of consumption and known as *man-eaters*, the one category of creature unaffected by the plague.

Wraith, Fain's wendigo, sat at Fain's side, his wolf-gaze locked on the descending airship. Wraith's gray pelt swished around in the wind, but his fluffy tail remained tightly wrapped around the side of his body. He had no antlers, just nubs where they had once been.

"Do we have to board that... thing?" Wraith whispered, his voice gruff.

Fain patted Wraith behind his skull mask. "It'll be fine."

"I've never flown before. It doesn't seem safe."

"I haven't heard of any airships crashing." Fain gave me a questioning glance. "Right?"

Airships were few and far between. Of course no one had heard of them crashing—most people had never even seen one. But I didn't want to spook him or Wraith. "I doubt it'll crash."

Fain stood a little straighter after my comment. His buccaneer coat fluttered in the wind, as did his dark brown hair. He kept the sides of his head shaved, which exposed his odd ears. The tips were frostbitten in appearance—black and dead-looking. So were his fingers. From what I had read, it was a side effect of bonding with a wendigo, as those wolf-like creatures stalked the snowy areas to the north, only bonding with people who were on the verge of death.

Fain kept his neck tightly wrapped in an ascot, covering the tattoo that marked him as a former pirate. When he caught me staring, he rubbed at it, as though self-conscious.

The airship didn't land. Instead, it hovered fifty feet above the ground, the gusts intensifying with its proximity. The bottom portion of the hull had been crafted with dragon and griffin bones—giant wings and a spinal cord down the center—all imbued with roc magic.

Rocs were gigantic birds with the power over wind and weather, and I suspected the magically enhanced bones were the cause of the intense breeze and the source of the airship's flight.

"Your assumption is correct."

Both Fain and I flinched.

The speaker, Adelgis Venrover, stood on the other side of me, half-hidden behind a tree trunk. He wore dark robes that matched his long inky hair, and if he held still enough, I suspected he would've blended into the darkness. His satchel, a dark brown, was the only color on his person.

Adelgis was thinner than me and Fain—the two of us were muscled from combat training—and that only contributed to Adelgis's minimal presence.

"The bones are imbued with roc magic," Adelgis continued. "And they're inside as well as outside the airship, keeping the vehicle airborne."

I hadn't spoken my mind, but that didn't matter when it came to Adelgis. He heard everyone's thoughts all the time thanks to his unusual magic. He was the only ethereal whelk arcanist I knew.

The mark on his forehead was a sea snail behind the seven-point star, the spiral shell almost eldritch in design. It was a bizarre creature that could hide itself in the light. Even now, I couldn't see the ethereal whelk, Felicity, but I knew she was nearby. Felicity rarely left her arcanist's side.

A rope ladder fell from the deck of the *Sun Chaser*. It hit the ground with a heavy thud. The bottom rungs were weighted, no doubt to keep the ladder steady despite the wind.

Once I boarded the *Sun Chaser*, there would be no going back. The Frith Guild would go one way, and I would go the other. Dread ate at my conviction. I walked to the rope ladder, my hands unsteady and my pulse high.

The shadows at my feet stirred.

Fain was a wendigo arcanist, and Adelgis was an ethereal whelk arcanist, but my eldrin was far different from theirs. Mine was a knightmare named Luthair—a full plate suit of armor crafted from darkness. He had no body, the armor was hollow, but he was just as alive as any other creature, even when he took the shape of a shadow at my feet. When he moved around like this, I knew he was agitated—or perhaps he could sense my apprehension.

"My arcanist," Luthair said. "You don't have to do this. You could return to the Frith Guild."

I shook my head as I grabbed the ladder. "No. I don't want to risk infecting any of them." If my tainted blood got anywhere near the others, I could spread the plague to them as well. I had to get it cured before I returned.

I had to.

I motioned for Adelgis to join me. He walked over, his long hair whipping around in the wind. When he reached the ladder, he furrowed his brow. "You want me to go first?"

Out of the three of us, he was the weakest. If he fell, I wanted the option to catch him.

Adelgis, who heard the rationale through my thoughts, replied with a solemn nod. "I see. That makes sense. Thank you, Volke." He grabbed the first few rungs and hoisted himself upward. He wasn't ridiculously weak, but fifty feet was a long way to climb. His eldrin stayed hidden in the rays of sunlight, however, floating along, untethered by gravity.

I motioned for Fain and Wraith.

A wolf couldn't climb a rope ladder, but my knightmare and I had the ability to travel through darkness. We could plunge into the void and reemerge on any surface a shadow could touch, like the darkness was our own personal pool of water. I would follow Adelgis up the ladder, and Luthair would take Wraith through the void, traveling like only a shadow could.

I would've taken them all up by traveling through the shadows, but my exhaustion wouldn't allow that. I hadn't slept the last few days, and less than thirty minutes ago I had dealt with the assassins in Thronehold. Luthair could handle one wendigo. I would use what little physical strength I had left to ascend to the deck of the airship.

"You go," I said to Fain.

He nodded and easily followed Adelgis up the rungs.

Wraith stared at his arcanist and whined, the wind sweeping away his noise in the next instant.

"Luthair," I said.

My eldrin rose out of the darkness around my feet, coalescing into a full set of armor, complete with a helmet and gauntlets. The black plate was made of shadows, but solid and lightweight. Luthair's helmet was empty, but he moved and saw without problems. His cape fluttered in the breeze, the hem tattered and worn. The cracks that ran across his body reminded me that Luthair was second-bonded, meaning I was his second arcanist.

"Take Wraith up to the airship," I said. "Please."

"Of course, my arcanist."

Luthair swished his cape over Wraith and then pulled him into the void of darkness. As a shadow on the ground, Luthair slithered up the ropes of the ladder, straight past Fain and Adelgis, and arrived on the deck of the *Sun Chaser* long before anyone else. Satisfied everyone had been accounted for, I started up the ladder myself.

Everything felt heavy. My legs. My arms. Even reaching a hand over my head required concentrated effort.

Halfway up, my boot slipped on a rung. I gripped the rope tightly, the threading rubbing my bare palm raw. I jerked my hand away immediately, fearful I would leave tainted plague-blood on the rope. Fortunately, I didn't stain the ladder. Unfortunately, I had shredded my hand enough that blood popped up as crimson droplets from the creases in my palm.

I waited for a minute, cradling my hand close. Arcanists could heal over time. It was much faster than normal, and reliable. As soon as my hand was repaired, I could climb again without fear of smearing my blood across the equipment.

Sure enough, my flesh stitched itself back together. I wiped the blood off on my shirt—everything I wore was soaked in crimson, most of it dried. I would have to change in the near future, though I didn't have any of my belongings with me. Hopefully someone on the *Sun Chaser* would have something I could borrow.

I ascended the last of the ladder, my breathing heavier than I would have liked.

How long had it been since I'd slept properly? Four days? A whole week? The toll for my foolishness was hefty.

With a final deep breath, I lifted myself over the airship railing and landed on the deck. My unruly black hair, disturbed by the wind rushing off the hull, puffed outward the moment I escaped the breeze. The deck was peaceful, and it had the appearance and parts of a standard sailing ship, including an anchor lift and drains for sea water. I suspected it had been a real ship once and had just been converted into an airship with the use of the bones and roc magic.

Adelgis, Fain, Wraith, and Luthair all stood near the top of the rope ladder, waiting.

I hated their expressions. They seemed like a mix between pity and concern. I didn't want to trouble them— and I also didn't want them to feel sorry for me. I had been infected while protecting someone, and I wouldn't change that no matter what.

"Oh, there you all are," a woman said. "I was wondering when you'd finally join us."

To my surprise, only two crew members of the *Sun Chaser* awaited us on the deck of the airship.

The first individual, the one who had spoken, I recognized right away—Karna the doppelgänger arcanist. The mark on her forehead was a star with a human wrapped around the points. She had her hands on her hips, her blonde hair spilling over her shoulders and down her waist like molten gold waterfalls. And she wore a dancer's outfit, a two-piece azure ensemble, the skirt long and loose, the top tight across her chest.

Karna motioned to the man next to her. "This is Captain Devlin, the proud owner of the *Sun Chaser* and a master roc arcanist of some renown."

The captain smirked. "Cordial introductions? Really? That's unlike you, Karna."

"Come now, Cap'n. I always love making a good impression."

Captain Devlin stroked his chinstrap beard—a thin line of black hair that outlined his jaw. His curly hair, just as dark as his beard, hung to his shoulders, held in place with a bandana and a tricorn hat. The man had the lithe build of someone who had spent years climbing the rigging on a boat, and his clothing was plucked straight off a pirate, complete with tall leather boots and a sash of a belt.

"This is Volke Savan, the knightmare arcanist," Karna said as she flashed me a quick smile. "And these two are his associates." She didn't even look at Fain or Adelgis when she introduced them, she just gestured with a wave of her hand.

The captain glared. "He needs to be cleaned up and his clothes burned."

"I'll ask Tammi to handle everything."

The morning sun lifted over the mountains on the horizon, backlighting Karna and Captain Devlin. I lifted an arm to shield my eyes from the rays.

"I'm sorry we had to meet this way," the captain said. "Karna says you have a plan to get a cure, so I'll help for now. But listen to me—if you so much as *scratch* anyone on this ship, I'll make you regret every decision that brought you here."

I nodded. "I understand."

"Good. Then we need to leave the Argo Empire as soon as possible. Follow instructions until you're properly cleaned up."

2

THE SUN CHASER

The Argo Empire was the largest nation around. Technically, it had been almost twice its size hundreds of years ago, but the late queen—assassinated last night—had allowed the edges of her territory to rebel and break away, resulting in several smaller kingdoms and island nations. With the capital city of Thronehold in turmoil, I assumed the Argo Empire would become even smaller.

The late queen's kin, Prince Rishan, had helped the assassins gain access to the castle, but not many knew of his treachery. Last I saw, he had assumed the throne and intended to rule the entire empire.

Only sovereign dragon arcanists were allowed to lead the Argo Empire due to the fact they had a prosperity aura that helped maintain growth and wealth. Prince Rishan was, in fact, a sovereign dragon arcanist, but he had been bonded for less than a full day and certainly hadn't trained enough to develop a magical aura. That meant the other sovereign dragon arcanists who ruled over territory in the empire would surely protest Rishan's power in the capital. It could lead to further rebellion or infighting. Perhaps civil war.

I understood why Captain Devlin wanted to leave as soon as possible.

Instead of dwelling on problems I couldn't solve, I instead focused on my surroundings.

The *Sun Chaser* had three decks, and I was taken down below to wash up. Since this was a ship in the air and not the sea, they didn't have much water, but they gave me as much as they could spare along with a washtub. Since Fain was immune to the plague, he accompanied me below and took away my clothing after I stripped.

I sat on a bench in the washroom, my feet in the shallow tub, my back against the bulkhead, and my gaze on the ceiling. The *Sun Chaser* creaked like any other ship, but not with the rocking of waves, only when it moved from one air current to the next. The howling of wind beyond the porthole was a new experience.

Luthair moved as a shadow from my feet to the bench. He didn't form into his suit of armor, instead remaining a puddle of darkness.

"My arcanist," he said.

I didn't move when I replied, "Yes?"

"Are you done bathing?"

I glanced down. All my injuries had healed thanks to my magic, and the water in the tub was a sickly pink from the dried blood I had scrubbed from my skin. As far as I could tell, I was clean.

"Yes," I muttered.

"It pains me to see you like this."

"Sick?"

"Despondent," Luthair said.

I didn't reply. What could I even say to that? Should I be

cheerful and carefree? Of course not. And I was exhausted, but my mind wouldn't stop replaying all the scenes that had brought me here. It was like nothing was right, and I was waiting for everything to fall back into place.

The door to the washroom opened, but the room wasn't large enough for it to swing all the way out. Fain stepped in, reminding me just how cramped the room really was. I moved down on the bench so he could take a seat next to me. His wendigo waited out in the hall.

"Here," Fain said as he handed over a new pair of trousers and a white button-up shirt. "But they said you should wait to dress until their surgeon comes to see you."

I set the clothes on my lap in an attempt to be modest, but it was difficult to care. "Thank you."

Fain cracked his frostbitten fingers. He glanced to me, then back to his hands. Then to the door. I didn't understand what he wanted—maybe to leave?—but he just sighed and leaned against the bulkhead. "After you get some rest, would you mind helping me with my magic?"

I lifted an eyebrow.

Fain continued, "I was never formally trained, and what little we did back in Thronehold helped me understand that I need guidance. I just thought, well, since we have to travel south to find Adelgis's father, that we might have time."

In theory, Adelgis's father, Theasin Venrover, was crafting a cure for the plague. He had left Thronehold weeks ago and headed south, though no one knew his destination. It would require searching, but in an airship, I suspected we'd be able to catch up to him.

But what if we couldn't?

I tried not to think negative thoughts, but they popped up faster than usual. Much faster.

Fain must've realized I had mentally drifted away from

the conversation because he placed a hand on my bare shoulder to get my attention. His blackened fingers had no warmth—just an icy touch.

"Hey," he said.

I waited, uncertain of why his tone had shifted from casual to low and serious.

"At one point I thought dying would be a lot easier than living."

"Fain," I muttered. "I don't—"

"You were the one who helped me then." Fain tightened his cold grip on my shoulder. "Let me help you now."

Although I wasn't sure if he could do anything, I answered with a slow nod. Perhaps magic training would distract me.

The door opened a second time and hit Fain in the knee. A woman stood in the doorframe, her curly brown hair framing her youthful, heart-shaped face. She wore pants with five times as many pockets as usual and even had a belt with several pouches.

"Hello," she said, her tone hesitant. "I'm Tammi, the surgeon for the *Sun Chaser.*"

Fain stood, offered a quick bow of his head, and then shuffled past her. "Pardon me."

She moved all the way into the washroom and shut the door behind him.

I held my new clothes tightly on my lap, wondering why they didn't want me to dress before Tammi had arrived. This seemed awkward. And unnecessary.

Tammi sat on the bench where Fain had been. She smiled, though it was forced. I tried to offer half a smile in return, but I couldn't muster the enthusiasm.

"You're remarkably... tall," Tammi said, a hint of nervousness in her voice.

I nodded.

I stood just over six feet, and I suspected Tammi was closer to five. The difference in our heights was exacerbated when she slouched.

"The captain said I should give you some bandaging." Tammi produced several rolls of gauze from her many pockets, all neatly bundled.

"I'm not injured," I said.

"No, but you might be. Since we want to prevent the spread of any plague-ridden blood, this will help." She unraveled the gauze and pulled on the sides, showcasing how durable it was. "This is made from wootz cotton. Have you heard of it?"

"I don't think so."

"It comes from copper plants to the west. They're minor magical shrubs with interesting colors and steel-like stems. The great thing about it is that wootz cotton is mighty absorbent. The plan is to keep you wrapped up, at least over the major organs, so that if you get hurt, the wootz cotton will prevent blood from going everywhere until your arcanist magic allows you to heal." Tammi scooted closer and motioned for me to sit away from the bulkhead. "I'm going to wrap you real quick, then I'll take the tub and dispose of the water, and you'll be free to walk around the ship. Sound good?"

Tammi seemed older than me, but only by a few years. I would be seventeen soon, and I suspected she was in her early twenties.

I held out my hand. "I can help with the wrapping."

She replied with a nervous laugh. "Actually, I'd prefer if you didn't move around much."

"Okay," I said with a shrug.

"And I'd also prefer if you stared at the opposite bulk-head while I worked."

I narrowed my eyes, confused by the request. When Tammi didn't explain, I exhaled and turned away from her. "If that's what you want."

What did it matter? Looking at the wall or looking at her —nothing would change.

Tammi set to wrapping my chest and stomach with the gauze, her movements quick and effortless, befitting any master surgeon. She didn't speak while she worked, nor did she hum or even make a noise. Then she wrapped my upper arms, shoulders, and armpits—moving my limbs with gentle motions and then waiting for me to hold still while she finished.

When it came time to wrap my upper thigh, I felt more like my normal, awkward self. I kept my new clothes pressed against everything scandalous as she bandaged the parts of my body with major arteries.

"Done," Tammi said as she scooted away on the bench. "It'll probably be warm while you wear this. I suggest you drink lots of water and stay in cool locations. Like... below deck."

"All right."

Tammi got up and left the washroom, the same forced smile on her face as she closed the door.

Once alone, I quickly dressed in the trousers and shirt. Tammi had been right. The warmth from the wootz cotton made it seem like the dead of summer under my clothes, but I appreciated the fact that I had a layer of protection if I were cut.

I exited the washroom.

Tammi and two other ladies were in the corridor, wait-ing. They all put on their fake smiles and waited for me to shuffle by before they entered the washroom. Since they weren't arcanists—they had no marks on their forehead—they couldn't contract the arcane plague. It was safe for them to dispose of the water and clean the room.

Luthair followed me in the shadows, slipping from one dark patch to the next. The lanterns in the *Sun Chaser* seemed new and bright, but most had their shutters half-closed, keeping the place dimly lit.

I could see in the dark, thanks to my knightmare magic, so I didn't mind. I just wondered why.

Karna waited for me near the narrow stairs that led above deck, her radiance dispelling the gloom of the corridor. She swished back her golden hair, motioned for me to follow her, and then leapt up the stairs with the fluid speed and grace of a dancer. As I went up the steps to follow, two other women went down, each carrying rigging for the sails. They didn't greet me or say a word, so I remained quiet as I stepped around them.

When I emerged on deck, I had to blink back the dazzling sunlight.

The *Sun Chaser* flew above the clouds, soaring between the white peaks of cumulonimbus and traveling at a faster pace than most sailing ships. The rush of air over the ship rustled everything. Without any cloud cover, the sun shone mercilessly over the deck and crew.

I couldn't help myself. I walked straight to the ship railing and leaned over to get a better view. The occasional wisp of cloud felt like a light misting of water. And the air—it was so crisp and fresh. Unlike anything I had ever experienced before.

How high were we? I couldn't see the ground, not through the thick layer of white below us.

"Excited?" Karna asked.

I hadn't realized she was standing next to me until then. "It's beautiful up here."

"I agree." She tied back her blonde hair with a shimmery piece of blue ribbon. Everything fluttered elegantly in the breeze, both dramatic and striking. "Nothing beats the view from freedom."

"How long have you been a crew member on the *Sun Chaser*?" I asked.

Karna tapped the railing, her gaze becoming distant. "Years, I suppose."

From what I'd heard, the *Sun Chaser* was home to mercenaries and mystic seekers—people who could be hired for any job, even if it were questionable in nature. That didn't mean they were blackhearts, just people floating between the order of guild system and the lawlessness of pirates. The crew of the *Sun Chaser* was made up of outsiders willing to work so long as they liked the price.

"I love it here," Karna said with a half-smile. "I basically recruited everyone in our crew." She pointed to a woman scrubbing the deck. "That's Lin, one of our gunners. And the girl next to her is Hanna. She's one of our deckhands. At some point you should meet Biyu—she's the cutest cabin girl."

"Do you have a position on the ship?" I asked.

Karna straightened her posture and touched her collarbone with one hand. "I'm the quartermaster. And in case you don't know what *that* is—"

"I know," I said. "It's a position directly under the captain. Some say it's more important than the first mate, since quartermasters are typically in charge of recruitment, supplies, and training." There were many stories of quartermasters recruiting people loyal to them and not the captain so that they could cause a mutiny.

Karna pursed her lips. "Hm. You must like sailing."

"I grew up on the Isle of Ruma. I know my way around ships." I glanced around, still squinting from the bright sunlight. "Where's the first mate?"

"We don't have one." Karna pushed away from the railing. "C'mon. Let me show you the rest of the ship, like any proper quartermaster should." Before I could answer, she grabbed my elbow and clung close.

I wanted to shake her away—to remind her I was still dangerous—but holding my arm wouldn't transfer the plague, so I decided not to act like a paranoid lunatic, and I kept the comments to myself.

Karna led me to the quarterdeck, a raised-up portion near the stern. It was a smaller deck, but with a better view, and I took a moment to stare off into the distance. The blinding white of the clouds almost hurt my eyes as much as the sun. In the distance, beyond gigantic peaks of fluff, a colossal bird burst out of the cloud line. With each powerful flap of its gargantuan wings, the bird went higher into the sky.

"That's the captain's roc," Karna said. "Her name is Mesos."

The roc, Mesos, had golden feathers, as though carved out of amber. Although huge, and somewhat frightening, I couldn't help but marvel at her majesty. She had to be larger than an elephant, perhaps the size of a small whale.

Karna pulled me across the quarterdeck, down a small set of stairs. "Over there is the galley. That's where you get your food. And there is where the lookout sits, on the forecastle deck. Captain Devlin uses his magic to steer the vessel, so the wheel and rudder are just for show."

The useless parts of the ship confirmed my suspicion: this had once been a ship for sailing. They had taken it from the waters and modified it for the sky, leaving vestigial parts around the airship.

Then Karna pulled me to a door that led below deck. Without boots, the grain of the wood felt odd on the soles of my feet. Everything seemed properly stored, cataloged, and clean, however, so I didn't fear stepping on loose nails or splinters.

"*I can't wait for you to meet our blacksmith,*" Karna said in a singsong voice, like she was teasing me by withholding some information.

I wasn't in the mood to play games, so I didn't bother asking.

We descended a short set of stairs, escaping the winds on the deck, and entered a narrow corridor with several doors. One was labeled: *Captain's Quarters*. Karna led me beyond that, all the way to the opposite end of the hall. She pointed to a door with no label.

"This is where you and your two associates will sleep." She smiled wide—genuine and filled with excitement. "Admit it. The *Sun Chaser* is ten times more wondrous and freeing than your guild back home. Think of this as an adventure."

I gritted my teeth, uncertain of what to say.

The Frith Guild was everything I wanted from life. Whereas the *Sun Chaser* was about making money and doing whatever they felt like to achieve it, the Frith Guild was about protecting people and places, especially from forces like pirates or the plague. Every one of my childhood heroes had served in the Frith Guild at one point or another —and if I could, I would've returned there in an instant.

Sure, the airship was a pleasant distraction. The view was undeniable. But it still felt foreign and cold.

"Everyone is always a little nervous when they come to

the *Sun Chaser*," Karna continued. She smoothed my shirt and undid the top button. I feared she would try to continue, but she stopped and fiddled with my collar. "But everyone comes to love it. You'll see. You just need a good night's rest."

"Why does it matter if I like it here?" I asked.

"I want you to stay," Karna stated, no hesitation. She met my gaze with her blue eyes, neither flinching nor backing down. "I don't usually trust arcanists, but you're the exception. Maybe once you spend time here—and spend time with me—you'll realize this crew could be your home."

"I barely know you," I muttered.

I had met Karna only a few months ago. She had been a dancer at an odd club in the Moonlight District of Thronehold, but even that had been a lie. She had been looking for arcanists to trick into taking her to the castle, and I had been the unfortunate soul she'd convinced. With her doppelgänger magic, she had helped me uncover the villains lurking in the back alleys of the capital city, and I was still grateful, but that didn't mean we were deeply or intimately connected.

My statement seemed to bother Karna.

She stepped away, her attention on the captain's quarters, far down the corridor. "Perhaps we don't know each other well now, but that'll change. Just keep an open mind, okay? You don't know everything about the *Sun Chaser*. You're going to be pleasantly surprised."

Again, she spoke like she was hiding something—like she wanted me to ask her what was going on.

But I didn't. Exhaustion and depression stopped me from continuing the conversation.

"Thank you for helping me," I said. It was the least I

could say. "Without the *Sun Chaser*, I doubt I'd be able to catch up to Theasin Venrover in time."

"In time?" Karna asked.

"I... only have a few months before the plague will be incurable, for lack of a better word. We need to find Theasin before then."

Karna nodded. "Of course. Don't worry about that now, though. Just get some sleep. We can talk more once you wake."

3

THE AIRSHIP CREW

I opened the door to the sleeping quarters and examined the contents of the room. A piece of me suspected the room had once been a storage unit. Hammocks were hastily hung in all four corners, and large crates were piled in between. Three barrels were tied together in the center of the room, each constructed with metal rings, which meant the contents were liquid. Perhaps rum?

Adelgis and Fain waited inside, each seated on a different crate. Wraith sat at his arcanist's feet, his tail swishing from side to side. They glanced up when I entered, but didn't say anything for a long moment.

"You look like you should get some sleep," Fain finally said.

The airship creaked as I walked around the barrels and avoided the crates. I took the hammock in the far back corner, the farthest from the door and safe from the light streaming in through the sole porthole window. The ropes holding my makeshift bed smelled of mold, and I wondered how long they would last before breaking. I sat in the hammock and rolled onto my back, my gaze on the wooden boards of the ceiling.

Fain took the hammock closest to the door. He jumped in and settled all in one motion, obviously familiar with life on a cramped sailing ship.

Adelgis withdrew a book from his satchel and went straight to a section in the middle.

I wanted to sleep. My body needed it. But every time I closed my eyes, a terrible sense of anxiety gripped my chest. It became difficult to breathe, so I held my breath, exhaled, and then started anew. It didn't help.

After a few minutes of staring at the ceiling, Adelgis slid off the crate and ambled his way over to my hammock. He stopped once he reached my side, and he stared down with a blank, unreadable expression.

"Adelgis?" I whispered, unnerved by his gaze.

He touched the side of my neck with the back of his hand. "You'll feel better once you've slept."

A fog overcame my thoughts, and my eyelids refused to remain open.

Panicked, I tried to throw myself out of the hammock, but it was too late. Adelgis's magic took hold, and I lost consciousness, even though I fought it every step of the way.

The place of my birth, the Isle of Ruma, had a distinct aesthetic. Blue stones fit into the sidewalks, depicting large fish swimming alongside giant schools of small ones. The iron railing around balconies had the depictions of waves bent into the metal, creating a quaint ocean scene across multiple houses. Statues of jellyfish and seagulls stood in the town square.

I walked down the main road of Ruma, basking in both the emotional and physical warmth. Island sunshine had its own special properties. It fell from the sky and bounced off the glittering waves, hitting everything twice. Skin remained tan no matter the season, and shadows never stayed for long. On the mainland, the gloom could last for months at a time.

Everything felt surreal, though.

There were no people in town. No birds in the sky. No ships at sea.

Off in the distance, on the outskirts of town, was a single cottage and graveyard. My heart leapt into my throat the moment I spotted it. Unable to contain my excitement, I ran for the fence surrounding the cottage, desperate to leap over and run inside. It was my childhood home.

When I slammed through the front door and entered the cottage, it took me a moment to realize there weren't any familiar scents. That didn't extinguish my enthusiasm. I ran through the kitchen and went straight to the back door. Everything was as I remembered it, right down to the dirty cooking pans stacked on the counter. But no one was inside. I exited the house and went into the graveyard, my eyes wide.

Where was Illia? Where was Gravekeeper William?

I almost lost hope, but then I spotted a large figure next to one of the gravestones, hunched over and digging a fresh hole. It seemed like an eternity since I had spoken with my adopted father.

Gravekeeper William stopped working and wiped the sweat from his brow. When he glanced over, he smiled wide. "There you are, boy. Come over 'ere and let me get a good look."

I jogged across the graveyard, smiling the entire way. "It's great to see you again." I threw my arms around him the second I could, half-amused by how large he was. He stood six inches taller than me, and he had to weigh nearly twice as much. Thick arms, legs, and a barrel gut—his size made me feel like a child in comparison. "I've missed you."

"Everything'll be all right," William said as he patted my back. "You have nothin' to worry about."

I tightened my grip, refusing to let go. He wore a pair of trousers, soiled with dirt, a long-sleeved shirt, and an apron he used whenever he handled dead bodies. I didn't care. I held fast, almost fearful to let go.

"I can't stop worrying," I muttered into his shoulder.

In my gut, I knew this was a dream. It was too strange and otherworldly—but I still wanted to hear William's voice, even if it was all a fantasy.

"This isn't like you," William said, chuckling. "You're the kid who rushed into a trial of worth ceremony, even when it was against the rules. And you were the one who fought plague-ridden monsters, even before you were an arcanist."

I remained still, unable to answer.

"You haven't even started this adventure yet and already you want to give up?" William asked. "That's not the Volke I know."

After a long exhale, I gritted my teeth and closed my eyes. "This isn't about *giving up*. It's about... doing what's right."

Everyone I knew who had contracted the arcane plague either went mad or killed themselves to avoid that outcome. Even Rylin—the griffin I had dealt with on the Isle of Landin—had known that his life was forfeit the moment he had been infected with that twisted sickness. He had *asked me* to kill him before he became a monster.

And the knight captain in Thronehold had done the

same thing. He had fought until the bitter end, killing himself so that the plague couldn't affect anyone else.

They had known what had to be done, and they had done it without hesitation.

Gravekeeper William returned my embrace. "Ah. Now I understand." He spoke as though he could hear my thoughts, but his tone was so comforting, I didn't much care.

I exhaled again, my breath hot, my body tense. "Is it selfish of me to look for a cure?" I whispered. "I risk everyone's safety by... by merely existing. If I hurt someone or infect them while I search for my own salvation, wouldn't that go against everything I had read about? All those stories of heroes and knights?"

The heroes wouldn't have questioned themselves or their decisions. They would've been noble and ended their lives before anyone had to do it for them.

"The assassins in Thronehold killed a lot of good men and women," William said.

So many. The queen, the knight captain, the Grandmaster Inquisitor—countless others. I almost hadn't made it out myself.

William continued, "That was their goal, wasn't it? To sow confusion and wipe away their enemies. You're in a unique position, boy. You aren't like the others. They didn't have any options. The knight captain had to fulfill his duty and stand at his post till the bitter end—but you don't. You have a choice. End everything now, just as the villains want, or spit in their face and find a cure, saving yourself and countless others."

I laughed once, more sarcastic than genuine. "What if I can't?" I asked. "What if—"

"What if you succeed?" William interjected. "That's what everyone wants, ya know. Illia, the Frith Guild, your mentor, your eldrin—they all want you to live. They want you to find a cure and bring it back, just like a hero of legend, the kind they write stories about. The only people who want you dead are the villains."

His words and voice soothed my anxiety, just like when I was a kid. I opened my eyes, thankful to have this moment, even if it was fake. Had Adelgis crafted this with his magic? Ethereal whelk arcanists could manipulate dreams, after all.

But this sounded so much like Gravekeeper William. He always had advice—always supported me—and part of me wished this were reality.

Only Illia's presence could make this moment perfect.

"I really do miss you," I whispered.

William smiled. "That's why you've got to succeed. Because I miss you, too. Come home once this is over. Tell me all about the adventure and how you eventually won the day."

"Okay." I closed my eyes, holding on to my sense of determination. "I will."

I awoke to the groaning of the airship.

At some point, someone had thrown a blanket over me, probably unaware that I wore wootz cotton over most of my body. I had never been so sweaty while lying perfectly still before. I tossed off the blanket and sat up, my head spinning for a moment. No light shone through the porthole, which meant I had slept the entire day.

The rest had done wonders, though. The clinging dread that had haunted me since my infection had faded to the back of my mind. I couldn't let the situation defeat me. I had a plan, and as long as I was careful, no one else would get hurt. Adelgis and Fain were here to help, and I always had Luthair, even in the darkest of moments.

I would make it through this. I would return to the Frith Guild—see Illia and the others—and eventually I would return to the Isle of Ruma to speak with Gravekeeper William.

I would be okay.

Someone grabbed me from behind. In one quick motion, they yanked my chin back and pressed a blade to my throat.

"Don't move." The feminine voice had a forced gruffness to it.

In that split second, I decided not to retaliate with my magic. As a knightmare arcanist, I could've manipulated the darkness to create physical objects made of coalesced shadow or I could've evoked terrors that sent people spiraling into their worst thoughts and fears. But the only people on the airship were the crew itself, and I didn't want to attack a potential ally, even if they were holding a weapon to my neck. Plus, I could slip into the shadows at any moment, escaping my attacker's grip, though I would risk getting cut. I didn't want to bleed anywhere on the *Sun Chaser*.

I held my breath.

The woman tightened her grip and held me close, my back against her chest. The blade at my throat was zigzagged, like a bolt of lightning. I couldn't see her or the weapon, however—the details I absorbed were from touch alone.

"Everyone knows what you are," she said, maintaining the growl in her tone, as though trying to hide her true voice. "And just because Karna brought you aboard doesn't mean we trust you."

I wondered about Luthair. Why hadn't he acted? Was he not in the room? Or perhaps he wanted *me* to handle the situation?

Before I could think of a reasonable response, the woman continued, "Every member of the crew has a weapon, and we'll always know where you are, even when you're sleeping." She pressed the blade as hard as she could against my throat without breaking the skin. "Do you understand?"

"Yes," I said, though the simple act of talking almost resulted in a cut.

"This'll be your only warning."

The woman released me and then hustled out of the room, her steps quiet. Given her insistence on stealth, and the fact that she had kept to the thickest shadows in the room, I suspected she didn't know I could see in the dark. I watched her leave as I rubbed my neck, curious about her weapon, the zigzag dagger. It had a golden sheen to the edge, and the hilt looked like it had been woven out of flax string.

Once the door snapped shut, I relaxed in the hammock. "Nice to meet you, too," I quipped. Then I examined my surroundings, hoping to spot Luthair's shifting form. The other hammocks sat empty. The crates and barrels hadn't moved.

"Luthair?" I asked.

No reply.

I stood and walked out of the room, no need to light the lamps. The hallway to the captain's quarters was just as dark and empty as the storeroom I now called home. Still bare footed, I made my way up the stairs to the deck. The night air greeted me with an icy gust of wind. The cotton wrapping under my clothes absorbed the chill.

Adelgis waited at the top of the stairs, his long hair tied back in a secure ponytail to prevent it from fluttering everywhere. His robes, on the other hand, twisted and tossed around, tangling around his legs and arms. He looked like an out-of-place scholar, though our blustery environment didn't seem to trouble him.

"I'm glad you're feeling better," Adelgis said.

I crossed my arms and scanned the deck. A couple of airship workers scrubbed the railings and checked the rigging, avoiding the side of the ship with Adelgis and me.

"Next time, warn me before you use your magic to induce sleep," I said.

"If that's what you want."

"Where is Fain? And Luthair?"

"In the galley, getting food."

I narrowed my eyes. "Luthair is a knightmare. He doesn't need to eat."

"I asked him to leave so that the odd crewmember skulking around our room would have a chance to speak with you." Adelgis tilted his head to the side, his gaze unfocused as he stared at the moon. "She was upset that you were allowed onboard, and I figured she would change her tone after meeting you, but perhaps this wasn't the best moment..." He kept his attention skyward, not even bothering to finish his thought.

I glanced up, surprised by the amount of color swirling through the darkness of night. The sky, speckled with a thousand stars, glittered like a horde of fireflies. A purple, blue, and indigo halo adorned the full moon, providing light enough for everyone to continue their on-deck duties without a lantern.

It felt like we were so close that, if I lifted my hand, the ink of the sky would stain my fingertips. The world seemed more mystical above the clouds. For a moment, I wondered if I were still dreaming.

"Um, hello," a child said, her voice so clear and sweet, it demanded attention.

I pulled my sights off the transfixing sky and found a little girl standing in front of me. She held a pouch of jerky and bread, but I barely took note of it. Her face—she wore an eyepatch over her left eye—had knife scars from the hairline down to her jaw. Despite the gnarled marks, she smiled from ear to ear and held out the pouch of food.

"This is for you," she said. "Oh! My name is Biyu. It's a pleasure to meet you." She bowed her head as she offered the pouch again.

If I had to guess, I'd say Biyu was eight or nine. Her shoulder-length brown hair, silky and straight, tossed in the breeze. She wore rough trousers and a coat secured shut in the front, but the most amusing piece of her outfit was the leather strap attached to a large book. It hung at her hip, the tome nearly as thick as her arm.

But her scars...

They reminded me of Illia. She had lost her right eye to pirates. Had Biyu lost her left eye for the same reason? I couldn't bring myself to ask. I didn't even take her pouch of bread and jerky. I just stared, momentarily forgetting myself while I thought back to my childhood—the many days with Illia when we were children.

Biyu furrowed her brow. "Um. Aren't you... hungry?"

Adelgis reached for the food. "It's okay. Volke's a little dazed. I'll take it."

"Absolutely not," Biyu said as she pulled the pouch close to her chest. "I said *I'd* give it to him, so that's what I've got to do." She offered it to me a third time, her one eye bright as she smiled again. "This is for you. Don't worry. It's good. Try some."

I took the food, my hand unsteady. "Thank you."

She waited, the wind tangling her hair. When I didn't say anything else, she gestured to me. "This is when *you* introduce yourself."

I almost laughed. I hadn't realized how rude I had been—just staring at her for a solid thirty seconds—and I took a deep breath to regain my bearings.

"My name is Volke Savan," I said. "I'm a knightmare arcanist. It's nice to meet you." I bowed my head. "Thank you for the food."

But my introduction didn't seem to please Biyu. She stepped back, her eyebrows knit as she gripped the leather strap that held her thick book. "Your surname isn't Savan."

The statement caught me off guard. "Yes, it is. Ever since I was adopted."

Biyu's expression snapped right back into a jovial smile. "Oh! Of course. That makes sense."

She grabbed her giant book, struggled to hold it in one arm, and then withdrew a quill from her coat pocket. The feather of her quill—both black and white—shimmered with a glint of magic. Biyu didn't need to dip it into ink. She just started writing on one of the pages in the middle, and the black spots on the feather shrank, as though disappearing to create the ink.

"There," she said once she was done. "I've made a note about your new name." Biyu slammed the book shut and carefully tucked the quill back into her pocket. "It's my job, as the world's best cabin girl, to keep *perfect records*." She had said the last two words with oomph and gusto, obviously excited to have the task, even though it was usually considered to be the least exciting on a ship.

"You know my previous last name?" I asked.

Biyu nodded. "It's Blackwater."

I caught my breath. Who had told her? Had it been Karna? No. I had never told Karna. Perhaps Adelgis, since he could hear thoughts? But I didn't think of it often. Perhaps Fain? I had told him. Once.

Biyu clapped her hands once. "I have to go now! I'll speak with you again, okay?" Then she dashed across the deck of the *Sun Chaser*.

I wanted to chase after and question her, but I also didn't want to interrupt her schedule. She entered a door that led below deck and disappeared from sight in a quick blur of energy and excitement.

The other crew members of the *Sun Chaser* picked up their work. Had they stopped to watch the interaction between Biyu and me? As I stared, I noticed they avoided making eye contact with me.

"They're skittish around arcanists," Adelgis said. "Both of them used to work for an arcanist who was driven mad by the plague. He tortured the staff of his estate and then later killed his family because he thought they were plotting to murder him."

"Have you been listening to the thoughts of everyone aboard the *Sun Chaser*?" I asked. "That seems... inappropriate."

"I told you. I can't stop anymore. I just hear everyone's thoughts. All the time."

I rubbed at my upper arm, more aware than ever of the disease coursing through my veins. "Did you hear what happened to Biyu? Was it... pirates... who took her eye?"

"Yes."

I gritted my teeth, but a realization settled over my thoughts a moment later. "The crew of the *Sun Chaser*," I muttered. "They all have questionable or painful back-grounds, don't they?"

Adelgis nodded.

The wind swept between us.

Karna said she had been in charge of the recruiting, and now I understood. She was trying to save people by giving them new lives after losing their old one. Her offer to have me stay aboard the ship made more sense, and while I still didn't want to, it made me appreciate the *Sun Chaser* more than before.

"We should get below deck," Adelgis said, his teeth on the verge of chattering. "I have a few ideas about where my father might be heading."

4

PLAN OF ACTION

"What did you think of your dream?" Adelgis asked as we descended to the lower deck.

"I was surprised how accurate you made Gravekeeper William," I said. "It felt so... lifelike."

"Oh, I didn't do that. I just manipulated the dream to recall memories of your adopted father. Your own subconscious made up his words and mannerisms, not me. I *could* have taken control, but I suspect I would've portrayed him incorrectly, and then you would've been angered."

I chuckled, amused by Adelgis's strange power set. Somehow, everything about the man was bizarre, but I appreciated that about him. He wasn't like anyone else I knew. Adelgis always had a different perspective, albeit odd.

"I helped Master Zelfree when he felt depressed." Adelgis half-smiled. "I can help with your sleep as well. What would you like to dream about? It could be anything."

I rubbed at the back of my neck, trying to think of pleasant dreams. I didn't want to see Gravekeeper William every night. The heartache would be too much. Instead, I wanted something to distract me from the reality of my situation. If I had something else to think about—something *other* than the tainted blood pumping through my veins—I suspected I'd have an easier time going about my day.

"Something fun," I said as we neared the door to the storeroom. "No. I take that back." Last time Adelgis had given me a "fun" dream, it had turned into an awkward nightmare of group dancing. "Something interesting. Something completely new and not from my memories."

Adelgis opened the door and walked to the nearest hammock, muttering, "*New, huh?*" before taking a seat on the ratty ropes of his makeshift bed.

I returned to my hammock, my food pouch in hand. Once settled, I nibbled on the jerky and bread. They sapped the water from my mouth, leaving me with a terrible thirst. To make matters worse, the flavor bordered on sawdust mixed with grease. It impressed me that the bread and the meat could somehow have nearly the same taste and texture, but that only brought about more disturbing questions.

The door to the storeroom creaked open and Fain slipped inside. His wendigo kept close to his legs as he shut the door, and Luthair slithered across the floor in shadow form. Fain had his own pouch of food—but he also had a bottle made of dark green glass. A beverage? I turned around in my hammock to face him.

"Have you two explored this rig?" Fain asked, his voice low. He quickly slid into his hammock. "I think the crew is mostly women."

Adelgis nodded. "The vast majority."

"Is that common on airships?"

"I'm not sure. I've never been on an airship before."

Fain relaxed and kicked off his boots. Wraith grabbed

them both by the laces and moved the pair toward the wall, his tail wagging the entire time.

"Pirate ships don't usually take on women," Fain muttered as he tore a piece of jerky in two. "Well, that's not true. I'm sure most pirates would *love* to have women as crewmates, but there weren't many who wanted to sail with the likes of Calisto. We did have a couple, though."

"Does it bother you?" I asked.

Fain shrugged. "No. It just explains a few things, that's all. Like why we aren't sleeping near the rest of the crew."

"They housed us near the captain because the crew doesn't trust us," Adelgis said matter-of-factly.

Fain snorted and laughed once. "Of course. *I'm* a renegade pirate, *Volke's* a plague-ridden madman, and *you're* some moon-faced weirdo. No one in their right mind would trust the lot of us."

I shot him a sideways glance.

Fain returned it as he ripped another piece of jerky in half.

"It's true," he finally said. "At least, that's how everyone sees us." He took a large bite of his food and cringed. With a pained expression, he forced himself to chew the meat. He swallowed long before appropriate, half-choking on the tough chunks. After patting his chest, and taking a swig from his green bottle, he managed to rasp, "What does it matter? They're just letting us ride away from the empire, right?"

As though prepared for the question, Adelgis withdrew a map from his satchel. It wasn't particularly large, but the precise nature of it was apparent, even from across the room. Longitude and latitude lines marked the entire drawing, along with a legend and a line for measuring distances.

Adelgis smoothed the parchment across his lap and scooted a bit closer to the lit lantern.

"We might have to ride on this airship for an extended period of time," Adelgis said. "I'm certain my father went to New Norra, far to the south, but he never stays there long."

He pointed to places on the map and then used his fingers to calculate the distance.

"New Norra is almost three hundred miles away," Adelgis muttered. "And if he went farther south, the next port city is more than fifty miles along the coast."

Fain exhaled. He handed the jerky to Wraith, and his wendigo gobbled it down without even tasting it.

"It still won't matter if the crew trusts us," Fain said. "If we keep to this room, I'm sure the trek to New Norra will be pleasant enough."

Adelgis shook his head. "I don't think you understand. The doppelgänger arcanist, Karna, said the captain would take us to New Norra, but she didn't guarantee anything else. My father probably stopped there, but he always moves on, which means we'll have to investigate and then travel to another city, perhaps several. If the crew of the *Sun Chaser* wants us gone—because they think we're weirdos, madmen, and pirates, as you put it—they'll abandon us as soon as possible, and we'll be stuck with slower means of transportation."

Fain glanced between Adelgis and me, a frown setting in. Then he ran his hand down his face, his frostbitten fingers contrasting harshly with the tan of his skin. "Damn. We're definitely gonna get kicked off."

"Why's that?" I asked. "People generally like Adelgis. He's kind, pleasant, and he's the son of a famous researcher. I think the crew will get along with him."

Fain narrowed his eyes into a sarcastic glare. "Are you

serious? Earlier today our friend, *Moonbeam*—" he jutted his thumb at Adelgis, "—told the crew he wanted to see what happened if they all asphyxiated to death."

"What?" I gasped.

Adelgis rolled his eyes. "It wasn't that dramatic."

"Some deckhand asked Adelgis about his eldrin," Fain said. "He told her it was an ethereal whelk, and the woman asked where they came from. Moonbeam said ethereal whelks are born from the corpses of children who drowned. That's when he followed it up with, *I wonder what would happen if the crew of this airship asphyxiated to death.*"

"I'm genuinely curious," Adelgis stated as he waved his hands around, flustered. "Maybe a new type of mystical creature would be born. We don't have much research on airships."

Fain lifted both eyebrows. Then he turned to me with an *I told you so* stare. "I'm not an expert on charisma, but even I know that won't ingratiate us to anyone. We might not make it to New Norra."

"Wait a moment," Adelgis interjected. "Volke is usually well-regarded. He looks normal. Mostly normal. And people like him. Well, after they get to know him."

"He's not himself right now," Fain said. "And I don't think we should push him to do anything other than rest."

"Because you're afraid Volke might become violent or deranged."

Fain gritted his teeth. "Let's just stop talking about it in front of him."

"You're the one who said he was a plague-ridden madman. I'm just elaborating."

"Stop," I said, holding up a hand. "It's okay. I'd rather we not hide the fact that I'm carrying the plague. I don't mind if you discuss it."

Shadows under my hammock moved with life and purpose. "My arcanist," Luthair said. "As much as I admire your truthful nature, this is one fact I think you should omit whenever possible."

I laced my fingers together and then unlaced them, filled with a fidgety energy as I mulled over the comment. I didn't want to trick anyone—being straightforward and open about the situation seemed like the right course of action.

"There are guilds who hunt plague-ridden arcanists," Fain said. "You know about the Steel Thorn Inquisitors Guild. And the Huntsman Guild. They're the most famous, but there are plenty of others. If word gets out about what you are..."

Adelgis traced the outer edge of his map with the tips of his fingers. "I suppose that would be troublesome."

The conversation died. Silence settled between us. Even the ship seemed to stop creaking as we hit a stream of gentle breeze.

Determined not to dwell on the subject, I tried to recall what we had been talking about before the argument.

The city of New Norra...

Although I had heard of the city from tales I had read as a kid, the truth of the matter was that I didn't know much beyond the border of my island nation. The farther south we traveled, the more foreign the world would become. Normally, I'd be excited for the adventure, but circumstances were dire. Theasin Venrover, Adelgis's father, was the only man I knew who could help me cure the plague, and the longer it took to reach him, the less time I had to deal with the problem.

What if Theasin could create a cure, but it required material from halfway around the world? That wasn't out of the realm of possibility. We had to find him soon, and if the

Sun Chaser was the fastest mode of transportation, we couldn't agitate our hosts.

"Why did your father go to New Norra?" I asked.

Adelgis held up the map and pointed. "Do you see this coast?"

He pointed to the southern edge of the Argo Empire. It stretched west for a considerable distance and then turned southward. According the legend, the farther south the coast went, the more it became a desert. The Amber Dunes —as the map referred to it—seemed barren. While several dots representing cities marked the rest of the map, the Amber Dunes had three. The largest dot, positioned halfway down the coast, was New Norra.

"This is the only port if you want to continue south," Adelgis said. "It's gigantic, and it has the largest bazaar I've ever seen in my life." He lowered his voice as he continued, "There are no laws about what you can buy or sell here, so my father frequents the place for unusual mystical creature parts."

"Like Port Crown?" Fain asked.

Adelgis replied with a nod. "Only with fewer pirates."

"But there are still *some* pirates?"

"It's a free port," Adelgis said, blasé and uncaring. "Pirates frequent the city quite often."

Fain paled a bit. He stared up at the ceiling, his brow hard-set.

"You don't think we'll run into someone like the Dread Pirate Calisto, right?" I asked Adelgis. "He sails up north."

"I hope not," Adelgis said. "But there's a real possibility."

For the moment, it seemed as though we would have to navigate dangerous waters. But even if we had to face pirates, explore unknown cities, and gain the trust of an airship crew—at least we had a plan. One way or another, we'd make it to Theasin and find a cure for this arcane plague.

At least, that was what I told myself.

The wooden boards beyond our door creaked.

We all looked up, even Wraith, his wolf-like ears erect.

The soft sound of boots echoed quietly in the hall, as though someone was trying their hand at stealth, but every other step was too hard to keep hidden.

"Who's that?" Fain asked.

"Probably the same girl who threatened me earlier," I quipped.

Fain shot me a questioning look, but before I could answer, Adelgis cleared his throat.

"No. The person in the hall wasn't a woman. It was the blacksmith." Adelgis forced a half-smile. "He's come looking for you, Volke. And I think your conversation with him will determine whether we stay on the airship for any length of time."

"Why's that?" I asked.

"Well..." Adelgis folded his map and placed it back in his satchel, taking due care to tuck it in between the pages of his book. "I think it would be best if the blacksmith explained everything."

I didn't know why, but his flippant answer irritated me. I didn't need surprises, not at this point in my life, and if it was important to staying on the airship, I needed all the information I could get before having a serious discussion.

"Just tell me," I said, barely holding back my anger. "Now isn't the time to be obtuse."

Adelgis stared at me with a neutral, almost callous, expression. "Very well. The blacksmith came to speak with you because he's your father."

5

A MURDER OF CROWS

My first thought was of Gravekeeper William, but my gut knew that wasn't who Adelgis meant.

When was the last time I had seen my father? On my fifth birthday, nearly twelve years ago. I hadn't spent the occasion celebrating or socializing with family—I had spent the day watching my father's murder trial. He hadn't been born on the Isle of Ruma, so they had sent him to the mainland for final judgment. I had never found out what had happened to him, and now Adelgis was telling me he was the blacksmith aboard an airship?

"My arcanist?" Luthair asked from the shadows.

I shook away my thoughts. "Yes?"

"You became quiet. I'm concerned about your wellbeing."

"I'm fine. Perfectly fine."

Fain swung his legs off the side of his hammock. "Do you have a bad history with your father?"

"No," I muttered. "I don't have much of a history at all."

The airship creaked as a strong gust of wind whipped past.

No one said anything, and I suspected they were waiting for me to make a decision. Did I even want to meet my father after all this time? What if he was just a blackheart, like they said in his trial? They made him out to be a cutthroat—someone who came to the Isle of Ruma to steal phoenix chicks.

But that was so long ago...

I could barely remember what had happened. I never enjoyed recalling the memories, so I pushed them from my mind whenever they surfaced.

"Your father wanted to talk to you," Adelgis said, dragging me out of my thoughts. "But he struggled with the words, and he's afraid of how you'll react."

Wraith swished his wolf-like tail from side to side. "If you haven't much of a history, what's the harm in speaking with him? I think you should."

"Perhaps it's best if you just ignore this," Luthair said. "You don't need any undue stress."

"Well, I agree with Wraith." Fain got off his hammock and walked around the crates until he was closer to my corner. "Family is important. You should speak to him."

Family.

Illia and Gravekeeper William were my family.

But perhaps Fain felt jealous. He had no family to speak of, not even an adopted one, yet here I had two. Squandering this opportunity would probably seem like a mistake to him. And I somewhat agreed. When I had been younger, I'd had a million questions for my father—now I could have resolution.

"Adelgis," I said. "Where can I find my father?"

"His quarters are next to the captain's. Down the hall and then turn left at the stairs."

"Thank you."

I stood and headed for the door. Luthair followed me as a shadow at my feet, offering no further advice on the subject.

Adelgis, Wraith, and Fain said nothing as I exited the storeroom. I walked the long hall to the captain's quarters, my head buzzing. Although I knew I was about to speak to my father, I wasn't sure what I would ask. I hadn't expected to see him—ever. A piece of me had written him off as dead, or at least so far gone that we'd never meet again.

I took the left turn and walked a narrow hall with three doors. One was labeled *Boatswain,* another had the word *Quartermaster,* and the last had nothing. The unlabeled door was the only one with light shining out from under it, and when I listened hard enough, I heard someone pacing, every second step heavy, as though the person's gait were uneven.

"Should I wait in the corridor, my arcanist?" Luthair whispered.

I shook my head. "I'd rather you were with me."

"As you wish."

I rapped my knuckles on the door, a chill running down my spine as I did so.

The pacing stopped, but no one said anything.

"Hello?" I asked.

But how was I supposed to follow it up? *It's me, your son. The one you haven't seen in over a decade. The one you abandoned because you're a murderer. Hope this isn't a bad time to speak.*

I gritted my teeth, hating even the idea of saying my name. Should I introduce myself as Volke Blackwater so that he'd know who I was?

Perhaps fate decided I was taking too long, because in the next moment the whole airship shuddered. I glanced around the empty corridor, wondering what could've caused such a tremble, when the ship quaked a second time, nearly knocking me to the floor. I braced myself on the bulkhead. The harsh clang of a bell sounded from above deck.

"Let's go," I said to Luthair.

I stepped into the shadows and moved through the darkness at a quick pace, slithering over the steps and reaching the deck of the airship in a matter of moments. I couldn't breathe when I shadow-stepped, but I had long become accustomed to holding my breath for the short trek between locations.

My body burned after the use of magic, however. It was a lingering side effect from being second-bonded to Luthair, but it was one I was overcoming. I shook away the dull aches and took stock of my surroundings.

Thunder rumbled from the dark clouds below the airship. The night sky, still as wondrous and beautiful as before, was now filled with the jittering bodies of birds. A couple dozen swarmed around the *Sun Chaser*, their flight irregular and their noises bizarre. Between the caws and the shrieks, I heard giddy laughter and manic howling.

I reached for the shadows, intending to pull out my sword, but nothing came.

My sword had broken—shattered during the queen's assassination.

When one bird flew close, I got a better look at it. A grifter crow—a mystical creature with low levels of magic, the kind that specialized in parlor tricks and sleight-of-hand. But it was riddled with the arcane plague, and the terrible sickness had warped its body. Instead of two wings, it had five—four functioning wings, and one deformed baby wing that hung off its chest like a wart or mole. Its eyes bulged out of its head, gray and jiggly, akin to a dead fish.

It laughed as it dove for one of the deckhands. She gasped and drew a flintlock pistol. The crack of the gunshot disappeared into the breeze washing over the deck. She had missed the grifter crow, even though the beast was the size of a small dog. They were slippery creatures.

As the deckhand tried to reload her weapon, the crow slashed at her with its razor talons, slicing open her forearm from her wrist to her elbow in one deadly cut.

I lifted my hand and evoked terrors. The crow screamed, tormented by unseen fears, and then it fell from the sky. It hit the railing of the airship and tumbled over the side, falling into the dark clouds below.

The deckhand didn't need any instructions. She ran below deck, holding her injured arm the entire way.

"My arcanist," Luthair said.

He moved to merge with me, but I held out a hand.

"No," I said. "Just help protect the crew."

Luthair formed as a suit of black armor next to me, his cape fluttering in the wind. He lifted a gauntlet and willed the shadows to lash out at any crows who drew near, his use of magic precise and without hesitation.

Technically, we were stronger when merged, but…

I feared somehow infecting him.

Of the dozens of plague-ridden monsters, four of them flew toward Luthair. They extended their claws—some had more than two feet—and they tried ripping at Luthair's cape.

But none came for me.

"Luthair," I said. "Stay back."

One wrong attack and Luthair could get infected with the plague as well. Since he was a mystical creature, the plague would affect him more thoroughly—and faster. I couldn't let that happen.

Luthair hesitated for a moment before melting back into his shadow form.

Fain and Wraith emerged from below deck. They stared up at the sky, their gaze unfocused, even though there were tons of birds swooping in close. They couldn't see in the dark, and the feathers of the crows rivaled the darkest of coal.

I dashed over and put my hand on Fain's shoulder. Master Zelfree had taught me about augmenting magic—granting my abilities to others for a short period of time—and I gifted Fain my dark sight. Then I touched Wraith and did the same.

"Thank you," Fain said.

Once they could see, they ran across the deck, trying to keep the birds from attacking anyone.

A few grifter crows went for the sails, tearing at the canvas and clawing at the masts.

"Dammit," someone shouted.

I glanced over my shoulder and spotted four individuals—Captain Devlin, Karna, and a man and woman I didn't know. They had come up from the officer's stairway, and the moment the captain could, he evoked the most powerful burst of wind I had ever felt in my life. A gale-force blast sent the grifter crows flying away from the airship, but it also sent Fain and Wraith collapsing to the deck. I shifted through the shadows to avoid losing my balance, but I could still feel the residual breeze of the attack for moments afterward.

The powerful winds didn't deter the crows for long. They laughed—giggled, even—and swarmed back toward the *Sun Chaser*, as though this were all a game. With renewed vigor, they tried to rip the airship apart.

"You'll all... *suffer*..." the crows chanted, their speech bizarre and hard to listen to.

Captain Devlin put two fingers in his mouth and let loose a whistle that pierced the night. I had to cover my ears, and I wondered if its potency had anything to do with his magic.

His roc—the giant golden bird larger than most beasts who walked on land—emerged from the storm clouds, answering the captain's whistle as though just waiting for a signal. She screeched, drawing the attention of the grifter crows. Then she turned and flew toward the distant clouds, leading the plague-ridden mass of birds away from the airship.

Karna ran to me, her appearance slightly different from earlier. She wore practical sailing clothes, including long pants and a coat. Her blonde hair had been braided and then wrapped into a tight bun.

"Are you hurt?" Karna asked.

I shook my head.

The other woman on deck pulled a zigzag dagger from her belt and pointed it to the sky. "Another one's coming!" The gold blade glittered with magic, and I knew right away she was the one who had threatened my life.

She wore an outfit similar to Karna, though her pants were striped and her coat went all the way up to her jaw. Her pixie-cut fiery hair reminded me of Zaxis. It fluttered in the breeze, but it was much too short to get into her eyes.

A beast dropped out of the sky. It landed on the deck of the *Sun Chaser* so hard and fast it almost broke through the wooden boards. It had the scales of a dragon, the wings of a bat, the stinger of a scorpion, and the short face of a snake. It only had two legs, marking it as a *wyvern*—a type of small dragon typically found up north. The beast was larger than a draft horse, and its wings stretched out twenty feet from one tip to the other.

A man rode on the wyvern's back. He held a long rifle in one hand and the reins of the beast with the other.

The wyvern laughed as it spread its wings wide. Its chest looked like a second wyvern was ripping its way out of the creature's ribcage, but then had become frozen in place. A half-formed head, wings, and a single leg dangled from the body of the plague-ridden wyvern.

"Die," the wyvern said with a rumbling chuckle. "Die, *die, die, die!*"

Then the beast vomited blood and chunks of flesh. It splattered across the deck of the airship. The vital fluid would've sloshed everywhere, but Fain leapt up from the deck and evoked ice. The frosty magic washed over the crimson fluid, keeping it from spreading. A slight dusting of rime covered everything from the railing to the sails.

Wraith went invisible and then appeared by the wyvern's leg. He crunched the beast's ankle, but the plague-ridden monster barely noticed. It laughed and gargled another round of infected blood.

The woman with the zigzag dagger also leapt forward. She stabbed the beast in the other leg, and a flash of lightning burst off the weapon and crackled up the wyvern's side.

The wyvern whipped its tail around and struck the woman, throwing her into the airship's railing.

The captain dashed to her side with unrivaled celerity, as though he were aided by the wind itself whenever he moved. He didn't approach the wyvern, however, no doubt because he was worried about contracting the plague.

"Can you handle the wyvern?" Karna asked me, her attention set on the rider. "I'll take care of its arcanist."

Before I could answer, Karna dashed across the deck.

When she got to the frosty blood, she leapt over the puddles, flipping and jumping, showcasing a whole host of athletic prowess as she nimbly avoided touching anything dangerous. When she neared the wyvern, it tried to bite her —both with its giant head, and then a second time with its half-formed head—but Karna was far faster. She arrived at the creature's side and then shoved her hand under the rider's pant leg.

The moment Karna touched the man's skin, the wyvern arcanist locked up, as though a puppet on strings and his puppeteer hadn't yet made him move. As a doppelgänger arcanist, Karna could manipulate people, but I hadn't expected her to have so much control during the heat of combat. With her magic woven throughout the man's body, she didn't even need to maintain contact to control him.

The plague-ridden man slid off the saddle of his wyvern. He pulled on the reins, but the beast didn't listen. Instead of fighting with it, the man walked to the side of the airship, his movements jerked and awkward as he fought against Karna's controlling magic. When he reached the railing, he planted the muzzle of the rifle against his neck, right where it met the jaw, and then pulled the trigger. The lead bullet slammed through his flesh and sent him staggering over the railing.

The wyvern laughed—unhinged and insane—like the whole event was the best comedy it had ever seen in its life.

Fain snapped his attention to me. "Now's your chance. *Do it.*"

I lifted my hand and manipulated the shadows to grab on to the wyvern, but I wasn't strong enough to keep it trapped for long. And without the added power of being merged with Luthair, I couldn't make the shadows into viable weapons.

"Attack it," Fain shouted.

I shook my head. "I don't have a weapon!"

The last person on deck—the man I didn't recognize—threw back his buccaneer coat to reveal several weapons. He had two swords of differing lengths, a whole host of daggers, and an intricately designed flintlock pistol.

"Take this," he said as he unlatched a sword from his belt and tossed it over, the blade still in its scabbard.

I caught the weapon and ripped it out of its protective casing. Fire flared to life the moment the sword was free, lighting up the deck of the airship like a brilliant ray of sunlight. Taken aback, I almost dropped the weapon, but I took a deep breath and regained my bearings.

The edge of the sword remained heated and glowing bright, as if the blade had just been removed from a forge. When I swung it to test the weight, it burned the air, sizzling even small particles riding the current.

The weapon was surprisingly light.

"You're one of... *us*..." the wyvern said, staring at the glowing blade in my hands, its dead fish eyes jiggling. "Help me..."

I stepped forward. Luthair shifted at my feet, and despite what I had told him, formed up around me, merging us together as one being.

I can't sit idle and watch, he said straight to my mind. *We're stronger together. Aim for the beast's chest.*

The wyvern vomited more blood.

I ducked into the darkness, taking the scorching blade with me and leaving the scabbard. When I emerged, I was directly in front of the monster, much to its confusion. With one powerful thrust, I drove the weapon deep into the creature's twisted chest. The blade sliced through the scales with shocking ease.

The wyvern screamed and tried to claw me with its feet. I dove back into the safety of the darkness and exited on the deck behind the wyvern.

The blade in my hand crackled with power, like it was getting hotter every second it wasn't in the scabbard. I slashed it through the air, leaving a wake of flame, and sliced through the wyvern's flank. It whipped its head back to savage me, but that was what I wanted.

I cut upward, not holding any strength back, and split its face in two.

The monster crumpled to the deck of the ship, somehow still giggling as it died.

My heart hammered in my chest, and it wasn't until that second that I realized how tense I had become. Something about the fight... I had never felt so certain about killing before. It had seemed right. Like I had needed to do it.

My arcanist, Luthair said. *You've done it. Dispose of the body.*

With a twist of my gauntleted hand, I created hooks and chains from the shadows and dragged the still-bleeding corpse of the wyvern to the side of the airship. After one unceremonious tug of the shadows, the monster fell over-board, ripping one of the sails with its tail on the way down.

6

JOZÉ BLACKWATER

I sheathed the scorching blade in its heavy scabbard. The heat subsided, as though the weapon had gone to rest. The wootz cotton under my clothes kept me warmer than I liked, though. Luthair unmerged, and I stumbled backward, sweat soaking into the bandages.

"I told you this would happen!"

I braced myself on a part of the airship, my head spinning. It took me a long moment before I realized the woman with the zigzag dagger was shouting. She pointed at me and then the gore splattered across the deck of the ship.

"These plague monsters never came for us before," she said. "It's because of *him*."

Karna leapt over the half-frozen puddles and shook her head. "No, it's not. You saw what happened in Thronehold. Those plague lunatics are becoming more brazen. They're making active attacks. Why would they come for one knightmare arcanist who's already infected? Get it together, Vethica."

The woman, Vethica, tucked her lightning dagger back in its sheath. She smoothed her short, reddish-blonde hair, her narrow face hardening into something resembling a mix between resignation and indignation. "I still think it's a mistake to have him here."

She turned on the heel of her boot and stormed off to the nearest stairwell.

Captain Devlin straightened his tricorn cap and sighed. "Throw me into the abyss," he muttered. "Flying used to be the *safe* option."

Deckhands cautiously trickled out from below deck, cleaning supplies in both hands.

The captain motioned to the mess. "Sorry 'bout this. Clean it as quick as you can."

After a few deep breaths, I regained my footing and wandered over to Karna and the captain. I didn't need to avoid the blood, but I did so regardless; otherwise, I'd have to wash my bare feet in the cramped washroom.

"You were amazing," Karna said with a smirk. "I expected nothing less."

Captain Devlin tipped his hat. "I do appreciate you puttin' in the work." He narrowed his eyes, his jaw tense. "You didn't summon those monsters to us, right?"

I shook my head. "No."

"I didn't think so, but I still had to ask. You understand."

The captain sighed afterward, his posture slumped. The winds continued to rush by, playing with his shoulder-length curly hair. He seemed like a man who had done this for a long time—it only took him a few seconds to harden back up.

I glanced around, looking for the man with all the weapons. He wasn't on deck anymore. I held his sword close, surprised by the considerable weight of the scabbard as compared to the blade itself.

"It's a fine sword," Captain Devlin said. He ran his hand

along the thin line of his chinstrap beard. "Jozé does good work. You should bring it back to him and have a chat. The man's been talkin' about you nonstop, ever since we watched your matches in the Sovereign Dragon Tournament."

I caught my breath, my grip tight on the weapon.

Jozé...

That was my father's name.

He had been on deck? We had been standing fewer than twenty feet apart, and I hadn't even gotten a good look at him—just the weapons he had flashed when I had said I had needed one. I couldn't even recall the expression or clothing he had worn. Why hadn't I paid more attention?

Karna smiled wide. "You haven't spoken to him yet, have you?" She rubbed my shoulder. "I knew this would be a shocking surprise, but I didn't expect *this* kind of reaction. What're you waiting for? Go speak to him."

I suspected she misinterpreted my silence as delight and wonderment, but it couldn't be further from the truth. My father obviously knew who I was, but he couldn't even look me directly in the face. *He* was avoiding *me*, and that only confirmed the guilt he harbored, either from abandoning me or from the crimes that had gotten him exiled from the Isle of Ruma.

With the blade held close, I headed for the stairs below deck. I would return the weapon. I would speak with him—hear him out—but if he didn't offer a proper explanation, I doubted I would ever interact with him again.

Luthair walked as a suit of armor behind me, his black plate clinking the entire way. He didn't normally remain a suit of armor, so I wondered why he maintained the form, but I didn't ask him about it. Most arcanists kept their eldrin nearby, no matter their sizes.

The crew of the *Sun Chaser* rushed to clean the frozen

mess. Fain and Wraith stayed with them and helped, and I appreciated their efforts. I didn't feel like participating, and Fain's icy magic would help with the containment. Most sailing ships sealed their hulls with pitch or tar—it kept water from seeping in—and I suspected the blood wouldn't leak into the airship, but we were better not taking any chances.

I returned to the narrow corridor before the captain's quarters, one level below deck. After a deep breath, I headed straight for the unlabeled door. There was no more need for hesitation. I knocked three times, loud enough to be heard throughout the deck.

"Jozé?" I asked, his name odd to say aloud. "I've come to return your sword."

The door clicked and then swung inward. I hadn't expected the quick response, and it took me a moment to step inside.

His living quarters were cozier than I had expected, but everything had been arranged with care and planning. Bookshelves with doors were built into the bulkhead, and the sole cot was positioned in one corner, while a solid desk and chair were positioned in the corner opposite. A small table and two benches took up the center of the room, but my attention went straight to the phoenix perched in the back.

I almost forgot to breathe.

Although I had seen several phoenixes in my lifetime—even one riddled with the plague—I had never seen a *blue* phoenix before. But there it was. Perched on a wrought-iron stand.

All the phoenixes I had known had gold eyes, red feathers, and bright orange bodies that looked like pure flame. This blue phoenix had silver eyes, like pools of molten metal, with sapphire feathers, akin to a lustrous peacock. Its body burned a bright white, hidden by its wings and feathers. When it moved, I caught a glimpse of the intense light, but only for a moment. Soot fell from its body, piling on a tray set on the floor beneath its perch.

"It's a pleasure to meet you," the phoenix said, her voice regal and her pronunciation perfect. She bowed her heron-like head, her eyes closed. "You may call me *Tine*. My arcanist and I are pleased to see you."

I had forgotten all about my father until that moment.

Luthair stepped into the room, and the door shut behind him.

My father stood with his hand on the handle, his gaze on his grip. When he finally mustered the courage to look at me, I could practically feel his apprehension.

We looked a lot alike. I didn't know why, but that irritated me.

No. I knew why. It was the association. Everyone on the Isle of Ruma thought I would become a man just like my father. I would be a murderer who followed in his dark footsteps.

We were both tall—he may have even been taller, like Gravekeeper William—and his dark eyes and black hair matched my own, down to the precise hue. He had rough stubble, though, like he hadn't shaved in days. And his honeyed skin was paler than mine, perhaps because he stayed below deck more often than not.

Jozé couldn't look at me long before averting his gaze. He pushed away from the door and walked around the edge of the room, favoring his right leg more than his left, resulting in a limp.

He wore a coat that went down to his ankles, and several belts and holsters held his many weapons in place. He also had metal and leather straps secured around his left knee—the one he refused to bend more than a couple degrees.

Despite his weak leg, he had the arms and shoulders of a man who worked with metal.

Jozé rested his weight on the end of his table. The furniture was nailed to the floor, just in case the airship took a tumble. Up close, I noticed the arcanist's mark on his forehead—sure enough, it was of the mighty phoenix. The Isle of Ruma was famous for their phoenixes, and there was no doubt in my mind where Jozé had met his.

"I saw your fights in the Sovereign Dragon Tournament," Jozé said, breaking the tense silence between us. His voice was deeper than mine, and gruff. Did he smoke? He sounded like a man who had run the habit for a long while. Jozé continued, "I was impressed, kid. Real impressed. I had money you'd win the apprentice division."

I nodded, unsure of how to follow up the statement.

The blue phoenix, Tine, watched our interactions with wide eyes. She glanced between Jozé and me, hanging on every word, but offering none of her own. Her dazzling blue feathers shone under the light of the lanterns on the wall, giving her an otherworldly halo.

Luthair positioned himself in the empty corner and waited. After a few moments, it was like he was another piece of furniture. He could've collected dust, he stood so still.

"Want some rum?" Jozé asked before the silence returned in full force.

I shook my head. "I don't drink."

"You look a little rough."

I ran a hand down my shirt. Sweat stained most of it. And I still didn't have any boots.

Jozé opened one of the bookshelves, his hands unsteady,

but he hid it well by keeping his grip tight on the door latch and then the bottle of rum. He uncorked the top and took a long swig. Once he'd gotten enough, he tipped the glass container in my direction.

"You sure?" he asked. "It takes the edge off."

Again, I shook my head.

While he took another drink, I tried to think of a question—any question—to ask him. I felt like I'd had hundreds before entering the room, but now they eluded me.

Jozé set the bottle on the table. The airship rocked a bit, but not enough to spill the beverage.

"I assume you know who I am," Jozé said, almost a whisper. He went back to avoiding my gaze, his attention fixated on the bottle. "I wanted... Well, I tried to see you several times during the tournament. To tell you I was there. But I never found an opportunity." He scratched at the back of his neck, hard enough I wondered if he was breaking skin.

"What about before that?" I asked, my volume increasing with each word. "What happened on the Isle of Ruma? Why didn't you ever send word? Where have you been? Why not see me before I reached the age of majority?"

I hadn't been able to speak three seconds ago, but now I couldn't stop.

He had wanted to see me, but couldn't find the opportunity? I didn't buy it for a second.

Jozé said nothing. He mulled over the questions, unmoving. His eyes contained a world of information, but he refused to give any of it words.

I threw his blade on the table. The scabbard clattered loud enough to startle his phoenix eldrin, but I didn't knock over the rum.

"Thanks for the weapon," I said, sardonic. "When you

have answers, I'll have the time." I turned to leave, hating every moment of this interaction.

"Wait."

I stopped.

"I've got answers."

My throat tightened as I turned back around and waited.

Jozé tapped his knuckles in the palm of his other hand. "Listen. Years before.... Well, before you were born, I was called to the Isle of Ruma to be a caretaker for the phoenixes."

His statement caught me off guard. I waited, one eyebrow cocked. If he didn't get to something relevant soon, I still intended to leave.

"That was... my profession. Before I became an arcanist. I was a caretaker for mystical creatures." Jozé exhaled. He closed his eyes and continued, "I watched over the phoenixes on Ruma until something unusual happened. When the new eggs hatched, one of the chicks was blue."

I glanced over at Tine. She met my gaze with a hopeful expression on her heron-like face, her feathers fluffing.

"I told the families who controlled the island," Jozé said. "They wanted me to keep it quiet and take the phoenix to the docks so they could sell it to a buyer on the mainland."

"What?" I asked.

The phoenixes of Ruma were meant to bond with people who completed the island's trial of worth. It had been crafted with the phoenixes of old in mind, including the oath of the arcanist that was etched into the 112 steps up the side of the Pillar. Why would they ever take phoenix chicks from the island?

Jozé motioned to his eldrin. "Tine was there. She can confirm what I'm sayin'."

"It's true," she said. "Please listen, Volke."

"I... found out who the buyer was, and I didn't want to help them sell Tine, so I intended to take her from the island."

Jozé spoke with guilt woven in his voice. Before I could interject with more questions, he hurried through the rest of the story.

"Hevil Ren, a man from one of the larger families, intercepted me and tried to take Tine. We got into an altercation."

"So, you killed him?" I asked, curt.

"It wasn't as simple as that, kid."

I held my breath, waiting for this *complicated* explanation. Jozé still couldn't bring himself to look at me.

"Did you kill him or not? It's not like I can—"

"*It was an accident,*" Jozé growled. He slammed his hand on the table, knocking over the drink and spilling the alcohol onto the floor. He grimaced afterward and ran a hand through his windswept hair. "I swear to you. I didn't mean for it to happen, but I wasn't gonna let them take Tine, either. You get that, right?"

His phoenix made a quiet chirping noise, but otherwise didn't add to the conversation.

"Why didn't you tell the people of Ruma?" I asked. "I never heard any of this."

Jozé snorted and pushed away from the table. His weak leg gave him trouble, but his lost-in-thought expression told me he didn't care.

"The judge, the jury—they were all people involved in the sale of the blue phoenix," he said. "They knew what I was tryin' to do, and they wanted me thrown in the ocean and drowned, just to keep their secret." Jozé sighed, and when he looked up at me again, this time it was more pensive. "I only got off that damn island due to a technicality the barrister brought before the court. *He wasn't born on the island*, is what the man said. *His judgment needs to come from the mainland*. The moment I got on a ship, I managed to get away. That's the end of the story."

I had never heard the specifics of the crime or of my father's sentencing. I had been too young to understand, and by the time I had gotten older, I had never had any interest. Hearing my father talk about the past... It made me wonder what else I didn't know about the situation.

It didn't seem unrealistic. The Isle of Ruma was so small that everyone knew everyone else. There were two families who basically ran everything, and if they had agreed to sell a phoenix chick on the side, I imagined they'd have been able to get away with it, so long as a random caretaker hadn't gotten involved.

"When did you bond with Tine?" I asked.

Jozé hesitated before answering, "After I jumped off the side of my transport vessel, I went to the buyer's home and... took her."

Tine puffed up her feathers, more soot raining down with each movement. "That was the outcome I wanted, though. You should tell your son that, my arcanist. Tell him I asked you to come see me."

But Jozé didn't follow up the statement with anything. It felt like he was waiting for my judgment—waiting for me to get upset or forgive him.

"You never tried to send me word?" I asked, much quieter than before. My anger had curdled into melancholy curiosity. "I lived on the isle until my fifteenth birthday. You knew where I was."

"I tried." Jozé limped around the side of the table, limiting the distance between us to a few feet. He stopped at that point, approaching no farther. "I returned to the Isle of

Ruma a few months later. I intended to take you away with me. I swear on the seas I did. But Will..."

"Gravekeeper William?"

"Yeah, well, he... convinced me to leave. He said I didn't have a plan—which I didn't—and he said I was a wanted criminal with no guarantee that I could keep us both safe. He made good points." Jozé sighed. "He promised me he'd take care of you."

I nodded along with the words, my blood icy. William had never told me that part of that story. He had never told me anything about my father, actually. He had always avoided it—said it was a thing of the past I should forget.

Jozé leaned back on the table. "Obviously, Will did good. Like I said, I saw you in the tournament. A knightmare arcanist. A talented fighter. Up and coming." He chuckled. "I'm jealous. I wasn't nearly as exceptional when I was your age. I, uh, transcribed books at a local abbey."

He drifted off and became quiet. His phoenix glanced between us, and I wondered what she thought of the interaction.

I still didn't know what to think.

Uncertain of how to deal with the situation, I placed my hand on the door handle.

"I appreciate that you told me," I said. "But... it's been a long day."

Jozé quickly motioned to the door. "'Course. Yeah. Sleep on it. I'll be here."

Luthair and I stepped out into the corridor, my chest twisted in unease. My father didn't try to stop us or even offer any more words. I figured that was for the best. I really did need time to process everything he had said.

7

REFRESHER COURSE

It took until dawn before the deckhands had the *Sun Chaser* cleaned of blood.

Filled with energy and restless from the fight with the plague creatures, I opted to remain on deck and practice my magic. The winds weren't as bad as earlier, and I wondered if the airship had changed speeds since we had left Thronehold.

Fain and Adelgis stuck close to me. I didn't mind—Fain had asked that I help him with his magic, and I preferred Adelgis close by since he acted a tad odd. They were probably sticking around to "watch me" should anything happen, but that was fine. I *wanted* a safety net. I didn't know if I could live with myself if I hurt anyone inadvertently.

The crew of the *Sun Chaser* stayed far away from us—for the most part. Biyu, the little cabin girl, sat nearby with her back against the railing of the airship, her giant book in her lap. She kept it open, her quill at the ready, her one eye fixed on everything we did. Anytime I coughed, I swore she wrote it down.

Fain stood opposite of me on the deck, his hands at his sides. Wraith watched from the railing, his skull face mask bright in the morning sun.

"The easiest uses of magic are evocation, augmentation, and manipulation," I said, parroting the first magic lessons I'd ever had. "With evocation, you create something. Like when I summon my terrors."

Fain waved his hand in front of him, and a blast of ice washed over the wooden boards of the deck. It made for dangerous walking, and he closed his hand afterward, helping the rime clear away faster.

Biyu scribbled in her book so fast I feared she would rip the paper.

"Augmentation is just adding your magic to something temporarily." I placed my hand on my chest. "Like how I can grant the ability to see in the dark for a short period of time."

"I can become invisible," Fain said as he demonstrated the skill. One second he was on the deck of the airship, the next second he shimmered out of sight, undetectable.

"Okay. Good. Then the last category is *manipulation*. That deals with things already in existence." I willed the shadows to move across the *Sun Chaser*, showcasing my control by hardening edges and creating shapes, like horses and rabbits—a puppet show with no narration. "Like this."

Biyu smiled as she continued her furious writing.

"What can you manipulate?" I asked, ignoring her odd documentation.

"I can't do anything like that," Fain muttered.

"Yes, you can. All arcanists can manipulate *something*." I motioned to Adelgis. "Ethereal whelk arcanists manipulate dreams."

"Well, I can't. I've been an arcanist for years and it's never come to me."

"You didn't know any other wendigo arcanists? Someone who used their magic more proficiently than you?"

Fain shook his head.

"We're going to fix that."

I walked over to him, trying to remember every little detail I knew about wendigo. They were creatures of consumption and cannibalism. They ate flesh, and they stuck to the cold north. Their fangs were laced in a debilitating disease that took hold quickly. Overall, wendigo were hunters that seemed to specialize in killing things, especially things that were close to death, either through sickness or frostbite.

"Can you manipulate ice?" I asked once I was close.

"No," Fain said. "I've tried. I just create it."

"Hold my forearm."

My command caught him off guard. He hesitantly reached out, pushed up the sleeve of my shirt, and took hold of my right arm. I shivered the moment his cold fingers touched my bare skin.

"Like this?" he asked.

I nodded. "Try using your magic to control some aspect of me."

Perhaps a wendigo could manipulate someone's strength or energy—something that would render them weak. That would make sense. They were man-eaters, after all.

Fain stared at my arm, his eyebrows knitted together. For a long while, he did nothing.

"It's okay," I said. "I'm sure it won't be anything we can't handle."

Wendigo were weaker than knightmares, and I assumed

Luthair could disable both Wraith and Fain should any magic get out of control. Right now, we just needed to focus on discovering what Fain could manipulate.

Fain tightened his icy grip. "How... do you do it?"

"It's like your magic is already *inside* the thing you want to manipulate, and you're just calling on it to answer your commands."

We waited on the deck of the airship, neither of us moving. I didn't want to discourage him by saying anything or acting impatient. When I had first used my magic, everything had been a mystery—the unknown aspects of my powers had been a fear that had eaten away at my confidence. Fain didn't need the doubt. It would only kill his ability to master his sorcery.

I hadn't braced myself for the sudden pulse of agony that emanated from Fain's hand. I shouted and jerked my arm away, the shadows across the airship stirring with my agitation.

Blood wept from my forearm as palm-sized slices of skin sloughed off, like a pancake sliding off the top of the stack. I grabbed at the injury and held it against my chest, allowing the crimson to soak into my clothing and wootz wrappings. I gritted my teeth, holding back a whole host of curses.

Biyu sat up, her brow furrowed. "I'll, uh, I'll get the captain!" She slammed her book shut and scampered off, just like a child running for a parent.

Wraith dashed over to me. Without any instruction, he lapped up the droplets of my blood that had landed on the deck. Then he proceeded to eat the thin slices of skin that had slid off my arm. He wagged his tail the entire time, the vision of a disgusting puppy who got to eat the scraps dropped from his master's table.

"Are you okay?" Fain asked, his voice shaky. "I... didn't know..."

As the shock of the event wore off, I managed to process what had happened. My arm wasn't seriously damaged, but the handprint in my skin was disturbing to look at. I kept it wrapped with my clothing.

"It's fine," I forced myself to say. "I'll heal this. Probably."

Adelgis ambled across the deck, his long hair tied back in a loose ponytail to keep it from getting in his eyes. He stopped next to my side and stared at the injury, offering no reaction other than deep curiosity.

"Seems wendigo arcanist manipulate *flesh*," he said, fascination in his voice. "That was what Fain was thinking about once he managed to get his magic to respond."

Fain frowned as he ran his frostbitten fingers through his hair. "I'm so sorry."

I shook my head. "I said it's fine. It doesn't seem like you did much harm." I wiggled my fingers, testing the muscles beneath the injury. "See? Fine. Everything's fine."

The pain, though...

Curse the abyssal hells—it took all my willpower not to break down. It subsided at a slow pace. Too slow for my liking.

"You should try your magic on me next," Adelgis said as he rolled up the sleeve of his coat.

Fain shot him a confused look, one eyebrow high. "You *want* me to use my abilities on you? Did you not see what happened?"

"I saw. But you won't master this without practice, and since no one wants you to spill Volke's blood, it logically falls to me to help." Adelgis held out his arm. "Don't worry. I have experience with bizarre happenings to the human body. I once had a giant leech living inside of me."

It took Fain a couple of moments to absorb Adelgis's statements. "You're a weird one, Moonbeam. Brave, I'll give you that. But weird."

The captain emerged from the officer's staircase, his cap secured to his head with his bandana. When he strode over, I took note of the energy in each step. It seemed odd, since he was so tired earlier in the morning, but I didn't know the man well, so I shook the thought from my head.

"What's going on here?" Captain Devlin asked.

"We're training our magic," I said. I kept my arm close to my body. "We didn't mean to cause any trouble."

"You're no trouble." He placed his hand on my shoulder. "Perhaps I could give you some advice. I've been around for a while. Seen a few things. You might like what I have to say." He squeezed my bicep and smirked.

Then everything fell into place. The walk. The mannerisms. The word choice. This wasn't the captain.

I jerked out of his grasp. "*Karna*. Please. You can just tell me it's you."

A slight smile crept across Adelgis's face. "Oh, you figured it out? I thought she would fool you with this one."

Adelgis was never fooled, not when he could hear thoughts like the average person could hear speech.

The fake Captain Devlin sneered. "You always catch me fast. A little *too* fast."

"It's the way you touch me," I said as I rotated my shoulder. "And the subtle way you act. It doesn't match the people you're portraying."

With a tip of the hat, Karna-Devlin chuckled. "That's because I'm never really trying that hard. One of these days —when you least expect it—I'm going to surprise you."

"Do you always change your... uh... body?" Fain asked as he gave the fake captain a once-over.

"We all have to get our training in somewhere."

Although I hadn't given it much thought, Karna *did* need to shift her appearance in order to practice her skills. Using magic was much like using a muscle in the body—the more exercise, the stronger it became. Additionally, the longer an arcanist was bonded to its eldrin, the higher the limits of their magic.

To an extent, anyway. Some mystical creatures were just weaker than others. At some point, they couldn't grow any more powerful.

How strong were doppelgängers? I couldn't remember. Perhaps Karna was building her skills and reaching for the upper capacity of her shapeshifting abilities.

Karna pushed back the curly hair of the captain and allowed her sorcery to change her appearance back to her normal dancer's physique. Her hair grew longer and blonde, and her height went down a considerable amount. Her clothes didn't change, however, leaving her wearing a pile of laundry draped over her athletic frame.

"Fascinating," Adelgis muttered as he observed the transformation. "Tell me, do you ever record changes? Height and weight and such?"

Karna narrowed her eyes. "No. Why would I?"

"I think if I had the ability to change from male to female, that would be the first thing I did. Is the weight the same? Or does the magic displace that? Obviously, the height would be different, but by how much? How would that affect one's perceptions?"

"Are you serious?" Fain asked. "If you could change into a woman, the first thing you'd do is measure your new height and weight? What's wrong with you?"

Adelgis regarded him with a neutral, almost sarcastic, glance. "What would be the first thing *you* did as a woman?"

"Knowing my luck? Menstruate."

"*Enough*," I barked, my cheeks hot. I ran my good hand down my face, trying to hide my embarrassment. "There's no reason to discuss this. Ever."

For whatever reason, the interaction amused Karna. She chortled as she glanced between us, and I wondered what her thoughts on the situation were. If I had to guess, I'd say she thought we were all acting like children, but perhaps she found the exchange endearing.

Then she noticed the injury on my arm, and her mirth disappeared. "What happened?"

"An accident," I said. "Don't worry. We won't be doing anything like this again."

"Hm. Well, you should also keep in mind how the crew sees you. If you're getting violent with your fellow arcanists, it'll disturb the deckhands. Biyu thought you two were trying to kill each other."

"She's a child," Fain stated. "Everything scares kids."

"Still. I don't want to have to storm onto the deck every time you two horse around." Karna placed her hand back on my shoulder, her slender feminine fingers softer than the gruff grip of the faux captain's. "You shouldn't injure yourself. Get some rest. Besides, don't you want to catch up with your father? I'm surprised you're not down there right now."

I hadn't thought about him—not once—while training with Fain, and I honestly still didn't want to. A part of me felt like it was a betrayal to William. *He* was my father. Adding Jozé to my life now almost seemed unnecessary. He could've just been another random member of the *Sun Chaser* crew.

But there was no real reason to hate Jozé, either. He hadn't abandoned me out of malice, and he seemed like he wanted to make things right.

"I need more time to think about it," I murmured.

Karna straightened her clothing to prevent it from spilling off her shoulder. She said nothing as she mulled over my comment. Perhaps now she knew my father and I didn't have a harmonious relationship.

The moment the pain in my forearm subsided, I exhaled and headed for the stairway below deck. "Adelgis, would you mind helping me sleep? I think it's time for me to get some rest." I glanced over my shoulder. "Fain, we'll do more of this tomorrow."

He nodded.

Wraith perked his ears up and watched me go, his gold eyes under the skull-mask following my every move until Adelgis and I disappeared below deck.

8

DREAMS OF DISTANT LEGENDS

Surgeon Tammi gave me a new shirt and replaced my bandages. Just like before, she asked that I not watch her work. I did as she instructed, and once she completed her task, she bid Adelgis and me farewell and left. It seemed odd how much she didn't want us interacting with her, but I suspected she had her reasons. I headed to the storeroom, Adelgis close by my side.

The lanterns in the narrow corridor on the first deck had been snuffed, resulting in a gloomy atmosphere. It didn't bother me, and I was ready to give Adelgis my dark-sight, but he motioned with a twist of his hand, and a bright flash of light appeared a moment later.

Crystalline shards appeared out of thin air and then coalesced together, forming into a single solid creature. The light became a shell and tentacles, the iridescent glow multicolored. The mystical creature was Adelgis's eldrin, an ethereal whelk named *Felicity*.

Once fully formed, she looked like a head-sized sea snail with tentacles hanging down from her soft snail body. The shine of her shell lit up the corridor better than any lantern.

"Thank you, Felicity," Adelgis said.

"Anything for you, my arcanist." Her voice was as bright as her light—happy and effervescent.

Before we reached the storeroom, I glanced down the hall to my father's bedroom. I still didn't know what to say to him. Tired and ready for a distraction, I entered the storeroom and headed straight for the hammock in the back.

"Volke."

I laid back on my ratty bed. "Yes?"

Adelgis stood at my side. Felicity played with his long hair, her tentacles weaving between the inky locks.

"Do you want me to investigate your father?" he asked. "I could ask him questions and listen to his thoughts."

I shook my head. "No, thank you." I rested my arm across my face, the crook of my elbow covering my eyes. "Just help me sleep. I'd rather not think about any of this."

"Very well. I have the perfect dreams for you."

Although the statement sounded ominous, I decided not to say anything. As long as he helped me sleep, I could overcome any dream-turned-nightmare that Adelgis threw at me.

Adelgis placed his hand on the top of my head, and the odd magical cobwebs quickly blanketed my thoughts. In a matter of moments, I was lost to a slumberland of his design.

I knew this feeling.

I was dreaming. But I wasn't experiencing the dream as myself—I was someone else. Leaner. More energetic. Lithe and agile.

I ran through a woodland area dotted in strange trees.

The white trunks and gray leaves made it seem like the color had been drained from the world, but the bright blue sky above the dull canopy proved otherwise.

Who was I? What was I doing? I watched the scene from behind the eyes of whoever's memory this was, observing from their gaze, but never hearing their thoughts.

I stopped near a thick tree, one so old and gnarled that the branches had twisted around each other, and the knots in the trunk were home to several birds. I ran my hand along the smooth bark, breathing deeply and enjoying the rush from a good sprint.

"Here it is," I called out.

A young man hustled his way out from between two trees. He wore an outrageous outfit, one with a puffy collar that circled his neck like it was trying to strangle him. I had seen paintings with that kind of attire, but they were old—it was a fashion from over a century ago.

The man with the puffy collar lumbered over, his breathing labored and his round face red. He took a moment to compose himself and even leaned heavily against the trunk of the tree. His leggings were tight, and he wore a loose and flowing red tunic, similar to those worn at formal lunch parties.

"So far out?" the young man asked between huffs. "Are you sure?"

"Have I ever lied to you?" I pointed to the branches above us.

The light caught something perched between two delicate twigs. The object glinted gold and shone for a second before the leaves rustled and blocked the light again.

I recognized the thumb-sized gem right away—a star shard. They were tiny fragments of magic that rained down from the sky. And everyone wanted them. They were rare and valuable and were used as the adhesive to bind magic to objects. Every arcanist could make use of them.

How had one gotten in the tree? Had it gotten caught in the branches when it had fallen to the earth?

The young man smoothed his tunic. "I can't believe you found it."

I offered a confident chuckle and swished back my windswept hair. "If I say I can do something, then I can. Why do you keep questioning me, Fennis?"

"But it's so high up. It must be thirty-five feet above us. And this tree doesn't look safe to climb."

Fennis finally caught his breath and straightened his posture. His curly brown hair and clean-shaven face seemed out of place in our wild woodland surroundings. Everything about him seemed out of place, actually. His clothing was a bit too clean, except for the sweat staining his underarms, and his short boots had a fine polish to them.

"Feh." I waved away his concern. "Easy. Watch this."

I put my foot into one of the tree's knots and hefted myself. My clothing—or whoever I was?—included dirty boots marked with a lifetime's worth of scuffs and a tunic that didn't fit quite right. It reminded me of when I had been an orphan living with Gravekeeper William. Everything I had worn back then had been a hand-me-down.

Much to my fascination, I easily scaled the giant tree. One branch, then to the next—I even kicked my legs up and hooked them around one of the tree's limbs, working my way higher and higher. If I fell, I imagined I'd have a hundred broken bones and several ruptured organs, but whoever was driving this dream-memory didn't seem to care.

It was the exact opposite. I swung from the branches as

though I were *trying* to be reckless, even going so far as to glance back down at Fennis and flash him a smirk.

"If you fall…" Fennis said, his tone an insufferable whine.

I laughed. "I'm not going to fall. Have a little faith."

Maybe *I* should've had more faith. I made my way to the star shard without incident, and even when the branch shook with my weight, I managed to stay in control just enough to grab the sparkling gem before it fell out of the twig.

The star shard…

The moment I grabbed it, I felt a pulse of inner power. The magic contained within could create something powerful—a trinket or an artifact—a permanent object with its own powers, much like the legendary Occult Compass.

I had technically held some in the past, but not for long, and it had been during a point of extreme turmoil. Holding this now, even in this dream memory, was a new experience.

I climbed back down the tree at a rash pace, practically dropping onto the branches below, no matter how much they shook or creaked. When I hit the ground, Fennis's eyes lit up, and my face went hot in response.

"Don't get weak in the knees now," I said as I tossed the star shard back and forth between my hands. "I'm just getting started. With *this,* we can afford passage through the Lightning Straits. We're going places. Real places. Far from here."

Fennis watched the star shard with an unblinking gaze. "We'll have more than enough for simple passage. So much more…"

I stopped tossing the shard. "I'll go into town and get it appraised."

"*No,*" Fennis said, a little too quickly.

"Why not? The sooner we get out of here, the better."

"Well..." Fennis waved his hand around, motioning to my entire body. "Look at you. If a dirty, unlicked cub strolls into town with a star shard, they'll think you've stolen it. Mark my words, they will. And then they'll take it and we'll have nothing."

I hated the assessment. It reminded me too much of my own youth. People had judged me long before they had known me—always on my appearance or family history.

"I should sell it," Fennis continued. He held out his hand. "My family is prominent. If I say I found it, everyone will believe me. And once I have the coin, I can purchase passage. For the both of us."

Whoever I was didn't answer. I fidgeted with the star shard, twirling it between my fingers. My palms were calloused, but I seemed skilled with my hands, like a sleight-of-hand entertainer or artist.

Fennis smiled. "Have a little faith."

After a long sigh, I placed the star shard in Fennis's soft hand. "Let me know when everything's set."

The dream faded at that point.

At first, I thought it might be over, and that I would finally awake, but a fog swirled around us, and it was like the world was rearranged. Somehow, although I didn't know how, dream-logic told me that time had passed.

When my vision returned, I stood at the edge of a waterfront town, staring out at the empty docks. Cobblestones filled every nook and cranny of the streets and alleys, and the houses were built close enough that someone could climb out one window and enter their neighbor's house through another. Smoke gushed from the many chimneys that dominated the roofs. Industry only had one scent, and this town reveled in it.

The sun set in the far distance while the waves lapped against the piers. I took a seat on a few empty crates stacked by the dock storehouse.

"There you are."

I turned toward the gruff voice, my shoulders tense.

A rough-and-tumble youth sauntered out of a dark alleyway, his copper hair so long and matted it looked like he had used a mop head as a wig, the locks falling straight to his shoulders. He wore ripped-up trousers and a tunic held in place with a leather shoulder pad.

His face had seen better days.

His nose had been busted, his lip split, and half his face was purple, as though his black eye had bled into the rest of his skin.

"What're you doing, Lynus?" I asked, my eyes narrowed. "What happened this time?"

Lynus was in no rush as he ambled over, his hands in his pockets. Blood trickled down from his busted eyebrow as he took a seat next to me. I realized then he had walked slowly because even his side was bleeding—a few scarlet dots marked his tunic.

"Eh," Lynus said with a shrug. "That's not important right now." He faced me, though his long copper hair was covering most of his mangled expression. "How come you aren't on a ship, sailing away with what's-his-name?"

"Fennis left without me," I said, my voice calm, but my blood cold. I forced a shrug, even if my tense body resisted. "So, I guess I owe you a drink. You called it."

Lynus pressed his thumb against his left nostril, closed it up, and then snorted hard. A glob of blood splattered onto the ground. "That prissy uptowner had frills for brains."

I laughed, though it was short lived and a little darker

than someone who was genuinely enjoying themselves. "I have bad luck with love, is all."

"You're cursed." Lynus chuckled. "We all are."

The waves continued their gentle song, and the seagulls added their sleepy chorus. For a long while, I sat next to Lynus, watching the sun finally set in the distance. The chill of twilight washed over the empty docks, blanketing us in the cold embrace of an autumn night.

"Are you done sulking?" Lynus asked.

"I was never *sulking*," I growled. "This doesn't bother me. I knew... Well, I knew someone like him wouldn't want someone like me." The tension in my shoulders worsened.

"Good. Because I got us passage to a port town near the Lightning Straits."

I snapped my attention to Lynus, his face still obscured by his blood-matted hair. "How?"

"I helped the tax collector *convince* some people they had to pay up." Lynus half-smiled, showing off his sharp canines. "They might've broken my face, but they won't walk right ever again."

"That's why you look like this?"

"Yeah."

"Why?" I asked, my throat tight and my voice at the edge of raw. I took a deep breath, and when I spoke next, I was practically yelling—it hid any sort of emotion other than anger. "What's the point if we don't have passage on a ship large enough to make it through the straits? Dammit, I don't need to *see* the narrow waters; I need to get to the world beyond it!"

Lynus didn't respond.

I grabbed his bloody tunic and shook. Through gritted teeth, I said, "Don't do these stupid stunts unless you think it through."

"Here," Lynus said as he withdrew a piece of parchment from his trouser pocket. "This is why."

The small poster read:

VOLUNTEERS
Aid Needed on the Open Ocean
THE FRITH GUILD
Arcanists of the Frith Guild need able-bodied men and women with the skills to tame the high seas. The queen has authorized expeditions to quell corsairs and discover distant lands and far-off places.
INQUIRE AT THE PORT OF RED FALLS
Speak with First Mate Gregory Ruma
Serve under Captain Liet Eventide
Bonuses will be given in addition to two months' advance.

"You want us to enlist with an arcanist's guild?" I asked, all anger gone from my voice.

"That's right."

"The Frith Guild?"

Lynus shrugged. "They have a good reputation. They won't fail to pay."

I ran my hand over the lettering on the poster. "You think they'll take men like us?"

"Won't know until we try. Better than staying here. Better than watching you sulk."

I laughed, this time with actual mirth. "Will you be able to handle taking orders from an arcanist? You're more feral than these organizations like."

Lynus rubbed at the bruise that covered half his face,

more blood seeping from the cut on his lip. "As far as I'm concerned, you're the only damn family I have left. If taking orders from try-hards will get you out of this depression, I guess I gotta tough it out then."

I smacked him on the side. He grimaced and ground out a curse.

"I'm surprised you managed this," I said. "A good plan? From you?"

"You always underestimate me, Everett. When have I ever let you down?"

I jerked awake, my heart pounding hard against my ribs.

It took a few seconds to realize I was in the storeroom of the *Sun Chaser*. Pale orange light beyond the porthole told me it was almost dawn. I had slept throughout the night, never waking once, all thanks to Adelgis's magic.

Everett.

Everett Zelfree.

Had that really been one of *his* memories? I had never realized my master from the Frith Guild—Master Zelfree— had once been a poor kid on the streets. All I had ever known of him were the stories and what I had learned over the course of studying under him. Why had Adelgis shown me those things?

"I thought you liked stories of legendary swashbucklers?"

I flinched and threw myself out of my hammock, my pulse quickening even faster.

Adelgis sat on the rum barrel in the middle of the storeroom. His ethereal whelk had disappeared from sight, no doubt so that the room could remain dark. Fain and Wraith were asleep near the door, neither of them stirring, despite Adelgis's question.

"What?" I asked, confused.

"I said, I thought you liked legendary swashbucklers?"

"I... I do. I read about them as a child."

"Perfect. Master Zelfree interacted with several of them, especially Gregory Ruma. Wasn't he the man your home island was named after? Memories of Gregory Ruma will be interesting, won't they? And you said you wanted *interesting* dreams."

I rubbed at the back of my neck as the rest of my body managed to wind down. "Uh, yeah. I suppose they would be interesting."

This was what I got instead of *fun dreams?* There really was no winning.

"It'll only take us six days to reach New Norra," Adelgis said. "I suggest you just relax until then. Fain and I can handle most everything the crew will need from us."

9

A SKY TREK

Training on the deck of the *Sun Chaser* kept me distracted.

Fain evoked ice often, making everything cool despite the rays of sun from a cloudless sky. While he attempted to increase the strength of his frost, I worked on my footwork. The slippery deck gave me a better understanding of how to keep my balance, even in the most difficult of terrains.

Luthair merged with me during those times, and although he didn't add weight, his shadow armor did help me keep my footing. Fain would blast ice over the wood as I rushed at him. He'd attempt to stop me, and I'd do everything in my power to keep from getting caught in the rime.

Although I didn't think it was the most efficient training, it did seem to help Fain. His ice became thicker and more powerful, even from just two days of solid practice and instruction. I suspected he hadn't been exerting himself before, for fear of his own powers. Now that he knew what he could manipulate, he seemed a bit more confident.

When I grew tired of running back and forth on an icy

deck, I unmerged from Luthair and waved at Fain. "I need to take a break."

Biyu waited by the railing again, her book open and her notes extensive. Luthair and I walked to her, and she stared at us the entire way, her one eye wide and locked on to Luthair's shadowy armor. I decided to take a seat next to her —a good three feet away, but still close—and Biyu made a quick note of it in her book.

"Are knightmares empty inside?" Biyu asked Luthair.

He took a position on the other side of me, his cape fluttering with dramatic flair. "Yes."

"Can you see things? Without eyeballs?"

"Yes."

"Can you smell things?"

Luthair mulled over that question for a long moment. "No," he finally said.

Biyu hunched over her book and wrote down the information as fast as her hand would allow. The black spots on the feather of her quill faded with each word she penned.

To my surprise, her handwriting was refined and almost elegant, even when she wrote at extreme speeds. I could read her writing, even at my distance, but my attention immediately went to the small accompanying pictures she had drawn in the margins.

"Is that Fain and Wraith?" I asked, pointing to the image of a dog and a man. The man's fingers were black, and the dog's face looked odd, as though drawn twice.

Biyu angled her book away from me. "I'm not done with those yet. You can't look at them."

"Well, they're really good from what I saw."

Her cheeks brightened to a soft pink as she touched the page of her book. "I, uh, like dogs. And wolves. And *especially* puppies." She glanced over, her one eye narrowed. "All the arcanists here have birds as eldrin, which are boring to draw. Except for Karna. But her doppelgänger isn't cute *at all*."

I scooted a tad closer, just an inch or two. "I'm sure Wraith would let you pet him, if you asked."

"I can't." Biyu held her book close and wrote a quick note. "Vethica says you three aren't to be trusted, and Captain Devlin says I should—" she cleared her throat and then deepened her voice in an attempt to match the captain's, "—*maintain a cautious distance and call for help if anything suspicious happens.*"

"Biyu!"

The shout got me tense, but I took a deep breath and relaxed once I realized it was the woman with the zigzag dagger—Vethica. She stood at the top of the stairs to go below deck, and her hard gaze spoke a thousand words of irritation.

"The captain wants to see you below deck, Biyu," Vethica said. "You should hurry along."

Biyu shut her book, tucked away her quill, and then offered me a quick smile. "Goodbye for now." She hurried to the stairs and flew down them two at a time.

I was starting to dislike Vethica. She walked straight to me, and I stood in order to greet her, but she huffed and waved away the gesture.

"What do you think you're doing?" she snapped.

"Resting after practice. Is that a crime?"

"No, but there's never a reason a man should be talking to a little girl like Biyu." Vethica brushed her short hair to one side, never taking her attention off me. "As the boatswain, I'll have you thrown from this ship."

"I don't mean Biyu any harm," I said. "She just reminds me of my sister. Illia also wears an eyepatch."

"A likely story."

I opened my mouth to make a heated retort, but I caught my breath before any words escaped. Vethica's forehead didn't have an arcanist mark, but once her bangs had fluttered to the side, I realized there were scars where one should have been. The faded etchings in her flesh seemed like wounds, and I wondered if she had once been an arcanist. If an arcanist's eldrin dies, the arcanist loses all their magic. It seemed a cruel and sad fate.

Vethica noticed my staring. She raked her fingers through her hair, bringing the orange-red locks back down in front, blocking the old arcanist mark.

"Mind your own damn business," she said. Then she crossed the deck, purpose in her gait.

I didn't try to stop her. All I could think about was how terrible it would be to lose Luthair. And if I didn't find a cure for the plague in my veins, that just might be the only outcome for us.

I had a night of vivid dreams, but not like I had been expecting.

All I saw were visions of ships, wide open oceans, and mystical creatures crashing out of the waves. It wasn't like the last dream, which had a coherent narrative told from Zelfree's memory. They were just instances of interesting scenes, like watching snippets of someone's life and only stopping to focus on the extraordinary moments.

When I awoke, I felt refreshed, but also... disappointed.

I had wanted to see how Master Zelfree had joined the Frith Guild.

The porthole for our tiny storeroom showed me the night sky. I had awoken early.

Anxious to stretch my legs, I slid off my hammock and then shadow-stepped to the door, so as to not make any needless noise. Luthair slithered after me—knightmares never needed to sleep, so I suspected he had just been waiting for me to get up and go.

I stepped into the shadows and emerged on the other side of the door, in the dark corridor that led to the captain's quarters. My heart seized in my chest when I almost ran into a man upon exiting the darkness.

"Whoa," Jozé said, his voice unsteady. He braced himself on the bulkhead and forced a chuckle. "It's you."

I shook my head. "Uh, yeah." Then I realized he had just been standing around in a dark hallway, no lanterns lit. "What're you doing here?"

Jozé rubbed his hand across the dark stubble on his chin. "I... came to speak with you."

"In the middle of the night?"

"Heh. No. Truth be told, I was here at twilight, but I kept debating about what I'd say." He leaned more of his weight against the wall of the airship. "Listen. The crew says you're practicing magic, but you don't have a weapon."

"That's true." My words came out curt, even when I was trying to sound normal.

Jozé opened his coat, flashing the variety of weapons I had seen he had earlier. "Here. Use this for the time being." He handed over the sword with the heavy scabbard, hilt first.

Although it seemed rude to reject his offer, the thought crossed my mind.

It was a good weapon, though.

I took the blade and held it close.

"I made that," he said. "Crafted it with a handful of star shards, the fang of a pyroclastic dragon, and my own phoenix magic. That blade'll get hot enough to sear a bonfire."

"Hm."

Silence settled between us as I stared down at the heavy scabbard. No wonder the blade burned with extreme intensity. Pyroclastic dragons were said to be the kings of fire.

"You know about imbuing magic, right?" Jozé asked, breaking me from my thoughts.

I nodded.

"Why haven't you made a weapon yet? I thought that was what knightmare arcanists did. They made a weapon with their eldrin."

"Well…" I tapped the hilt of the sword, wondering how much information I should give my father. When I determined it wouldn't hurt to explain, I said, "I made a shield with Luthair, but I left it with my sister. And before Luthair was bonded to me, his first arcanist had crafted a sword from a behemoth fang, but that was broken during the attack on Thronehold."

"That means you don't have one anymore?"

I shook my head.

"Kid, I know you're still deciding whether you'll speak to me, but if there's one thing I'm good at in this world, it's crafting magical items."

I glanced up, my eyebrows knit. "They say you're the ship's blacksmith."

"Yeah. I make all sorts of magical things for the captain and crew, with metal or bone or mystical wood." Jozé patted his stiff leg. "I'm not really good at anything else, so I focused hard for these last twelve years."

"What're you trying to say?" I asked.

"I'm good at making weapons. You need a weapon. Let me help you with this." He pushed off the bulkhead and stood as straight as his bad leg would allow. "Obviously, I can't make up for the years lost between us, but I can at least be useful to you now, right? We're heading straight to New Norra—I'm sure we can find something interesting to use as the base material for a weapon."

"Base material?"

"Like a fang or claw or shard of bone. Maybe we could even find some rare metals floatin' around. We could make something unique, and I can show you how a master arcanist crafts a magical item."

Excitement and hope laced his words.

I had to admit—it sounded good. Although my father and I didn't have much in common, we were both arcanists, and if he could teach me to craft brilliant trinkets and arti-facts, perhaps we could find common ground to bond over. He had been absent most of my life, but this sounded like a plausible route to reconciliation.

"I'd like that," I said. "I've only ever made the one item, so I don't know much about imbuing magic."

Jozé let out a half-laugh, half-sigh. "*Good.* Great, even. Once we land, I'll take you to the bazaar."

A new day. More terrible food from the airship galley.

I continued my training on deck, working with Fain, my mind on distant possibilities while he practiced simpler things. When I merged with Luthair, it was easier to focus, but whenever I wasn't, my mind wandered like a dinghy lost at sea. Practicing magic wasn't distracting me like it had before.

The sun set, ending the day.

With all the enthusiasm of a shambling corpse, I ate dinner and headed back down to the storeroom. I threw myself on my hammock, my gaze on the roof. Adelgis placed a hand on my temple, and once again, I drifted into a dream world created by his sorcery.

But again—it wasn't like the memories from before.

Sure, I saw Gregory Ruma. He was just like the old legends said. Brave. Bold. Gallant. Without peer. The flashes of memories showed him toppling ships with his control of water and blasting cutthroats with lightning.

And while I enjoyed seeing it, the context wasn't there.

I awoke with another profound sense of disappointment and then flinched when I realized Adelgis was leaning over me, staring as though he had been watching me sleep.

"What're you doing?" I whispered, now fully awake, my heart hammering out of control.

Adelgis sighed. "You seem unhappy."

"I like my personal space."

"I don't mean right now. I meant in your dreams. You're not amused by them anymore."

I rolled out of my hammock and took a few steps away from Adelgis. Once my nerves had calmed, I ran a hand through my matted hair. The sweat and grime from multiple days of training caused me to shiver. I probably smelled horrible.

"We're stopping to resupply," Adelgis said as he pointed to the porthole. "Look outside. We're at a village on the edge of the Amber Dunes, right where the forest meets the sands."

The porthole beckoned me with the soft glow of a beautiful dawn. I ambled over, curious to see a village near a desert. The thick glass obscured my vision, but not enough to hide all detail. I could make out the houses and dirt roads, and the tree line—a bright green—clearly ended at the edge of a vast, dry valley.

"We'll be getting water," Adelgis said. "You can bathe before we continue on our merry way."

I tucked my hand into my underarm and scratched. "Probably a good thing."

"Definitely a good thing," Luthair said from the darkness at my feet.

I chuckled. "When clothes can talk, these are the things they say."

"Destiny decided that I needed to guide *two* arcanists through the sweaty period of their life people call *young adulthood*."

"Good thing you don't have a sense of smell."

"I'm thankful for the little things in life, my arcanist."

I examined the storeroom with a quick glance. Besides the crates and barrels of rum, Adelgis and I were alone.

"Where's Fain?" I asked.

"He's getting us food."

My stomach grumbled in protest. "Hm."

"You know I can give you dreams of bountiful banquets or lavish feasts." Adelgis pulled his black hair free from the ponytail and allowed it to fall past his shoulders. It had gotten longer, and he combed it with his fingers. "At least then you could experience something tasty."

"No, thank you. That would only be more depressing when I awoke."

"What would make you happy, then?"

The Frith Guild.

I missed them.

That was why I wanted to see how Master Zelfree had joined. I wanted to see him interact with others when I couldn't—be with the people I missed when it was impossible for me to return. And in a strange way, Zelfree and I seemed to share a few life details I hadn't known before. It made me feel... more connected to the man.

"He doesn't like it when people know his personal history," Adelgis muttered, obviously hearing every one of my thoughts. "Master Zelfree wasn't pleased when he realized I could see everything in his life."

"Did he tell you not to share anything?"

"No."

I crossed my arms, well aware that Zelfree disliked people knowing anything about him. "Maybe just... give me the memories that aren't personal-*personal*. If that makes any sense."

"I'll try to think of a few to show you," Adelgis said. "Until then, we should freshen up and perhaps mingle with the crew."

10

THE CITY OF NEW NORRA

The *Sun Chaser* didn't land, it remained fifty feet in the air, the gusts below the hull powerful enough to bend the nearby trees and rip away leaves. Fain, Adelgis, and I left the ship along with the captain, Jozé, Karna, and Vethica. Deckhands were left in charge of loading the airship with supplies. They used a pulley and crane to lift all the heavy materials onto the deck, and while I found it fascinating to watch them crank up several crates and barrels of water, I decided to head to the edge of the village.

The captain's roc, Mesos, glided down from the clouds and landed on the ground with a few powerful and controlled flaps of her massive wings. Her talons dug into the dirt, leaving deep holes wherever she stood.

I walked close to her, shocked at how tall she was once standing on the ground. I had only ever seen a roc up close one other time in my life—when I had visited Port Crown, the pirate's den. A roc had stood guard at the rocky water gates.

Mesos stared down at me with bright, round eyes. The

gold of the irises matched the brilliant gold of her feathers, and she lowered her head so that her beak came within a few inches of me. With each exhale, her crisp breath washed across my shirt and shoulders.

Captain Devlin approached with his arms wide. Mesos fluffed her feathers and made a *cooing* noise, but due to her huge size, it sounded closer to a deep rumble, akin to a monster or some other spooky creature only conceived of in nightmares. The captain hugged his gargantuan eldrin, his arms unable to wrap all the way around Mesos's neck.

"How's my favorite lass doin'?" he asked as he scratched between her feathers.

Mesos cooed again and then leaned on him.

"Hey, hey, hey!"

The roc gently fell forward and laid on the captain. It reminded me of a chicken covering her eggs, and she "snuggled" him like only a giant bird could.

The crew of the *Sun Chaser* snickered and laughed. Some even patted Mesos on her black beak, despite the fact that the edges were sharp enough to slice a man clean in half. Mesos exhaled, her breath becoming an icy fog that froze people's hair in odd cowlick shapes. This seemed to amuse her, as she laughed a chirp-like laugh.

"This isn't funny," Captain Devlin said as he dragged himself out from her feathered body. "You're making us look ridiculous, you know that?"

My father's phoenix, Tine, circled down from the sky, her radiant blue feathers glittering with powerful magic. Her peacock-like tail twirled at the end, and the green-azure "eye" markings seemed more mystical than a normal phoenix's.

Tine landed on Mesos's back, and although Tine was the

size of a large turkey, she looked like a baby chick when perched on a giant roc. It was a bird dog-pile on the captain.

"Did you know that female birds of prey are larger than their male counterparts?" Adelgis asked so close to my side that I almost jumped when I realized his proximity.

Although at this point, I was almost fully accustomed to his weird timing.

"I didn't know that," I muttered.

"Female rocs, phoenixes, hawks, and eagles are all larger than their males. That means that Mesos will probably double in size before she's fully grown."

"Interesting. Did you learn that from your father?"

Adelgis tensed, his expression of fascination disappearing under a mask of neutrality. "Yes."

"Are you... worried about seeing him again?"

"I've decided I need to have serious words with my father." Adelgis forced a smile. "It's nothing you need to concern yourself with. I should be the one to deal with my family."

"Okay." I patted him on the shoulder. "Let's go into the village then. Take our minds off things."

"That's why I came to speak with you. I think it'd be better if you went back on the airship."

"Why?"

Adelgis pointed toward the village. The houses were built tall with airy roofs, no doubt to help keep them cool. The stones used in the bases were large and wide, and the wood for the walls reminded me of cabins I had seen in old paintings. Adelgis motioned to the fields beyond the housing. Goats roamed in herds, fenced in with sturdy posts. On the other side of that, I spotted a group of horses with impressive riders. They wore leather and chain armor, and most were carrying nets, lanterns, and large satchels, as though they were traveling far.

"They're hunters," Adelgis stated.

He didn't need to explain further. "Plague hunters," I said.

"If you wait near the airship, we can avoid them."

Although I dreaded the idea of separating from the others, I agreed with Adelgis's assessment. Instead of tempting fate by wandering through a village where people wanted me dead, I waited back at the airship, despite my urge to explore.

When I had been younger, I would've given my right arm to travel the world in an airship filled with extraordinary arcanists. Now that it was happening, I couldn't enjoy it. I smirked to myself. Sometimes fate had a cruel sense of humor.

Adelgis waited with me, though. He remained quiet and smiled whenever I looked over. He could hear every one of my thoughts, but I suspected his were beyond fascinating. The last time he had seen his father, Theasin Venrover—the man who was potentially my salvation—it had been to have an abyssal leech ripped from his side. His father had treated the entire ordeal like a chore. Theasin's responses to their interactions had made me wonder if the man was emotionally dead inside.

What would Adelgis possibly say to his father?

Captain Devlin, having freed himself from his roc, smoothed his long coat and straightened his tricorn hat. He regarded Adelgis and me with a jut of his chin, like a reverse nod, and I offered a quick wave of my hand.

Before I had to make small talk with the man, Karna skipped out of the village and headed over, energy in her steps. The captain crossed his arms and watched her, like he already knew she wanted to speak with him.

"Good news," she said in her songstress voice. "I found two new girls who want to join the ranks of the *Sun Chaser*." Karna came to a halt next to the captain, her blonde hair bouncing twice more after she stopped moving, her large curls somehow spring-like. She wore large trousers secured with a belt and an oversized coat, and I wondered if she had been impersonating someone moments prior.

Captain Devlin growled something under his breath. Then he replied, "And what're we goin' to pay them with? We didn't make coin in Thronehold—not when you failed to follow through with the assignment, and definitely not when Jozé gambled the remainder away."

"We'll be fine," Karna said as she rubbed his shoulder.

"These supplies set us back. We might not have enough to pay the crew we do have."

"Oh, but we will once we reach New Norra." Karna reached into her baggy pants and somehow withdrew a circlet crown from her clothing, as though it had been hiding somewhere in her undergarments. "We'll make back everything we lost in Thronehold and more."

She twirled the circlet around on her finger. The black-and-red coloration reminded me of sovereign dragon scales. Why was she carrying around a crown?

"She stole the late king's crown," Adelgis whispered.

I snapped my attention to him. "The late king of Thronehold?"

"Yes. That's the artifact Karna was supposed to steal *for* our enemies. Apparently, she decided to steal it *from* them instead."

"When?"

"The night of the queen's assassination."

I never did understand why the dastards who had attacked Thronehold had wanted the crown. I had assumed because it was powerful beyond reason, but the simple circlet didn't look like a magical item of vast ability.

"You worry too much," Karna said to the captain, still twirling the crown around with one finger. "Besides, I can always entertain some wealthy arcanists to get us the money, if needed."

"Do we really need more crew members?" the captain asked.

Karna grab the crown and held it tight. "They've been through a lot, and they have nowhere else to go." Her somber tone wasn't like her. I didn't think I had ever heard her so serious.

Captain Devlin sighed. "Fine." His soft tone betrayed the fact that he had probably capitulated hundreds of times in the past. "But only the two new deckhands."

"Aye, aye, Cap'n." Karna winked, her melancholy expression vanishing in an instant. And while she was beautiful, even in ill-fitting clothing, Devlin had no reaction other than a pained groan.

Four days of travel.

It wasn't long, but I only had a limited amount of time to solve my plague problem. Six months, at the most, before looking for a cure would become moot. Each day spent on travel was a necessary evil.

The winds became hotter and hotter the farther south we traveled. Soon, there weren't even clouds beneath us—it was just clear skies from the sun to the ground. Occasionally I'd glance over the railing, admiring the vast ocean on one side of us and the vast sand dunes on the other. More than once, I spotted interesting sights. Giant whales beneath the waves, tall rocks jutting out of the desert—I wanted to show them to someone. Illia would've loved to see the sea life, and I suspected Zaxis would say something along the lines of, *that rock isn't so big, I've seen larger when I travelled with my family. You're such an island bumpkin, Volke.*

Imagining his childish insults got me smiling. I missed them.

A harsh whistle sounded across the deck.

I glanced up, my heart in my throat. Then I spotted it, off in the distance—New Norra.

It had to be. There were no other cities around, just the never-ending waters of the ocean and the sands of the desert.

A river sliced its way inland, forming a delta where the ports for New Norra had been created. They called it the Lion's Tail River, and since the city was the only one for miles, hundreds of boats floated at or around the docks, waiting for their turns to load and unload.

Boats of every shape and size dotted the water. A two-masted schooner, a lug-rigged bilander, a ship-of-line, a man-of-war, dozens of merchantman vessels, and even a couple of brigs, just like our airship. The bright white sails were so numerous, they appeared to be clouds resting on the waves.

New Norra sprawled out in every direction, but it never got too far from the life-giving Lion's Tail River that made up the heart of the city. Boats could travel the waterway, and bridges had been constructed with the ability to lift up and down—something so marvelous and ingenious, I wondered why other nations didn't use them.

In all my excitement, I didn't even realize how overheated I had become with the wootz cotton under my clothing. I stood in the bright daylight, staring out over the delta, river, and massive trade city, my breath stolen by the wonder of adventure.

If only Illia were here to see it.

And Nicholin, and Atty, and Titania, and Hexa, and Raisen—they would all enjoy the sight.

"My arcanist?" Luthair asked.

"Yes?"

"We have now officially gone to a place I never visited with Mathis."

I didn't know why, but that information made me smile. "I'm glad, though it looks like we won't have much in the way of shadow." I lifted my hand to shield my eyes as I tilted my head back. The radiance was enough to cook an egg inside its shell.

"Perhaps you're right," Luthair said. "Look at the walls of the city."

I couldn't believe I hadn't seen them sooner—giant crystals made up portions of the city's sandstone walls, glittering with a myriad of colors. When light filtered through the twenty-foot-high crystals, it cast rainbows across the sand, watch towers, and walkways. The mystic glow they all emanated made me wonder if they were magical. I'd bet my life they were.

"Maybe they're a part of the city's protections?" I said.

"Protections from what?" Luthair asked. "They're a city-state that borders no other nations."

"I don't know. Maybe there are things in the sands."

Luthair didn't reply.

As the *Sun Chaser* flew closer and closer, the crew hustled to secure everything for a more anchored landing.

They avoided me, always maintaining a distance of ten feet or more, and I made my way off the deck to give them space.

"You should be careful inside the city, my arcanist," Luthair said. "Without any information on the people and surrounding territory, we're at a disadvantage."

I nodded. "Don't worry. I intend to find out where Theasin went and then leave as soon as possible."

11

THE KHEPERA MYSTERY

To my surprise, New Norra had a sky dock, a small platform built off the city's outer wall to allow for airships to tie down. The dock wasn't as large as the several such docks dotting the delta—some so giant they could accommodate fifty ships—but it allowed for four airships to remain secure at the same time.

Once the *Sun Chaser* had been tied down, Captain Devlin, my father, Karna, Vethica, Fain, Adelgis, and I disembarked. Unlike with normal sailing ships, where the gangplank was nothing more than a wide board of wood, the *Sun Chaser* had rope railings. Obviously, it was to prevent people from falling, since one misstep wouldn't result in diving into the ocean—it would result in a 150-foot drop to the dunes below.

The afternoon sun beat down without mercy. The wootz cotton made everything worse, and by the time I reached the end of the gangplank, I was ready to call it a day and head back onto the airship.

My mouth became so dry, it felt stuck in place.

Twitching my lips reminded me they were on the verge of cracking.

"Welcome, Captain Devlin," one of the city dockhands said as she approached.

She wore loose, baggy trousers, a cloth belt, and a flowing shirt with sleeves down to the wrists. Her helmet came with a flap of cloth that hung over the back of her neck and ears. A rifle was slung over her shoulder, and she kept a knife at her side, but otherwise, she didn't look weighed down or encumbered with heavy equipment. At first, I thought having so much clothing would be bothersome in the heat, but I quickly realized it was meant to protect the wearer from the unforgiving rays of the sun.

The captain stepped forward, straightened his leather belt, and then motioned to the city. "What's going on? It looks like people are stalled in the delta."

"It's the Marshall of the Southern Seas," the dockhand said. "She's making it difficult to travel down the coast."

"Why? What's that old salt biscuit want?"

"She wants to investigate New Norra, but the governor isn't allowing her soldiers beyond the shipyard. It's made things real tense around here."

Captain Devlin lowered his hat over his face and sighed. "Nothing about this trip has gone to my liking."

Vethica pushed the captain aside. "This doesn't have anything to do with the khepera, does it?" Her tone matched her panicked expression.

The dockhand took a hesitant step backward. "I'm not sure."

Khepera?

Those were a rare type of mystical creature. From what I could recall, they were giant scarabs, about the size of a human head, with shimmery iridescent shells and glittering wings. Much like phoenixes, they were creatures of rebirth, but they were also creatures of renewal and the sun itself. Could they be found somewhere out in the Amber Dunes? That made sense. Khepera preferred to live in sand, after all.

Why did Vethica want to know about them? Perhaps she was hoping to find one?

"Forget about it," Captain Devlin said. "We have more important matters to deal with." He gave a quick bow of his head to the dockhand.

Instead of bowing her head back, the dockhand placed three fingers over her heart—her thumb, pointer, and middle. I had never seen such a gesture before, and I stared for a long moment afterward, wondering why she made it.

My gaze obviously didn't sit well with her, because she glowered in my direction and then motioned to the sandstone steps that led to the city wall. "Quickly now."

I followed the captain, shadowing his path. Fain and Adelgis flanked me, neither saying a word. I couldn't help but notice the harsh sting of stray sand whenever the wind sped up enough to carry it.

"*No one has managed to bond with a khepera in over two decades,*" Adelgis said, his voice in my mind rather than my ears.

I wasn't unaccustomed to telepathy, but I hadn't been expecting it, either. I half-slipped from the steps, and Fain grabbed my upper arm to prevent me from tumbling down onto the city wall. I corrected my footing and muttered a quick *thanks*. I could've shadow-stepped if anything had gotten too serious, but I still appreciated his help.

Adelgis continued as though nothing had happened. "*There used to be a bonding ceremony every two years, but my father says no one celebrates anymore. He said the creatures have disappeared.*"

While I mulled over the odd information, I kept my attention on the cityscape unfolding before me. Sandstone spires dominated New Norra's silhouette, some with needle-points so fine, they practically vanished at the tip, disappearing into the brilliance of the blue sky. Great efforts had been made to paint the bricks of the walls and buildings all throughout the city. Red, blue, and golden yellow were used on almost every structure, giving the city spots of color despite the universal use of sandstone.

As I stared, I noticed a pattern. Red bricks and roofs were primarily used on homes, the gold was used on shops and merchant areas, and the blue seemed exclusively designated to the drinking fountains, baths, and river access paths. The color-coding of the city struck me as ingenious. Even if someone couldn't read the signs posted on most corners, they could still quickly find what they wanted inside the city.

The denizens of New Norra kept themselves covered from the neck down past their ankles. Most wore hats—some with large brims, others with long veils—but no one covered their forehead, not even with long bangs or messy hair. Everywhere I looked, men and women alike wore their hair back and in a tight ponytail or they kept their hair short enough that it couldn't hang across their face.

Arcanists kept their forehead apparent because of the mark designating them as someone who had bonded with a mystical creature, but non-arcanists didn't need to do such a thing. It made me wonder whether there was a law against hiding one's forehead or if that was just a custom for the gigantic city.

"I already hate it here," Fain muttered under his breath.

Sweat soaked his button-up shirt, and he tugged at the front of it, unsticking the fabric from his chest every couple of seconds. I couldn't see Wraith—no doubt he was invisible, to hide his frightening visage—but I could hear his constant panting. Halfway down the stairs, Fain used his magic to frost his clothing, keeping him cool for a grand total of ten seconds before the rime evaporated in the heat. Then he did it again.

Once we stepped onto the top of the city's wall, I got a better view of the main street. The river of bodies flowed in both directions as merchants, traders, soldiers, craftsmen, and sailors made their way through the city. The citizens of New Norra had a distinct dress, but the many individuals in the main street wore clothing from all around the world, including the buccaneer attire I was accustomed to seeing from the islands—long coats, high boots, and button-up shirts.

I observed the people, wishing the sun would set. Heavy steps broke my thoughts, and I turned around to spot my father still descending the stairway. His blue phoenix had flown off, blending with the cloudless azure of the sky, leaving him alone as he carefully made each step.

His bad leg pained him, I could see it in the restrained grimaces, but he still smiled when he noticed me watching.

"You excited for the city, boy?" he asked as he stepped off the stairway and then clasped my shoulder.

"It *is* fascinating," I said. "But..."

I wanted to enjoy it, I really did, but I feared the crowds and the mingling of people from far off places. Much like in Thronehold, there were too many people here to sift through them with any sort of efficiency, and because of my condition, I didn't want to accidentally infect someone who would then jump on their ship and take off to distant lands, harming even more people in the process.

How was I going to find Theasin Venrover in a city as massive and populated as New Norra?

"I want to speak to the visiting mystic seekers," Vethica said. She pulled a cowl over her head, using the hood to shield her face from the sun. "Karna... would you accompany me?"

Karna swished back her hair. The sweat dappling her skin only heightened her attractiveness, as though she were the human personification of an oasis. "Of course." She gave me a smirk when she caught me staring and then offered a quick wave goodbye as she headed off with Vethica. "Don't get into too much trouble without me."

"Be back before it gets dark," the captain said.

"Aye, aye," Karna replied with a sarcastic curtsy.

The captain opened his mouth to say something more, but he was cut off by a loud shout.

"Wait!"

Biyu flew down the steps, her book clutched tight to her chest, even though she had a leather strap to carry it like a satchel. With only one eye, I figured there was a good chance she would trip, so I readied my control of the shadows to catch her, just in case. Thankfully, it never happened. She hopped down the last two steps and landed in front of us.

"Cabin Girl Biyu, reporting for duty," she stated in a cheery tone.

"I told you to wait on the ship," Captain Devlin said, annoyance in his voice.

"But I have to document everything!"

"It's dangerous in the city. You'll be safer on the *Sun Chaser*. Take notes there."

Biyu frowned, and her one eye practically grew in size from the welling tears. I considered it more adorable than sad, and in that moment, I'd never be able to tell her *no*, regardless of the request.

The captain groaned. "Don't look at me like that." He pulled his hat off his head and then placed it firmly on Biyu. It was too large and fell straight past her eyebrows.

Biyu lifted the hat enough to peek out. "What's this for?"

"If you're going to walk around town with me, you'll need a hat. A little lass like you could get heatstroke."

Her fake tears dried up in an instant, swallowed by the biggest smile she had yet. "You won't regret taking me along!" She rubbed at her nose and then added, "But won't *you* need a hat? Old men get heatstroke, too."

"I'm not—" Captain Devlin gritted his teeth. Then he took Biyu by the shoulder and led her along the city wall. "You know what? I need a new hat, anyway. That'll be our first stop."

Once they had wandered a fair distance, I realized it was just Fain, Adelgis, and my father remaining.

"I've visited New Norra tons of times." Jozé motioned to the same walkway the captain had taken. "I'll show you around, if you like. Keep you out of trouble. That kind of thing."

Fain and Adelgis gave each other a knowing glance. Then Fain shrugged and motioned to the distant docks. "I wanna see the free port, anyway."

"I'll head to the research labs and library," Adelgis said. "I know my father visits them whenever he stops in New Norra. Someone there might know his location."

I wanted to go with Adelgis, to help in the search, but he gave me an odd look.

"*I'll be fine,*" he said, his telepathic voice different than when Luthair spoke to me while merged. "*You should take advantage of this time to explore the city with someone who knows their way around. Perhaps you can gather useful information.*"

I knew he was just giving me an excuse to spend time with my father, but he still had a point. Perhaps knowing a little more about my surroundings would help lessen the ever-building anxiety.

"Lead the way," I said to Jozé.

He took a breath, straightened his posture, and led me down the city wall. Although he had a bad leg, he hid it well now that we were walking on a stable, flat surface—no rocking from a ship, no steps down a stairway. Tine flew down so she was closer, but she remained a good twenty feet in the air, her soot fluttering down like black snow.

A chorus of bells rang out.

I stopped and stared out over the many buildings, wondering where the music was coming from.

"The sun is setting," Jozé said.

"That's why they ring the bells?"

"It gets pretty cold at night, and the heat can get brutal on certain days. That's why they ring the bells—to warn people about the impending sunset and sunrise."

The sun remained in the sky, and I suspected it wouldn't fully set for another hour. They were giving us *that* long to prepare? How cold could it possibly get?

My father took another set of stairs down the wall. It led to the interior of the city, and soldiers stood at the top and bottom, all with pistols and scimitars—curved sabers that hung from their belts, easily pulled in the thick of battle. I examined the men as we passed, and each returned my stare with cold calculation. I wondered if they thought we were pirates, but since they said nothing, I decided not to engage.

"The Amber Dunes are home to some of the deadliest

mystical creatures," Jozé said once he reached the bottom step. "The desert is so unforgiving that even the animals become vicious, ya know what I mean?" He said everything with a smirk, but I didn't quite understand.

"What creatures?" I asked.

Luthair shifted around my feet. "Manticores, death worms, cockatrices, and basilisks are all found in the Amber Dunes, my arcanist."

A shiver ran down my spine. Manticores were practically an evil version of a griffin, complete with a deadly scorpion tail. Death worms moved through the ground like water, their crimson skin deadly to the touch. Cockatrices had gazes that could turn things to stone, and basilisks had potent venom—not as potent as the king basilisk, but still powerful enough to kill an arcanist.

All of those things came from the same desert? Impressive and frightening—it started to feel as though the city were a safe haven from the many forms of death lurking in the sands and waters around us. If I didn't die from the heat, a random mystical creature could get me. Or, worse yet, a pirate in the delta. I'd have to stay on my toes.

My father and I walked into a narrow alley between sandstone buildings and then stepped out into the street. The brick roads gave New Norra a sophisticated appearance, as though the city had been planned out in advance. I marveled for a moment—most cities I visited had dirt or cobblestone thoroughfares. Red, blue, and gold painted bricks were placed together to form guiding lines. I followed the gold line with my gaze, watching it continue down the main road and head straight for the markets.

I started to head in that direction, but Jozé placed a hand on my shoulder. "Not that way." He gestured down the road. "C'mon."

"You don't want to purchase anything?"

"It reeks of nobility in the center bazaar." He scoffed and urged me away from the hustle and bustle of the market crowd. "And to be honest, I'm not comfortable with the upper crusts of the arcanist world. We should avoid areas where aristocrats might show their dainty faces."

Although I wasn't sure if I shared his sentiment, I knew I wanted to avoid as many arcanists as possible, so I didn't fight him. I allowed him to lead me away from the center bazaar and straight for the delta docks.

The denizens gave us quick glances before stepping aside to allow us room to walk. I didn't meet anyone's gaze and instead kept my hands shoved deep in my pockets the entire time. At one point, a merchant riding a slender horse tried to get my attention with two toots of an emasculated horn. I glanced up, surprised to see the merchant was actually trying to sell me some fine cloth. She held it out, muttered something I didn't catch.

"Get out of here," he growled, cutting her off.

The merchant kicked at her horse and trotted off in the opposite direction.

"What was that?" I asked.

"We look out of place," Jozé said as he motioned to our clothes. "And some of the locals will try to fleece you. Just ignore them."

Most buildings were two stories, and I enjoyed walking in their shadows as we continued our travel. After a few blocks, my father slowed his gait.

"So," he muttered. He rubbed the hip of his bad leg. No other words escaped him.

Clearly, he wanted to speak, but it would fall to me to start the dialogue.

"Have you had any other children?" I asked. Perhaps I had a larger family than I expected.

Jozé shook his head. "I was afraid. I had already left one, so why would I take that risk again?"

His melancholy tone didn't help my mood. I should've asked something a little more... not depressing.

"Favorite food?" I asked. Innocuous questions were safe.

"Eggs. Lots of eggs. Yours?"

"Fish soup."

He nodded. Then he patted me on the shoulder and flashed a half-smile. "Is there a girl or boy or someone you're smitten with? You look like you could break hearts."

"Uh..." I rubbed at the back of my neck. "It's complicated."

"Heh." Jozé smiled wider. "What an understatement. Nothing is as complicated as love. Don't let anyone tell you otherwise."

"Volke."

Adelgis's unexpected telepathy didn't startle me like it had before. I glanced around, hoping I would see him, but the crowds on the main street were too thick.

"I'm sorry to interrupt you, but I have potentially good news."

Could I answer? I didn't know how. When I spoke telepathically with Luthair, it happened naturally, but with Adelgis, it felt like a one-way communication.

"I couldn't help myself. I started asking around about the khepera and why they had disappeared."

He wanted to know about the magical scarabs? That made sense. Adelgis always had a fascination with mystical creatures.

"No one can explain why they started disappearing, but several of the city's Watch Battalion knows why the Marshall of

the Southern Seas is here. The marshall wants to search the city for any khepera that might be hiding. She thinks their magic of renewal can be used to cure the plague."

I stopped dead in my tracks, my heart hammering hard.

"Really?" I asked aloud, even though that was foolish.

"I think there might be some real merit behind her conclusions," Adelgis continued, likely without having heard my question. *"Khepera are creatures of powerful renewal. Perhaps we won't need to find my father if we find a khepera instead."*

THE REAPER ARCANIST

"What's wrong?" Jozé asked, his eyebrows knitted.

I massaged my temple. "Do you know much about the khepera? And about their disappearance? I'd like to know more."

"Really?" There was more excitement in his voice than I had expected. "I didn't think you were the scholarly type."

I gave him a sideways glance, uncertain of how to reply.

He relaxed and then exhaled, his expression shifting to something between amused and apologetic. "I saw how well you fought in the Sovereign Dragon Tournament, and I just figured you were more about brawn. Not that there's anything wrong with that."

He motioned for me to follow as he turned away from the main street. We abandoned the blue line that led to the shipyard as we traveled down one narrow alleyway and then to the next.

"I've always preferred academic pursuits," Jozé said. "I guess it runs in the blood."

"I do enjoy reading." I kept close to him as we walked, hoping he wasn't leading us through a bad part of town.

"Did you ever read about all the grand arcanists of the past? The swashbucklers and heroes, like Lark the Gallant and Gregory Ruma?"

"You mean those really old tales?"

I nodded.

Jozé chuckled and shook his head. "Those are for children. I've always been fascinated by trinket and artifact creation or unexplained magical mysteries. Real things worth my time."

His dismissive tone ate at me, but I didn't say anything. Perhaps they were kids' things.

We walked by a group of homeless individuals huddled together in a fraternal circle, hiding from the sun in the shadows between buildings. Their ratty clothes and unkempt hair bothered me—a piece of me wanted to stop and see if I could help them—but I had no coins, and even if I had, I suspected New Norra had its own currency. What could I do for them? My magic didn't lend itself to aid.

My father continued through the city, rubbing at his leg occasionally.

"Aren't you a phoenix arcanist?" I asked, matching his pace, even if I could walk faster. "Why not have Tine heal your leg?"

"Blue phoenixes are a little different," Jozé said. "Their fire is beyond compare, but they don't *heal* like the red phoenixes do."

I nodded along with the words, remembering the book Adelgis's father had written on mystical creatures. Theasin had stated something similar—blue phoenix fire could burn even those immune to the destruction of heat.

"How did you get the injury?" I asked.

Jozé gritted his teeth. He didn't answer right away, he just scratched at his stubble. I almost told him to forget I had asked, but then he replied, "I got it when I... killed the man... on the Isle of Ruma. Because my injury had begun to heal before I became an arcanist, it's stayed with me."

"I see."

Arcanists could heal themselves of many injuries, but wounds that had happened before bonding were considered permanent. Like Illia's missing eye. In theory, there were creatures with magics capable of repairing such wounds, but they were rare.

Perhaps the Grand Apothecary, Gillie, would be able to help my father?

The sky shifted from blue to blazing orange the longer we traveled. I had read a book once that said desert sunsets were unlike any others in the world, and now I understood why. The vibrant scarlet of the dying sun soon bled into purple, creating a sky that could only be described as an evening rainbow.

With my head craned and my attention on the colors, I didn't even notice the people around me. I ran into someone and muttered an apology. They started out angry, but became apologetic upon seeing my arcanist mark. I had become accustomed to the deference, though I considered it more a failing on my part than a sign of respect. I wished people wouldn't fear me.

And now with the plague...

I crossed my arms over my chest.

The winds picked up and a chill washed over the area. One second it had been too hot to think properly, the next second the temperature had plummeted to pleasant levels.

"We're almost there," Jozé said.

"Where are we going?"

"There's an entrance to the underground right over here."

"Underground?"

"You heard me. It's where the khepera live. Just come look."

Another gust of wind and goosebumps sprouted across my body. I wasn't sure how, but it was already cold enough that I wanted a coat.

It didn't take us long to reach an open area of the street. It was circular and wide, like it had been built to accommodate a marketplace, but no stands or traders were around. Instead, there was a single building in the middle of the circular plaza—open and with no door. It housed a stairway leading straight down.

"There it is," Jozé said.

No one approached the building or attempted to go down, they just detoured around it. I would've said they were pretending it didn't exist, but no one even looked at it, like it was bad luck.

"Where does it lead?" I asked. "I know you said *underground*, but is there anything down there?"

"The Grotto Labyrinth." Jozé stepped close to the wall of a nearby building and leaned against it, giving his bad leg a rest. "The khepera live in the center. Their trial of worth involves navigating the maze."

An underground maze intrigued me more than I wanted to admit. It reminded me of all the tales I had read about arcanists of the past—all the adventures people would go on to meet their eventual eldrin.

Jozé narrowed his eyes. "What's that look on your face?"

I rubbed at my jaw, unaware I had been smiling. "Oh, uh, the Grotto Labyrinth just reminds me of Master Arcanist Quinna. She navigated the maze-like mines of a saline dragon as part of her trial of worth. It was an epic tale."

"Huh..."

"And she had to do it blind because of the dragon's unique breath." I tried to contain my excitement, but it started to spill over as I remembered the entirety of the adventure. "She actually used the echoes of her own voice to find new passages to explore." When my father's expression remained stiff, I forced a chuckle and rubbed at the back of my neck. "It's not important. Forget I even mentioned it."

A long moment stretched between us.

Jozé tapped at his belt, his gaze distant as though he were momentarily lost in deep thought. He didn't dwell long, and before I could remark on his pensive state, he said, "Well, the Grotto Labyrinth *is* a thing of legend. I've never looked for myself, but supposedly there are traps and riddles down there."

"Truly?"

"Like I said, they were made for the khepera trial of worth."

I mulled over the information and decided to get a better look. With energy in my step, I walked across the circle plaza and headed straight for the entrance to the Grotto Labyrinth. It would be legendary to solve puzzles and avoid traps, all to find a mystical creature waiting at the center.

My father grabbed my elbow and held me back. "What're you doing?"

"I'm going to investigate," I said.

"Hey. Look around."

The people of the city were giving us odd looks. Three soldiers dressed in light leather—one woman and two men—stood around the edge of the plaza, their eyes on me. When they noticed me staring, each placed a hand on the hilt of their scimitars.

"The Grotto Labyrinth is sacred," Jozé said under his breath. "It's a crime to mill about near the entrances, and it's a bigger crime to enter when you shouldn't. We don't need that kind of attention."

"But I thought the khepera weren't around anymore?"

Jozé moved us away from the entrance. The soldiers relaxed, but they didn't stop their staring. Once we made it to the opposite side of the street, the sun had fully set, blanketing everything in an oppressive chill. I had never been in the snow, but I imagined this was what it felt like. I rubbed at my arms, my breath becoming visible. Even the wootz cotton couldn't protect me from the icy wind.

Oil lanterns and streetlamps were lit, giving the city a warm glow, despite the decreasing temperature.

"Listen," my father said, "for the last two decades, no one has found any khepera, but that doesn't necessarily mean that they don't live in the labyrinth."

"Adelgis's father said they're not here anymore."

"Theasin Venrover? The famous artificer?"

I nodded.

Jozé waved away the comment. "That man can drown in the abyss. He's exactly the kind of arcanist I despise. *Artificer.* Ha. *I'm* a better artificer than that man."

"I thought your title was blacksmith?"

"I work well with metal," Jozé said, his voice terse. "But that doesn't mean I can't use other materials for my trinkets and artifacts. Men like Theasin are the height of pretentious. His whole damn family has irritated me at one point or another. Except for your friend, I suppose."

"Theasin is fairly knowledgeable about mystical creatures, even if he's unpleasant."

Although I tried to hold it back, my teeth chattered on the last few words. My father lifted an eyebrow and then took hold of my hand. His phoenix magic reminded me of Zaxis—just better. The heat that radiated from my palm to the rest of my body chased away the cold in an instant. He released me, but the magic remained, fighting back the weather.

"Thank you," I muttered.

"Trust me, boy. As someone who has witnessed people doing devious things to get their hands on special mystical creatures, I'm willing to bet my life there are still khepera in the Grotto Labyrinth—they're just being kept from people."

That thought hadn't yet crossed my mind, but now that my father mentioned it, I could see it being a possibility.

"Khepera don't actually die," Jozé said. "Well, they do. It's just, once they do, they're reborn at the center of the Grotto Labyrinth years later, even if they died halfway across the world. These creatures don't breed, you see. There's a finite number."

"Do their arcanists stay arcanists while the khepera reform?"

"No. At least, that's what I've heard. The khepera die, and then they're reborn without their old memories and names, though the folklore is that a piece of their old arcanist is always with them. The old ladies in the market call the khepera the *wise men of mystical creatures* because they have experiences and personalities from all time periods."

I hadn't heard any of that before. My excitement to investigate the Grotto Labyrinth increased. I stared at the entrance, wondering if I could just shadow-step my way inside. That way no one would see me. If the place was sacred, I wouldn't damage anything, but if the khepera's renewal magic could cure the plague, it was worth breaking a few traditions to find one.

"Did you ask about the khepera because you wanted an adventure?" Jozé asked.

"I think the khepera can help me."

Screams and shouts echoed down the street. Adrenaline rushed into my system, and I turned, tense from head to toe. The crowds on the brick road jumped out of the way of a fleeing individual—a man running toward us. He ran at a reckless pace, terror fueling his speed rather than purpose. Was someone trying to harm him? His baggy trousers and loose shirt fluttered around his body, both marked in wet crimson. He was bleeding.

The soldiers in the plaza moved to defend the entrance to the Grotto Labyrinth, not to deal with the bloody man.

I ran forward. My father tried to reach out and grab me, but he missed.

"Volke!"

When I got within twenty feet of the running man, I opened my mouth to offer my aid, but an odd realization washed over me, and I held my breath.

The man was plague-ridden, just like me.

I just... I just *knew*. Like a whisper from a dream, the information entered my thoughts, and my very blood understood it to be the truth.

I hadn't been able to sense that before, not when the wyvern had landed on the deck of the *Sun Chaser*, so why could I feel it now? The knowledge disturbed me, and my sense of urgency drained away, leaving me confused.

The man—an arcanist with the mark of a grifter crow woven throughout the star—continued running into the plaza. When he passed me, he looked over, no doubt sensing me as well. I dove back into the shadows, behind people on the edge of the street. A part of me wanted to attack him, but another part of me drowned in hesitation, caught off-guard by this new revelation.

Thankfully, the grifter crow arcanist was being pursued.

A man wearing a black cloak dashed through the street, a bizarre scythe in his hands. It didn't look like a functional, well-kept weapon. The blade—curved and at least two feet in length—appeared rusted and chipped. The ebony hilt seemed worn from time, scuffed at the sides and base.

And chains hung around the man's waist, like an impractical double set of belts.

Although the outfit seemed damn near ridiculous for combat, I recognized the many elements. The individual chasing the bleeding man was a reaper arcanist. Reapers, like knightmares, merged with their arcanists, becoming a single entity that lived and died as one. Unlike knightmares, reapers were creatures purely excited and fueled by death.

Once the reaper arcanist neared his fleeing target, he held up his hand and evoked terrors. I knew the feeling because knightmares could do the same, but I was immune to fear effects. The citizens of New Norra weren't, however. And neither was the grifter crow arcanist.

People cried out and cowered away. The fleeing arcanist tripped on a brick and collapsed to the ground, practically sobbing the entire time. I ducked down, trying to stay out of view, irrationally afraid the reaper arcanist would discover I was plague-ridden. But I also wanted to see the conclusion of this pursuit.

It wasn't a fight. Stabbing a man in the back while he cried on the ground came closer to straight murder, but I at least knew why the reaper arcanist had had to do it.

I backed away from the people around me, well aware *I* probably deserved a similar fate.

The reaper arcanist's scythe glowed a sinister red as the plague-ridden man twitched and died at the end of the blade. A name burned itself into one of the links of the chains hanging from the reaper arcanist's waist, blazing with each letter one at a time as the dying man experienced his final breaths.

The moment the grifter crow arcanist died, his body shriveled, like a husk drained of blood, and that disturbed me more than the rest of the process.

The terrors in the area lifted, allowing the men and women around us to get to their feet. Most hustled away, obviously done with the encounter, but some lingered nearby, whispering questions of concern and bewilderment.

"Have no fear," the reaper arcanist said, his voice a mix of his and his eldrin's—somehow dark and slimy at the same time. "I'm a master arcanist with the Huntsman Guild. I'm here to help clear your streets of the arcane plague."

His reaper separated from him. The cloak, scythe, and chains fell away and then floated to his side, as if an invisible person wore them now. The hood of the cloak "looked" from side to side, as if scanning invisible eyes over the crowd. Although it had no hands, it held the rusty scythe close and even twirled it twice. The blood from the kill had long since vanished.

The man held up both his hands and faced the largest group of citizens.

I recognized him.

He had a thin mustache and goatee, both as black as his slicked-back hair. His narrow frame was wiry from combat, and he wore light armor, but it was the condescending and somewhat arrogant way he spoke that gave away his identity.

Jevel Balestier.

He had been at the Sovereign Dragon Tournament. His apprentices had fought us in the tournament, and he had been the one obsessed with fighting Master Zelfree and winning in one-on-one combat. Although I didn't really know this man, I already disliked him.

How was he already in New Norra? Had he taken an airship as well? Probably not. He'd probably left Throne-hold during the tournament, after he and his apprentices had lost, days before the assassins and the commotion.

People around us muttered quiet thanks and a few cheered, but there wasn't a celebration.

"What shall we do with the body, my arcanist?" his reaper asked, its voice dark and hollow.

"Take it with us, Ruin," Jevel snapped. "The fools around here won't accept a name on a chain as proof."

"As you wish."

The reaper picked up the body, but it was like watching an invisible person. The corpse "floated" up into the air, held by phantom hands. It was flung over Ruin's shoulder—over his cloak—and the reaper secured it in place with an invisible arm.

Someone touched my back.

I whirled around, ready to fight, but I stopped myself when I realized it was my father.

"We should return to the *Sun Chaser*," he said. "I don't want any run-ins with guild arcanists."

13

JOINING THE FRITH GUILD

My father's phoenix lit up the cold sky as she flew back to the *Sun Chaser*.

Jozé and I walked at a casual pace, though my heart continued to hammer. The streets of New Norra thinned and quieted, creating a peaceful atmosphere, a harsh juxtaposition to my thoughts. Nothing calmed me, but I kept my dread hidden well. Occasionally, I could hear music wafting up from the far side of town—all the way at the ports— which surprised me. In the city of Thronehold, it was too lively at all points in the night to hear things so far away.

"Do you feel any different?" Jozé asked. "Now that you're sick?"

No one was around, but I still tensed when he said it aloud. "I haven't noticed anything." Except for the feeling I'd had before the man had died—how I'd somehow known he had been plague-ridden. That still haunted me.

"I know I haven't been there for you in the past." My father said the words without looking at me. His voice had an edge of seriousness. "So, you might think these words are empty, but I'll do everything in my power to help you."

At first, I wanted to dismiss the statement and brush it aside with a quick *thank you*. But there *was* a chance he could help me. He knew about mystical creatures. He made trinkets and weapons and artifacts. And if he came through for me now, perhaps the years he had been away could truly be forgiven.

"That's why I want to find a khepera," I finally said. "Adelgis thinks they might be able to help with... my problem."

"Is that right?" Jozé let out a quick exhale. "Well, this may be a bit of good news. Vethica has been investigating the khepera for years now—every time we stop in the city, or anytime she finds an arcanist who knows about mystical creature legends."

"Do you think she'll help me?"

Jozé laughed. "No."

I frowned.

My father held up a hand and quieted himself. "Once she bonds with a khepera, I'm sure she'll get a lot friendlier to the idea of helping, but until then, she can be quite abrasive. And she hates plague-ridden arcanists and mystical creatures."

Who didn't? But I didn't ask anything further.

We reached the sandstone steps to the city wall. Before Jozé started climbing, I took hold of his arm. Now that it was night and darkness surrounded us, I wanted to test the strength of my magic.

I motioned to the stairs. "Hold your breath."

I didn't know if he complied, because I didn't wait for acknowledgment. I stepped straight into the shadows, shifting us through the inky void, slithering up the steps, and exiting on top of the wall. Relief washed over me when I realized I had successfully taken my father, but the toll it took hurt me. Not only was I second-bonded to my eldrin, but taking someone else into the shadows was like doing jumping jacks while running—it wore me down fast.

Jozé staggered, but caught himself before falling. He glanced around, momentarily confused by our surroundings. "Interesting... I didn't know you could do that with other people."

I shook my head. "It's nothing."

We made our way across the wall until we came to the sky port steps. Again, I took my father through the shadows, both to practice and because he seemed genuinely impressed. The moment we were aboard the *Sun Chaser*, Adelgis hurried across the deck until he reached me.

"Volke," he said, almost breathless. "We have several problems."

I glanced around the airship, half expecting to see a plague monster somewhere nearby. Instead, the deck was quiet. A few crew members secured the rigging or untied empty barrels and readied them near the gangplank. Lanterns had been positioned near the railings and doors, illuminating the ship enough for simple work. No one was in distress—they appeared more tired than anything else.

"What's wrong?" I asked.

"The Huntsman Guild is here in the city."

"Yeah. I saw that reaper arcanist from the tournament."

"The city is offering a hefty reward for the death of plague-ridden arcanists and mystical creatures. Other hunters have flocked here as well."

I nodded, unsure of what to say to that.

"There are several dread pirates in the port," Adelgis continued. "Apparently, the Marshall of the Southern Seas isn't allowing them to pass, and now they're semi-trapped in the city unless they want to go back north."

"Okay."

Dangerous, but not the worst news. Pirates in free ports tended to mind their own business. While the city wouldn't enforce bounties from other countries, it still had its own laws, so pirates were welcome to stay so long as they didn't cause too much trouble.

It probably meant we should stay away from the docks and shipyard at all costs, though.

"And although I didn't make it to the labs or library, I did overhear thoughts about the khepera," Adelgis muttered. "I'm sorry I got your hopes up, but it seems as though no one in New Norra has seen any. I thought maybe the khepera were being smuggled out or hidden, but I couldn't hear anything that would indicate that."

My father stepped forward. "Don't rule out that possibility yet. Let me speak to Vethica and the captain. If we search the Grotto Labyrinth, we might be able to find clues."

Adelgis, unfazed by the interjection, said, "The denizens of New Norra won't enter the underground maze, unless for official matters. Some think that the khepera left because too many people violated the rules of no entry in the past." He smoothed his long hair, his voice becoming distant. "If we solve this mystery on their behalf, it might actually be a boon for everyone. The citizens of New Norra considered the city cursed now that the khepera aren't around."

I slowly nodded.

Could the khepera really cure the arcane plague? Theasin seemed to believe abyssal leeches had the capability, but that didn't mean it was limited to them. Khepera were mystical creatures of renewal, and that could equate to unique forms of healing. On the other hand, the longer we stayed here and searched, the less time I had to find Theasin.

"I think it's worth investigating," Adelgis said, obviously replying to my thoughts. "I can search for my father's whereabouts while the rest of you discover the location of the missing khepera. If I find my father before you find the creatures, we can reopen this issue about whether we should stay. If you find the khepera first, then perhaps our problem will be solved."

That meant I would get a chance to explore the Grotto Labyrinth, and that fact alone swayed me to the option. Some of us could search for the khepera, while others searched for Theasin—a decent plan.

"Don't do anything until I speak with the captain," Jozé said. "I mean it. He'll be upset if we do anything without him knowing."

I nodded. "We'll wait."

"Good. Maybe you two should get some rest, then. In the morning, we'll get this all settled."

I was dreaming.

Adelgis's magic influenced my sleep so often, I knew the moment I entered one of these "memories" from the past. This memory was different from the last few, however. I felt like I had returned to a coherent narrative and I recognized the narrow streets and gloomy atmosphere of Master Zelfree's rundown childhood town.

I stood on the docks, blue skies above me, calm waters under the pier. Actually, *Zelfree* stood on the docks, but I watched the events through his eyes, and it gave the scene a more personal touch, like it really was my own memory. The smell of the sea salt felt so familiar and real.

Young men and women waited in line, each of them in

their early twenties or younger, their clothes ragged and their frames scrawny. The ships in port had sailors standing near the gangplanks, some with pieces of parchment, some with bits of charcoal. The people waiting in line would walk up to a ship, sign their name on the paper, and then hopefully board their new vessel.

I had seen this before, not in Zelfree's memories, but when I'd lived on the islands. Ships would often come to port recruiting people, and it was always the same. Sign a two-year contract and begin work as the lowest level of deckhand. If you worked hard enough, perhaps you could move up in the ranks. It was tough, but ships would hire anyone, even if people were unskilled. It meant they got a lot of orphans, third or fourth children, and ex-convicts who hadn't been sentenced to death.

Most individuals waiting in line held small pieces of paper. It was the advertisement for the Frith Guild, and each one of them took it over to a man standing next to a dinghy. The small boat belonged to the massive ship-of-the-line waiting out in the bay.

A ship-of-the-line was a three-masted warship known for superior naval battle. The side of the vessel had the name emblazoned in the side: *The Red Falcon*. Ship-of-the-lines were too large to fit in port, so *The Red Falcon* had to send the tiny dinghy back and forth to take on new crewmembers.

I waited my turn in line, my feet hurting and my clothes itchy.

A man walked away from the Frith Guild crewmates and headed back down the pier. His shoulder-length copper hair shone in the morning light, giving the locks a dark-red hue that looked akin to rusted metal. The people in line snickered and stared—but any time the man shot them a glare, they all looked away.

I recognized the man as Lynus—the same one who had told Zelfree to apply to the Frith Guild in the previous dream-memory Adelgis had shared with me.

"How'd it go?" I asked. Zelfree's voice was familiar, but not entirely the same, just like the other dream. Younger. More energetic. It was why I hadn't recognized him straight away, but now that I knew, I was certain this was Zelfree.

Lynus pushed back his hair. His face was still swollen and bruised. He couldn't even open his right eye, and the cuts on his eyebrow and lip looked like they could split open again at any moment.

"They want you pass a *test* first," Lynus growled, his emphasis on the word *test* like it was venom.

"Oh, yeah?"

I pulled Lynus close. He was... larger than me. More muscle. Taller. It made me nervous, but Zelfree didn't tense or act differently.

"What kind of test?" I asked under my breath. "Those whimsical tests they give new apprentice arcanists?"

Lynus rubbed at his face. It appeared he had trouble breathing with his mouth closed, and I suspected his nose was broken. "Math or some nonsense."

"Math? Hm. Arcanists get all the fun, it seems." I stared at Lynus, one eyebrow raised. "You're good at math. I taught you all your numbers."

"My head hurts." Lynus groaned as he grabbed at his temple. "It's hard to... concentrate."

My head hurt just looking at him. I was surprised Lynus didn't have a concussion—maybe he did?—and even walking around without falling over was a major accomplishment. The longer I got a good look at him, the more impressed I became. He seemed sturdier than most people I knew, including Zaxis.

"Get in line for that ship," I said as I pointed to a brig out in the bay. "It's a vessel of mystic seekers."

Lynus stared down at me with his one squinted eye, his face resembling purple, pulverized meat. "Mystic seekers?"

"They hunt mystical creatures and star shards out in the wilds. Then they bring them back to civilization. You can handle that, right?"

"I suppose." His voice shifted to something quieter. "What're you gonna do?"

"I'm going to take this math test," I said with a chuckle. "Just to see how well I'll fare. I'll come join you afterward."

"Tch." Lynus moved away from me and ambled over to the next line. "Don't take too long."

The line moved at a steady pace, and I noticed only about one in ten were accepted as crew members of the Frith Guild's *Red Falcon.* Then I was called over to the dinghy. I sauntered over, my hands in my pockets, the ocean winds playing with my hair. Well, Zelfree's hair. The man at the dinghy was a ship officer, I could tell by the four buttons on his fancy black coat and because his boots were as shiny as a mirror.

But the moment I looked at his face, I knew his identity.

Gregory Ruma.

The legendary swashbuckler—the man who named my home island—the man who had been brought low by the arcane plague. He had kept his wife's barely animated corpse in an abandoned building while he had tried to find a way to fully resurrect her. The plague had played tricks with his mind, stripping away his hold on reality.

Now here he was. Young and fresh, the first officer of the *Red Falcon*, long before he had even had his adventures far to the north. A cluster of work contracts stuck out of his coat pocket, all identical except for the blank lines meant for someone's name.

Zelfree didn't seem impressed, though. He didn't catch his breath or even flinch. He gave Ruma the once-over, focusing for a long moment on Ruma's short brown hair—windswept and lush—and then on his arcanist mark. A leviathan was woven through the star, a long serpent-like creature with fins and a dragon face.

"Good day," Ruma said. "Are you here because of the flyer?"

I nodded.

"And can you read?"

He didn't ask in a way that offended me, but my entire stance changed once the question had been asked. I tensed and crossed my arms, my teeth practically hurting from clenching my jaw so tightly.

"I can read," I said, my tone carefree and jovial—the exact opposite of how I felt.

"Excellent. I'm Gregory Ruma the Leviathan Arcanist, first mate to Liet Eventide and journeyman arcanist of the Frith Guild. I have a couple of questions before I can offer you a worker's contract."

"I'm ready for whatever you've got."

The confidence in Zelfree's statement bordered on arrogance, and if I could have chuckled, I would have. Master Zelfree had never seemed cocksure when I had interacted with him. Then again, I didn't know *young* Zelfree. They almost seemed like different people.

Ruma forced half a smile. "All right. Have you ever worked as a mariner before?"

"No."

"Ah. Well then, indulge a few hypotheticals. Let's say you

have fifty copper coins, and a rogue steals eighteen. How many do you have left?"

I tightened my grip on my arms and smirked. "How about I give you the imaginary thirty-two coins to jump right to your most difficult question?"

Ruma lifted an eyebrow, his gaze hardening as he searched mine. For a brief moment, it felt like there was something unspoken between us.

"All right," Ruma drawled. "Let's say you have eighty copper coins that you need to divide among three ship-mates. The second man will need twice as much as the first, and the third will need five less than the second. How much do you pay each?"

The first math question I could answer without much difficulty. This question, however, left me momentarily confused. I couldn't hear Zelfree's thoughts, even though I inhabited his body, so I didn't know if the complexity of the question puzzled him or not.

Ruma withdrew a scrap piece of paper and a bit of char-coal from his pocket. Then he handed them over. "You can write it out, if you need."

I gave Ruma a pointed look—something that screamed, *are you serious? You think I need help solving this problem? I* grew tenser and turned away. "The first man gets seventeen coins, the second gets thirty-four, and the last gets twenty-nine."

While Zelfree had solved the question, I hadn't yet. Were those really the answers?

Ruma's hard edge transformed into a genuine smile. "That's correct."

"Have you got any more questions?"

"No. That's all I needed."

Ruma reached for one of the duplicate work contracts in

his coat pocket, but stopped before he took one out. Instead, he opened one of the pouches on his belt and withdrew a different piece of parchment. "Here's your contract." Again, he offered the charcoal bit. "Sign your name and you can board the dinghy. One of our crewmembers will take you to the ship and show you to your new quarters."

I snatched the work contract from Ruma's hand. "I'll think about it."

"You're not going to join? No one here pays as well as we do."

"I'll work with whomever I want to," I stated. "There's more to life than coin, and I won't be controlled by it."

I walked back down the pier without even looking at the contents of the contract—I just shoved the paper into my trouser pocket, my whole body still stiff. I didn't stop until I reached the line for the mystic seekers' ship. For some reason, despite the fact that mystic seekers usually paid more than other types of crews, the line seemed shorter than most.

When I reached Lynus, he glanced over, and just his proximity seemed to relax me. No longer agitated, I returned my hands to my pockets and exhaled, as though this were where I was meant to be.

Lynus stared for a long moment. "What's wrong?"

"Nothing," I said.

"You had that *look* when you walked over here. Don't tell me you failed the test?"

"Of course not."

"Then what happened? I figured you'd *love* the Frith Guild recruiter, what with his perfectly coiffed hair. Or did he turn you down?"

I smacked Lynus in his side, right in one of his injuries. He chuckled through a groan and then grimaced. It didn't feel like I had hit *that* hard, but it had still been a solid strike. Lynus continued to chortle, even after he had straightened himself.

The people in line—thugs and cutthroats, every one of them—shot us glowers. I stepped closer to Lynus, who practically blended in with the rough crowd.

"Well?" Lynus asked as he rubbed at his wounded side. "Let's see the contract. C'mon."

I shrugged. "They assumed I couldn't read. You know. The same song and dance. I don't wanna sail with them."

"Heh. Can you blame them? You do look like a vagabond."

Although I hadn't noticed it before, my ill-fitting clothes and scuffed boots registered in my thoughts. I glanced down, and I knew Zelfree must've felt the same in that exact moment. Dirt and tree sap dappled the sleeve of my shirt.

"It doesn't matter," I said. "It's not like I'm going to take an assignment on a ship that isn't with you. I just love opportunities to prove how talented I am."

"I still wanna see it."

I pulled the crumpled piece of paper out of my pocket and handed it over. Seagulls flew close, and I wondered if they thought the paper was a bit of food they could steal. Lynus growled in their direction, and the birds had enough sense to take wing and head farther down the pier.

Lynus read over the contract with the one eye of his that would actually stay open. His busted eyebrows narrowed and knitted. He handed the paper back, hesitant.

"You're not gonna take this?" he asked.

I shook my head. "Weren't you listening?"

"They wanna make you an officer-in-training, Everett."

I flipped the page over for a moment. I had only

managed to read two sentences before I shoved the contract back into my pocket:

First Mate and Journeyman Arcanist of the Frith Guild, Gregory Ruma, hereby offers ____ the position of Trainee Navigational Officer (Nautical Apprentice). The duties shall include all manner of deck officer and navigation training.

"They probably handed me the wrong contract," I said.

Lynus scoffed. Then he shoved my shoulder, almost enough to knock me off the damn pier, but I maintained my balance. "You'd be a damn fool not to take it," he said.

"I'm not leaving you with the mystic seekers."

"Nah, you're just saddling me with the guilt of holding you back."

I snapped my attention to him. Lynus managed a smirk in return.

"You really want me to take a position on a different ship?" I asked.

"'Course not." Lynus ran a calloused hand through his matted hair. Then he pointed to the edge of the bay, right were two mountains almost connected. The mountains created a natural barrier—a narrow passage all ships had to sail through. "Everyone has to go through the Lightning Straits, right? Even if I join these mystic seekers, we'll probably see each other on the other side. There aren't many ports from here to the Argo Empire, either. Think about it."

"You're saying we'll still see each other, even if we're not part of the same crew."

He nodded. "Just take your officer position and be

thankful at least one of us is lucky. I'll work with these sea cows. And maybe someday *I'll* join the Frith Guild, too."

The way he had said those sentences—it was a lot softer than everything before.

It reminded me of Illia. She never hesitated to push me toward my goal. And like Lynus with Zelfree, she could always read my emotions, even when others couldn't. If Illia and I were in this situation, I had no doubt in my mind it would play out the exact same way.

I rubbed at my nose and then said, "Just promise me we'll stay solid. Even if we take separate ships, travel with different crews, see unrelated sights—you and I will stay the same."

Lynus chuckled, though it sounded odd through a busted nose. "Gettin' sentimental already? We haven't even left."

"I just want to make sure we'll stick together. Even if times somehow get rougher than they already are."

"Don't worry. I promise things will always be good between us, no matter what else happens." Lynus shoved me and then growled, "Now don't make me throw you into the water. Go on. *Get outta here.*"

I rotated my shoulders and left the line, my steps sluggish.

It was a shame I couldn't hear Zelfree's exact thoughts in the moment. It was obvious he didn't want to leave.

I awoke in the *Sun Chaser*, my back hurting from the awkward way I had tossed in my hammock. I pulled myself up into a sitting position. Nothing moved, and that seemed odd for a ship. An airship wasn't tethered to the water, but I still expected to hear the waves lapping against the hull.

My dreams lingered at the edge of my thoughts. Why hadn't Master Zelfree ever mentioned Lynus? If they really did have a relationship similar to Illia and me, wouldn't he have at least brought it up in passing? Or perhaps the unspeakable had happened...

Adelgis sat in his hammock, his attention glued to the book in his lap.

"Hey," I said, my voice rusty from sleep.

Morning light trickled in through the porthole, giving us plenty of light, even if the lanterns were snuffed.

"How're you feeling?" Adelgis asked without looking up.

"Fine."

"I'm glad to hear it."

"Uh, Adelgis," I said as I rubbed my sore neck. After a long stretch, I continued, "You've seen all these memories you've given me, right?"

He nodded, but still didn't look up from his reading.

"There's this man in the dreams that seems close to Master Zelfree. His name is Lynus. Does he... die at some point?"

"No."

I exhaled and smiled. "Oh, good. I was a little worried."

Adelgis froze halfway through turning a page. A moment later, he continued with his reading, not bothering to voice his thoughts.

The door to our storeroom creaked open. Fain slid inside, still wearing the same trousers, shirt, and coat he had been the day before.

He glanced between us, his eyes narrowed. "You're both awake."

"Where have you been?" I asked.

"Searching the city."

"Did you find anything?"

"Well, this place is a little weird. Jittery. I get the feeling something is wrong. I was hoping you and Moonbeam could help me once I get some sleep."

I nodded along with his words. "Yeah, our number one priority should be scouring this entire city." It was the only way we were going to find traces of Theasin or the khepera.

14

THE TRAIL OF THEASIN VENROVER

Fain was right. The city seemed jittery.

It was difficult to pinpoint what caused that feeling, and the longer I thought about it, the more I realized it was the culmination of several factors. The ports were full, and sailors had become restless. Coupled with the growing number of pirates, I understood why some people were on edge.

Then came the rumors.

As Adelgis, Fain, and I walked through the brick streets of New Norra, I heard more and more whispers concerning the Argo Empire. Tales of the queen's assassination had finally reached the common folk, but nothing was accurate. One woman said the queen had been decapitated by her own sovereign dragon. A merchant claimed that islanders had killed the queen to start a war. A group of children joked that the arcane plague had run through Thronehold, corrupting most of the arcanists.

A few details remained consistent: the queen was dead, and Prince Rishan was poised to take her place on the throne.

No one knew of the prince's dastardly involvement, and no one mentioned the runestones. I found the latter fact the most interesting. The runestones had been the whole reason the assassins had shown up in the first place. The villains had wanted them so that they could unearth godly mystical creatures, the kind so powerful their magic could alter the terrain or turn the tide of war.

As I rounded a street corner, my thoughts went straight to the Frith Guild.

I had given them six of the twelve runestones, including the runestone for the world serpent. Were they out searching for the creature right now? Maybe they had already found it—Illia had the Occult Compass, a powerful magical item capable of locating mystical creatures. That, along with the runestone, would make finding the world serpent an easy task.

"What building is this?" Fain asked.

I hadn't even been paying attention to our surroundings. Flustered, I glanced around, surprised by the presence of black sandstone bricks, instead of the blue, yellow, and red in the rest of the city. The buildings around us were taller, some with pillars in the front and most with short staircases up to the main door. Small groups of individuals wandered the road, and it didn't seem like anything was for sale. If I had to guess, I would've said we were in some sort of government district.

The city wall loomed over the area, casting a long shadow down the street.

"This is Norra Library," Adelgis said, pointing to one of the larger buildings. Although there were several thick glass windows lining the walls, they were dark amber in color, making it impossible to see inside. "My father says it's one of the best in the world."

A group of scholars walked by, each with a long robe covered in embroidery. Instead of shapes or designs, they had words stitched into their clothing, most of which seemed to relate to mystical creatures and magic. They hustled past us before I could get a better look, however.

Fain pulled the ascot up higher on his neck. I suspected it was warm, but he never took it off, no doubt to keep his pirate tattoo hidden. "I don't think I belong here."

Adelgis wore a simple cap, but his long, black hair hung straight down from the sides. He took a moment to smooth the raven locks. "My home city of Ellios has evergrow trees for making paper. They take the fibers of the wood, beat it down until it becomes fine, and then dilute it with water to make the pulp for the paper." He just continued to speak as though Fain had said nothing. "But New Norra, they use *wool* fibers from their desert ibex to make that pulp. Ibex are goats, in case you weren't aware. Their horns can—"

"*Moonbeam*," Fain said, cutting him off. "I get it. If I have any questions about paper, you'll be the first person I ask."

"Hm. Yes, well, I think my father would've visited this place before leaving the city, so we should check inside."

"This sounds like the perfect spot for you and Volke." Fain tugged on his sweat-soaked shirt and frosted it over for the hundredth time. "Wraith and I can search near the Lion's Tail River in the meantime."

"Thank the good stars," Wraith said through his panting.

I nodded. "We'll cover more ground that way."

"I think this is an acceptable plan," Adelgis said.

I held a hand over my eyes as I glanced up into the sky. It wasn't yet noon. "Let's meet up after the sunset bells chime. Didn't Karna say she would be at a cantina?"

"She said she would be at the *Painted Cactus*."

"We'll meet there."

Without any more words, Fain went invisible and headed in the opposite direction. Wraith kept his pace, breathing shallow the entire way. Once I couldn't hear the wheezing, I faced Adelgis.

He took a sip from a canteen, the kind made of a glass bottom wrapped in a woven basket cover. When he was done, he offered me some, but I turned it away.

"Does it bother you when Fain calls you *Moonbeam*?" I asked. "You never react, but it's difficult to tell what you're thinking nowadays."

"I don't mind." Adelgis corked the canteen and then tied it to his belt. He wore a simple shirt and trousers, and his cap offered shade for his face. It was the least amount of clothing I had ever seen him wear around outside his room. "I like to think *Moonbeam* is my honorary pirate name."

I snorted back a laugh. "What?"

"Fain said pirates give up their real names and take new ones when they join a crew. I like to think Moonbeam is the name I would take."

"Moonbeam the Pirate?"

"Yes."

"You know the name is supposed to be *intimidating*, right?" I ran a hand down my face, on the verge of disbelief and half-chuckling. "That's not a name that instills fear."

"I think my name would invoke a sense of confusion."

"Oh, it does that," I quipped.

"Besides, Fain's thoughts are rather grim. He always frets over every interaction, sometimes believing that one mistake will cause us to leave him at some port. But when he started joking with me—and calling me *Moonbeam*—he grew a little more confident, seeing this as us bonding, rather than necessarily insulting me."

I thought Fain had gotten over his fear of rejection when

we had brought him into the Frith Guild, but perhaps joining me on this trek had gotten him worried again. I wasn't sure how to assuage his fears outside of telling him I didn't intend to ditch him at the nearest port.

"I'll talk to Fain at some point," I said. "But for now, let's focus on the library."

Norra Library was three stories of books, bookshelves, ladders, tables, and wide desks meant for transcribing. The place smelled of paper and ink, and the amber windows filtered the harsh light from outside, creating a sepia aura that color-washed everything into a monotone reddish-brown.

Adelgis went straight for the librarians, but I lingered back to examine the contents of the library. Some tomes were so old it was difficult to see the writing on the inside. I sifted through those and specifically looked for books written by Adelgis's father, Theasin Venrover. While I didn't care for the man on a personal level, I had appreciated having his mini-encyclopedia during the Sovereign Dragon Tournament. Perhaps I could find something else useful from him?

"My arcanist," Luthair said. "Look here."

The shadows pointed to a book on the top shelf. It was titled: ABYSSAL CREATURES. It wasn't written by Theasin Venrover, but the title intrigued me. I plucked the book from its perch and slowly flipped through the yellowed pages.

"Why did you like this one, Luthair?" I asked.

"I suspected it might have information on the abyssal leech."

That hadn't crossed my mind, but the moment it did, I

rushed through the contents of the book, searching for any section that could relate to the mystical creature. According to Theasin, the abyssal leech could manipulate magic, which would ultimately be the key to solving the arcane plague problem. Theasin had a single leech—I watched him remove it from Adelgis—and hopefully, this would solve our problem, but in the meantime, I wanted to know more about this bizarre creature.

I arrived at a section with drawings of leeches and stopped.

Abyssal Leech

This creature feeds on the magic of others. It embeds itself into the flesh of an arcanist or mystical creature and slowly saps away their strength over an extended period of time. Unlike other creatures, which must bond in order to grow and mature, abyssal leeches simply need to find a magical host and suckle from the magic. If bonded, an abyssal leech can manipulate and augment the magics of anything it embeds itself into, and its arcanists can warp magics around them.

I flipped the page, engrossed in the information.

Abyssal leech arcanists have the ability to unweave magics from items and even other living things.

· · ·

I didn't like the use of the word "unweave." I didn't know why, but it conjured disturbing images in my mind's eye, and it made it difficult to concentrate on the rest of the passage.

Because of this powerful unweaving ability, most magical fortifications pose no problem for abyssal leech arcanists. During reproduction, abyssal leeches implant egg sacs into other creatures. Having more than one infesting a body causes certain death, and once the host dies, the hatchlings spread out and embed themselves in new hosts. If they grow large enough, they'll implant their own eggs, creating an epidemic.

The late queen of the Argo Empire had ordered the extermination of the abyssal leeches, and I was starting to understand why. They sounded destructive—not just to people, but to physical locations as well, if they could undo magic. This was a creature that would stop the plague?

Abyssal leeches have long been associated with bad luck and disastrous omens. They are presumed extinct.

"There wasn't nearly this much information in the book penned by Theasin," Luthair whispered from the shadows.

"That's true," I muttered. "Do you think Theasin doesn't know as much, or do you think this was written after Theasin did his initial research?"

"I think he's hiding information."

I stared at the shadows on the floor. "Why?"

"I don't know. But it's obvious he enjoys having more knowledge than others. Especially if he can use it to his advantage."

"Are you trying to say he's going to do something questionable with the abyssal leech he took from Adelgis?" I didn't want to think of Theasin as an enemy, not when he was supposedly creating a cure for the plague. "Keeping information to one's self doesn't necessarily mean something dubious is happening."

"And while that is true, I would advise caution when dealing with someone whose motives are unknown. I hope for everyone's sake that we can find the khepera and cure you with their magic, rather than relying on Theasin Venrover."

I flipped through more of the book, but there wasn't much else on the abyssal leech. I returned it to the shelf, my pulse higher than it had been moments ago. Thinking about Theasin and the leech only reminded me of my dire situation. I hated drowning in the doubt, so I had to take a quiet moment to refocus myself. If I was lucky, we would find the khepera, and I wouldn't even need to worry about all of this.

"Volke," Adelgis said as he walked down the aisle, "we have a problem."

"What is it?"

"My father isn't in the city anymore."

"Okay. That's not necessarily a problem. We already figured that might be the case. We'll just head to wherever he is."

Adelgis shook his head. "That's the real problem. No one knows where he went once he left New Norra." He crossed his arms, his expression pinched. "The librarians here said the last they saw him was at the labs."

I rubbed at the back of my neck. "Then why don't we go there and ask? Surely someone knows where he went."

Adelgis furrowed his brow. "I don't have access to the Grand Laboratories of New Norra. It's a special research facility for arcanists registered with a union of guilds. My father is a member, but that doesn't extend to me."

I forced a sarcastic chuckle. So we weren't allowed in? Even though Theasin's own son needed information? How private was this damn lab?

"No one will help us?" I asked.

"The thoughts of the librarians are filled with secrets and doubts. They were told not to tell anyone of my father's visit. I think if I head to the labs, I'll get the same response. Denial."

"What do you want to do, then? How can we find him?"

"My father keeps detailed records and often writes letters to his peers. If we're somehow granted access to the Grand Laboratories of New Norra, I think I can figure out where he went through a combination of mind reading and old-fashioned investigation."

All we needed to do was get inside.

There were several ways we could attempt to gain access. We could ask one of the research arcanists to help us, we could physically sneak in, especially with my shadow-stepping and Fain's invisibility, or...

As I dwelled on the problem, a plan formed alongside my smirk. "Well, we do know a doppelgänger arcanist."

"I liked the plan the moment it started forming in your thoughts," Adelgis replied, his excitement spilling into his hands, giving him a nervous tic. "If Karna walks us into the labs disguised as my father, we could accompany her to my father's personal quarters without opposition." He poked my shoulder with his pointer finger. "You should be the one to ask Karna to help us, since she actively dislikes both Fain and me."

"I can do that."

His jovial enthusiasm waned for a minute as his gaze fell to the floor. "But it would be unusual if my father arrived at the labs unannounced, especially since he left there a week prior. Standard procedure, to which he always adheres, demands a letter of announcement. If we really want to fool the researchers and artificers of the labs, we would need to send one in advance. Which means the earliest we'll have access is in a day or two."

Adelgis's attention to detail impressed me. Could we actually pull off impersonating his father? Adelgis made it seem possible. All we needed to do was search around Theasin's personal lab for any clues to his whereabouts. We could be in and out without anyone becoming the wiser.

"Do you mind?" Adelgis asked.

I lifted an eyebrow. "Do I mind what?"

"Waiting a couple of days, so it appears as though the announcement letter arrived before my father's ship."

Wasting a few days to fake our way into the labs was time I wouldn't regain. But it had to be done.

"It'll be fine," I said. "We can search for the khepera in the meantime."

"Then I'll write the letter straight away."

15

ADELGIS'S FATHER

Once the sunset bells rang, Adelgis and I headed toward the *Painted Cactus* on foot. While the trek was easy, it was dark by the time we arrived.

The *Painted Cactus* was a cantina located on the edge of the city proper, right before the gate that led to the ship-yards. My father had insisted it was a pleasant establishment, but the moment I drew near, I questioned his definition of the word "pleasant."

The entire two-story building was bursting with patrons, food, and drink. Even the outside had groups standing around or sitting on benches, loud and rowdy, speaking in ever-increasing volumes to get their voices heard. The sounds of smashed glass or the occasional cheering echoed through the cantina, spilling into the street.

It wasn't a place of high etiquette or restraint, and while that didn't bother me, it wasn't a place I considered relaxing. If anything, I grew tenser. Arcanists, mostly sailors and merchants, made up most of the patrons. One arcanist caught my attention because the star on his forehead had the picture of a skeleton whale woven between the points. It was a bake-kujira—known as the "ghost whale"—the *bringer of misfortune* and the *dead lord of the tides*. I had only ever heard of them in old tales, and I almost stopped to ask the man about his eldrin, but I decided against it.

With the plague running in my veins, I didn't want to mingle with random arcanists for longer than necessary.

Perhaps I would see the undead whale in the delta, and that would be enough to sate my curiosity.

"It's quite cold," Adelgis said as we maneuvered our way through the crowds to the front door. He rubbed at his arms, his simple outfit not enough to fight the evening chill.

The wootz cotton kept me a little warmer, but it wasn't enough. "Hopefully, the inside is better."

Once we got through the front door, a cloud of alcohol-scented smoke wafted over us, but at least it was warm. Almost everyone had a mug filled with an odiferous white substance. It had to be alcoholic, given the way everyone drunkenly conducted themselves, but I wasn't familiar with the drink.

Adelgis pressed himself close to me as we navigated the cantina, speaking loudly, but I still couldn't hear him well. "It's desert milk."

"Milk?" I asked.

"Not actual milk from an animal. The drink just turns white when water is added. It's an alcohol made from grapes and figs."

Adelgis's random knowledge always astounded me, but now that he continually heard thoughts, perhaps this was just a result of information osmosis. How else would Adelgis have known about the specific drink people enjoyed in New Norra?

The many tables inside the *Painted Cactus* were dedicated

to card games or dice. I had never been good at gambling, and since I didn't have any coins, I didn't bother paying much attention. Instead, I focused on the stage in the far back. A couple of men sat on a long bench, each with a string instrument on their lap. They plucked at the cords, creating a pleasant melody that didn't demand too much attention.

Karna, dressed in a long skirt with slits to her hips, danced to the gentle tune, her slow but precise movements causing her flowing attire to swish around her. The inside of the outfit was lined in shimmery scales, and when she flipped backward—landing gracefully on her feet every time—the shine of the scales demanded attention. Anyone sitting at the tables near the stage only half-focused on their game. Even I almost forgot I was walking through the cantina.

Her long, blonde hair was tied in a loose ponytail, and her top was a tight half-shirt that covered her shoulders and chest and nothing else.

The moment the song stopped and Karna took her bow, coins flew onto the stage from men and women alike. Karna offered winks and a slow wave as she gathered the copper and headed backstage.

Adelgis placed a hand on my shoulder. "You should speak to her. I want to ask the bartender a few questions."

The woman behind the bar glowered in our direction, her cutthroat appearance a little intimidating. She stood taller than most men, scars on her face and neck, and her shoulders had been carved out of small boulders. The arcanist mark on her forehead had the design of a half-goat, half-fish—a legendary capricorn—and she appeared to have weapons not-so-hidden in her oversized robes.

"Just be careful," I said.

Adelgis nodded as he headed over to the bar and kitchen area, not a hint of concern on his face.

Now that I was alone, I got near the closest wall and then stepped into the shadows and moved through the crowds in a matter of seconds. One moment I was in the gambling area, and the next, I was behind the curtain of the stage, back with the performers and musicians. The dim lighting didn't bother me, as I could see in the dark, but it was obvious some of the entertainers couldn't see well in the gloom. A dancer leapt up in surprise the moment she managed to catch sight of me, a quiet gasp escaping her as she staggered backward.

"I'm here to speak to Karna," I said.

As though summoned by saying her name, Karna stepped out from behind a rack of clothing. She pushed back her hair with a flick of her wrist and sauntered over. "It's okay, Telli. This is a good friend of mine."

The woman touched three fingers to her chest and left us without another word. Karna hooked my elbow and guided me off to the side, away from everyone preparing for another round of entertainment.

"You look like you need something," Karna said, amusement in her voice.

"I was wondering if you could help us gain access to the Grand Laboratories of New Norra." Guilt crept into my thoughts, like we were planning a heist or some other overt criminal activity, and I felt compelled to explain myself just to make sure she didn't get the wrong idea. "We need to figure out Theasin's location, and the lab isn't open to the public. We're not going to take anything or disturb their research. If you could impersonate Theasin Venrover, just for a short while, that would be helpful."

"I can do that," she said.

I exhaled and half-smiled. "Really? Thank you. We'll be at the lab in two days and—"

"But I want something in return," Karna interjected.

The request caught me off guard. With my eyebrows knit, I said, "I don't have any coins."

For a split second, Karna's expression hardened, but the look disappeared as quickly as it had come. She turned around, grabbed a leather pouch off a nearby table, and then opened it up to reveal hundreds of coins—most were copper, but the occasional silver shone through. She took my hand and then dumped a small pile into my palm.

"There," she said with a sarcastic edge. "Buy yourself something nice in the market."

"I didn't mean I needed this."

"Your father wants to help you craft a weapon, right? You could probably buy a mystical creature part or two, if you know how to haggle." Karna tossed the pouch back on the table, a sly smile creeping back into her expression. "I don't want your money." She grazed her fingers down my chest. "I want you to sleep in my quarters for the rest of the trek."

"Wait, what?"

"At least until we find Theasin Venrover." She gave me a coy smile. "Do that and I'll lend you any and all of my magic whenever you want."

"Karna," I muttered, my face growing hot. I pocketed the coins and stepped back, unsure of how to word everything. I hadn't expected such a demand. "I can't. You know why. You're an arcanist, and if you were infected through... well, through *intimacy*, and—"

She gently placed her hand over my mouth. "You're cute when you're flustered, but I don't want that. I truly just want your company. And I know you're the type of man to be beyond respectful."

Once she removed her hand, I exhaled and stared at the floor. It was flattering to hear she wanted my presence, but the nature of the arcane plague meant it could be transferred in numerous ways. My ever-growing fear of infecting someone else made this otherwise flirtatious proposition seem needlessly dangerous.

"Fine," I eventually said. "But I'll leave if *anything* happens." I said the word with awkward emphasis, and I felt foolish for doing so, but what did she want from me? To say all the details aloud? "And only after we investigate the labs."

Karna gave me a quick embrace, her arms around my chest. "Perfect. You just let me know when you need me."

With an unfortunate amount of time to waste, I trained with Fain, helping him improve his magic, as well as practicing my own.

During one of our sessions, Fain stopped after evoking ice across the deck of the *Sun Chaser*. He stared at his frostbitten fingers for a long moment and then turned to me.

"Did your evocation become more powerful as you used it?" he asked.

"I'm not sure." I recalled back to the many times I had used my magic. "But I have gained better control of it. At first, I evoked terrors that affected everyone in the area—friend and foe. Now I can control it. Pick specific targets. What about you? Have you gained any sort of subtler control?"

"I create ice, but I'm not sure what else I could do with it."

"Your ice coats the ground… Have you ever tried to frost something else? Like the air?"

"How would that help?"

"You could create a fog. It could obscure vision?"

"An ice fog is different than normal fog," Fain said. "It's filled with crystals—frozen bits of water in the air. It'll do more than just fill the area with thick mist."

I rubbed at my neck. "I've never seen ice fog before."

Fain lifted an eyebrow. "Really? It's common up in the north, where it snows for four months straight. Breathe too much of that ice fog and you'll get sluggish—plus, you'll have a hard time getting enough air."

"Try making some," I said.

Fain held up his hand, his concentration visible on his face. I held still, trying not to distract him in any way. When he used his evocation, a thin layer of rime washed over the *Sun Chaser* again, but a second later, small portions of the ice wafted up, creating streams of fog that lifted from the deck, like ghosts rising from the grave.

After a long moment, Fain gasped and lowered his hand, his breathing becoming labored panting. The ice on the deck faded.

I jogged to his side. "Are you okay?"

"It's too hot," he said through gritted teeth. He bent over, posting his hands on his knees and gulping down air. "It was difficult to do even that much…"

I patted his back. "I'm impressed. You did a remarkable job for your first time."

"Yeah, you really did," a cute voice chimed in.

Fain and I looked up. Biyu sat on the far side of the airship, her one eye locked on to us, a smile across her face. She scooted a little closer and rested her chin in both hands.

"Don't give up," she said. "I believe in you! You should

try again. Maybe this time with your wendigo? I want to see you two do magic together."

Fain's cheeks shifted to a shade of pink. "Uh…" No other words came to him.

"Not right now," I said. "But perhaps later. At night, when it's colder."

"I won't get a good view at night," Biyu said, frowning.

"I'm a knightmare arcanist. I can make it so you see in the dark."

Her sadness vanished in an instant. "Really? That's amazing!"

I couldn't contain my smile. "Then you should come back at night, Illia—er, *Biyu*." I ran my hand down my sweaty face, trying to clear my thoughts and focus. "We'll train for a few hours after it gets dark," I said.

Biyu pulled on the strap holding her book and tugged it into her lap. "I'll be there taking notes."

I found nothing about the khepera when I searched the city, other than the few entrances to the Grotto Labyrinth, each guarded by soldiers. Most of New Norra had depictions of the scarabs in their decorations—even some of the bricks had carvings of the mystical creatures—but none of it indicated where they had gone. When I questioned the citizens, they grew irritated. *If mystic seekers couldn't find the khepera, what makes a random arcanist think he could solve the mystery?* Their question lessened my confidence.

Vethica, on the other hand, wouldn't give up. She would go into town every day with a handmade map and a stack of notes. According to my father, she had personally mapped out all the entrances to the Grotto Labyrinth and had even snuck inside the underground maze to document the many passageways. But she still came back empty handed—no explanation on where the khepera might have gone.

On the morning we were to sneak into the Grand Laboratories of New Norra, I spotted her leaving the *Sun Chaser* before dawn had fully settled. Again, she carried her materials, and she barely glanced in my direction as she made her way for the gangplank.

I hustled over to her, determined to get answers.

"Vethica, do you have a moment?"

"No," she said, curt.

"I want to help you find the khepera."

Vethica continued to the gangplank, her eyes narrowed. "Don't. You should stay as far away from the khepera as possible."

Her terse attitude prevented me from getting in another word before she left the airship. I just stood by the railing and watched her go.

Adelgis, dressed in the same minimal clothing as before, hurried over to me. "Volke, it's almost time to go." He glanced in the same direction I stared. "Don't worry about that. We can speak to her afterward."

"Do you know why she holds such animosity toward me?"

"Oh, yes. She thinks about it all the time."

I glowered at Adelgis, waiting for him to explain.

He must've heard my impatient thoughts, because he met my gaze, his dark eyes searching mine. "She was once plague-ridden," Adelgis whispered. "Both her and her eldrin, a thunderbird. She was forced to kill it, and she hates that you haven't done so already."

The information hit me hard. I knew she had once been an arcanist, but killing her own eldrin? I couldn't even imagine. No wonder she hated me. She probably thought this whole situation unfair.

My focus went straight to the shifting shadow around my feet.

"I see," I muttered, barely aware of anything else around me.

If Luthair became plague-ridden, I didn't think I would have the willpower to kill him. It would be my fault, though. I would have to take responsibility.

The sound of boots up the airship stairway dragged me out of my spiraling thoughts of depression. I caught my breath the moment a figure emerged from below deck.

Theasin Venrover.

He crossed the deck of the airship, no hurry in his steps, his crisp, black trousers and silk shirt free of sweat or soil. Instead of wearing long robes with hoods to cover his head and face, he wore a dark cloak with a hood. The gloves on his hands were just as I had remembered—thin and hugging so close to his skin, they might as well have been tattoos.

Damn. Adelgis and his father looked a lot alike, from their shiny, black hair to their tanned skin. Adelgis kept his hair long, though—a little past his shoulders—and his father kept his cut short, especially on the sides. Well, that and Theasin was more imposing. He had a confidence and athleticism that Adelgis lacked.

I opened my mouth to say something, but Theasin sneered, stopping me cold.

"What're you waiting for?" he asked, his voice icy and condescending. "We don't have time for your gawking."

With wide eyes, I turned to Adelgis. I wanted to ask if this were really Karna, but all I offered was a confused stare.

Adelgis nodded. "This *is* Karna. I gave her some dream-memories of my father so she would know what he looked like, how he spoke, and what he liked to wear."

The Karna-Theasin scoffed. "Really? *This* needed an explanation? You were the one who concocted this plan. Or have you already forgotten?"

I was still shocked at how well Karna had pulled off Theasin's demeanor. I had seen her impersonate others before, and I had always managed to detect the differences between the person and her duplicate. Not this time. She was everything I remembered of Theasin—a perfect copy. Why was she so much better at imitating Theasin over Captain Devlin?

"Uh, we should probably get to the labs before the sun is fully in the sky," I muttered.

"Lead the way," Karna-Theasin commanded.

16

THE GRAND LABORATORIES OF NEW NORRA

Walking through the streets of New Norra made me long for Thronehold. The trollies there were a wonderful convenience, and I swear the merciless sun that hung over the Amber Dunes wouldn't set until it had evaporated every last drop of moisture in the city.

We followed the golden yellow lines until a black line appeared on the brick roads. Instead of heading back to the massive library, we made our way west, along the Lion's Tail River, far from the delta. The farther inland we got, the less crowded the streets became. Once we passed the center bazaar, the atmosphere became quiet and peaceful.

To my fascination, I spotted two stone golems standing on separate street corners. They were gigantic—sandstone boulders made up their body, arms, legs, and bulging shoulders. Their heads were small rocks, and everything looked to be held together by an invisible force of magic.

Each golem's arcanist stood next to them, though they were short in comparison, only half the height of the eleven-foot golems. The arcanists wore similar clothes, no doubt uniforms—black, flowing pants, black tunics, and copper armor over their chests and thighs. Their helmets shaded their heads, and scimitars were on full display, hanging from thick belts on their hips.

"*Those are members of the Watch Battalion,*" Adelgis said telepathically as we walked by. "*They're employed by the governor of New Norra to maintain order and guard the city buildings.*"

The members of the Watch Battalion shot us harsh glowers, but they didn't move from their posts.

"I didn't see any when we were at the library," I muttered as I glanced over my shoulder to get another look at the stone golems.

"*They were there. Stone golems are capable of hiding in stone that matches their type.*"

I almost laughed. The entire city was basically made of sandstone. Did that mean the Watch Battalion was hiding everywhere in the city and I just hadn't realized it?

My thoughts drifted back to our surroundings. It seemed the longer we followed the black line, the wealthier the city became. The houses were mini-palaces, the people rode on slender horses with sorrel coats that glistened in the oppressive light, and there were actual plants around—grass, trees, and even a dozen flowers.

I slowed down to get a better look at a couple of birch trees. Their white bark and eye-like knots were intriguing, but did they grow in the desert? I didn't think so.

Karna-Theasin stopped dead in his tracks and turned back to face me with a sneer. "Are you done?"

I quickened my pace to reach Adelgis and his faux father. "Sorry. The scenery intrigued me."

"The arcanists here like to foolishly defy the climate," Karna-Theasin said in a matter-of-fact tone. "No matter the monetary or magical cost."

Karna's dedication to Theasin's character still impressed me. Even the gait—she walked in front of us, each step forceful and precise, just like the real man.

I jogged to her—his?—side, examining the movements.

"Have you ever met the real Theasin?" Karna-Theasin asked, his voice a perfect duplicate of Adelgis's father.

"I met him once," I said. "He left an impression, that's for sure."

Karna-Theasin narrowed his eyes. "I detest him."

If Adelgis heard, he made no indication. I worried because Adelgis always spoke highly of his father, but after the abyssal leech had been removed from his side, he had opted to just avoid the subject most of the time. The situation had to hurt, but I didn't know what to say to him.

"What exactly are we getting from these labs?" Karna-Theasin asked.

"I need to find out where my father went after he left the city." Adelgis crossed and uncrossed his arms, his restless movements making me nervous. "I'll hear the thoughts of the other researchers and arcanists, but I also want to read any and all correspondences my father made while here. It shouldn't take too long."

"Good. I don't want to have this body for a second longer than necessary."

The day grew hotter and hotter, but thankfully, it didn't take us long to reach the laboratory. I knew it immediately thanks to the signs, but also because of the tall, wrought-iron fence surrounding the massive plot of land around the building. The Grand Laboratories of New Norra were shaped like a U, with a fountain in the courtyard spraying precious water into the air.

When we approached the gate, I straightened my posture and squared my shoulders, hoping we wouldn't look out of place. One of the Watch Battalion stood at the entrance, his stone golem standing next to him.

The man's eyes widened when he got a good look at "Theasin."

"Artificer Venrover," the watchman said. "You came by foot?"

"Unfortunately," Karna-Theasin replied, bite in his words. "Good help is hard to find these days, and I couldn't wait for a street cart or carriage."

"Oh, I see. It must be important if you came straightaway."

"Obviously."

The watchman placed three fingers on his chest and then hurried to open the gate. His movements were shaky and a little uncoordinated, but he eventually opened everything up and motioned us in.

"Welcome back, Artificer," he said.

Karna-Theasin strode in and passed the watchman without even a *thank you*. That was how I imagined Theasin would do it, but I still thought it was rude. I offered my own thanks as I passed the man, even if it garnered me an odd glance.

We traveled the long walkway up to the front doors of the labs, the glitter of water from the fountain reminding me how dry my lips had become.

The ornate double doors opened before we reached them. When we stepped inside, I took note of the non-arcanist servants who stood behind the doors. It seemed their sole responsibility was to open the entrance whenever someone approached. A dull profession, but I supposed it was easy.

Cool air washed over us, billowing outward like a sigh of relief. It helped focus my thoughts.

Stepping into the laboratory's open reception room felt like stepping into a perfect painting. Somehow, the floors were immaculate—not a speck of sand nor scuff from a boot anywhere on the polished sandstone tiles. Scholars went about their business, but they, too, kept themselves unusually stiff, as though wrinkling their fine silk robes would result in punishment.

A woman wearing the uniform of the Watch Battalion walked straight toward us, her steps betraying years of strict military training. Unlike the men outside, she possessed several additional pieces of copper armor, medals on her shoulder, and she carried a flintlock rifle. Her black hair had been cut at chin-length, and she wore no helmet.

Her arcanist mark intrigued me. It was a star with a swirl of flame around the points, a faint face in the fire. A djinn. A rare type of desert creature who could hide itself, much like knightmares and ethereal whelks. They had flame-like bodies they could shift from corporeal to incorporeal.

"This woman is Watch Commander Bashir," Adelgis said, his telepathic voice echoing in my thoughts. Was he speaking to Karna as well? I hoped so. He continued, *"The watch commander is concerned. Her thoughts are about my father. Apparently, he's supposed to bring something back for her, and there's no way he could've arrived at his destination and returned so quickly."*

"Artificer Venrover," Watch Commander Bashir said. She stopped a foot in front of us and touched three fingers to her chest. "This is most unexpected. Welcome back."

The interaction made me nervous. I wasn't a master of subterfuge, and I hadn't even considered the fact that there might be people monitoring Theasin's movements for their own personal reasons. If we were discovered—especially inside the Grand Laboratories of New Norra—I suspected we would be arrested, perhaps worse.

And once they found out I carried the plague, they would execute me without hesitation.

"There are only two things in this world that continue to surprise me," Karna-Theasin said. "Human stupidity and human incompetence. Unfortunately, both were at play when my assistant left valuable notes behind in my lab. I'm here to retrieve them. I understand this will put a delay in your delivery, but it couldn't be helped."

I slowly turned my gaze, amazed at how smooth and effortless Karna acted out the scene. It was perfect, right down to the word choice.

The watch commander eased her stance. "Ah. I see. Unfortunate for all of us, then. Let me know if there's anything I can do for you." She stepped out of the way and motioned for us to continue into the labs.

A wisp of fire flashed around her shoulders—no doubt her djinn moving along with her—but it never manifested.

Watch Commander Bashir didn't bother acknowledging Adelgis or me. It seemed as though she considered us unimportant, or perhaps just accessories to Theasin's work. Or better yet, Theasin's ego overshadowed everything around him, making everything else trivial.

We strode deeper into the laboratories, past the clean front room, through an arched doorway, and then into a long hallway. The only people inside were researchers and arcanists, all of whom wore the scholarly robes I had seen in the library. Most individuals had books or notes, but some carried the dead bodies of mystical creatures and a handful of star shards. The glittering gold of the shards caught my eye. If I were going to make a weapon with my father, I would need a few star shards of my own. They were the magical glue used to create permanent items.

There were no windows. Light was provided by glowstones mounted to the walls. Their bluish-white hue made everything seem mystical, even the mundane artwork and tapestries of the desert.

We came to a four-way intersection in the hall.

"Where are we going?" Karna-Theasin muttered under his breath.

Karna had behaved so confidently that I had forgotten she had never been here before.

"*Turn right,*" Adelgis said telepathically. "*Then at the next intersection, turn left. My father's lab is at the end of that hall.*"

Although they were simple instructions, the building was larger than I had expected. It took us several minutes before we made it to the correct corridor.

To my amusement, no one beyond the watch commander attempted to speak to Theasin. They all averted their gazes when we walked by, and a handful of people fled into rooms as though they had remembered something urgently important the moment they realized Theasin had arrived.

The door to Theasin's lab was just as ornate as the front doors and made of heavy redwood. The polished brass hinges were in the shape of dragons, similar to a relickeeper, the mystical creature to which Theasin was bonded.

Karna-Theasin attempted to open the door, but it held shut.

Locked.

There was a keyhole, but we didn't have the key...

I met Adelgis's gaze. Every moment we stood awkwardly in front of the door was a moment we could get caught.

Theasin would never forget his keys, and if anyone asked, what were we going to say?

Adelgis fidgeted with the sleeves of his shirt, his brow furrowed.

I turned around and examined the hallway. Most everyone had left in the wake of Theasin's return. Once the last researchers disappeared around the corner, I grabbed Karna and Adelgis.

"Hold your breath," I said.

I had never taken *two* people with me when I shadow-stepped, but I figured traveling a few feet wouldn't be too difficult. We slid into the darkness, slithered under the door, and then emerged on the other side, the cool sensation of the shadows a welcomed comfort.

The instant I exited the void and took a breath, however, pain flared from my chest throughout my body, burning me unlike anything before. I cried out and hit my knees on the tile floor, my arms wrapped around my gut, my whole body trembling.

What had happened? Was this a result of second-bonding with Luthair? Was it his incompatible magic?

"Volke," Adelgis gasped as he knelt next to me, his voice unsteady.

"My arcanist." Luthair emerged from the shadows, his full-plate armor clinking as he, too, knelt at my side. He touched his lightweight gauntlet to my back. "What happened?"

I leaned forward, unable to speak as I bit back the pain. I pressed my forehead against the tile, sucking in breath through my teeth.

Karna-Theasin walked off and returned with a damp cloth. He patted my neck and cheeks, the cool touch of water helping me to regain composure.

"I'm fine," I forced myself to say.

Adelgis rubbed my shoulder. "Volke, why don't you rest? I know my father well enough to know where he likely hid his notes."

After a shallow breath, I nodded, hoping I could recover in time to walk out of this place without being suspicious.

Adelgis stood and then headed deeper into the lab. Karna-Theasin remained nearby. He massaged my shoulder, and if I were feeling well, I would've found the interaction distasteful. I couldn't even imagine Theasin comforting his wife on her death bed—there was no way in the abyssal hells he would attempt to soothe *my* injuries.

Luthair stayed by my other side. He even removed his cape and draped it over me. "Next time, allow me to slide under the door and unlock it."

I tried to offer a nod. The pain subsided, but slowly. My breathing returned to normal, and the agony in my intestines faded into a dull ache, like a sore muscle.

Curse all the ships at sea—what had happened?

After a few moments, I pushed myself to my feet and stood, my legs a little shaky.

"Rest, my arcanist," Luthair said.

"It's okay." I used the damp cloth to wipe the sweat from my face. "It doesn't hurt as much."

"I could've taken someone through the shadows. You don't need to push yourself."

"I'm sorry. I hadn't thought about it—I just wanted to get us in and out as fast as possible."

Luthair remained by my side as I took stock of our environment. The sprawling lab consisted of four rooms, though the doors between each had been removed, resulting in what felt like a large singular room with dividers.

There were operating tables, one desk, three bookshelves, a glass container with jars inside, loose papers everywhere, a coat rack with several cloaks, and even post-marked letters on the countertops that lined the walls. Almost every surface had something, yet it didn't feel disorganized, just cluttered—papers were kept clean, nothing was mixed haphazardly, and all writing utensils were stored in a single spot.

How much work was Theasin doing here? There was enough research in this lab for a whole team of people.

I kept Luthair's cape close as I shuffled forward, determined to explore the area myself.

Adelgis sifted through paperwork at an impressive pace. He glanced over the words and quickly determined whether something was relevant or not. Then he moved on to the next set of paperwork, his focus unbreakable.

Karna-Theasin, on the other hand, approached the coat rack. I didn't know why, and I didn't ask. He just fidgeted with each piece of clothing.

I examined the bookshelf-sized glass cabinet. Jars and vials sat within, each with strange contents. Eyeballs, thick black liquid, and even a few with eggs suspended in mucus. Were these mystical creature parts? Perhaps Theasin used these to create items?

My attention went straight to something I had seen before.

Two vials filled with sand. One was tan and the other was pink.

I opened the cabinet, the squeak of the hinges causing me to cringe. Neither Adelgis nor Karna-Theasin seemed to care, and there was no way someone could have heard it outside of this lab, so I took a deep breath and calmed myself. With a shaky hand, I picked up the vials. The grains of sand shimmered in the light of the glowstones.

Adelgis's brother, Niro, had given me these types of sands in the past. He had said the tan sands healed the body, and the pink sands healed the soul. I had used the pink sand to help Adelgis recover from the ill effects of the abyssal leech, so I knew it worked. I just didn't know why.

"What're those?" Karna-Theasin asked, though the cold edge to his voice was gone. He sounded more like the playful Karna, which made the interaction odd.

"I don't know what they are," I muttered. "But I know they heal things."

"Like the arcane plague?"

I hadn't considered that, but I doubted it. My soul wasn't injured, just infected. And Adelgis's brother said the pink sand would kill someone who wasn't injured.

"I don't think so," I said.

"A pity."

I wanted to take them—since they were so useful—but I couldn't justify stealing from Theasin, even if I considered him unpleasant at best. I placed the vials of sand back into the glass cabinet.

Curiosity got the better of me, though. I wandered over to the nearest operating table, Luthair walking close by, and examined everything on top. Parts of a dead creature were strewn across the surface, along with paperwork and a journal. I recognized the type of creature. A hydra. The alligator-style body, stumpy legs, and snake-like head were unmistakable.

It reminded me of Hexa, and a new kind of pain lanced my chest. It hurt like only nostalgia and longing could. I wished she were here so she could tell me the specifics about this hydra. Maybe she would've had some insight.

I gently pushed the bloodless body parts to the side, somewhat disgusted by the stiff way they rolled. At least they were odorless. Why keep them in such a state? Was Theasin going to make hydra trinkets? Why hadn't he put them away?

I searched through the paperwork, trying to concentrate on anything other than the disembodied limbs. Without much effort, I stumbled upon a map. Gravekeeper William loved cartography—he had been a navigation officer when he had served in the navy.

I picked it up and narrowed my eyes. This wasn't a map with longitude or latitude. It wasn't even a map of the city. It looked like a maze—a long, complicated map that required a legend and several notes. It wasn't labeled, but up in the corner was the drawing of a scarab.

"Adelgis," I muttered as I walked around the table, never taking my eyes off the map. "Is this the Grotto Labyrinth?"

I made it to his side, but he hadn't answered. He just stared at the paperwork on Theasin's personal desk, unmoving.

"Are you okay?" I asked.

Adelgis snapped out of his frozen state and hastily gathered up the papers, his hands shaking. "Y-yes. I apologize. What was your question?"

"Is this the Grotto Labyrinth?"

Adelgis gave the map a single glance. "I... I think so."

"Are you sure everything is okay?"

He folded the paperwork and kept it close, almost as if he didn't want me to see it. "Yes. I'm sorry for worrying you. I heard thoughts. Strange thoughts. Everything is fine now."

Although he seemed panicked—and weirder than even his normal self—I decided not to question him further. Adelgis had never lied to me, and he had been a stalwart friend who deserved the benefit of the doubt. If he didn't want to tell me what was bothering him, he didn't have to.

"Do you think we have time to copy this?" I asked. "Maybe we can show it to Vethica."

"Take it," Adelgis said. "Take anything you want."

I lifted an eyebrow. "I don't want to steal from your father."

"Don't worry about it." Adelgis clenched his jaw, his gaze fixed on the paperwork. "This is all property of the Venrover estate. If anyone will get in trouble for it, I will. I give you permission. Anything you want—it's yours."

I stepped away from Adelgis, holding the map close. There wasn't much I wanted, so perhaps I would take the sand and the map and be done with it.

With a conflicted conscience, I returned to the glass cabinet. Karna-Theasin was now kneeling next to the chair at Theasin's personal desk. He lifted it and examined the legs. I had no idea what was going on, and again, decided not to ask.

"Perhaps Theasin has star shards," Luthair said, drawing my attention. "We could use them for trinket creation with your father."

I chuckled to myself. How had I forgotten so quickly? I had thought of the shards as I walked in here. If Adelgis didn't mind me taking things, perhaps searching for star shards would be prudent.

I glanced around, hoping to catch sight of their golden glint. I saw none.

Karna-Theasin set the chair back down and then stood. He stretched his arms in the air and then scratched his backside. "Uh. It gets tiresome being that uptight." Karna still had Theasin's voice, just not the same tone or inflection. "Adelgis, have you found what you were looking for yet?"

"Almost."

I grabbed the vials of sand out of the cabinet and shoved them in the pocket of my trousers.

Then I looked again for the star shards. Surely, Theasin would have some...

Adelgis whirled around, his eyes wide.

"*Someone's coming*," he said telepathically. "*She has keys to the lab.*"

A second later, someone fiddled with the handle of the door.

17

THE LEGEND OF GODS

Karna-Theasin straightened his clothes, and Luthair slid back into the shadows.

The door opened, revealing a young woman with hair and eyes the color of chestnut. Her hair had been tied back in an elegant bun, with loose locks that seemed strategically placed for aesthetic appeal. It was the same with her robes —at first glance they appeared thrown on, but the way the cloth dipped in the front, displaying collarbone, and the manner in which the belt had been cinched tightly around her waist, hinted at intentional design.

The arcanist mark on her forehead had a bird, but before I could determine exactly what her eldrin was, a creature flew into the lab. It was a brown owl wearing tiny bits of battle armor, all crafted from bronze. Its talons were metallic, and some of its feathers shone as though made from polished steel.

It was a minerva owl—intelligent beings who lived far to the north, much closer to my island nation than to the Amber Dunes. The bird landed on the counter, its giant golden eyes flitting from one person to the next.

The woman's expression blossomed into excitement the moment she caught sight of Theasin. "You really are here. I thought the servants had to be mistaken, but I'm pleased they're not."

"*Her name is Setti*," Adelgis telepathically said, the speed more frantic than his earlier communications.

"I needed to retrieve something," Karna-Theasin said, curt and cold. "Do you care to explain what you're doing in my labs?"

Adelgis gritted his teeth, his expression shifting to visible concern. "*She's my father's mistress.*"

The information surprised me, but not much. Theasin was married, but apparently, Adelgis and his brother, Niro, had different mothers. Learning that Theasin had a lover in a far-off city only confirmed what I already suspected of the man—he had all the loyalty of a feral cat.

Setti narrowed her eyes, and her minerva owl twisted its head all the way around to stare at the fake Theasin. Would Theasin have snapped at his lover like this? It didn't seem so —not by their reactions—and a piece of me suspected we would need to force our way out of here if Setti guessed we were impostures.

After a quick exhale, Karna-Theasin ran a hand through his short black hair. "It's been an infuriating couple of days," he said, apology in his tone, even if he didn't say it—I suspected the real Theasin would never utter such words. "Returning to the labs has delayed my schedule."

That was all Setti needed to hear, apparently.

Her posture relaxed, and she stepped closer to Karna-Theasin, a slight smile forming. "Well, everything is better now." She caressed his arm from his elbow to shoulder, her slender fingers twirling into the folds of his cloak. "I have all the information you asked for, *and* I'm free for the rest of the day."

The owl once again turned its giant eyes to everyone else in the room. "Where is Essellian?"

"*That's the name of my father's eldrin*," Adelgis said, filling in the blanks at lightning speeds.

Karna-Theasin grazed his fingers along the side of Setti's neck. "I left Essellian on the ship. I have no time to waste. You understand, don't you, my desert flower?"

Although I thought it risky to throw out a pet name when Theasin seemed barely able to remember his own children's names, the comment obviously affected Setti. Her sun-soaked skin deepened to a dark red, and she pressed herself up against Theasin in a seductive manner.

"Surely, you have a few minutes?" she whispered.

Sound echoed in the lab, carrying from one end to the other, even at low volumes.

I faced Adelgis, growing more uncomfortable with each passing second. She *had* seen us, right? But Setti continued with her sweet nothings as though she were alone in the room with Theasin, her hands trailing across his body. What was I supposed to do? Continue acting like a piece of furniture? Watch them like a perverted lamp as they nuzzled each other?

Perhaps I could shuffle into the corner and feign interest in one of the many mystical creature parts Theasin had lying about.

"You there, *dog*," the minerva owl said.

"Me?" I asked, glancing back.

"Yes, you. Come take my arcanist's paperwork."

I stood dumbfounded for a prolonged while. What about me indicated I was Theasin's *dog*? And why was the woman's eldrin giving me orders?

The minerva owl puffed up his feathers, its round eyes squinted. "Quickly now. Or are you one of the dumb ones?"

I gave Adelgis an inquisitive glance. He returned it with a look of confusion and said nothing. Uncertain of what to do, I decided to play along. I walked over to Setti and Karna-Theasin and held out my hand. Setti didn't bother acknowledging me. She handed over her paperwork and then shooed me away with a couple of flicks of her wrist.

Should I say something? Bow? Place fingers on my chest? I wasn't sure, so I backed away, turned on my heel, and then walked to Adelgis's side, my movements stiff.

"Did the Autarch give you those two?" Setti asked, an eyebrow raised. "They seem... less competent than normal."

The Autarch?

"*I'm not sure what's going on,*" Adelgis said, his telepathic voice exuding confusion. "*Setti and her eldrin keep thinking we're agents of someone called the Autarch, but they don't seem to know who that is. All they know is that it's someone powerful and important. And they hold this Autarch in high regard, almost with mystical reverence, seemingly just because my father has spoken well of him in the past.*"

Autarch was an archaic title. It meant *absolute ruler* and was used to denote someone more powerful than kings, queens, or emperors. Who would have had the audacity to use such a title nowadays? There was no kingdom, nation, or empire that still had it on the records, at least not that I knew of. Perhaps some distant land still clung to the old ways?

"Never mind them," Karna-Theasin said. "People like us can never escape idiocy."

I bit back a laugh, amazed by how much Setti appreciated such cruel remarks.

"Artificer Mixxin doesn't know much about the Second

Ascension," Setti said. "That's everything I found in his desk." She got up on her tiptoes and kissed Theasin on the side of his neck. "If he figures anything else out, I'll be sure to let you know straightaway."

The paperwork in my hands became my sole focus of interest. I didn't care about this unknown Autarch, nor did I care about Setti and her demanding eldrin. *The Second Ascension* was the name of the group who had the queen of the Argo Empire assassinated. They were the ones who had helped Prince Rishan usurp the throne. They were the ones who had killed all those arcanists in Thronehold.

They were the ones who had infected me with the arcane plague.

Karna-Theasin lifted Setti's chin and brought his lips down on hers. Their embrace—and kiss—lasted longer than I thought necessary to pull off an impersonation, but I wasn't about to interrupt. Once they finished, Setti stepped back, her face flushed worse than before.

Karna-Theasin smirked. "It's a shame I can't stay, but I need to leave as soon as possible. Before I go, can I count on you to do me one last favor?"

Setti rubbed at her hot cheeks. "Anything for you, my love."

"Can you gather all known information on frost snails? They're crucial to my upcoming research."

"Frost... snails?" Setti repeated, her eyebrows knitting.

"Yes. They're extremely rare mystical creatures. Only a handful of arcanists have ever seen one. I'm certain the Norra Library has details, but they'll be difficult to find." Karna-Theasin ran his knuckles down the side of Setti's face. "Well, difficult for someone of lesser talents."

She kissed his hand. "I'll gather all the information you need." Then she stared up at him through her eyelashes.

"And I'll be here waiting for you once you're done with your business."

"I look forward to it."

Apparently eager to please, Setti flashed a confident smile and then sauntered out of the lab. Her minerva owl flew off after her, not a word to anyone else. The door shut with a slam, echoing throughout Theasin's lab.

"What're *frost snails*?" I asked.

Karna-Theasin whirled around on his heel and shrugged. "I made them up. I wanted to send her on an impossible witch hunt because it amuses me."

I couldn't stifle my chuckling. "I see."

Normally, I wouldn't condone such behavior, but Setti and Theasin weren't the types of people I wanted to protect from trivial harm.

"I also cut all the bottoms to Theasin's coat pockets," Karna-Theasin said, walking over with a smirk. "And I shaved down one of the legs on his personal chair, making it uneven and wobbly."

Again, I couldn't stop the laughter. I didn't know why, but the petty revenge made the risk of getting caught seem all the more worthwhile. Theasin had implanted an abyssal leech into his own son, after all. He deserved to lose everything out of his coats—he deserved the irritation of an unsteady chair.

He probably deserved a whole lot more, but that was a discussion for a different day.

Karna-Theasin offered me a playful smile. "I need to get my jollies from somewhere." Then he crossed his arms. "But I've gotten that all out of my system now. Are you two done?"

Adelgis hadn't joined in on the fun. He folded his father's paperwork and carefully stuffed his pockets, his eyes downturned and his expression haunted with melancholy. I didn't push him. I just waited, not saying anything. Once he had all the papers, he glanced over.

"Volke," he whispered. "You were thinking about star shards earlier."

I nodded. "I don't see any, though."

"My father always keeps valuables in the bottom drawer of his desk."

More than happy to take the shards, I walked around the desk and yanked on the drawer handle.

Locked.

Of course it was.

I exhaled, but before I gave in to frustration, Luthair shifted through the shadows and entered the drawer. A soft click floated up from the lock. I pulled on the handle, and to my delight, the drawer opened with ease.

"Thank you," I said.

"*Careful*," Luthair hissed. "Something is in here."

I jerked my hand away and stepped back.

The half-opened drawer didn't move. I waited, expecting a plague-ridden monster to leap out. But nothing happened. Karna-Theasin and Adelgis both stared, their stances tense, like they, too, had been preparing for a fight.

"What was in there?" I whispered.

"I'm sorry, my arcanist. I just had... a terrible feeling. A chill that I had never felt before. Like a presence."

Luthair's odd description didn't sit well with me. An odd *presence*? What could possibly be in the drawer that would scare a knightmare?

I knelt down and carefully opened it to its fullest extent. Sure enough, a dozen star shards sat in the far back corner, all nestled in an open leather pouch. I didn't reach for them. Instead, I stared at the only other items in the drawer—six long pieces of *something*, all black, and all wrapped in white silk cloth.

I stared at the fragments for a moment. They appeared to be familiar. They had the rough porous texture of bone, but their ebony coloration threw me off. I had never seen black bones before.

Scorched? No. Just black.

"Adelgis," I said. "Do you know what this is?"

He stared down into the drawer, one eyebrow cocked. "I'm not sure. It's probably from a mystical creature. I'm not sure which."

I picked up the bone fragments, careful to hold them with the cloth. They were as long as my forearm and sharp at the points. What creature was big enough to have these? I turned them over, examining them from all angles.

The bones reminded me of knightmares, since they were creatures of darkness and terror. Perhaps this was somehow related? Could that be the reason Luthair was afraid?

I touched one of the bones with my other hand, the tips of my fingers brushing the side. A strong sense of power sparked at my fingertips. For a brief moment, it felt like the bones had been jerked awake, shocked into life because of my contact. They didn't move or display any type of magic— they just felt... alive.

Adelgis held out a hand. "Alive? Let me see one?"

I handed Adelgis one of the fragments. He held it for a long moment.

"I feel nothing," he said.

Karna-Theasin held out his hand, obviously wanting to partake in the experience. I handed him another one. Again, no reaction. Karna-Theasin just stared at the bone, underwhelmed.

But *I* could feel it. Something was different about these

bones. Something that called forth a deep feeling in my chest. I wanted to keep them. Close.

And they *had* to be important. Why else had Theasin kept them in the drawer with his valuable star shards?

"This reminds me of the crown I stole," Karna-Theasin muttered. "It looks like the same material. Maybe it's rare?"

I spun the bone between my fingers. "Maybe my father will know what this is. He said he was a talented artificer in his own right."

"We can find out more about these later," Adelgis said as he handed back the bone. "Now isn't the time. The longer we dally, the more likely we'll run into someone else who knows my father." He took the pouch of star shards and tied them to his belt.

Karna-Theasin relinquished his bone fragment as well.

I stood and tucked the bones into the waist of my trousers before covering them with my shirt. They were too long to fit into my pocket, and I didn't want to carry them through the labs, just in case someone recognized them and tried to take them away. The sensation of them touching my skin directly kept me invigorated. Why didn't the others feel what I did? How could they not sense the draw of these bones?

Karna-Theasin gave me the once-over. "What did that woman bring us, by the way? She seemed concerned about the paperwork."

"Setti brought us information on the Second Ascension," I said. "It's not much. Just minor details that I already knew." I hadn't yet had time to read over it all, but I had skimmed most of it. "These are a findings report, basically."

"What's the Second Ascension?"

Although I had kept the information secret from Karna in the past, things had changed. She had helped me in more ways than one, united me with my father, and even helped us infiltrate the labs—a crime she could be punished for as well, if we were caught. She was an ally. I could trust her with the information, and it was probably prudent to start disseminating facts as soon as possible.

I exhaled. "The Second Ascension is a group of lunatics who created the arcane plague just so they could spawn a bunch of world-altering god-creatures."

Karna-Theasin snapped his gaze to Adelgis, like he needed this statement to be confirmed by an outside source.

Adelgis nodded. "That's what we suspect, anyway. They were the ones responsible for the attack on Thronehold. They call themselves the *Second Ascension* because this will be the second time god creatures have entered this world."

"How many god creatures?" Karna-Theasin balked. "And when was the last time?"

"Twelve. Maybe thirteen. And a very long time ago. Back when star shards first rained to the ground." Adelgis straightened his coat and headed for the door. "The Second Ascension knew of the legends that said that gods would spawn during the *turning of an age*—a time period of fundamental magical change. *That's* why they created the arcane plague. They wanted to alter magic enough to force the god-creatures into existence." Adelgis grabbed the door handle. "And even as we speak, the Second Ascension is out hunting down the first god—the world serpent. If any of them bond with something that powerful, I'm sure everything we know and love will eventually be destroyed or enslaved."

He said each word in a blasé tone, like this was a trivial conversation about the weather.

"So that's what you were all flustered about when we were in Thronehold," Karna-Theasin muttered as he stroked his chin. "You were trying to stop this *Second Ascension* group."

I stared down at Setti's paperwork. This was just a simple report about the existence of the Second Ascension. It barely went into detail. Why would Theasin want this? Setti said she had stolen it from another researcher. Did Theasin just want to know what they knew?

"And you know all of this for certain?" Karna glared with Theasin's face—which was actually intimidating. "And you're not doing anything about it?"

"We told the Frith Guild," Adelgis said. "They're handling it even as we speak."

"You trust one of these *guilds* to handle a problem of this magnitude?"

"I do." Adelgis opened the door. "And once we cure Volke, we're going to return and do what we can to help. Isn't that right, Volke?"

I nodded as I jogged across the laboratory. "Yes." I motioned to the hall. "Now let's go. I don't want to be here once Setti realizes *frost snails* aren't real."

DAMAGED

We exited Theasin's personal lab—Setti had left the door unlocked, making our departure simple, though we couldn't secure the door shut when we left.

The bone fragments touching my skin remained a constant presence in my thoughts. Something about them made me fidgety, almost restless. Having them close felt like standing on the edge of a wellspring, one filled with vast amounts of magic. I couldn't seem to tap into it, though. It was just *there*. Like staring at something through a window. Able to see it, unable to touch it.

The three of us walked the long corridor, Karna-Theasin in the lead. Adelgis watched me the entire trek, his neutral expression more odd than usual.

"Are you okay?" I asked him.

"*Are you?*" Adelgis replied telepathically.

The question didn't sit well with me. "I feel fine."

"*You've never had thoughts like you just had,*" he said. "*That worries me.*"

I wanted to wave away his concerns, but a piece of me knew he was right. An obsession with magical power hadn't been something I concerned myself with. Then again, I had never been so close to something like this before.

What was I going to do about it now? Think of something else?

"What do you think the others in the Frith Guild are doing right now?" I asked as we took one of the corners.

"They're probably searching for the world serpent."

"You don't think they've found it yet?"

"I suspect the creature is far away—the travel times would limit the likelihood that they've already succeeded."

Karna-Theasin glanced over his shoulder with a frown.

I probably looked ridiculous, considering I was the only one talking aloud.

Imagining the Frith Guild on an adventure of a lifetime did distract me, though. I no longer thought about the bone fragments and instead dwelled on my memories of the others. Illia had desperately wanted to find the world serpent —not because she wanted it for herself, but to keep it out of the hands of the Dread Pirate Calisto. I imagined her at the helm of the ship, demanding the fastest routes to the serpent, using the Occult Compass to guide the guild straight there.

We entered the reception room, and I stared at the double doors that led outside. Soon we would be free.

"Wait a minute," someone said, drawing my attention. "I know *you*."

The voice sounded familiar. I stopped and then caught my breath.

The reaper arcanist, Jevel Balestier, walked over, one hand in a pocket, the other hanging at his side. His reaper, Ruin, floated alongside him, the empty cloak fluttering as though caught in a gentle breeze, even though there was none. The hood was up, but there was nothing there, much like Luthair's vacant helmet whenever he formed out of the shadows. A rusted scythe hung in the air around the reaper, occasionally twirling in a slow rotation.

Jevel wasn't nearly as intimidating up close. He wore a ragged set of seafarer's clothes, including the high boots and long coat. His goatee had grown long and scruffy, and he scratched at it when he neared.

"You're Zelfree's apprentice," he said to me, his narrow eyes squinting farther.

My chest tightened. I didn't know what to say, and I definitely didn't want to answer any questions.

"He's with me now," Karna-Theasin answered, not missing a beat.

"As an apprentice?" Jevel asked.

"If that's the new word for *lackey*, then yes. My *apprentice*."

If anyone other than Theasin had said that, I was certain it would garner odd glances. No one in the reception room —not the members of the Watch Battalion, not the researchers, not the servants—seemed to think that was an unusual statement, though.

Jevel huffed. "A pity. I was hoping Zelfree would be in town. I never got to have my fight with the man."

"It's a good thing for you he's not here, then," I muttered, unable to hide my sardonic tone.

Ruin stopped twirling its scythe. "No *mimic* has ever bested a *reaper*." Its voice was hollow and haunting. "And in some places around the Shard Sea, Everett Zelfree has a bounty on his head. It's only a matter of time before the Huntsman Guild finds him in a place he doesn't belong." Ruin swiped the scythe around in front of him, close enough I felt the *whoosh* of air.

The shadows at my feet stirred in agitation, and I was half-tempted to settle this myself.

"Behave, Ruin," Jevel said. "The boy isn't with Zelfree anymore. Though it is cute how much he admires the man." He laughed to himself as he turned away, obviously uninterested in me now that I wasn't a part of the Frith Guild. "Now that I have all these new toys, though, Zelfree's name is as good as on my chains."

The metal links hanging from the reaper rattled as it glided after its arcanist. The many names burned into the chain were records of arcanists the beast had killed.

Why was Jevel so obsessed with fighting Zelfree? He'd had the same single-minded determination during the Sovereign Dragon Tournament.

"We should avoid that man at all costs," Adelgis said telepathically, his message somehow laced with contagious concern. *"Apparently, the Grand Laboratories of New Norra have crafted an item that can detect individuals with the arcane plague, and they're giving one to Jevel for his services rendered to the city."*

Detect the plague?

The information sank into my gut.

"Let's take our leave of this place," Karna-Theasin said. He placed a hand on my shoulder and guided me toward the door.

The sun began to set on the trek back to the airship. Soon, the cold would descend upon us.

I stepped onto the *Sun Chaser*, but my anxiety didn't leave me.

Although Adelgis had taken plenty of paperwork from

his father's lab, he said he needed time to sort through it all. Without a word, he headed to our sleeping quarters, keeping the papers close. Karna didn't waste time, either. She dropped her disguise, transforming back into a beautiful female dancer. Theasin's short black hair extended out into a brilliant blonde waterfall that reached her waist. Then she headed below deck, wringing out her hands, as though the slimy feeling of being Theasin wouldn't leave her until she scrubbed them clean.

Before I could rest, I headed below deck and then down the corridor to the officer's rooms. My father was the blacksmith, Karna was the quartermaster, but Vethica was the boatswain. I knocked on her door, determined to give her what little I found in the labs.

"Come in," she said, her voice muffled behind the wood.

I entered, surprised by the mess I found myself in.

Papers and books were scattered everywhere—the floor, in two hammocks, on a bookshelf with a locked door. There was a cot built into the bulkhead and nestled in the corner, and it was the only space without the clutter. Even Vethica's chair had several tomes propped against the side.

Vethica leaned over a book, her elbows on her desk, her attention focused. She wore just a pair of trousers and simple tunic, her frame thin and her eyes underlined with dark bags. It made me wonder if she had been neglecting herself.

"I told you I was busy," she muttered. "If you brought food, just leave it on the bed."

"That's not why I'm here," I said as I shut the door.

She stopped reading and shot me a glare, realization hitting her at a visible rate. "What're *you* doing here?"

Vethica wouldn't tolerate my presence long, so I decided to just hit all the major points I wanted to say.

"I know what happened to you," I said. "I know about your thunderbird and the plague."

She stood from her chair so fast, it flew back and hit the ground, toppling books in the process. Rage built in her expression, her hands balled in fists.

"What do you want?" Vethica asked, her words slow and cold, a harsh contrast to her demeanor.

I pulled the map from my trousers and handed it over. "I found this in the Grand Laboratories of New Norra. Adelgis thinks it's a map of the Grotto Labyrinth. I thought it could help you."

A long, strained moment passed between us. For a second, I thought she might not have heard me. She just stared, her eyes darting between me and the map.

I held it out a bit farther. "I, uh, wanted to ask you something. If you don't mind."

Vethica took the map with an unsteady hand. Was she trembling from rage or confusion? I couldn't tell. "A question?" she whispered, her voice strained, as though she were fighting to keep it under control.

She said nothing else.

"Why are you so obsessed with the khepera?" I asked. "I mean, if I... if I end up losing Luthair to the plague, I think I would want to seek out another knightmare to bond with. If I were going to become an arcanist again, I mean. Why not find another thunderbird?"

Vethica ran a hand through her short, red hair. If she stood in the lantern light just right, she'd practically be a sibling to Zaxis—they had the same hardened gaze and tense stance.

Before she answered, she opened the map and examined the contents. Over time, her aggression bled away. She fixed her chair, took her seat, and then gently placed the paper on her desk, covering everything else she had been working on.

"I'm damaged," she said.

I wasn't sure what she meant by that, but I waited for her to explain rather than demanding answers.

"I had the arcane plague too long." Her voice grew quieter, and she stared at the map rather than meeting my eye. "At first, I didn't feel any different. I thought I could hide it. I thought maybe it wouldn't affect me like it had the others."

I had yet to notice any real changes, but knowing Vethica had experience with this intrigued me. I moved closer to her, wanting to hear every word she whispered.

"But things changed," she said. "I couldn't control myself sometimes. And my thoughts... they became frightening and disjointed. It was as if I were losing a grip on what made me who I am." Vethica leaned onto the desk, her shoulders bunched at the base of her neck. "And one day... I thought..."

She moved a couple of books on her desk, revealing a glass jar that had been tucked into the far corner. Two blazing gold feathers were held inside the container, occasional sparks of electricity flaring off of them.

Thunderbird feathers.

"There were these whispers," Vethica continued. She touched the jar. "I was convinced I needed to infect my eldrin."

I didn't know how to respond.

Vethica shoved the books back in front of the jar. "*I* was the one who spread the plague to... to my thunderbird."

The statement clawed at my thoughts. I imagined myself in her situation, slowly losing myself to some disease and then infecting Luthair because I thought it was a good idea.

I crossed my arms, my heart pounding hard enough I could feel it on my forearm.

Vethica sighed. "I wasn't entirely a lost cause. Karna convinced me to kill my thunderbird, and I thought all my troubles would be over, but... I can still feel myself slip from time to time. Don't you get it? I'm damaged. The plague ran its course, and now the scars remain."

"I'm sorry," I murmured.

I had been told that an arcanist had six months—within that time, if they got rid of their magic, the plague would leave their body, and they would return to normal. However, if they carried the sickness longer, beyond six months, the damage would become permanent, even if they lost their eldrin and magic.

Which was what had happened to Vethica. She had carried the arcane plague in her blood for far too long. Now she was no longer herself.

"I need the khepera," Vethica said. "I've read all about them. I don't know if they can cure the plague, but I *know* khepera can heal a tarnished soul. Dozens of stories confirm it. That means... if I can bond with one... I can get my old self back. I can finally be free of this. Free of these *terrible thoughts*."

Everything made a lot more sense. From Vethica's hate to her new obsession, it seemed a good portion of her life had been focused on clearing away the plague.

The vials of sand in my pocket popped into my mind. I withdrew the pink sand and turned it over in my palm. "Vethica, I don't know if this would help you, but I have something that's supposed to heal injuries to the soul."

She glanced over, and I showed her the strange sand.

Vethica narrowed her eyes. "What is it?"

"I don't know," I said. "I just know it works. Adelgis had a problem, and I used this sand to heal him. However, I was warned it could kill someone if they didn't have injury to their soul—so I'm not entirely sure it would even work, but—"

"I don't want your guesswork." She exhaled. "I just need to find a khepera."

With a sigh, I pocketed the vial of sand.

Vethica pushed herself up from her desk, her jaw clenched and her whole body visibly tense. "I guess I should thank you. That said... nobody on this ship really understands what it's like to be plague-ridden, except for me. I know the kinds of horrible things you'll do once it sinks into your mind and rakes through your thoughts. You're an honorable man now, but it won't last."

I stepped toward the door. There was no need for the dreadful reminder.

"I should be going," I said.

"If you had any spine at all, you'd free yourself from this curse. Like you said—you can just search out another knightmare to bond with."

"And like *you* said—when you were first infected, there was no difference. I still have time. If I fail, then I guess I'll have to search for a new eldrin." I gripped the door handle, defiance welling in my thoughts and conviction. "But I won't fail."

I left Vethica's room before she got in another word.

19

THE LIGHTNING STRAITS

The corridor welcomed me with an icy embrace, but the wootz cotton under my clothes refused to let me feel it. Luthair shifted around my feet, his shadowy presence a comfort.

I gritted my teeth. "I didn't mean it, Luthair."

"What didn't you mean, my arcanist?"

"Searching for a new eldrin. I wouldn't do that if I had failed you."

"In your grief, you have confused yourself. I am a creature of protection, and the plague in your blood is hard evidence that I was the one who failed *you*. If I can't assist in discovering a cure before it's too late, then you deserve to find another mystical creature to become your eldrin."

"That's not—"

"I failed to protect my first arcanist," Luthair interjected, his melancholic tone hard on my ears. "But I refuse to fail my second. We no longer need to discuss this—we're both determined. Together, we'll make this right."

"Okay," I said, my throat tight.

If I doubted, I would surely succumb to despair, so I had to believe we could make it through this. I had to.

The door across from Vethica's was labeled, *Quartermaster*. I stared at it for a long minute, steeling myself to the reality of the situation. Karna wanted me to sleep in her quarters, against my objections. I wasn't opposed to her, or her presence, or even her flirtations, but her ever-escalating advancements made me nervous. The arcane plague seemed more than just an illness—it was malevolent. It twisted the bodies of mythical creatures and messed with the minds of arcanists. It had clearly harmed Vethica and continued to do so in ways beyond sinister. It had manipulated her into infecting others, even the one closest to her, which seemed almost too horrific to fathom.

Why was Karna willing to risk all that to have me close? True, I wasn't villainous *yet*, though why chance anything?

But a deal was a deal.

I stepped forward and knocked on the door. It opened the second time my knuckles struck the wood.

Karna waited with a smile and a tunic—and nothing else. The easygoing garment hung to her mid-thighs, made of tannish linen. It was better than what I had expected her to wear to bed, so I didn't make a comment.

"And here I thought you would avoid me," she said as she opened the door wide. "I don't usually have to fight this hard to get someone to agree to spend time in my quarters."

"Well, you finally got me," I quipped.

Karna grabbed my elbow and guided me into the room. As she shut the door, I took note of the simple interior. Unlike Vethica's quarters, which were covered in the work that consumed her life, Karna didn't have anything. There was a bed built into the bulkhead of the ship, complete with a feather mattress and blankets—things a normal sailing ship wouldn't necessarily have because of the risk of water. Against the opposite wall were three wooden trunks and a single lantern, providing all the light.

That was it.

Not even a desk or cabinet for books and materials.

If the trunks were taken out, no one would ever know the room had been inhabited.

"It's... clean," I said, grasping for any sort of compliment.

"Let me guess—you're messy?"

"I wouldn't have said so." I approached the trunks, wondering what was kept inside. "But I've never had much personal space. I had a room at the Frith Guild, but we were frequently away. And when I lived on the Isle of Ruma, I basically stayed in a cleaned-out closet."

"Is that right?"

I pulled the black bones from the waist of my trousers. The six fragments still felt as powerful as ever, and I almost didn't want to put them down, but sleeping with them seemed silly. I removed some of my wootz cotton and wrapped the bone pieces together. Then I placed them on top of one of the trunks like a tied bundle of kindling.

I turned around and found Karna sitting on the bed. It wasn't especially large—clearly built for a single person, to save on space—and I wondered what she intended. I didn't see a hammock or even another blanket.

Karna leaned forward and placed her chin into her palm. "You've never slept beside a woman before, have you?"

"Not really." I rubbed at the back of my neck. "It's not that I don't want to. It's just that now seems like the most inopportune time imaginable."

"When I was younger, I would sleep next to someone every night," Karna said, her tone a mix of playful and wistful. "One of my siblings, mostly. But sometimes others. I like listening to the sound of someone's heart—it's soothing."

"I see," I muttered. "I never thought of that."

"Well, I went a long time where I didn't want anyone to share my bed." Karna smoothed the blankets on her mattress. "It no longer... felt right." When she glanced back to me, she offered me a coy smile. "But you're different. You've always been different. I still can't decide what I think about that."

She patted the bed, beckoning me over.

My face grew hot as I took a seat next to her. When she placed her hand on my back and slid her palm up my shoulder, I tensed.

"Karna, I don't think—"

"Relax," she said, cutting me off. Then she smacked my side. "You act like I'm about to attack you. Everything will be fine."

I rubbed at my ribs, unable to unwind, not with her so close. She was warmer than I imagined, and strands of her hair caught the lantern light in such a way that they shone like gold. Just a few, like precious metals hidden in a field of amber wheat.

"Aren't you tired?" she asked.

"Yes."

"Then lie down."

I did as she instructed, enjoying the soft mattress. I wondered if roc feathers had been used in creating it. Or perhaps roc down? That would have been interesting.

"You aren't going to take off your boots?" Karna asked. "Or are you so afraid of something happening that you'll sleep fully clothed?"

I hadn't given any of that thought—mostly because I had been avoiding it—and my face reddened further as I sat back up, slid off my boots, and then undid my belt. Normally, I didn't wear anything when I slept, but when in close quarters—like in the storeroom of the *Sun Chaser*—I kept my shirt and trousers on.

I did the same here, even though the wootz cotton would make things uncomfortable.

Once situated, I rested onto the mattress, my gaze on the ceiling. Karna crawled into a position between my arm and my body. She placed her head on my chest, just beside the armpit. She was soft, and her touch gentle, but we had no spare room on the bed for any tossing or turning. It wasn't too bad—she was lighter than I had anticipated.

"See?" Karna asked. "There's nothing to worry about." She pointed to the lantern. "You can snuff that without getting up, right?"

I manipulated the shadows to turn down the wick until the flame went out, blanketing us in darkness. The simple trick amused me. Once upon a time, I wouldn't have had such fine control. Now I didn't struggle with it, even next to a light source, and that pleased me.

Karna gently ran her fingers over my chest, breaking me out of my self-congratulatory moment. The airship didn't creak, not while we were tied at the sky port, which heightened the silence. Occasionally, the hull still groaned from the weight of passengers and cargo, but it wasn't the same. I concentrated on every breath and movement—hers and my own—and that made it next to impossible to sleep.

To my surprise, Karna shifted deeper into position and pulled her arms in tightly, nestling in close to me, half her face buried in my chest. I wrapped my arm around her waist, trying to get into the most comfortable position. I felt her smile through my shirt.

Karna never said anything, though. In a matter of moments, her breathing grew even and steady.

Although it was cold outside, Karna's room retained heat as well as the wootz cotton. I closed my eyes, trying to force myself into sleep.

***

I didn't know how or when, but I was dreaming.

It was the same kind of surreal feeling I had with all Adelgis's manipulations, and I was glad he had the ability to continue the dreams even when he wasn't within arm's reach.

The familiar sway of a ship under my feet excited me. The bay waters lapped against the distant piers. Was this Zelfree again? It had to be. I half-recognized the shabby town and its dirty cobblestone roads out across the water. Did that mean I was now aboard the *Red Falcon*?

Watching through Zelfree's eyes, I faced a woman next to the ship's railing. She wore an officer's uniform—long coat, fitted white trousers, high boots with a lustrous shine, a black tricorn hat—and she had long, chestnut hair that hung past her shoulder blades and fluttered in the bay winds. When she smiled, it had a warmth that reminded me of Gravekeeper William.

Her appearance surprised me. Taming the waters of the ocean was a rough job that usually eroded all beauty away from a person. Not her. She maintained a youthful vigor.

"It's nice to meet you," she said.

I nodded, but didn't return the greeting.

"I'm Captain Eventide."

If I were in control of what was happening, I probably would've gasped. I had never seen Guildmaster Eventide so *young* before. Powerful and striking—obviously charismatic. She seemed like the idealized version of an arcanist I had always imagined as a child.

Her arcanist mark was, of course, the atlas turtle—a giant creature that grew plants on its back—but it was just a normal mark in this dream-memory, not glowing soft white like I knew in my timeframe. I wondered when she would get her true form atlas turtle.

"I'm Everett Zelfree," I said. "An interesting crew you have here."

"If life isn't interesting, it's not worth living," Eventide replied.

"Words only uttered by those who had a pleasant childhood."

The almost sardonic response got Eventide smiling. She had a certain confidence of her own that shone through in that moment. The winds of the bay rushed by, bringing with it a fine dusting of salt and smoke from the city's chimneys.

"Well, Everett," the captain said. "Let me ask you—have you ever been to East Jinko?"

"That tiny backwater fishing hole they called a town? Of course not. It was burned down by pirate raiders. No one knew for weeks. That's how insignificant it was."

Eventide laughed aloud. "Hey, now. That's my hometown you're talking about."

My eyebrows shot to my hairline. "*You* lived there?"

"How's that for a *pleasant childhood*?" She kept her smile as she turned her gaze to the water. "Mudfish, reeds, and squirrel made for an interesting stew—my mother's specialty. Everyone knew everyone, and when the pirates came, we all holed up in the same room under the town hall." When she returned her attention to me, the charisma hadn't faded—it seemed reinforced. "Hard times—interesting times—they've made me who I am today. I wouldn't change that for the world."

"I see..." I said. "I'm sorry I jumped to conclusions."

"No need to apologize. You just owe me a little bit about yourself now."

I opened my mouth, a protest on my tongue—I could tell from my stiff posture—but Eventide cut me off by lifting a hand.

"You're one of my officers," she said. "It's only right."

"How much time do you have?" I asked as I leaned against the ship's railing.

"Give me a quick rundown."

"Okay," I said. "Wanted posters would have you believe I'm a thief with a terrible mustache. Former lovers will have nothing but the highest praise. And my schoolmaster would have you believe I'm a class clown."

"And why would they say all that?"

"Probably because I'm a suave trickster with a penchant for theft."

Eventide lifted an eyebrow as she chuckled. "Is that right?"

"You would've known that had your recruitment process involved more than just math questions." I crossed my arms. "Consider that my first suggestion as an officer-in-training."

A part of me figured Zelfree would be thrown from the ship, but no matter how sarcastic and dismissive he became, Eventide never reacted like how I had imagined. Instead of growing upset, she actually laughed aloud, her mirth carried away by the increasing breeze. She held her hat in place until the wind calmed itself.

"Ruma told me all about your recruitment," Eventide said. "He typically asks more questions, but he said you displayed a fierce desire to prove yourself."

For the first time in the conversation, I tensed. I pushed away from the railing and lowered my arms. "What do you mean?"

"He said you had this look in your eye—a look of someone who wouldn't allow anyone, or anything, to hold him back."

I rubbed my trousers, a fidgety restlessness overcoming me. "And that's all you want in an officer, huh?"

Eventide patted my shoulder. "In my experience, people with your attitude inevitably find themselves at the top of their social structure. If you stayed a thief in your hometown, I'm sure you would've become a master burglar. But now you're an officer on my crew."

"So you're assuming I'll become ship-shape for some pats on the back?"

"No. I'm assuming you won't be satisfied until everyone here acknowledges your talents—and you're smart enough to know that tricks and thievery won't get you there."

I said nothing, though I wondered what Zelfree thought of all that.

"Besides, Ruma is an excellent judge of character." Eventide tossed back her long hair. "I trust his recommendations, no matter how much work a person might need." She stepped around me and headed for the quarterdeck. "I look forward to seeing your career, Everett."

I had always enjoyed Guildmaster Eventide, even though we had rarely spoken. She was always so easy to talk to, so effortless to like. Few people had that quality to put others at ease. I wished I had it.

The world shifted and moved, melting away like water thrown on a fresh painting. The colors rearranged themselves afterward, forming into another memory, this one likely in the future.

Once again, I stood on the deck of the *Red Falcon*, my head craned back, my attention focused on the sky. The ship-of-the-line sailed out of the bay at breathtaking speeds, no doubt aided by magic. I leaned onto the railing, taking in as much of the surroundings as humanly possible.

Waves broke against the hull of the ship, spraying white mist into the air and soaking my hair. I slicked it back with a quick swipe of my hand, excitement coursing through my veins. Had Zelfree ever ridden on a ship before? The way he acted, it made me wonder.

The port town grew smaller and smaller as it disappeared into the distance. The seagulls, which had once been numerous, dwindled in number until none were left. Although Zelfree probably had work to do, he remained at the railing, watching the water with rapt fascination.

I didn't know how much time had passed—perhaps a few minutes, perhaps a few hours—it was a dream, and some things blurred together.

Giant mountains in the distance caught my eye. They were dark in color, like granite, and the tips reached so high, it seemed as though they would tear through the sky.

Lightning flashed between rocks and boulders, crackling and sparking, filling the air with rumbles of thunder. The deckhands rushed to secure everything as I just stared at the wondrous phenomenon.

All over the mountains, from one edge of the horizon to the other, lightning arched at random moments. Sometimes from the ground, sometimes from the thick clouds overhead, but they never stopped. There wasn't even any rain—just the lightning and the echo of frightening thunder.

Gregory Ruma strode out onto the deck. He spotted me and jogged over, his gaze also turning to the sky.

"We're getting close to the Lightning Straits," he said.

I gripped the railing of the ship, my fingers strained. "We aren't going to sail through immediately, right? You have to wait until the lightning storms have died down before taking the ship through the straits."

I hadn't seen many straits. They were narrow waterways, bordered on either side by land, usually mountains, connecting two large bodies of water. Straits were dangerous to sail through normally—one wrong move and the ship could crash into rocks or be crushed by something falling from above—but going through straits that actively had lightning surging from the terrain was another matter entirely.

"We don't need to wait for the lightning storms to die down," Ruma said with a smirk. "Not when we have our captain with us."

I glanced around until I spotted Eventide at the bow of the ship. Her coat fluttered behind her. She planted one boot on the railing and leaned forward, her attention on the flashes of lightning.

"What kind of arcanist is she?" I asked.

Ruma pointed over the starboard railing.

I hustled across the ship, dodging the busy deckhands, and then looked over the edge. A giant turtle swam next to us, her whole body perhaps twice as large as the *Red Falcon*.

Gentel.

I had met her several times, but she had always been gigantic—large enough for an entire guild house to be positioned on her back. In this state, she was still large, but not big enough to have more than a hammock and a few tables on her back.

And to my fascination, her shell was covered in a bulb, like a flower that had yet to bloom. The thick, green leaves protected her shell from taking on sea water, saving the many plants growing there from getting drowned in salt.

Gentel looked up at me, her round eyes glistening and shiny.

"How will the captain protect us?" I asked as Ruma walked to my side.

"Atlas turtle arcanists can create powerful barriers. They're unrivaled in protection, lad. Just you wait and see—this light show might stop other ships, but it won't stop the Frith Guild."

"But there's a timing to the storms. They stop and start with a bit of regularity. What if the captain fails to protect us? Why take that risk? We should just wait."

"Eventide has done this countless times," Ruma said. "You have nothing to worry about."

The *Red Falcon* sailed straight for the narrow waterway between the giant thundering mountains. My whole body remained tense as we traveled toward it. The booming of the storm grew in intensity, and the very air sizzled with unseen power. My hair stood on end, frizzy and puffed, from my head to my toes.

Nervous deckhands filtered down below deck, but I remained.

When the ship drew near the strait, a massive bolt of lightning flashed from the rocks and arched toward our mainmast. If it hit, there was no doubt in my mind the wood would explode into a thousand splinters, just like a tree struck in a storm. The sail would probably also catch fire and spread the flame to the rest of the ship.

Luckily for everyone involved, the lightning struck a semi-invisible force field of magic. The barrier shimmered when hit, but disappeared again once the lightning had died down. No harm came to the *Red Falcon*, not even a singe.

When another bolt of lightning flared, it, too, smashed against Eventide's barrier to little effect.

The *Red Falcon* sailed into the strait, and all light left us. The mountains went so high up that the shadows cast between them were also as pitch black as tar. Eventide remained at the bow of the ship, but Ruma headed to the stern to take control of the helm. If anyone lost control, the ship would smash into the mountains.

I refused to move from my position on the deck. Lightning arched between the mountains, creating electric rainbows overhead. The constant flashes illuminated the straits in short bursts. I watched for a prolonged period of time, my mouth open and my eyes wide.

I hadn't known before, but the Lightning Straits were considerable in length. Even in the dream, it felt like hours went by. The rocking of the *Red Falcon* became severe as the waters splashed between the two mountains.

A creature beneath the waves—not Eventide's atlas turtle—seemingly helped calm the currents, keeping the ship steady. Although I hadn't seen it, I already knew who was responsible.

Decimus. Gregory Ruma's eldrin.

And Decimus was a leviathan, a king of the waves. The massive creature could manipulate water and was no doubt helping Ruma guide the ship through the safest route. It occurred to me then—Eventide and Ruma had complementary eldrin. Her atlas turtle magic protected the ship from attack, both magical and mundane, and his leviathan magic propelled the vessel at safe and swift speeds. The cleverness stuck with me. For a brief moment, I was awash in the nostalgic feelings of my childhood, back when I had read about every legendary arcanist and their swashbuckling adventures.

The *Red Falcon* sailed close to the mountain walls, and I hurried to the railing. The narrow passageway became so tight that the crackling stones of the mountain were nothing more than a foot away. I didn't know why, but I leaned onto the railing and reached out to grab a small stone, something no larger than my palm.

To my surprise, I managed to pluck one from its perch among boulders. I pushed myself back to the deck of the swaying ship and held the rock close.

Its dark speckled coloration intrigued me. I spun the rock around in my hand, marveling at the static bursting off the surface. More than once, it shocked my fingertips.

Before I could put the stone down, a powerful burst of electricity pulsed outward from it.

The dream-memory went black, and when I could see again, I was on my back.

Had the stone zapped Zelfree? I wanted to laugh, but I had no control over what was happening. Instead, I just coughed and wheezed, my mouth filled with a bizarre taste, like I had sucked on metal.

Ruma was at my side, giving me the once-over. "What happened?"

"The ship's surgeon said he was bored," I murmured, "so I thought I'd give him a challenge."

"You touched one of the surgestones, didn't you?"

"Fondled it, really. That might be why it got upset."

He helped me to my feet, chortling the entire time. "This whole mountain range is made out of surgestone. That's what causes these storms. Why would you ever touch it? You're not an arcanist—if you get harmed, it'll take months for you to recover."

"I..."

The words never came. The tight feeling in my chest

spread to my gut, and for a brief moment, it felt like I might vomit. I held it together, and Ruma guided me toward the stairs below deck.

"You need to rest," he said. "I'd hate for our newest officer-in-training to get himself killed on his first voyage."

The dream melted away a second time, taking away the Lightning Straits and the *Red Falcon* and rearranging different images. Somehow, I knew time had passed. The ship made it out of the straits unharmed and then sailed across the Shard Sea.

Something about pirates.

Something else about finding lost merchants.

I saw fleeting moments of adventures, but in each one it was the same. I waited on deck—or rather, *Zelfree* waited on deck—while Ruma and Eventide handled the problems. In each dream-memory, I had an overwhelming sensation of frustration, almost irritation. I felt the same—I wanted to see the action. I wanted to participate. I understood why Zelfree stood at the edge of the ship, watching as close as he could.

Then the dream-memory shifted one last time.

It was the dead of night. I walked out of a bar at the end of a pier. There were hundreds around, all drinking and gambling. The merriment kept everyone awake, which kept the party going. It was a drunken cycle that refused to quit.

I had seen it before at ports where sailors came in for a rest. After months at sea, the men just wanted some freedom.

The evening chill followed me away from the bar, all the way out into the woodlands around whatever town this was. I had no lantern and just kept to the dirt road, my hands in my coat pockets. The sound of celebration died off in the distance.

I stopped at a grouping of trees, the gloom thick, and a chorus of crickets played as though competing against one another. I would've said I was alone had I not heard the heavy breaths and steps of someone larger than me.

"Everett," a person said. "It's been a while."

Although I couldn't see him through the darkness—Zelfree had no knightmare magic, after all—I knew who it was.

I smiled. "Lynus, I'm glad you came. Surprised, really."

"Your letter made it sound serious."

"It is." I leaned against the tree and exhaled. Exhaustion gripped at my limbs, making me sluggish. "But first, how have you been? You never send me letters. I was worried you weren't getting mine."

"Same ol', same ol'," Lynus replied, his voice steelier than I had previously remembered.

"Talk to me. You only say that when you don't want anyone to know what's going on."

Lynus leaned against the same tree on the opposite side. The slosh of a canteen told me he was drinking, and strong odor confirmed what kind.

"Human cruelty knows no bounds" he said. "But I can handle it. My next of kin is misfortune, remember? There's nothing I haven't seen."

"How's your new captain? What's his name? Redbeard? I've heard... stories."

"He says he knows how to find the rarest of mystical creatures." Lynus took a swig of his powerful alcohol. "He says he'll get us things that'll satisfy desires both subtle and gross."

"Yeah..." I crossed my arms and took a deep breath. "Does he *actually* know how to find rare mystical creatures?"

"Seems like it. Captain Redbeard's never been wrong."

"Well... that's the main reason I wanted to see you."

Lynus capped his drink. I heard him scratching at his neck before he replied, "Want me to arrange an introduction?"

"No. Nothing like that. I want you to help me get a mystical creature."

"As in, take one from the ship?"

"No," I said. I leaned the side of my head onto the tree and whispered, "I want you to tell me where one is before he sends mystic seekers out to retrieve it."

The information startled me. I knew why Zelfree wanted this—mystic seekers didn't have claims on mystical creatures they hadn't yet taken into their possession—but it was considered a serious offense to interfere with their search. Mystic seekers were paid by monarchies and governments, after all. It was their duty to find creatures out in the wilds and bring them back for potential trials of worth and bonding. Anyone stealing from them was effectively stealing from the nation that had hired them.

"Redbeard kills anyone who lets slip this information," Lynus said.

I pushed away from the tree, my arms still crossed tight. "If you don't want to do it, that's fine. Just let me know now so I can go talk to someone else."

Lynus chuckled. "Don't get huffy with me, Everett. You know damn well I'll do it."

"Yeah?"

"I've always got your back. I was just thinkin' aloud."

I relaxed my posture and walked closer to him, feeling more at ease with Lynus nearby. "When do you think you could get me any information?"

Lynus moved away from the tree, his boots crunching the dead leaves and twigs harder than my own. The darkness made it impossible to see any details; all I saw was his shadowy silhouette. "I know of a creature right now. Everyone who's gone to see it can't convince it to come back to the ship, and everyone who tried to take its trial of worth earned themselves a horrific death."

"Sounds pleasant," I drawled. "Why tell me about this one?"

"Because it's nearby. That's why we've been stalking this town for weeks now."

I nodded along with his words. "And you think I can handle its trial of worth?"

"I dunno. Not sure what it entails. But I know you're clever. You'll figure it out."

"Then tell me where it is."

"Here's the thing." Lynus grabbed my upper arm and pulled me close. He lowered his voice and spoke directly into my ear. "Captain Redbeard says it's ancient and powerful. He calls it the *Mother of Shapeshifters*."

20

RETRIBUTION

I jerked awake, swimming in confusion and gulping down air. For a split second, I didn't know where I was or what I was doing. Where was Adelgis? Fain?

Where was Illia?

The pounding of my heart helped me focus. I counted each beat until I reached thirty and then I took a deep breath. I didn't know why, but the dream-memory had felt ominous in the last few moments, like it had been about to shift into a nightmare-memory.

Another deep breath. I would've relaxed had I not looked up.

Waiting by the door, slightly hunched and leaning against the bulkhead, was a scarecrow. Not a normal scare-crow made from a stick and hay and discarded clothes, but an amalgamation of a scarecrow and a living person, as though the two had conceived a hideous child.

Grayish skin had been stretched over tawny hay, forming a complete, albeit lumpy, humanoid body. There were no eyes, just a smile-slit cut into the taut skin with stitching at the corners, keeping it from ripping farther along the face.

Dried blood spotted the creature at the ends of all limbs—the "fingers" and the "feet" were the worst of all—and anywhere that hay poked out of the body.

I leapt off the bed, more awake and tense than I had ever been in my entire life.

In my haste to get up and get combat ready, I looked away from the disgusting creature for half a second, perhaps less. When I returned my attention to it, the freakish scarecrow was gone. In its place was a short man with a pot belly. He wore a scuffed top hat, breeches that hugged his legs, and an open doublet, like he was a fancy noble who had taken a tumble in the gutter and thought that was a good look.

"Whoa, there," he said, holding up a hand with a fingerless glove. "Didn't mean to startle you. I thought you'd be asleep for a little bit longer."

I ran a shaky hand down my face, not surprised by the amount of sweat I wiped away. My heart had been pounding before, but now it threatened to break through my ribs.

The man motioned to the door. "Karna tried to wake you, but when that didn't work, she went to check up on the rest of the crew. She told me to relay the message."

"What... are you?" I forced myself to say. It wasn't an eloquent or polite question, but I didn't care—I just wanted the answer.

"I'm a doppelgänger." He took off his hat, offered a formal bow, and then stood straight. "Karna's eldrin, to be specific."

"I... uh... I've never seen one before."

"And you probably never will again. Only a rare few ever do."

I found myself fishing for words, but nothing came up. The adrenaline in my veins waned, leaving me with a jittery restlessness. The doppelgänger didn't seem dangerous, and it simply smiled as I gave it the once-over.

"Since you're awake, I'll take my leave now," he said.

He grabbed the door handle, and I held up a hand.

"W-wait."

The doppelgänger glanced back with a raised eyebrow.

"I'm sorry," I muttered. "I really was just taken by surprise."

"Think nothing of it. All that matters is that you didn't attack me. Doppelgängers aren't known for their fortitude, ya see."

"Right..."

The bizarre man placed his top hat back on his head and then exited the room with a graceful couple of steps. When he shut the door, he did it gently enough to avoid making any sound. I was equal parts impressed and worried. Obviously, Karna's doppelgänger had been with us for the entire trek. Where had it been? Who had it been? Did it sneak around all the time?

I hadn't even asked for its name.

"That was weird, right, Luthair?"

No answer.

I stared down at the shadows. No movement. I checked the corners of the room and then around the sides of the trunks. Nothing. He must have left.

I picked up my black bones and hurried out of Karna's room. Bright light streamed into the airship through the portholes, and the intense heat told me that morning had come and gone. How long had I slept? I wondered if the length of the dream-memories had anything to do with it.

Several crew members shuffled in and out of the corridor. I avoided them as best as possible, not wanting to bother anyone.

But where was I going?

I wanted to ask Adelgis about the whereabouts of Theasin, since he now had his father's letters and notes, but at the same time, I wanted to deal with the black bones. I figured that Adelgis would contact me the moment he knew something—he had telepathy, we could talk at any time—so I opted instead to see Jozé.

I knocked on the door labeled, *Blacksmith*. My father answered a moment later. His face didn't have as much stubble as before, and he seemed livelier when he smiled.

"There you are, boy." He clasped my shoulder and guided me into his room. "Your friend brought me a pouch of star shards, and I figured we could try making you a weapon."

"Which friend?"

"Adelgis. Theasin's son."

"Right."

Jozé opened one of the cabinets mounted on the bulkhead. His phoenix sat on a perch nearby, her blue body adding a gentle hue of sapphire to the room. When she noticed me staring, she fluffed her feathers and held her long neck tall.

"I'm not sure how much you know about imbuing magic," Jozé said as he gathered materials. "Think of it like an equation. It's your magic, plus the magic of the objects you're imbuing, plus the number of star shards. Now, you're a knightmare arcanist, so I have just the thing." He set everything in a leather pouch, shut the cabinet, and then motioned to the door. "Let's get to the deck."

I did as he instructed and headed for the stairway. He followed behind at a slow pace, rubbing at his leg from time to time. Tine, his phoenix, waited until there was a clear shot through the corridor and then leapt from her perch.

She couldn't spread her wings, but with a few half-flaps, she made it a good distance. Soot covered the floor wherever she touched down.

When we got up on deck, the afternoon sun shone all around us. It took fewer than ten seconds for me to bake inside my clothing.

Jozé placed his pouch down and opened it wide. He had several materials—steel, iron, copper, some metal I didn't recognize, leather straps, and even bits of fine string. The metals were in ingot form, shaped like rectangles and perfect for forging.

"So, if we were using a normal forge, I would have to instruct you about metallurgy," Jozé said. "There's a science to that, but since I have blue phoenix magic, we can skip a few steps." He picked up a steel ingot and then turned it over in his palm. It only took a short moment before the metal heated to the point that I could see mirage-like waves floating off it.

"You're going to heat that here?" I asked as I motioned to the wooden airship.

"I don't need to hammer it," he said. "There won't be any sparks. So long as it's not dropped, it won't be a problem. And even if I *do* drop it, the harm will be minimal. Everything fire is my domain."

He was the master, so I took his word for it.

"While I'm heating this, why don't we try something simple?" Jozé reached into his trouser pocket and withdrew a single golden star shard and a blue phoenix feather. He handed them to me. "Why don't you try imbuing your knightmare magic into that feather?"

I held both items close, uncertain of what I was doing. "Maybe I should get Luthair."

"Your eldrin? You don't need him to make a trinket."

"He helped me last time."

Jozé rubbed at the slight stubble on his chin with one hand and continued to heat the steel ingot in the other. "I think you should try this by yourself."

I regarded the star shard and phoenix feather with a bit of skepticism. "What will I make?"

"Ah, that's the fun part. I said this was like an equation, but there are plenty of nuances. Knightmare magic deals with shadows, armor, weapons, and fear, so you'll be adding one of those elements to the feather. Phoenixes are known for their healing and fire, but the physical body part used will dictate what you get."

"I don't understand," I said. "Different body parts do different things?"

"You got it." Jozé snapped his fingers. "If you imbued a talon, you'd surely make something offensive. If you imbued a mystical creature's heart, you'd get something powerful. The feathers of a phoenix tend to draw more on the healing aspect, but since I have a blue phoenix, it'll likely deal with fire."

Long ago, the Grand Apothecary of Fortuna, Gillie, had crafted me a simple trinket. She had used a red phoenix feather and her caladrius magic to create a bracelet that prevented diseases. Where had it gone? I shook my head the moment I remembered I had given it to Master Zelfree after I had saved him from the Dread Pirate Calisto.

So, what would knightmare magic and a blue phoenix feather create?

"How do I do this?" I asked.

"Hold the star shard to the feather and imagine yourself giving the shard your magic. Think of it like a sponge, and you're the water. Let it take what it needs."

I closed my hand tightly around the star shard and

feather and imagined the time Luthair and I had created a shield together. It had been in the middle of a dangerous fight, but I could still recall the entire event with decent clarity. I shut my eyes and allowed my magic to rush into the crystal.

A smile crept across my face as I felt the star shard melt away. It was like ice under the harsh rays of the sun—once solid, then liquid, then gone forever.

Magic drained from me, but unlike with my shield, where it demanded more and more until I had to free myself from its thirst, this feather barely took anything. It stopped a second later, filled to capacity.

When I opened my hand, the blue feather was now marked with black at the tips—an inky substance that moved a bit while I stared.

"What does it do?" I asked.

"Give it here." Jozé held out his free hand.

I gave him the shadowy feather and watched as he reached into an inner coat pocket and produced an old piece of parchment. "So, there are mystical creatures called *relickeepers*," he said as he juggled the objects with the one hand, still heating the metal in the other. "And relickeepers have the ability to know the materials of an object, how many star shards were used, and what kind of magic was imbued. They can also detect a trinket's function."

"Adelgis's father is a relickeeper arcanist."

Jozé rolled his eyes. "Well, good for him. Luckily for us, I have a relickeeper trinket that will do the same damn thing." He wrapped the parchment around the feather and then unfolded it. The parchment had been blank before, but now golden letters floated to the surface, revealing a short set of information. "See? Now we don't need a bizarre dragon to tell us what's happening."

He handed me the parchment.

It read:

Blue phoenix feather
Knightmare magic
Single star shard
A knightmare arcanist's shadows won't be as easily destroyed
by fire

"Why does the number of star shards matter?" I asked.

"The more you use, the more you can imbue into an item. Once you use enough, around ten or so, the item becomes an artifact, not just a trinket. Artifacts are much harder to break and are typically more powerful."

Jozé handed me the feather back. Although it didn't do much—a slight fortitude to flame didn't seem extremely useful—I still treasured the trinket. It was the first one I had ever made by myself, and it had been with a feather from my father's eldrin. I had never thought a day like this would ever happen. I had always imagined my father a criminal and that I would need to be the exact opposite of him to prove myself to the world.

The odd situation filled my thoughts, and it took me a long while before I tucked the feather into my pocket. In doing so, I was reminded of the black bones.

"Will your parchment identify bones? Or random scales from creatures?"

Jozé nodded. "Yes."

I withdrew the bones from the waist of my trousers. "Can you identify these?"

Using his one hand, Jozé wrapped the parchment around the bones. When he removed it, nothing happened. He stared at the paper for longer than thirty seconds, like he thought it might eventually awaken and do its duty.

"That's odd," he muttered.

Jozé wrapped the parchment around the bones a second time.

Again, nothing.

"Why isn't it working?" I asked.

Silence passed between us as Jozé mulled over the question. Before I could say anything, he said, "Relickeepers can identify anything less powerful than they are."

He had said it like a perplexing matter-of-fact statement. It reminded me of when I had met with Theasin. He was a relickeeper arcanist, but he hadn't been able to identify the material my shield had been made of. I had used a world serpent scale, and since the world serpent was considered a god-creature, beyond the power of a relickeeper, that would explain why he hadn't been able to name the material.

And it was a possible explanation now.

This had come from Theasin's personal lab, after all. It could be anything—perhaps even bones from the world serpent.

"Do you think I can create a weapon out of these?" I asked. I held up the six bone fragments. "My sword was broken during the attack on Thronehold. I need a replacement."

"Do you know what they are, boy?" Jozé asked.

I shook my head. "No. But if you can't identify them, they must be *something* interesting."

"Really think about this. A part of being a good artificer is calculating what you're trying to make. Mystical creatures that fight—like manticores—have magic suited for weapons. Mystical creatures that care for or heal others—like caladrius—would make terrible weapons. If you use bones from an unknown creature, you're gambling. Your weapon might not be as useful as, say, a blade of flame, crafted from a blue phoenix."

"These are powerful, though." I held them closer to my father. "Just touch one."

He exhaled and did as I asked. Then he ran a single finger along the length of one, his eyebrow knit. "Hm."

"Don't you feel it?"

"I feel nothing."

His statement shocked me. I figured, out of all the people on the airship, *he* would be able to sense the same thing I did. There was power in these bones—great power. Why didn't anyone else see that?

"I still want to use them," I said. "I don't know why, but they feel different to me."

"Give them here."

Hesitant, I handed over the six bone fragments. My father brought them close to the white-hot ingot in his other hand. The once-rectangular piece of steel was now a half-melted mess, threatening to drip onto the deck and start a fire. I almost wanted it to happen so I could tell Jozé *I told you so*, but he expertly held on to the molten steel, no damage to his palm or flesh.

Phoenix arcanists were immune to fire, and it was amusing to watch the metal slide around his skin without hurting him.

Jozé slowly placed a bone fragment into the steel.

"*Hey*," I barked.

He shot me a stern glower. "It'll be all right, boy."

His phoenix moved in close, her silver eyes on me. "Volke, don't worry. This is common when forging magical weapons. The bone will become part of the metal, and once Jozé shapes it into a blade, you'll be able to imbue it with knightmare magic."

I crossed my arms, my stomach grumbling. It had been a long while since I had eaten, and the shock from this morning—and the odd dreams from last night—still haunted my thoughts. I wasn't entirely myself, so I stepped back and forced a calming breath.

Jozé fed the rest of the bones into the steel. Once everything was mixed, he used both hands to pull the metal-like clay. The molten heat subsided faster than with normal metal—no doubt the temperature was controlled by my father's magic—and he worked the steel much like an expert baker worked bread. He kneaded it and then folded it, and then smoothed it. When he wanted it to be solid, he removed heat, and when he wanted to mold it again, he heated it up.

If we had been using an actual forge, this would've been days' worth of work.

"My arcanist."

I spotted Luthair slithering across the deck in his shadow form. Karna followed behind him, her eyes on the bright hot metal that Jozé tossed around in his hands.

"What're you two doing?" she asked.

"Crafting a new weapon for the boy," Jozé muttered through gritted teeth, his concentration narrowed on his task.

I hadn't noticed until then, but most of the crew was on deck, watching from afar. They stood near the railing or up on the quarterdeck, staring down. Whenever I glanced over, they looked away and feigned work, but they always went right back to watching once I turned away.

Even Biyu stood with them, her giant book half-hiding

her from my view. She wrote at a fearsome pace, and I wondered just how much detail she took down.

Jozé took a couple of deep breaths as he lengthened the metal. Typically, metal was poured into a cast, but he managed to harden the hot steel fast enough to actually create a blade in his hands, no need for a mold. He had done it so quickly, and by turning the metal around to keep it from spilling, it almost looked like a performance. I considered it more art than blacksmithing.

When he finally had the basic shape of a sword, he cooled the steel and then set the weapon down on the deck, tip first, so that the hilt rested against his gut.

The blade I had before was considered a short sword—about two and a half feet in length—but the rough blade my father had created was four feet, which most considered to be a *longsword*.

It wasn't done, though. Everything was dull and just shaped in the form of a sword.

The metal was blackish, no doubt tainted from the bones that had been fed to the molten steel.

"That's not the same kind of blade I had before," I said.

"The beauty of knightmare magic is that it creates lightweight weapons," Jozé said, somewhat winded. "And I figured you could use a blade that could switch from one-handed to two-handed, if needed."

I had trained in sword-and-shield style, so the thought of fighting with a two-handed blade didn't sit right. On the other hand, I no longer had my shield, and I didn't know if I'd ever get it back. Perhaps my father was right.

"Okay," Jozé said. "Let me finish, and then you can do your thing."

He took a deep breath, picked up the rough blade, and

then slid his fingers over the entire weapon, slowly shaping the last of the details.

I would've said it was impossible for someone to use their hands to craft something straight, but I suspected his magic was somehow helping in the process. The metal seemed to do what he wanted, and when he pinched the edges of the blade, they sharpened and didn't fold away.

He made both sides deadly—some blades could have just one sharp edge, but the double edge allowed for more versatility when fighting. Then he smoothed the hilt and added a guard. It seemed to take a lot out of him, though. His breathing became heavier the longer he worked.

When he was done, the longsword looked ready for combat, even if it was still a little rough.

"Don't worry about how it looks now," he said after a deep breath. "Once you imbue your knightmare magic into it, the sword will take on a slightly different appearance. It'll never dull, and it won't weigh as much as it does now."

Jozé wrapped the hilt with leather and then burned it into place. He handed me the weapon, pommel first.

I took it with both hands. Although I hadn't worked with swords for long, I knew to check for the balance—a point where the weapon's weight is equally distributed to each end. If there was too much weight on the hilt, my strikes would be slow and clunky. If there was too much weight at the tip, it'd take me longer to recover from each strike.

To my surprise, the sword had a fantastic balance, centered about three inches up the blade. My father had done that with just his hands and magic? It impressed me, though I didn't know how to articulate that without sounding childish.

Jozé withdrew two star shards from his pocket and handed them over.

"I need more," I said.

"How many more?"

"I need to make this an artifact."

Luthair moved around my feet, Karna gave me an odd glance, and my father snorted back a laugh.

"You don't *need* to, boy," Jozé said. "Besides, you didn't even know what those bones were, so you might be wasting star shards on something trivial."

"You don't understand. The villains I intend to fight are... they're..."

I closed my eyes, remembering the attack on Thronehold. During the commotion, the villains of the Second Ascension had unleashed something I had never seen before. It was a type of dust made from nullstone—anti-magic rocks that prevented arcanists from using their abilities. The dust had broken down trinkets, disintegrating them. That was how I had lost my sword. But it didn't break artifacts. The dust hadn't been able to harm my shield.

If I was going to face the Second Ascension again, I had to be ready.

"There's a group of madmen who know how to destroy trinkets," I said as I opened my eyes and stared at my father. "They do so with ease. If I can cure myself, then they're the ones I'll be fighting next. I can't afford to make dozens of weak magical items just to practice. I need to make sure this weapon will hold up when things get dire."

Jozé ran a hand through his black hair. "Star shards aren't cheap."

"I understand."

"They're finite. You don't mine them, you can't create them—they fall from the sky at random points, no one knows when. They're rare, you get it? Hard to come by."

I nodded.

"You still want to?" Jozé asked, one eyebrow raised.

Karna shot him a glower. "You should let him try."

He replied with a long sigh.

"I already sold that crown," Karna retorted. "We have money to pay the crew for a few months. And if you need more star shards for your work, you know Captain Devlin will get them for you."

Perhaps my father thought I couldn't handle creating an artifact, and he was afraid I would waste the shards. But I knew I could. I already had, even if I hadn't done it with any sort of finesse. Now that I knew the basics of item creation, and Luthair was with me, I could get it right.

Jozé reached into his pocket and withdrew eight more star shards. He handed them over, his expression hardened into an unreadable neutral.

"You'll have to let the weapon take as much magic as it needs from you," he said. "Don't let go until you feel the draining sensation stop. And focus on one star shard at a time—it helps, trust me."

Again, I nodded.

With a shaky breath, I set the longsword on the deck of the airship and then knelt next to it. The eyes of the crew weighed on me as I set the ten star shards on the blade. I hadn't anticipated this being a show, but their presence didn't unnerve me.

What would Zaxis do in this situation? He would probably give everyone a speech about how amazing he was—about how glorious his weapon would be—maybe even give them a bow and utter a few more thank-yous.

I smiled to myself.

Atty would probably just make her weapon perfect the first time, no theatrics at all.

I touched the weapon and shook the thoughts from my head. Now wasn't the time.

"My arcanist," Luthair said. "Let me help."

I touched the shadows on the deck. "Okay."

He formed up around me and merged with my being. Although I was plague-ridden, as long as we weren't injured in this form, it seemed it wouldn't pass to him.

His shadowy plate armor engulfed me in a cold sensation of power, and it felt pleasant after standing in the desert sun. Together, we placed a gauntleted hand on the weapon and poured our combined magic into it.

The sensation was familiar. Just like with the shield, the longsword wanted an intense amount of magic. The star shards sank into the blade, taking my essence with them, imbuing the weapon with knightmare powers. Every second that went by drained more from me. Then it started to burn, like when I used my second-bonded magic too intensely. I gritted my teeth and continued.

My whole body trembled.

The weapon wanted *so much*.

It was like having all my breath stolen, and every time I tried to inhale, I received a mouthful of water. Worse and worse it became, but Jozé said not to let go. I continued, fearing I might pass out. At least I had knelt on the deck. If I had been standing, I would've surely toppled over.

It's almost done, Luthair said telepathically, straight to my mind.

I refused to fail and let the sword take the very last of my strength.

Only then did it seem satisfied.

I released the weapon and gulped down air.

Karna knelt beside me. She touched her fingers to the shadow-plate on my shoulder. "Are you okay?"

I tried to nod, but it probably looked like I was dizzy.

It took my father a bit of effort to kneel down, thanks to his bad leg. He touched the longsword and gingerly scooped it into his hands. The blade was the same shadowy metal as my armor, dark and filled with an inner void. The sharp edge gleamed when Jozé turned the weapon over.

"It's lightweight," he said. "Just as I predicted. This would fetch a nice price. Knightmare magic is so rare. There's only one talented knightmare artificer I know, and she works with the Steel Thorn Inquisitors."

Karna narrowed her eyes. "Are you going to have him create weapons for your patrons now?"

"Maybe." Jozé chuckled. "We would make a decent living." Then he brought his attention to me. "What're you going to name your new blade?"

"Name it?" I rasped, my voice a combination of my own and Luthair's.

"Of course. This isn't some ordinary trinket. You made an artifact, remember? It deserves a name."

All the greatest heroes in the storybooks had weapons with names. What had Ruma named his pistol? In my fatigued state, I had forgotten. I remembered liking it, though.

I thought about names while I regained my strength. Something to do with justice. Something to do with the arcanists of old. Something to do with defeating evil or saving the innocent. There were so many possibilities.

A sword is used to fell the wicked, Luthair said to me. *Its name should instill fear in those who revel in their sins.*

What would Illia name it? Something practical. Something unique.

What would Zaxis name it? I half-laughed to myself imagining all the over-the-top names he would concoct.

What about Hexa? Perhaps something blunt—like *Devastator*. That sounded like her.

Once recovered, at least a little, I forced myself to stand. Luthair was right, and I knew what I wanted to name it.

Luthair unmerged with me and then kept me steady with a hand on my shoulder.

"Retribution," I said. "I'll name the sword *Retribution*."

My father lifted both eyebrows and replied with a slow nod. "I see." He placed his palm on the blade closest to the hilt and then dragged it up. He emblazoned letters across the shadow, bone, and steel.

RETRIBUTION

A slight ember remained in the lettering, keeping the name alight, even after he took his hand away. Then he handed me the longsword.

"That's a fine name," he said. "Let's hope it lives up to it."

21

BIYU AT THE BAZAAR

I had never trained with a sword that felt so effortless. Even Mathis's old blade—crafted with knightmare magic and a behemoth fang—didn't slice through the air like Retribution did. I spent the rest of the day going through my standard training routines, getting myself used to the extra length of my new weapon. Although it was longer, it was still light enough to wield with one hand. The hilt was long, allowing for an easy transition to two hands, just as my father had said.

It would take time to master, but this was a superior sword.

The crew of the *Sun Chaser* watched for a while, and I didn't mind. It was better than them fearing me.

And I hadn't noticed it at first, but apparently my father had "signed" the sword with a bird symbol on the hilt. It was his trademark—all the weapons he forged had it. Crafting guilds always had unique marks, but I had never met an individual who had a specific design. I thought it interesting, and I wondered how many of my father's weapons were out in the world.

The city bells chimed. I continued training regardless of the drop in temperature. One of the deckhands brought me some jerky, and while I thought it was closer to dirt than edible food, I gobbled it down.

As the sun set, Jozé returned to the deck of the ship. He carried a scabbard—the same kind of sheath he kept his flame sword inside of—and he limped over to my side.

"Here," he said as he handed it to me. "It should be the right size for your new blade."

"Do I need it?" I asked. Hadn't he said the longsword would never dull? I took the heavy scabbard. It weighed twice as much as Retribution, perhaps more.

"It's lined with nullstone," he said. "When your blade is sheathed, others won't be able to detect its magical nature. Trust me. It's always good to have the element of surprise."

Nullstone intrigued me. It had so many useful applications, but at the same time, it was a terrible substance that restricted magic. Having a nullstone scabbard could potentially have more than one function in combat.

"If my scabbard is lined in nullstone, I won't be able to take the sword with me when I shadow-step," I said.

Jozé smiled. "Hey, now. You're talking to a master arcanist. Nullstone can be altered with magic—it can be attuned to certain magics, block out specific magics, and even make trinkets, believe it or not. It's just... difficult. And costly. Nullstone requires almost twice as many star shards to craft it into something."

I didn't know much about nullstone, but I knew my father spoke the truth. Thronehold castle had been protected with a nullstone aura that was attuned to sovereign dragon magic, and the villains within the Second

Ascension had created *decay dust* out of nullstone—a vile cloud that destroyed trinkets.

"So I need to attune this?" I asked as I examined the scabbard.

"It won't be difficult. I've done it a few times."

An icy breath on my neck alerted me to Fain's presence before he whispered, "Volke, do you have a moment?"

I didn't know why he had decided to speak with me while invisible, but I opted to humor him. I held the scabbard close. "Thank you for this," I said to Jozé. "I appreciate it." I stepped around him, and the chill of Fain's presence stayed with me as I headed for the stairs.

"It's Adelgis," Fain muttered. "He's been acting strange since yesterday."

"How so?" I asked as I reached the bottom steps.

"Ever since you two returned from Theasin's lab, Adelgis has sequestered himself to the corner of our storeroom. He's reading over a pile of paperwork, and he avoids speaking with me at every turn."

I reached the storeroom door and opened it without bothering to announce myself.

Just as Fain had described, Adelgis sat on the floor of the room, hunched over a myriad of paperwork. His long hair hung down, blocking his face from my view. His reading materials consumed a quarter of the small space, the papers stacked on the crates and barrels, organized in such a chaotic way that I couldn't make sense of it all. It reminded me of Vethica's room.

A glowing sea snail hung in the air—Adelgis's ethereal whelk, Felicity—and she faced me as I entered. Her tentacles wiggled, similar to a wave, just more bizarre. The crystal of her shell glittered as she floated to the side, allowing me a straight line to Adelgis.

"Adelgis?" I asked.

He placed his hands over the papers he had been reading. "I'm busy. I apologize, but I have a lot of material to analyze. Can we speak another time?"

"Uh, sure. But are you okay?"

He didn't move. "I'm perfectly fine."

"What's so important about this?"

"I'm using it to find the location of my father." Adelgis drew some of the papers close and stacked them with restless energy. "Several people have written him letters, but they don't specifically list their locations. They do, however, discuss landmarks and other points of interest nearby. I believe I can deduce my father's location once I have all the facts."

"Okay." I walked over. "Do you need help?"

Adelgis tensed. "I'd prefer if I did this on my own. If you attempted to help, I fear it would only add to the overall time. Some of the locations mentioned require a firm grasp of geography and history, and I would have to stop to explain things. We're short on time. You want me to find my father as fast as possible, don't you?"

"How long do you think this'll take?" I asked, skeptical of his reasoning, but unwilling to demand a different explanation.

"I don't know. Perhaps a few days. I haven't gotten through half the paperwork yet."

I nodded and then moved away. It seemed to ease Adelgis's anxiety—he loosened and fanned the paperwork out again.

"Okay," I said. "Let me know if there's anything I can do for you."

"I just need time. Please. No disturbances."

Felicity slowly spun in midair. "My arcanist just needs to concentrate," she said.

I didn't want to leave him—Adelgis always conducted himself in an odd manner, but this seemed worse than usual. On the other hand, I didn't want to agitate him any further. Perhaps the paperwork involved a lot more than locations, and the disturbing information had gotten under Adelgis's skin.

I decided to trust him and assume everything he had told me was accurate.

One day.

Two days.

On the third day, I started to regret my decision to leave Adelgis to his own devices. He sat in the storeroom morning, noon, and night, barely interacting with anyone except for the crewmates who brought him food. I only had a limited amount of time, and I had to remind myself that I couldn't force anyone to work faster than they were capable.

I just had to wait.

To keep my mind busy, I trained with Fain. My thoughts occasionally dwelled on Adelgis's wellbeing, though. The last few nights, he hadn't given me any more dreams. Was he doing anything other than reading? Was he even sleeping?

Fain rushed across the deck of the ship, went invisible, and then—while I was distracted—grabbed my forearm and manipulated my flesh, ripping away layers of skin with just a gentle touch. Pain flared throughout my body.

I growled through gritted teeth, unleashing terrors and manipulating shadows without any real control.

Fain's invisibility dropped as he staggered backward, grabbing at his head, tormented by unseen horrors. He hit the deck on his knees, his eyes scrunched shut.

Claws of darkness ranked across the deck, gouging wood, mauling barrels, and snapping rope.

A deckhand fussing with the rigging crumpled to the ground, her scream startling.

I throttled my magic, my breathing heavy, frustration building in my veins.

"I'm sorry," I said to the woman. "It was an accident." I jogged over, intent to help her up, but she shook her head, tears at the corners of her eyes, and hustled off the deck.

Shame twisted inside my chest. The crew of the *Sun Chaser* had just started to tolerate my presence, and now they probably wouldn't get within twenty yards of me. Why had I lost control like that?

Fain got to his feet and shook the last of my terrors from his mind. "Is everything okay?"

"Yes," I said, curt.

I gripped my injured arm and glanced back at the crimson droplets on the deck of the ship. After a short exhale, I cleaned everything, determined not to leave even a single speckle. Fain helped, his ice making things easier since he could prevent the liquid from spreading.

"I don't normally catch you with my attacks," he said. "You must've been pretty distracted."

"Hm," I replied, the agony subsiding slowly.

Once I finished, I went to the railing of the ship to grab a bucket reserved for waste. I spotted Biyu hurrying down the gangplank, her head ducked low, her little legs carrying her away from the airship at a stealthy rate. No one accompanied her, and she glanced over her shoulder like only a guilt-ridden child could.

"Fain," I said. "I think Biyu is trying to sneak away."

He stepped up to the railing and watched the little girl quietly descend the steps to the walls of New Norra.

"Looks like it," he muttered. Then he motioned to the deck. "So, how about we train evocation again? The ice will feel refreshing." He shielded his eyes from the blazing afternoon sun. "Maybe the deckhands will also enjoy it."

"I think we should go after her."

"Who? The deckhand you scared?"

"I'm talking about *Biyu*," I stated, trying to hide my sardonic irritation, but failing. "C'mon. I don't think she should go anywhere alone."

Fain shifted his weight from one foot to the other. "I'm not, well, a *kid* person. I'm not even a *person* person, either, if I'm being honest."

"Think of this as social training, then." I pointed to the city walls. "Meet me down there."

Before he could answer, I stepped into the shadows and traveled through the darkness. I emerged at the base of the sandstone steps of the wall, and Biyu almost collided with me. She managed to stop on the last step, her one eye huge the instant she realized she had been caught.

"V-Volke," she stammered.

The injury on my forearm had healed a decent amount —no longer bleeding—but it was still raw. I removed some wootz cotton from my bicep and wrapped it around the injury as I said, "I saw you heading into the city. Does the captain know where you're going?"

Biyu held the leather strap of her book, her lips pursing. "He can't know. It's a secret."

"I don't think he'd approve of you leaving. And I think you know I'm right or else you wouldn't be sneaking off."

She pressed her sun hat down until it covered her face,

muttering angry things under her breath. She must have been talking to herself, because the words shifted from confrontational to calm between sentences. When Biyu finally lifted her hat, her eye was glassy.

"I want to get the captain a present," she said. "So he can't follow me to town or else it won't be a surprise."

"You have coins?"

Biyu reached into one pocket of her coat and then another. Each had something useful inside, like a piece of charcoal or a blank piece of paper. The last pocket contained one silver coin and four copper coins. She held them up, beaming a smile that could be seen from Thronehold.

"Here they are!" she declared. "I earned this, you know. By being the best cabin girl ever!" Biyu leaned closer to me and lowered her voice. "Captain Devlin said I'd get paid a silver coin every moon, but he gave me these coppers as a bonus because I did such a good job."

I hadn't realized the captain was paying her, considering how young she was. If I had been given money at her age, I was certain I would've used it immediately and frivolously.

Fain leapt down the stairs until he was behind Biyu. She gave him an odd glance over her shoulder.

"Fain and I can accompany you to the bazaar," I said. "And we promise we won't tell the captain about your surprise."

"I dunno... Vethica said you can't be trusted."

"What do you think?"

Biyu stroked her chin as though imitating someone who scratched at their beard while they thought. "Will the wendigo come, too?"

"Wraith is with us," Fain said. He motioned to his side. "Show yourself."

Wraith appeared a moment later, his invisibility melting off his gray fur and revealing his skeletal frame and skull face. Nothing about Wraith looked pleasant to me, but Biyu stared at him as though she were looking at a majestic flower that only bloomed once every decade.

Biyu let out a girlish and excited gasp. Then she reached out her hand. "Can I pet you?"

"I suppose," Wraith muttered. He lowered his head and Biyu stroked the grooves of the skull all the way up to Wraith's ears.

She yanked her hand away, turned on her heel, and then leapt off the last step of the staircase. "Okay. You two can be my bodyguards, but you have to promise not to tell anyone!" She pointed toward the glittering delta in the distance. "Let's go to the port bazaar. Karna says that's where all the best stuff is."

***

The gold and blue lines painted onto the bricks of the street led us straight to the port bazaar. It was larger than I had imagined, with stalls and stands for every desire. Food, guns, knives, clothes, live animals, maps—anything I could think of, there was someone selling it. The concern of thieves and pirates drifted into my thoughts, but the weight of my new weapon attached to my belt dispelled the fear.

"—and that's the first time I ever ate octopus," Biyu said.

She hadn't stopped talking since we had left the city wall. At first, she had focused on her life, her hobbies, how she had learned to read and write... And once that had all been over, she'd gone straight to innocuous topics, such as her favorite colors—surprise, all of them—what kind of dreams she had, and now all about her least favorite foods.

I would've answered her, but it was clear she didn't want to engage *me* in conversation. Or Fain, for that matter.

Biyu patted Wraith on the scruff of his neck. "What's *your* least favorite food?"

"I'm not sure," Wraith said. "I haven't eaten something I didn't like."

"*Wow*. So amazing. If you don't dislike anything, what's your favorite?"

"Human fles—"

Fain cleared his throat with a loud cough and then grabbed his eldrin by the side of the skull. "Hey, aren't you looking for a gift, kid? You should focus." He pointed to the merchant stands all around us. "Pick something."

Man-eating mystical creatures could eat all types of meat, but they occasionally *needed* human flesh to maintain themselves. I had never asked Fain what he did about Wraith, but now that Fain knew what he could manipulate, I wondered if this problem would be easier to solve. Or perhaps... it was his own flesh he fed to his eldrin, since arcanists could heal themselves?

I shook my head, dispelling the disturbing thoughts.

The port bazaar had hundreds of people, but the area was spacious enough to provide plenty of room.

The three of them walked to the next stall over, Wraith wagging his tail, Fain frosting his clothes every thirty seconds, and Biyu pointing to everything on display. Just as I went to follow them, a group of five children—around four years old—charged into my legs. They hadn't been watching where they were going, but fortunately they weren't large enough to knock me over.

They wore simple robes, nothing fancy, and dirt caked their faces, typical of children no matter the culture, apparently.

"Run," one cried, her voice filled with excitement and mirth.

"He's going to catch us," another said.

"Oh, no," a little boy said with a giggle.

No one said a word to me. They probably didn't see me through their merriment. They just ran around my legs—one going between—and then continued through the bazaar.

A sixth child hurried after them, a red chicken held tightly in his arms. Someone had drawn a silly arcanist mark on the boy's forehead. Each point of the star was a different size, and the creature drawn over it was none other than a chicken.

He also collided with me, despite the fact that I was tall and visible.

The little boy rasped and hugged his chicken close to his chest. "Stand aside," he said between breaths. "I'm an arcanist, coming through!"

I chuckled. "*You're* an arcanist?"

The boy glanced up, really seeing me for the first time. His eyes went straight to my arcanist mark. He squeezed his chicken, which answered with a strangled *bagok*!

"I'm... I'm a chicken arcanist," he whispered.

"I don't think so."

The boy frowned, and his posture wilted.

I grabbed a green sash from the nearest vender and knelt, surprising the lad.

"You're a *cockatrice* arcanist," I said as I wrapped the green sash around the fluffed tail of the chicken. "Much more dangerous than a chicken arcanist."

Cockatrices were deadly mystical creatures that lived in the harsh sands of the desert. They had the bodies of chickens, the tails of serpents, and the wings of bats. I fashioned the sash into a snake-like tail as best I could before offering the boy a smile.

"Now you can turn people to stone," I said.

The boy patted his chicken along her red feathers, a shy smile growing at the corners of his lips. "Y-yeah. I *am* a cockatrice arcanist."

I pointed down the road. "Your friends went that way."

"Thank you. Thank you very much!" He ran off, holding his chicken high.

The woman selling colored sashes gave me a long glower.

I reached into my trouser pocket and gathered a few coins Karna had given me. I handed them over, and the woman placed three fingers on her heart. I mimicked the gesture, even though I didn't know if that was appropriate for the situation.

Fain ran toward me, shoving a man out of the way in his haste. He had been more than fifty feet away.

When had he gotten so far from me? Last I had seen, he and Biyu had been shopping just one stand over.

"*Volke,*" Fain shouted as he reached my side. "We need to get the captain."

The panic in his voice sent me right to the edge of restraint, and I placed a hand on the hilt of my blade. "What is it?" I asked. "Where's Biyu?"

Sweat dappled his face. His frostbitten ears and fingers stood out against his paled skin. With shaky hands, he pointed away from the bazaar. "We need to go. He's here. They took her. Captain Devlin has to—"

"*Who's* here?" I snapped. "Calm down and tell me what's happened."

"*Calisto.*" Fain grabbed my upper arm, his grip tight. "His crew took Biyu. I saw the tattoos..." He ran his hand idly over the ascot around his neck—the only thing hiding the tattoo that marked him as a former member of the pirate crew. "Calisto is here. At a cantina near the edge of the ports."

It would take us over an hour to get to Captain Devlin, even if we ran.

The Dread Pirate Calisto was an agent of the Second Ascension and a madman who had destroyed dozens of ships. He had cut the eye out of Illia's face, and he had almost killed Zaxis, Illia, Master Zelfree, and me.

And now he had Biyu.

I shoved Fain off my arm and stormed down the road, my pulse high and heat in my system worse than I had ever felt it. I didn't care what it took—I wouldn't let Calisto harm a little girl, not when I could do something about it.

"Volke?" Fain asked, his panicked tone laced with confusion.

"You get Captain Devlin and alert the Watch Battalion," I commanded. "I'll retrieve Biyu."

THE RETURN OF DREAD PIRATE CALISTO

"*Y*ou *can't,*" Fain said as he stepped in front of me. "If there's a fight—"

I pushed Fain aside a second time, harder than before. When our eyes locked, Fain hesitantly backed off, his protests dying.

"I'll get the Watch Battalion," he said.

With no more arguments, Fain draped himself in invisibility and dashed off. Fueled by anger, I headed in the opposite direction. I didn't know where they had taken Biyu or even where Calisto was staying, but I knew his ship, the *Third Abyss.* It was larger than most—a man-of-war style battleship with over 100 canons—and constructed using *ghostwood.* The special lumber created a perpetual fog, and once I reached the piers, there was no doubt in my mind I would either see the effects on land or out in the delta.

"My arcanist," Luthair said, his voice echoing from the darkness around my feet. "Do you intend to fight him?"

I stormed through the dock bazaar, my expression enough that people moved out of my way when they noticed me approaching. "I just need to rescue Biyu," I said, terse.

"You've improved your sorcery significantly since last you faced Calisto, but he's still a master arcanist. If we wait for the Watch Battalion, they'll help us retrieve Biyu with little risk to ourselves."

New Norra was a free port, which meant Calisto's previous crimes of piracy wouldn't be punished by the governing authorities, but any crimes he committed while in the city were fair game. Kidnapping a little girl meant the authorities could arrest him, but *would* they? Surely, there were strong enough arcanists to handle him, but perhaps he would escape them, or injure several innocents in the resulting melee.

I couldn't stand the idea of Calisto harming Biyu. Not even for a second.

"I'll try not to start a straight brawl," I said as I stepped around a group of merchants on black horses. "But I won't sit idle."

"If that's how you feel, I'll fight with you as one."

"Wait until we see him. Maybe we can attack him before he knows what he's dealing with."

"As you wish, my arcanist."

Luthair stayed close to my feet, blending with my natural shadow, ready to merge with me at a moment's notice.

Halfway to the piers, I spotted a man near a stand selling leather. He wasn't dressed in the usual clothes of the New Norrian citizens. He wore a long coat, baggy pants, and a thick belt. The weight of his many earrings stretched his ear lobe an extra inch, and his neck was marked with a distinct tattoo—three horizontal lines: ☰ . Fain had the same tattoo, as did anyone who served on Calisto's ship. It designated them as pirates and crewmembers of the *Third Abyss*.

I moved a man out of my path as I headed straight for the pirate. I never took my eyes off the cutthroat, even as I wove through the crowds traveling down the brick road. When I reached the man's side, I grabbed his shoulder and yanked him around, barely able to control my rage.

The grizzled pirate—who had more beard than face—regarded me with confusion.

"Where's Calisto?" I demanded.

The cogs of his mind rotated at half speed. He stared at me, absorbing the words like a rock absorbed water.

"Shove off," the pirate finally growled, his breath mist-thick with alcohol. He jerked his shoulder away. "You ain't gonna get anything from me."

I grabbed the front of his coat, and in one quick, powerful motion, threw him to the ground. I slammed his back against the bricks and loomed over him as I, once again, asked, "Where's Calisto?"

The patrons of the bazaar scattered, but no one fled the area. They watched from twenty feet away with a sort of morbid curiosity, whispering to each other and pointing. I suspected someone would get the Watch Battalion if anything got out of hand, but I was likely given the benefit of the doubt because I was an arcanist, and the pirate was not.

The cutthroat, shaken, reached for a pistol inside the folds of his coat.

I manipulated the shadows and ripped the weapon from his possession, the darkness tearing at his clothing in my haste. I tossed it across the street.

Defenseless, he held up both his trembling hands. "Calisto's at the *Waterside Notable*. It's r-right over there." Without moving too much, the pirate pointed one dirty finger down the road, straight to the cantinas and gambling halls.

I left the man on the bricks, doubt creeping into my thoughts. Calisto would have his crew, and inside a dock-side cantina, it would be a confined location. Then again, Biyu would be terrified in a dark and dank cantina meant for pirates. I had to go no matter what.

The *Waterside Notable* didn't stand out from the other sandstone buildings. It was two stories tall, shutters over the windows, a heavy lock on the door—standard fare for a drinking establishment. There was, however, a skull painted in gray over the front door. Men with cutlasses and pistols guarded the entrance, their arms crossed as they leaned against the outside wall.

I strode over, expecting to fight my way inside, but both men eyed my arcanist mark and allowed me entrance without a word. I stepped between them and entered the *Waterside Notable*, a cloud of smoke washing over me.

Three women played music in the corner, two with oboes and one with a string instrument similar to a lute. They wore the same long robes meant to block the sun, despite the fact that all the windows were shut.

A couple dozen individuals filled the room. There were high tables with tall chairs, and low tables with pillows on the floor for seating. Some tables even had a personal fire pit in the center where the patrons cooked their own meat. The vaulted ceiling made the place feel gigantic, and a small inside balcony was reserved for arcanists. The arcanists sat at the tables that overlooked the room, the railing posts spaced far apart, to allow for a generous view.

"Capt'n!" someone shouted. "Capt'n Calisto!"

A shiver ran down my spine as I panned my gaze across the cantina. The lingering smoke stung my eyes.

Conversations quieted down.

"Capt'n Calisto!"

"Is there a reason you're disturbing the whole cantina?" a man answered back, his voice familiar. It was smooth, but weighty—and laced with a threat he hadn't yet put into words.

Everyone stopped talking. Even the band silenced their instruments.

"We found her, Capt'n. The one you wanted."

"*Who*? If it's not someone important, tell me about it later. *I'm busy.*"

Then I spotted him.

Calisto sat in the balcony portion of the cantina, in the farthest and darkest corner. Others sat with him—his arcanist crewmates, I was sure—but that didn't matter. I tried searching for Biyu, but she was so short, and everyone in the nearby vicinity was so much taller.

I hurried around the edge of the room, moving past other patrons, trying to find her.

"It's the girl with the missing eye, Capt'n. She was here in the city. We got her."

"You *what*?" Calisto asked, his tone shifting to excitable. "She was *here*?"

Calisto stood from his chair, kicked it aside, and then leapt over the railing. He slammed onto the floor of the first story, landing between tables, with no apparent harm to himself. Several people jumped away, knocking over a table and several chairs in their panic. Desert milk spilled across the floor, the stink of alcohol hidden by the smoke.

"I can't believe my luck," Calisto said. "This trip *will* be interesting after all."

He stood straight, an amused smirk across his face. His arcanist mark contained a fearsome manticore, and unlike most arcanists, his glowed with an inner light. Calisto's eldrin was true form—something rare and precious, and it made his magics deadlier than before.

He wore a coat that hung to his ankles, one with crimson lion mane stitched into the collar and parts of the shoulder, accentuating his already broad shoulders. His copper-auburn hair complemented his dark shirt and black pants, and I knew he wore a trinket of poison immunity around his neck. He carried pistols on his belt, knives on his boots, and various bracelets on his wrists.

But...

A second realization hit me. His voice, his appearance—they were more than just *familiar*. My heart sank into my gut as the pieces of this puzzle fell into place.

The Dread Pirate Calisto was the man in Zelfree's memories.

He was Lynus.

That fact drained me of urgency. The rage in my system stagnated. Confusion replaced everything, and I wanted nothing more than answers. Why hadn't I realized sooner? I had met Calisto before, over a year ago, so why hadn't I put one and two together? In all the dream-memories so far, Lynus had been beaten, bloodied, or in the dark. I hadn't seen him completely, and his voice never registered as Calisto's.

I supposed I never expected Lynus to be anything other than a friend to Zelfree. Maybe I didn't want to see it.

How could this have happened?

Everyone inside the *Waterside Notable* cleared away from Calisto and the two goons who had called for his attention. That was when I spotted Biyu. She was trapped between the two pirates, each holding one of her arms.

"Here she is," one man said as he pushed Biyu forward.

Biyu stumbled a few steps, but managed to stay upright. She held her book close, both arms wrapped around it, as though it was something sacred and worth defending. She trembled as she tilted her head back to stare up at Calisto—she was four feet tall, while he was well over six.

Calisto rubbed at his copper-stubble-covered chin as he gave Biyu the once-over.

"What is *this*?" he asked with a sneer.

The pirate lackey motioned to Biyu's eyepatch. "You said you wanted the girl who was missing an eye. We found her in the bazaar, and—"

Calisto shot him an icy glare, ending the other man's will to speak.

"I wanted the *rizzel arcanist*," Calisto stated. "The one who attacked my ship, fool. I don't want whatever this is."

No one said anything and the tension thickened. Calisto clenched his jaw as he glared down at Biyu. He was muscular and athletic—she wasn't. He carried weapons and knew how to use them—she didn't. Someone like him, harming someone like Biyu, was unforgivable. My anger came back in full force. I couldn't allow it to happen.

"My arcanist," Luthair whispered. "There are others arcanists here, most on Calisto's side. You must be cautious."

Calisto grabbed Biyu's eyepatch and ripped it to the side. She gasped and tried to step back, but he held her in place.

I shoved past two patrons, my hand on the hilt of my blade—I'd get one good surprise attack, and now was the perfect time to test out Retribution's powers. Luthair offered more protests, but I knew he'd merge with me when the moment came.

"Didn't you already cut this girl's eye out?" one of the pirates asked. "Maybe you want the rest of her?"

"This isn't my handiwork," Calisto stated. "It's sloppy. Someone else did this."

Ten feet away from Calisto, I forced myself to slow, uncertainty creeping back into my thoughts. He sounded *much* more like Lynus when he had said that—the tone in his voice changing slightly, as though he might've been forcing himself to sound a certain way.

"I told you," a woman from the balcony area said.

I backed up, closer to the other patrons, and removed my hand from my weapon. My heart refused to cease its rapid beating.

Calisto glanced over his shoulder. "What's that?"

The woman leaned over the railing to speak, her low-cut shirt exposing more of her bosom than considered acceptable. "I told you Captain Redbeard had returned, didn't I?" Her long, black hair hung free, spilling over her shoulders. "He's trying to lure out a manticore and make it white. Maybe he's jealous of yours?"

I knew the woman. I had fought her in the past. She was Spider, Calisto's first mate and a kappa arcanist.

"Redbeard?" Calisto repeated. He had a growl on his breath as he muttered something I couldn't hear. "He thinks he can come back to these waters, does he? It's time I went and set the record straight. We have unfinished business."

The Dread Pirate Redbeard was famous for his exploits all throughout my island nation back home. He targeted ships with mystic seekers specifically—or anyone carrying magical resources. Redbeard's name had come in Zelfree's dream-memories, but I didn't realize they were one in the same.

"Where're you going?" Spider asked.

"I'll be back soon. Keep the game goin'."

Calisto stepped around Biyu and headed for the door.

He shoved a man aside, but before he exited out into the streets of New Norra, one of the pirates held up a hand.

"Wait, Capt'n! What should we do 'bout the girl?"

"Throw it back in the gutter where you found it," Calisto replied, cold and sarcastic. "What do I care?"

His crew didn't bother following that up with a response.

Then Calisto slammed out into the streets of New Norra, his superhuman strength on display when he busted one of the hinges straight out of the stone doorframe.

Manticore arcanists were in a league of their own when it came to physical prowess. I could still feel the sting of the time Calisto had broken my sternum in a single attack—even *while* I had worn Luthair.

With everyone focused on the door swinging by the last functional hinge, I shadow-stepped next to Biyu, wrapped my arm around her, and then pulled her into the darkness. I should've warned her about the suffocating sensation, but I didn't want to risk losing her. Instead, I quickly shifted through the shadows, feeling my way out of the cantina and around the corner into the dark alleyway between buildings. Only then did I exit the darkness with Biyu still in my grasp.

She gasped for air. I struggled with my loss of energy and burning magic, but I knew I'd survive.

"Are you okay?" I asked as I set her down. I knelt to get eye-level with her. "Did they hurt you?"

Biyu tried to fix her eyepatch, but her whole body shook, making it difficult. I reached out to help, but she flinched away, her shoulders bunching at her neck. Finally, with some effort, she managed to get it on over the scarred eye socket.

The alleyway was deserted. We were alone.

I scooted closer and offered my hand. "Biyu, I think we—"

"I'm sorry," she whispered, her throat tight.

I shook my head. "You don't need to apologize."

"I'm sorry."

The repetition confused me, so I decided to ignore it. "Biyu, let's get back to the *Sun Chaser*, okay? I can get us there fast. We just have to go through the shadows a few times."

She gulped down her breaths and then turned her one eye to me. "Please don't tell Captain Devlin." Her voice and chin both quavered. "Please. I'm so sorry."

"We need to tell him what happened. He has to know those pirates almost hurt you."

Biyu grabbed the sleeve of my shirt, silent tears falling from her eye. "Please don't. *Please*."

"I... don't understand. Why wouldn't we?"

"*I don't want him to throw me away*," she said, desperation in her voice. "Please. I'll be happy again. I'll be the perfect cabin girl. I won't make trouble for anyone."

"He wouldn't—"

"Yes, he would!" Biyu pulled herself onto me. She threw both her arms around my neck and squeezed tightly. "Everyone does," she said, her voice thick with emotion. "Mother said... Father said I wasn't.... I wasn't..." Biyu pressed her face into my shoulder. "I want everyone on the *Sun Chaser* to love me. I w-want... I want them to be my family. Don't tell them I broke the rules. *Don't tell them I caused trouble.*"

I embraced her, unsure of what to say.

For a long while, I just patted her back, hoping it soothed her to have a calming presence and a shoulder to cry on. In my heart, I knew a man like Captain Devlin wouldn't abandon Biyu because some pirates had abducted her. How could I convince Biyu of that fact?

"My arcanist," Luthair said from the darkness. "A member of the Watch Battalion approaches."

I released Biyu and stood.

She held her hands together, her face one of genuine fear. "Please don't tell."

"Don't worry," I said. "I'll handle this."

After one short trek through the darkness, I emerged at the end of the alleyway. Luthair stayed behind, no doubt to guard Biyu, and I appreciated his forethought. It would be beyond frustrating if something happened to her a second time.

An arcanist in black-and-copper armor headed straight for the *Waterside Notable*, her scimitar in hand. Fain walked along beside her, and the ground near her feet rippled like water, despite the fact that the street was made of bricks.

I jogged out to greet them. Fain pointed to me, and the arcanist turned with a harsh glower. Her mark had a stone golem laced through the points.

While I wanted Calisto punished for his many crimes, the city of New Norra would only take action on crimes committed here, and the kidnapping and release of a girl without any harm wouldn't amount to much. If I wanted to keep this a secret from Captain Devlin, as Biyu wanted, I couldn't report this. Calisto was lucky. This time. The last time.

"Everything is okay," I said to the member of the Watch Battalion. "Our cabin girl was mistaken for someone else, but I have her now. It was all just a misunderstanding."

The soldier narrowed her eyes. "You don't need assistance?"

"No," I said.

"And you don't want to take anyone to the hall of justice?"

"No. That won't be necessary."

The woman shot Fain a disgruntled glare. "Next time I'd appreciate it if a pair of arcanists attempted to solve their own problems before notifying the Watch Battalion."

"Yes, of course," Fain muttered.

The stone golem arcanist sheathed her sword and then turned on her heel. The rippling in the bricks followed her away from the *Waterside Notable*. Was it her stone golem hiding in the sandstone? Probably.

"It was a *misunderstanding*?" Fain repeated once the woman had disappeared down the street.

I motioned to the alleyway. "I'll tell you later. For right now, we're not mentioning this to Captain Devlin, do you understand? Not a word."

Although he gave me an odd glance, Fain eventually nodded. "If that's what you think is best."

23

A MOVING LABYRINTH

Biyu, Fain, and I left the dock bazaar and headed for the sky port, the heat of the day intense, even in the shadows. Although I hadn't been paranoid when we had traveled together before, now I couldn't help but examine everyone who drew near, no matter how frail or unassuming they appeared to be. I kept Biyu within arm's reach, concerned Calisto's pirates would search for her.

If she had been Illia, I would've done the same.

"Look forward, not back," Biyu whispered. "Have hope, not regret."

Wraith appeared by her side. Biyu lit up, despite his ghastly visage. He wagged his tail and allowed her to pet the skull over his face. For a few blocks, she said nothing, but once we rounded a corner and headed for the city walls, she muttered to herself once again.

"Look forward, not back. Have hope, not regret."

Fain stepped closer to me, and under his breath, asked, "Is she okay?"

"Biyu," I said.

She glanced up, her usual smile right back in place. "Yes?"

"How are you feeling? You keep repeating that phrase."

"That's my chant for when I'm trying not to be anxious or sad," she said matter-of-factly. "I memorized it when I was learning my letters. Don't you think it's good?"

"It's okay to occasionally be anxious or sad. You don't need to force the happiness."

Biyu frowned and folded her arms. "It's called *being optimistic.* That's what Karna said. She said I'm *optimistic.*"

My thoughts drifted to my home island. The Pillar—a 112-step staircase—had bits of wisdom for aspiring arcanists on every step. I half-smiled, reminded of one when Biyu spoke.

"Optimism," I said. "Without it, we lose ourselves to misery."

Biyu's eye lit up, and she somehow smiled wider, even though I thought that impossible. "Yes! Exactly."

"Are you sure it's good to tell her things like that?" Fain asked. He shoved his frostbitten hands into his pockets and exhaled. "It's foolish to skip around like a jester drunk on joy. If she realizes now how dark the world can be, she won't be as sorrowful in the future."

"I'm lucky I can get sad," Biyu said, her voice never losing its pep. "It means I have things I care about—things I don't want to lose. If I couldn't get sad, it would mean I didn't care anymore." She had said everything like a mother lecturing a child, but her cute voice and waggle of a finger made her seem more child-like than ever.

Fain shrugged, his expression telling me everything I needed to know. He didn't believe her, and he certainly didn't care for the advice from the Pillar.

As long as Biyu wasn't crying, I was content for the moment. I could always speak with Fain later.

We returned to the *Sun Chaser* without any other words between us.

Scarlet soaked the sky by the time we returned. The bells chimed, warning of the impeding cold, and the deckhands quickly loaded the airship with our new supplies. They avoided me as I walked by, and I didn't blame them. Perhaps it was best.

The moment we stepped onto the deck, Karna ran to meet us. Biyu locked up, frozen in place, her one eye wide. Had the others become worried about our disappearance? Would they yell at Biyu, like she feared? Or worse?

Karna didn't even look at Biyu. She grabbed my elbow and pulled me close.

"Vethica, Adelgis, the captain, and Jozé are all waiting in the captain's quarters," she said. "Come with me. You need to hear this."

I motioned for Fain to follow, despite Karna's quick look of irritation. She didn't voice her protest, though, which meant Fain's presence would be tolerated.

"Watch the girl," Fain said to Wraith.

His wendigo nodded his wolf-like head. Biyu took the moment to wrap her arms around his neck, half-burying her face in his fur. She trembled, but only slightly. Under her breath, she chanted the same thing she had used earlier to calm herself.

Convinced Biyu would be okay, I followed Karna down the stairs and below deck. She took me straight to the captain's quarters without delay. She offered nothing in the way of conversation, not even a whisper of explanation. Why had all the arcanists gathered? Were they changing their minds about helping me? Or were they fearful of the plague?

Karna opened the door to the captain's quarters and guided me inside. I thought it would be a bedroom, much like Karna's, Jozé's, and Vethica's quarters, but it was actually a sitting room with two glass cabinets filled with books, a large map table, and two couches. I suspected the door on the opposite side of the narrow room led to Captain Devlin's sleeping quarters, but I wasn't certain.

The two portholes allowed the red glow of sunset to invade the room. It affected the colors of the space, giving the place an almost sinister feel. Combined with the serious expressions of everyone already in the room, I found myself growing nervous.

Captain Devlin, Jozé, and Vethica sat on one side of the map table while Adelgis sat on the other. The map didn't have any markers, nor did it have the texture of the terrain. It was a simple map drawn on thick paper, the topography, latitude, and longitude all marked, but lightly.

I took a seat next to Adelgis, and right before Fain could sit on the other side of me, Karna slid onto the couch. Fain sat on the other side of her, his posture stiff.

"I'm glad Karna finally found you," Jozé said, his attention on me. "Vethica has some interesting news."

Before I could ask what, Vethica stood and threw down two pieces of paper across the table. I recognized the first—it was the map I had given her, the one I had taken from Theasin's lab. The second was a similar map, nearly identical, and officially labeled: MAP OF THE GROTTO LABYRINTH FOR THE GOVERNOR'S OFFICE.

"I know why no one has found the khepera," Vethica

stated. "It's because no one has actually made it to the center in over two decades."

Only Fain and I seemed shocked by the statement. The others didn't even react with raised eyebrows.

Vethica continued, "You probably don't know this, but the labyrinth isn't a fixed maze. It's constantly moving with timed rotations. There are over a hundred sections that spin and realign. Look here. This map shows how the walls connect, disconnect, and then reconnect when everything moves."

I sat forward and examined the maps. There were drawings that included latches, similar to doors that indicated the walls could move and then attach together.

"I don't understand," I said. "The entire labyrinth moves?"

Vethica nodded.

Clever. That would prevent people from easily finding a path through and would probably result in trespassers getting stuck.

I rubbed at my neck. "But... this map says the Grotto Labyrinth is nearly half the size of the city. That's gigantic. What powers the maze's movement?"

"The Lion's Tail River," Jozé said. "Look here, boy. This is where the river connects with the main power wheel for the maze. The flowing water keeps the walls and rooms spinning."

I stared at the drawings, surprised to see a detailed explanation of how the water was used to keep everything functioning.

"Wouldn't it need to be repaired?" I asked. "Or oiled, at the very least?"

"There are oil chutes in most of the temples around the city," Jozé said. "New Norra's caretakers are the ones who continue the labyrinth's maintenance."

While this was all fascinating, I didn't understand why it was so important. "Why does this mean no one has made it to the center? Wouldn't a path open eventually?"

Vethica pointed at both the maps. "Look. Can't see you see the differences? The governor's map contradicts Theasin's map. If you used the official map to make it to the khepera, you would end up in the wrong final chamber—at least, if Theasin is to be believed."

"My father doesn't make mistakes," Adelgis muttered.

"Which means the individuals who went to bond with a khepera never made it to them. And if you compare the turning of the maze with a calendar, you'll see that the maze is now always impassible whenever they hold the bonding ceremony in New Norra. Someone *intentionally* changed the flow of the maze to ensure people would never find the mystical creatures."

"How do we fix this?" I asked. "Do we tell someone? Damage the water wheel? Or stop the priests from doing their maintenance?" If the maze broke, it would eventually need to be repaired and recalibrated.

Vethica shook her head. "We should use this to our advantage. With Theasin's map, I can determine a path to the center. Since certain sections are spinning, the maze is impossible to solve the majority of the time. The correct path to the khepera nest is passable infrequently, but fortunately for us, one will open in three weeks' time."

"Three weeks?" I balked.

That wasn't long, I knew that, but when I had a limited amount of time, it felt like a life sentence. We would have to wait around in New Norra for twenty-one days? I didn't know if I could handle it. I already felt antsy, and we had only been here for half a week or so.

I turned to Adelgis. He stared at his lap, his long hair tied back, revealing his neutral expression.

"How long do you think it'll take you to find your father?" I asked.

"I think we should try this," he said. "Honestly, if we have a khepera, there's a chance Jozé could help create a trinket to keep you from succumbing to the negative effects of the plague."

"But—"

"*Volke,*" Adelgis spoke telepathically. "*I've discovered complications about my father's location. I don't think we can get there, not even with this airship. This option, while not guaranteed, is worth the risk.*"

I wanted to argue with him, protest his assessment. Hadn't we broken into the labs to get to Theasin? Hadn't we done everything to this point to find Adelgis's father? Why would we delay now? What had Adelgis found that caused him so much doubt, and why wouldn't he tell me?

"*I know you've shown me a lot of trust already, Volke, but please give me this last little bit. I think it's wiser to find a khepera than to head to my father.*"

The situation seemed less than ideal on many levels. Then again, finding a cure in three weeks would be a boon. Perhaps I had to just trust that we could do this.

"What about the Watch Battalion?" I asked. "How will we get into the maze when all the entrances are guarded?" And it wasn't *just* the guards. If any citizen in New Norra saw us going into the maze, they would alert the authorities. It was a sacred place, after all. How could we hope to avoid so many prying eyes?

"I've ventured into the Grotto Labyrinth before." Vethica turned to the captain. "Do you think you could distract the guards of the city like you did before?"

Captain Devlin relaxed back on his couch, weariness in his expression. Then he rubbed at the bridge of his nose and exhaled. "Probably. I could create a sandstorm again—it always keeps the locals preoccupied."

"Wait, what?" I asked.

The captain half-chuckled. "Roc arcanists can create a hurricane aura. It disturbs the winds and when used in a desert—like this—kicks up the sand."

"Isn't that a bit extreme? Sands caught in gale force winds can shred a person's skin or scrape through an eyeball. You could kill someone."

Captain Devlin held up a hand. "Calm down. New Norra has climate crystals built into the outer wall that calm the winds once they reach the city. My hurricane aura is strong, but those crystals significantly dampen the effect. Last time we did this, sand got everywhere, and it was a pain, but no one got injured. It's the perfect distraction."

I mulled over the new information and then asked, "You won't get caught?"

"Well, since the hurricane will be magical in nature, I'm sure it'll clue the Watch Battalion in on the fact an arcanist is creating it. If I'm caught causing the trouble, it'll mean more than a slap on the wrist, I guarantee."

Vethica sat back down on the couch, next to the captain. "You're willing to do it, though, right?"

The room remained silent as Captain Devlin considered her question. He stroked his chinstrap beard and then stared at the ceiling. "I'm willing," he said with an exhale. "But this'll be a risk, lass. If we want to make sure we don't get caught, I'll have to stop it within an hour or so—any longer than that and I know the Watch Commander will find me. Can you solve the whole damn maze in that time?"

"With the map—and Karna's help—I'll be fine."

Karna placed a hand on my knee and squeezed. "I told you my magics aren't useful for traps and puzzles. I think we should take Volke and his associates, just in case."

Although we weren't members of the crew, I understood why she wanted Fain, Adelgis, and me. My father's bum leg would prevent him from moving with any sort of haste, and if Captain Devlin had to maintain his hurricane aura, I imagined he had to remain outside—or else the hurricane would occur *inside* the maze.

There were no other arcanists on the *Sun Chaser*. The duty of helping Vethica acquire a khepera fell on the rest of us.

Adelgis and Fain turned their attention to me, inquisitive looks on both their faces.

"We'll help," I said.

The two of them seemed content that I had answered on their behalf. At least I assumed they hadn't secretly wanted me to refuse.

"All right, then," Captain Devlin said. "We'll do it."

24

THE MOTHER OF SHAPESHIFTERS

Dreaming.

I had to be.

The cold gloom of a strange forest enveloped me. Whereas I could see in darkness, Zelfree could not. I saw the dream-memory through his eyes, so now I could barely see anything. I stumbled down a rough path created by woodland creatures, the roots of trees trying to trip me at every opportunity. Fragments of moonlight pierced the canopy above, but just barely.

I stopped and leaned against a thick trunk, the bark sharp enough to poke at my skin through my coat. It took a few moments, but I managed to yank off my right boot and rub at the sole of my foot. The soreness told me I had been walking for a long while.

"What's wrong?"

Lynus.

I recognized his voice now more than ever.

Or should I call him *Calisto*? They didn't seem particularly similar, but the voice was unmistakable. They had to be one and the same.

"Nothing's wrong," I said. "How much longer until we reach the Mother of Shapeshifters?"

Lynus stepped close, but the absence of light made it difficult to notice details. His breath came out as warm fog, and when he pointed, all I saw was the silhouette of his arm and finger.

"Brennis died over there," Lynus said. "And Renk died a mile back. This portion of the woods is the beast's temporary hiding place."

"How did they die?"

Lynus lowered his arm and stepped closer to me, mere inches separating us. "Brennis had been fanged by something. His neck was swollen, the flesh purple. Seemed similar to a snake bite, but from something larger, like a bear. Renk looked as if his head had been smashed against a rock. They found bits of his brain a good ten feet away."

He spoke of the gore without any feeling or emotion—not even apathy, just matter-of-fact.

"Two different causes of death?" I asked. "How do you know the Mother of Shapeshifters was responsible?"

"Simple." Lynus chuckled. "Their clothes had been taken and skin from their chests, arms, and legs had been flayed off. Captain said it happened after they had died. He's sure of it—handiwork of the Mother of Shapeshifters."

"Is there anything else you can tell me?"

"'Bout what?"

"How they died?" I slipped my boot over my foot and laced it tight. "Any detail, no matter how insignificant you think it is, could be helpful."

"Tsk." Lynus opened his canteen and took a swig of his alcohol. After he gulped down a few mouthfuls, he exhaled and secured the cap back in place. "You and all your damn questions." He rubbed at his face. "I dunno. What kind of details?"

"Did you find footprints around the bodies? Something to indicate the Mother of Shapeshifters's size?"

"No." Lynus mulled over the question a bit longer. "Nothing around the bodies."

"Were there any broken twigs? Tousled shrubs? Cracked tree branches?"

"No. Nothing like that."

"So there wasn't a struggle," I muttered. "Interesting."

I had never heard of the Mother of Shapeshifters, and the conversation fascinated me. I wished I was still in contact with Master Zelfree, just so I could question him about the incident. Obviously, since he was a mimic arcanist and not a Mother of Shapeshifters arcanist, this plan had to end in failure, but he also wasn't dead, so...

"What about with Renk?" I asked as I tapped my toes on the ground before resuming my walk. "You said his head looked smashed in by a rock. Was the rock nearby?"

Lynus chortled. He kept my pace, but slightly behind me. "No rock. His skull was just flat on one side. Like... it had come from one strike."

"Or perhaps he fell?"

"Maybe. If he had gone head-first, like diving into the top of a boulder."

We walked for a few more minutes until a dense fog crept between the trees and overtook the narrow pathway. Lynus slowed his steps, and I did the same. Somehow, through the darkness and the mist, I knew *something* was nearby. Watching.

"Lynus," I whispered. "I'll handle it from here."

"Are you sure?" he asked.

"It's a trial of worth, right? I need to do it on my own."

Lynus shifted around in the darkness, a low growl on his breath. He eventually placed his large hand on my shoulder. Then he gripped tight.

"I've been meaning to tell you something," he whispered.

I placed my hand on his and met his gaze as best I could through the fog. "What is it?"

The direct question seemed to unnerve him. He jerked his hand from my grip and murmured a curse under his breath.

"Just know that... if anything happens to you, I swear I'll kill this creature even if it's the last thing I do."

This time, I laughed. "No need for poetic vows of vengeance just yet. I'll return as an arcanist. You'll see."

Although I spoke with utter confidence, the quick beat of my heart told me Zelfree wasn't as confident as he presented. And I could understand. What were we dealing with here? I had no idea, and it seemed failure resulted in a gruesome death, so there wasn't much time to piece together the puzzle.

I patted Lynus on the shoulder and then headed deeper into the forest. The fog thickened, and ambient noises of life increased in frequency, as though the creatures all around us were agitated. Owls hooted, crickets sang screeching songs, and bushes shook with the quick movement of small creatures.

A shape moved around in the distance, but it was much too dark to see what it was. What little moonlight there was had almost been lost. It was person-sized, though.

Then another shape moved at the edge of my vision. Then another. Three in total.

I swear they looked like scarecrows.

My steps slowed, and my breathing turned shallow.

Although I moved with caution, a sudden drop in the path caused me to tumble down a short hill. I landed at the base and then scrambled to get up into a sitting position, my pulse high. Mud covered my trousers, hands, and half my coat. I still couldn't see more than a few inches in front of me, but the swirls of movement in the fog increased.

"Hello?" I asked, my voice steady, despite the tension knotting in my chest.

"Another one," someone whispered.

"That makes three," another replied. "Soon we'll have a sibling."

Their words drifted through the air at different volumes, each raspy and laced with the harsh scratch of dry hay.

"Hello?" I asked again. "I've come seeking the Mother of Shapeshifters."

More movement, this time faster and excitable.

To my surprise, the fog parted and spread away, revealing a wide, circular clearing. The shadows of night clung to everything like tar, but at least the chill of water hanging on the wind had vanished.

"Welcome," a deep rumble of a voice said.

I locked up, frozen in place.

Straight across the clearing, somewhere hidden between the trees and covered in darkness, was a giant *creature*. Its silhouette didn't make sense. Several *limbs* hung off it at weird angles. Dozens of arms? Multiple legs? I couldn't tell. Was there a head? It just appeared like massive shoulders. When it had spoken, the rumble rustled the trees and sent shivers down my spine.

"H-hello," I replied in a quiet tone.

It opened two eyes, and they shone like a cat's when they caught the light just right. The eyes remained opened—no blinking, perfectly round—staring at me so intently it bothered me to match the gaze.

Even Zelfree couldn't handle the beast's stare.

I turned my attention to the ground.

"My name is Everett Zelfree," I said. "I'm searching for the Mother of Shapeshifters."

"Search no further. *I* am the Mother of Shapeshifters."

Hesitant, I glanced up, and instead of two eyes, there were now four. I looked away, my breath caught in my throat.

After a quick exhale, I continued, "I'm here to take your trial of worth."

"Is that so?" When the creature moved, it seemed as though the trees shuddered in response. It stepped closer, but not into the clearing.

I glanced up again and instantly regretted it.

Sixteen eyes—four of which appeared as though they were melting. They slid down the beast, still glowing bright with a cat-like quality. All of them unblinking. All of them on me.

I looked away. What was this thing? Was it trying to frighten me?

"You must do something for me," the Mother of Shapeshifters said, its tone becoming serious and haunting. The forest went quiet, the scarecrows in the forest stopped moving—the world tensed in anticipation.

"What is it?" I whispered. "I'll do anything."

When I had taken the phoenix trial of worth on my home isle of Ruma, there had been a task I had needed to complete. I had to gather a charberry and bring it to the phoenixes—only the most ripe and beautiful would do. What would a freakish shapeshifter require of Zelfree? And how would that determine his worth?

"You must tell me your greatest, deepest fear," the Mother of Shapeshifters said. "Then you will conquer it. Only once I'm satisfied with your victory will you be allowed to bond with one of my kin."

"Fear?" I whispered.

"That's right. Reveal to me your greatest fear." The creature moved closer, the trees shaking, their leaves rustling in protest. "Only then can I test you. Do you have the spine for it? Are you worthy of a shapeshifter?"

Snickering echoed from the fog in the forest.

I remained quiet and still. Was Zelfree thinking about his deepest fears? I didn't know if I could answer properly, if I were in the situation. What was *my* greatest fear? The longer I thought about it, the more abstract my answer became. Sure, I was afraid of the plague, and plague-ridden monsters, and I was afraid of death—who wasn't? Those weren't my greatest fear, though.

It was failure.

Failure to live up to the heroes of old. Failure to protect my friends and family. Failure to cure the plague in my veins —failure that I couldn't step up to the challenges life threw at me.

How would the monster make me face that? A certain piece of me wondered if this was all a trap. Or perhaps a test?

"Well?" the Mother of Shapeshifters asked. "What do you fear the most?"

It stepped into the clearing, a foul odor of rot and blood wafting all around it.

I half-gagged. Then I cleared my throat, and without looking up, I said, "Let me guess— Brennis said he was afraid of snakes. And Renk said he was afraid of heights."

The Mother of Shapeshifters didn't reply. It continued

closer and closer. Fallen branches snapped under its weight. Nothing slowed its movement. Then it loomed over me.

I ran a hand down my face, the pounding of my heart waning. What had Zelfree realized that made him so confident?

"But Brennis and Renk didn't die because they failed to overcome their fear. They died because they failed to realize what they were dealing with."

The creature chuckled, its breath hot and washing over my body. Drops of saliva and bits of chewed flesh dripped onto my shoulder.

Still, I didn't look at it.

"Oh?" the creature whispered, though due to its close proximity, it was easy to hear.

"Shapeshifters are known for their deception. A doppelgänger could be anyone. A mimic could have any magic. Isn't that their greatest strengths?"

"So, then—what is your answer?"

"Nothing," I replied. "I have no fears."

A blatant and bald-faced lie. Would the Mother of Shapeshifters accept that? Was Zelfree's conclusion correct?

Or perhaps the creature wanted to see someone's willingness to deceive.

The beast waited for a long moment before taking a step back. "There are only two correct answers, and you have chosen the answer of the *mimic*. Its potential is great, but it's dependent on others. Just like you."

The last statement struck me as interesting. Why had it said that?

The sound of slick liquid sticking and then unsticking filled the forest clearing. I closed my eyes and waited. A soft *plop* and then something landed in my lap. It was... round... and soft... and pulsated. Again, I found myself gagging.

"Farewell, Everett Zelfree."

Just then, I opened my eyes.

The Mother of Shapeshifters exploded into a swarm of birds, each one a different size. They shot toward the canopy of the forest, ripping through leaves and branches and shooting into the night sky at a fearsome pace. They left a pillar of moonlight streaming into the clearing, illuminating the area enough for me to see what had been dropped in my lap.

An apple-sized egg sac—the kind spiders left clinging to a wall.

The webs of the sac were laced in crimson, and the whole thing jiggled with each pulse from within. The fibers stuck to my trousers, and when I picked it up, the strings stretched out like melted cheese.

The sac felt hot to the touch, but not enough to burn. The web walls caved into my fingers, and I had to gently cradle it.

The fog cleared away, and the scarecrow creatures had disappeared. It was just me and the grotesque egg sac.

I was about to get up and leave when the sac jerked in place. It moved more than before, and then a crack formed down the center. I waited with bated breath, unblinking. The head of a kitten jutted out of the sac, its fur slicked with blood.

The kitten gasped and then pushed one of its paws out.

"Help," it whispered.

I snapped back to reality and pulled the sac apart from either end. The webbing ripped and the kitten had enough room to slide out. It meowed and squirmed, and I held it close, despite the sticky fluids dripping from its tiny body.

The kitten's tail—longer than normal—wrapped around

my wrist. For long moment, I just petted the baby animal, soothing it and muttering reassurances.

A strong urge overcame me. It was the offer to bond, and Zelfree took it without a moment's hesitation. His arcanist mark burned onto his forehead, branding him with a star that had no creature behind it. He had become a mimic arcanist.

"My arcanist," the kitten said with a mew. "My arcanist…"

I stroked her wet head with only two fingers. She was too small to use a full hand. "Shh," I muttered. "You're okay."

"My name…"

I stopped my petting. "I'm Everett."

"Traces. I'm… Traces."

"Everett?" Lynus yelled out from the forest. "*Where are you?*"

"Here," I called back.

It only took Lynus a few seconds to reach me. He leapt down the slope in the trail and landed in the clearing. He had to glance around before he spotted me sitting on the ground.

"I heard branches breaking," he said. "Are you okay?"

With trembling hands, I held up the bloody kitten. "I did it."

"What is that *thing*?"

"A mimic."

Lynus knelt by my side. "A cat? Not the Mother of Shapeshifters?"

"I don't think the Mother of Shapeshifters was even an option," I said. Then I smirked. "But at least she knew I was a cat person." I cradled my new eldrin close, my arms trembling—not from fear, but relief.

"Heh. Dogs are better."

I grabbed his shoulder. "Help me up."

Lynus did as I commanded, but I made sure to keep Traces comfortable at all times.

"Cats are better," I muttered. "They're lucky, independent, and capable of living anywhere." I offered Traces more pets as she drifted off to sleep.

"Cats, huh?" Lynus said.

"That's right. You'll see."

"Cats..."

A hand grazed the side of my face.

I opened my eyes, groggy to the point of confusion. Where was I? My dark-sight had returned, and I stared at the wooden boards of a bulkhead. Was this the *Sun Chaser*? It had to be. Where else would I have been?

"I thought you'd never wake up," Karna said, her voice low and straight into my ear. "I can't sleep." She took my hand and placed it on the natural curve of her side, right above the hip. "Keep me company."

AURA TRAINING

I rubbed at my eyes, but I couldn't clear away the exhaustion. Details from the memory-dream lingered in my thoughts, and I had a million questions. My mind muddled everything together the moment Karna slid her hand over my chest.

"Um," I muttered. I had forgotten her previous statement.

"It's been nearly a week since we started sleeping next to each other," she said, her silky voice practically lulling me back into a comfortable sleep. "You haven't asked me for anything more than this."

"Do you want me to?" I ran a hand down my face, shaking away the worst of the grogginess.

"I must admit, I was a little disappointed."

I sat up on the tiny mattress, my back stiff from the awkward positioning. I hadn't moved around much, to make sure Karna wouldn't be thrown from the bed, and it resulted in odd pains every time I awoke.

Combing my hair with my fingers, I took a couple of deep breaths.

Karna sat up next to me. "I would've said *no*," she said. "But I still wanted you to ask."

I stared at her through the dark. Her eyes remained unfocused, since she couldn't see in the gloom, but she crossed her arms and glowered in my general direction regardless. Her statement and attitude confused me—or perhaps I just wasn't accustomed to someone with her forwardness—but it seemed as though she didn't desire my touch, but my desperation. Or maybe *frustration* would be a better word.

I didn't appreciate her games.

"I know you're worried about spreading your illness to others, but I've spent my fair share of time around those who were plague-ridden," Karna stated. "You may not know this, but Vethica was infected for a long while. We still managed to enjoy each other's bed before she... well, before it became a problem we could no longer deal with."

"I don't like taking unnecessary risks," I muttered. "I can already hear William scolding me."

"William?"

"Gravekeeper William. He..." I shook my head. "Never mind."

I never wanted to disappoint William. He was the epitome of a father figure and just as much my role model as any heroes from legend. He had served his nation, loved only one woman with all his being, and cared for two orphaned children when no one else on our island would—the definition of chivalry and honor. What would Gravekeeper William say if I lost myself to lust and later regretted it?

Obviously, I wasn't forcing myself on Karna—it was almost the opposite. If I weren't tainted by the plague, perhaps this would be different. She was beyond beautiful. My whole body reacted when she was near.

But none of that was a good enough reason to risk spreading this malady.

Karna loosened a bit as she leaned against my side. She uncrossed her arms and placed a hand on my leg. "You're so high-strung. Don't you want to unwind?"

"That's not—"

"I can make you forget all about your worries," Karna said in a quiet, half-breathless voice. "And I'll just use my hands. Nothing else."

Somehow, even when I tried to deny her, Karna had a way with words that stilled my thoughts. My face reddened, and I was thankful she couldn't see me properly. I hated feeling *uncertain* and *feverish*. I found it hard to formulate coherent arguments when her fingers grazed my forearm.

Karna chuckled under her breath, soft and feminine. "Take off your clothes and lie down. Once you see it's harmless pleasure, you'll realize how foolish you've been."

I was running out of reasons to say *no*, and I didn't stop her from unbuttoning my shirt, even if I was worried that she would feel the exuberant beating of my heart. The thrill of the moment brought with it a heightened sense of perception. She still smelled of flowers, even though we had been sleeping for hours prior.

"My arcanist," Luthair said from the darkness, his gruff voice a jarring reminder of the outside world.

Karna flinched at the words and glanced around. She grabbed my arm, her eyes wide, but unseeing.

"I wish to make a formal protest," Luthair continued. "This goes against the wishes you've expressed in the past."

Her shoulders tensed as she slowly turned her attention

back to me. "Your eldrin is here?" The faux-curiosity in her voice betrayed her underlying irritation.

"He's always with me," I said. "He's been here every night."

"You didn't think to send him away?"

"No..." I rubbed the back of my neck. "I mean, I barely have any privacy nowadays. What does it matter if one more person knows what I'm doing at all times?"

Karna flipped back her long, blonde hair and glared at me. "Who else is here?"

"Well, he isn't *here*, but Adelgis can hear thoughts. Always. And I'm pretty sure he's not sleeping."

She gritted her teeth and turned away, her body becoming tenser with each word I spoke. "I had forgotten about your creepy little friend."

"And Fain is often invisible, hovering nearby. I doubt he's here now, but he's surprised me on a couple of occasions, so I'm not certain. If he revealed himself to be in the corner of the room, I wouldn't be shocked."

"You could have at least said something," Karna stated. "I'll have you know I sent my doppelgänger away every night so that we had time alone."

Although we were embroiled in a tense moment, the instant I heard the word *doppelgänger*, the events of the dream-memory came rushing back at full force. There had been doppelgängers in the woods all around Master Zelfree, and their scratchy hay voices echoed in my thoughts.

"Karna," I said. "Did you ever meet the Mother of Shapeshifters?"

She slid off the side of the narrow bed and stood straight, her posture stiff. "How do you know about that?" Before I could reply, she turned on her heel, facing away from me. "No one but... shapeshifters know of that."

"My master, Everett Zelfree, is a mimic arcanist and—"

"Zelfree? The renegade pirate?"

"Well, he was never really a pirate. He pretended to be one to help the Frith Guild." I waved away the comment. We were getting off-track, and I had a burning question I wanted to ask. "Do you remember what you answered when the Mother of Shapeshifters asked for your greatest fear?"

Karna walked away from the bed, more uncomfortable than I had ever seen her. She kept her arms tightly crossed, and her gait became stiff. "I don't want to talk about this." She shook her head. "I haven't slept, and your ability to change the subject is masterful." Karna flounced from the room, opening and shutting the door in one quick motion.

That was... bizarre.

I hadn't meant to *change the subject*, per se, but the mystery of the Mother of Shapeshifters intrigued me. What was that creature? It obviously wasn't a mimic or a doppelgänger, even if it was creating them. And it seemed unique —I had never heard of another one existing. Where had it come from? Where was it now?

I kicked my legs off the side of the bed and let out a long sigh.

"I'm sorry, my arcanist," Luthair said from around my feet. "I didn't mean to add an element of contention to the evening."

After another exhale, I tilted my head back. "What did you mean when you said this went against my wishes?"

"You told me on numerous occasions what you were looking for in a partner. And I was there when Atty Trixi- belle asked to be with you."

"Atty..."

I gritted my teeth. I had been trying to avoid thinking

about the other Frith Guild apprentices. It brought nothing but anguish, and Atty especially left a dull ache in my chest.

"I barely know her," I stated, anger lacing my words. "We didn't spend much time together, and when we started to change that, I was infected with the plague. So what does it matter?"

Luthair shifted through the darkness of the room. "Should I keep these comments to myself in the future?"

"No." I ran a hand through my hair. "I just... I thought I didn't have to rush anything with Atty. I could take it slow. I thought I had more time. Now even *thinking* about Atty... I'm just an idiot."

"You have more time than you realize. Nothing is set in stone."

"What're you trying to say?" I asked.

Luthair mulled over my question before saying, "All I know is that I want you to live without regrets, and I fear your dire situation may lead to you acting in ways you normally wouldn't. I merely wished to remind you that I intend for us to overcome this. Please, just don't act rashly."

"I'll try. Thank you, Luthair."

***

Days crawled by.

Karna refused to speak to me about the Mother of Shapeshifters and even released me from her request to share her room. After that, I couldn't find her, but I supposed she *was* a doppelgänger arcanist. For all I knew, she remained nearby as one of the crew.

Why wouldn't she speak to me about her trial of worth?

I tried to distract myself with training or reading, but nothing worked. My mind wandered, and multiple alternative plans took root in my thoughts. Out of the many preposterous schemes, one seemed plausible, and I had to speak with Jozé.

I knocked on the door labeled *Blacksmith* and waited.

My father answered a good thirty seconds afterward, the sound of his heavy steps easy to detect, even through the bulkhead. When he caught sight of me, his eyes widened, and then he offered a tepid smile.

"What can I do for you, boy?" he asked. He wore nothing but loose trousers and a button-up shirt, though most of the buttons remained undone. His relaxed stance and stubble told me he probably hadn't been expecting visitors.

"Can I speak with you about the Grotto Labyrinth?" I asked.

He opened the door to allow me inside. His phoenix sat on her perch, her head curled around her body and her beak tucked behind a wing. Strange noises squeaked out of her occasionally, but otherwise, she slept soundly.

Keeping my voice low, I asked, "Do we truly have to wait eighteen more days before we can explore the Grotto Labyrinth? Why not enter now and force our way through the moving parts of the maze?"

Waiting drove me crazy. Every hour that ticked by added to my anxiety. Were the khepera worth it? Adelgis seemed to think so, but the price of patience was worse than the price of a glass of water in the desert.

"I can step through shadows," I continued. "It allows me through narrow spaces. Even the slightest crack between moving walls would allow me to slip by."

"It won't work," Jozé stated. "The walls of the Grotto Labyrinth are made from nullstone. It'll stop all magic."

"Nullstone? I thought the nullstone mines were in Thronehold. That's hundreds of miles from here."

"New Norra used to be ruled by the Argo Empire. During that time, nullstone was brought in for all sorts of reasons—the main one being the Grotto Labyrinth. The khepera are considered sacred. I told you that."

Although this didn't change anything, the knowledge upset me. I turned back for the door, uninterested in further conversation.

"I see," I said, curt. "Thank you."

"Wait."

I hesitated at the door.

"Why don't you have a drink with me?" Jozé asked. "I can get you water if you like."

"I can't waste my time while I wait for the khepera," I said as I opened the door, my grip on the handle tight. "If I sat and had drinks, it'd only add to my stress."

"Okay. Why don't I show you more about magic? You don't have your mentor anymore, right? You need someone to help you along."

"We don't have any more star shards. How can we imbue any more items?"

Jozé chortled as he stepped closer. "We don't need to practice imbuing right now. We can focus on something else. I saw you at the Sovereign Dragon Tournament. You never used your eclipse aura. You can't manifest it, can you?"

I shook my head. "Master Zelfree said learning how to use an aura was one of the last things an arcanist should focus on."

"But you need a challenge, right?" Jozé tapped my chest. "What's more challenging than learning a complicated magic? You won't have time to dwell on... well... *lost time.* Trust me."

Although I hadn't come to him seeking a distraction, my father presented a good argument. If I practiced creating a magical aura, I would at least have a new tool in my box, should the situation arise. Knightmare arcanists created a forced eclipse whenever they manifested their aura—the magical darkness snuffed out lights and empowered anything that used shadows. As an added benefit, the enhancements from the eclipse aura negated the ill effects of my second-bonding.

It would be helpful to master, and I wouldn't feel like I was wasting my time.

"I helped Vethica and Devlin develop their magical auras," Jozé said. "I'm damn near an expert on the matter."

Also impressive. Auras were the most difficult to master. An aura wasn't like imbuing or evocation or manipulation—it affected a large area and could even do things like bringing added prosperity to a people. The potential was great, but so were the requirements for mastery.

"You helped the captain with his hurricane aura?" I asked. "What does he use it for besides distracting the city of New Norra?"

"He'd capsize sailing ships or defeat enemy airships. It's a useful aura on the offensive and less for everything else."

"And what does a thunderbird aura look like?"

"They create a *thunderclap aura.* Lightning fills the air and strikes out at most metals. Anyone carrying anything—and especially those wearing armor—are caught in electric powers that lock up their muscles."

"*All* muscles?" I asked.

"It depends on the strength of the arcanist," Jozé said with a shrug. "But I've seen thunderbird arcanists fight armored soldiers. If those soldiers were wearing full plate armor, they were as good as dead, and any metal weapons attracted enough power to keep people paralyzed for a prolonged time."

A roc's hurricane aura was devastating—hurricanes always were—but what if there was a thunderclap aura mixed into it? A terrible one-two combo that would end most non-magical threats.

Perhaps my father could interpret my furrowed brow, because he tilted his head and smirked.

"Blue phoenixes have an exhaustion aura," he said. "Years ago, when Vethica, Devlin, and I were attacked, we combined our efforts. It worked well... until it didn't." Jozé chuckled to himself as he shifted his gaze to the floor. "Let's just say the attackers didn't know what hit them, but we hadn't anticipated the backlash to our own forces. It was an *interesting* couple of weeks after that."

My father's reminiscing got me smiling. "Sounds similar to some of those old tales I used to read."

He lifted an eyebrow. "Hm. Well, maybe they're not as bad as I thought they were."

I had been anxious and frustrated before, but now that I had spoken with my father, the stress melted from my being.

"When do we start?" I asked.

"Tomorrow night. When it's cold. Out on the sand dunes."

"Do you mind if I invite Adelgis and Fain?"

He shrugged. "I don't know if they're ready for this kind of training, but they're more than welcome to try."

EQUALIZER

The freezing sand dunes of the desert stretched on for miles, all the way to the horizon in both directions. It reminded me of the ocean, especially since the glow of the moon gave the sand a blue hue. The dunes were waves frozen in time, forever rolling with the wind.

I disliked walking on the desert sands. It wasn't like the beach, where the water kept everything packed together. The desert shifted under my feet more often than not, and it required more of my attention than I had anticipated. I shadow-stepped whenever possible, thankful for the night, even if the clear skies kept it lighter than usual.

Fain had a difficult time, but he never said a word. He trudged through the dunes, sand filling his boots with each unstable step. Adelgis followed close to him, even going so far as to keep a hand outstretched and half on Fain's shoulder. He wobbled a few times when he went up a sandy hill, but he, too, never complained.

I imagined it was even more difficult for Jozé, but he had walked out here long before I had. He and Tine waited on the top of a crescent dune, his coat fluttering in the winds, embers from his phoenix flaring in the night.

He smiled as I drew near.

"There you are," he said. "It's a good night for practicing."

A harsh chill swept over us. I rubbed my arms. "If you say so."

Fain and Adelgis made it to the top of the dune a minute later. Adelgis shivered the entire time, but Fain didn't show any indication he was bothered.

Although I had only known him a short period, I could already tell when things genuinely interested my father. Jozé clapped his hands and rubbed his palms together, his enthusiasm apparent in the way he glanced around, his dark eyes scanning the environment. He obviously loved magic—whether imbuing, studying, or discussing it. He had been excited to craft my sword and discuss the khepera, and now, when we were going to study auras, he couldn't stop smiling.

"*Our fathers are a lot alike,*" Adelgis spoke telepathically.

I nodded as the realization hit me.

They *were* similar.

"Take a seat," Jozé said as he motioned to the dune. "Don't worry about the sand. You can wash up afterward. And sit on your coat."

I did as he instructed, even though I thought it strange. "We won't have to stand to train?" I asked.

"No. Auras aren't like evocation or manipulation. They require more inner focus." Jozé removed his own coat and placed it on the sand. Then, with some awkward movement, he sat down, keeping his bad leg outstretched. "I want you to imagine an empty cup slowly being filled with water.

When the liquid reaches the lip, it clings there for a moment before finally spilling over."

Fain, Adelgis, and I—all seated on coats, our legs crossed—waited and listened. I imagined the cup, though I found it difficult to visualize while under such stress.

Jozé leaned forward. "Pretend *you're* the cup, and your magic is the aura. You must fill your being and then allow the magic to pour from you and affect the environment."

"That's it?" Fain asked, his brow furrowed. "That sounds easy."

"Well, you might succeed in creating an aura quickly, but that's not why it's difficult to master. Ya see, a lot of arcanists learn this technique incorrectly. They *force* the magic outward as fast as possible, and when that happens, you'll create an aura, but you'll have to focus on it—like with your evocation. However, if you've created an aura properly, you won't have to force it. The effects will happen naturally, and you'll be able focus on other things while it persists."

I had only seen a knightmare's eclipse aura three times in the past—once with the Grandmaster Inquisitor, once during my fights in the Sovereign Dragon Tournament, and once when the castle at Thronehold had been attacked. When the Grandmaster Inquisitor made his aura, he did so with little effort. The eclipse *happened* and then remained, no stress to him. During the tournament, when the Inquisitor's apprentice had created an eclipse aura, it obviously had required a vast majority of his concentration.

Which meant the apprentice had been doing it incorrectly.

It had still worked, it had just been inefficient, and that was the reason he had lost.

"What's the first step to manifesting an aura correctly?" I asked, eager to test myself with this new challenge.

Jozé sat straight. "Clear away your thoughts and emotions. You need to be an empty cup."

Adelgis dropped his gaze to his lap, his shoulders slumped.

Could he clear his thoughts when he heard everyone else's? *Perhaps if we were all blank, he would be as well.*

Without his coat on, Adelgis's shivering intensified. Fain let out a soft sigh before picking up his coat and throwing it over Adelgis's shoulders. Then Fain sat back down in the sand—*I could only imagine it would get everywhere.*

When Adelgis gave him an odd look, Fain just turned away, like an entire silent conversation and argument had happened between them in a matter of moments.

"You should all focus," Jozé said. "Try it."

I closed my eyes and took a deep breath. The cold of the night burned my nose, and it took me several minutes to shake off the lingering concerns of the chill. Once tangled in my own thoughts—far from the world around me—I inhaled again.

At first, I thought I would have a clear mind in a matter of moments. Then I wondered...

What would a wendigo aura look like?

What would an ethereal whelk manifest?

What would Illia's rizzel create?

Illia...

During the attack on Thronehold, I had seen a plague-ridden rizzel. It had manipulated gravity—a power Illia hadn't yet mastered. Had she learned it now? Was Master Zelfree showing her how that would be useful both on the battlefield and off?

What would her aura look like? Would she control the gravity for miles around? Would she create the ability for others to teleport? Would something else happen?

I was certain, whenever she learned of her ability, Illia would master it. She wasn't like Atty—who wanted perfection—but Illia was dedicated, capable, and intelligent. There was no doubt in my mind she would become a stunning master rizzel arcanist.

But would I ever get to see it?

"You aren't clearing your thoughts, Volke," Adelgis said.

I gritted my teeth and tried again.

How quickly would Illia have cleared her thoughts?

I shook my head, silently chastising myself. It was difficult to imagine life without Illia, and if I couldn't find a cure for the plague, I would never see her again.

Again, I reprimanded myself for stray thoughts. What was wrong with me? Images of her filled my head. Illia smiling, Illia worried, Illia laughing, Illia determined—I tried never to think of her because of the ache in my chest, but whenever I did, it was hard to imagine anything else.

"Jozé," I said as I opened my eyes. "What if I can't completely clear my thoughts?"

He frowned. "Instead of imagining yourself as a cup, imagine you're a tea kettle. Have you ever seen what happens to water in a tea kettle?"

I nodded.

"Well, your thoughts and emotions will be the fire under the kettle. If you're not in control, you risk having the aura become *unstable*, for lack of a better word." He waved away his own statement. "But don't worry about that. Take your time. Relax. Focus. The tea kettle is an analogy I use to warn arcanists against manifesting an aura when under duress. You're not under duress right now, right?"

I wasn't under duress, but...

"I'll try again," I muttered.

I closed my eyes, determined to master this first step before proceeding to the next.

An entire week of training, and I still couldn't clear my thoughts away to nothing.

Neither could Adelgis, it seemed. Was I the cause of his failure because I couldn't clear my thoughts? He wouldn't tell me. He just said he found it difficult to concentrate, and each night we practiced, he sat silently and still, never voicing his situation to my father.

Fain said he had cleared his thoughts, and while he had moved on to the next step—allowing his magic to spill out into the environment—he had yet to manifest an aura. I didn't know what a wendigo arcanist would create, and the mystery excited me. I figured Adelgis would know, or perhaps he could look it up, but I refrained from asking him, just to keep the sense of surprise.

On the seventh night, when I returned to the airship, two of the deckhands greeted me with smiles. Caught off-guard, I returned the gesture, but they had never done that previously, even before I had accidentally lashed out with magic at one of them.

When I went below deck, Tammi, the ship's surgeon, waited near the storeroom door, a tray held in both hands. I had forgotten how short she was until I walked up next to her—she had to be a full foot shorter than me, perhaps a foot and a half.

She held out the tray, and I noticed it was covered by a shallow lid. "I came to give you some food for whenever you wake up next," she said.

The airship's jerky and crusty vegetables made my

stomach churn. I had used most of Karna's money just to purchase fresh food from the markets of New Norra.

"This is from the galley," Tammi said. "Our cook made it special for you." She lifted the lid and showed me an assortment of breads, dumplings, and fresh jerky. It smelled beyond wonderful, to the point I could taste the savory flavors with a deep inhale.

"Your cook knows how to make things that don't taste like salt?" I quipped.

Tammi offered a nervous chuckle. "The galley members had been feeding you and your friends the food they'd usually throw out."

That explained a lot. "Why?"

Tammi shook her head. "It won't happen anymore. Everyone knows about what you did for Biyu."

"You mean, she told you about the Dread Pirate Calisto?"

"Yes." Tammi held out the tray a second time. "She told us not to tell the captain, but most of the crew knows now. It's only a matter of time before he does, too."

I took the tray, happy to have any food that wasn't garbage. "Thank you."

Tammi shook her head. "Everyone here cares for Biyu like family. Thank you for looking out for her. We hope you'll find whatever you need to cure yourself."

I nodded, and Tammi stepped around me and headed for the stairs, though this time she didn't flee as though she thought her life were in danger.

It did a lot to ease my tension.

On the fourteenth night, I not only thought about Illia, but also about Zaxis, Hexa, Atty, and Master Zelfree. Adelgis hadn't given me any more dreams, so my imagination ran wild with all sorts of possibilities and scenarios.

In my frustration, I tried forcing the magic, despite what my father had warned about, but even that didn't work. I just hurt myself with my double-bonded pains and left the desert feeling sore.

When I got back to the airship, I had yet another strange thought. I waited until my father returned to his quarters before approaching him. I knocked on his door, and he let me in with a smile.

"Let me get us some drinks," he said.

"No, thank you."

"Don't worry. It'll help you with this aura manifestation, trust me."

"I didn't come here to talk about that," I said as I took a seat at his table. After imagining all my old friends and hometown, my thoughts had gone to one last strange place I thought I had locked away forever. "I was hoping you could tell me something about my mother."

Jozé, in the middle of pouring himself some rum, nearly lost his grip on the bottle. He fumbled with it, spilling alcohol across his glass, and then onto the table. He chuckled to hide his mistake, but his hands shook.

"Your mother," he repeated. "That's a formal way of addressing her."

"I can't remember her name."

I hated that I couldn't, but it was the truth.

Jozé rubbed at the back of his neck while he took a seat. "Right... Her name was Aarona."

I waited, hoping he would just elaborate.

"She was born on the Isle of Ruma," Jozé continued. "And she was branded a thief at an early age. Her family died at sea, and when she had problems with her forced apprenticeship, she turned to petty theft to get by."

"Oh…" I muttered. It was probably an accurate rendition of her history, but I had been hoping for something more.

Perhaps Jozé sensed this, because he continued, "When I met her, I knew she was very clever and resourceful. I wasn't a member of the community, so I didn't have any preconceived bias against her, and Aarona appreciated that. We became fast friends—she helped with my studies of the phoenixes, and before long, we became something more."

Jozé said nothing else on the matter.

I held my hands together, my fingers interlaced. I waited a long while, hoping he would continue, but when it became clear he wouldn't, I decided to move on with the conversation.

"I can't clear my thoughts," I muttered. "I'm always thinking about the other apprentices, or Master Zelfree, or the Frith Guild."

Jozé nodded. "You miss familiar things."

The moment he said those words, I knew them to be true. I *did* miss familiar people and places. That's all I wanted. "What can I do about this?" I asked.

"Memories are to cherish, not dwell on. You need to treat them as gifts and not as something to return to."

The statements cut hard, but it didn't help. I couldn't escape the memories—*that was the problem.*

Jozé pushed himself up and waved around a pointed finger. "I think you're on the right track. You need to focus all your effort and energy on something else. Don't let your mind wander. Keep it controlled." He walked over to a coat rack tucked in the corner of the room.

His phoenix lifted her head. "What're you doing, my arcanist?"

"Getting something for the boy. Don't worry."

She fluffed her brilliant blue feathers and said nothing more.

Jozé grabbed a holster and pistol from a hook on the rack. He hobbled back, retook his seat, and then placed the gun on the table.

"Your birthday is coming up, right? You'll be seventeen?"

I nodded.

He pushed the holster and flintlock pistol over to me. "It's a trinket. I made it myself." Jozé pointed to the bird emblem he had branded onto the grip. "I want you to have it."

Although I wasn't certain about accepting, I picked up the weapon and removed it from its holster.

The weapon had a beauty most didn't. The grip was made of scarlet wood, while the trigger guard, hammer, and barrel were made of silver and crafted brass. The fine artistry of the swirled hammer and wave-like trigger made the gun feel like someone's personal project.

"Careful," Jozé said as I slid my finger over the trigger. "That pistol doesn't need gunpowder. I imbued magic so that only a bullet was required for firing. It still only shoots one at a time, but it's a much faster reload than modern flintlock weapons."

I turned the pistol over and examined every inch. Emblazoned on the side in a shimmery fire, just like my sword, was a single word: EQUALIZER.

"Is this the pistol's name?" I asked.

Jozé nodded. Then he got up again and walked over to his wooden cabinet. "Oh, I almost forgot. This is the best part." He opened the cabinet and withdrew a small leather pouch. "You'll need these." He tossed the pouch onto the table. It landed with a heavy *thunk*.

I picked up the pouch. Tiny balls rolled around inside. "Bullets?" I asked.

"Not just *any* bullets." Jozé walked to the end of the table and leaned on it. "They're made with the venom of a manticore. Do you have any idea what that does?"

"It neutralizes magic," I intoned.

"That's right." He smiled. "You're a quick study."

The Dread Pirate Calisto had a manticore eldrin, and I remembered with frightening clarity what the venom of a manticore was capable of. Once injected, an arcanist couldn't use their abilities—it was why Master Zelfree had so many scars on his body. Calisto had tortured him and then used his manticore's venom to prevent Zelfree from healing.

And they were once friends?

I narrowed my eyes, glaring at the pouch, but not really seeing it.

What had happened between them?

"There are only ten bullets," Jozé said, oblivious to my dark thoughts. "And if you hit someone, there's only enough venom to prevent their magic for a few seconds at most. That doesn't sound like a lot, but—"

"It's a long time in a fight," I interjected. And it was enough of a *surprise* that it would give me the advantage in a tricky situation. "Thank you for this."

"Of course." Jozé ran a hand through his black hair. "I'm sorry... I missed so much of your life before."

"Don't bother apologizing. It doesn't bother me anymore."

He knocked on the top of the table, almost like a nervous tic. "Well, just know that I'm impressed with everything you've done so far. You're young, but you're talented."

I nodded, absently staring at the pistol.

Talent alone wouldn't save me. I had to succeed in finding this khepera, no matter what.

Finally, the day arrived.

I hadn't slept the night before. I had rested in my hammock, staring at the ceiling, waiting for the sun to dispel the cold with the arrival of morning. I remained fully clothed, with both my sword and my pistol ready at a moment's notice. I even had Theasin's pink and tannish sands in the pouch of my belt. If anyone was injured, I would have "medicine" for them.

Adelgis was already awake. He waited, sitting on his hammock, his ethereal whelk floating in the air and casting lights across the room.

Fain snored. He always managed to sleep, no matter the pressure.

"The captain is preparing for his hurricane," Adelgis whispered. "He'll create it before the sun rises, while the majority of the city is already in their homes. Once the Watch Battalion has taken shelter, we'll make our way to the Grotto Labyrinth."

"Won't we get caught in the hurricane?" I asked. "Or should we head to the entrance now?"

"If the Watch Battalion sees us, they'll remove us from the streets." Adelgis stood from his hammock. "Karna has a way for us to move through the gale-force winds. We'll travel as a tight group and enter the maze together."

I leapt from my hammock, my heart pounding hard. "Good. I'm done waiting. Let's go get us one of these khepera."

INTO THE MAZE

Karna and Vethica waited for us on the deck of the airship. They spoke in hushed whispers, so engrossed in their conversation that they didn't notice Adelgis, Fain, and me approaching. The darkness before the dawn, unique in its opaqueness, likely also hid us as we traveled across the deck.

Vethica wore thick trousers, a wide belt, and a rough tunic. Slung over her shoulder, and heavy from the contents, was a leather satchel. Attached on her belt was her zigzag dagger. She carried nothing else, not even a hat to protect her red hair and pale skin from the sun.

Karna, on the other hand, seemed more concerned with maneuverability over protection. She wore thin clothes, and little of it, not even a shirt. Her chest was bound by wool straps, I assumed for modesty and to keep everything in place. Her boots covered most of her shins, but her trousers were closer to breeches—tight and flexible. That was it.

The howl of fierce winds picked up in the desert. Although I had only lived through a handful of major storms, I knew the warning signs well. The air smelled of minerals, animals vanished, leaving behind an odd silence, and small objects shuddered. This was a desert, and not my home island, but the signs were the same.

Fain tucked his hands into his armpits. "How are we making it through the storm? I know the captain said it wouldn't be rough in the city, but I don't want sand in my eyes, either."

"With this," Karna said as she reached into Vethica's satchel. She withdrew a chain necklace and amber talisman. Inside the amber was a feather—or at least a piece of one. "It's a roc feather imbued with thunderbird magic. It'll cause the winds to avoid us."

"Is that right?" Fain gave the trinket a quick glance, but his attention went straight to Karna's "outfit" afterward. When I gave him a pointed look, he turned his gaze to the cloudless sky.

Adelgis held out his hand. "May I see the item?"

Karna handed him the amber pendant, and Adelgis turned it over in his palm. The feather inside was tiny and curled, and I wondered why they used that feather instead of one of the roc's giant wing feathers.

"Did you make this, Vethica?" Adelgis asked.

She replied with a curt nod. "Jozé helped."

Adelgis handed it back.

The winds ripped through the desert dunes, carrying sand straight into New Norra. Giant crystals built into the city walls glowed with an inner magic the moment the hurricane became too powerful. They dampened the weather, shielding the city. Captain Devlin had been right— sand everywhere—but the storm wasn't strong enough to damage the buildings. The denizens of New Norra locked everything down tight, keeping the inside of their homes safe from even the inconvenience of sand.

The trinket Karna held created an invisible bubble, no more than five feet in diameter, diverting the winds around us, preventing our small group from being affected.

"We should go now," Vethica said. "The Watch Battalion is already moving."

She pointed to the city walls, and the guards typically stationed at the steps had run into the streets to help foreigners get into safe places. Most grumbled and protested, but they eventually did as they were told.

We made our way as a group, staying close together to fit inside the protection of the roc talisman. Wraith, invisible, ran into my legs more than once, but I kept my balance.

"Sorry," he muttered, a dog-like growl in his voice.

The more ferocious the hurricane became, the harder it was to hear anything. The talisman protected us, but the howling of the storm still echoed down every street and alleyway. Shutters rattled in their sills. We jogged our way to the Grotto Labyrinth entrance, never encountering another person.

Our distraction had worked perfectly.

Once inside, we remained close, even as we descended the stairs. Glowstones on the walls illuminated the path with a gentle golden light.

The steps, carved with sandstone, had been decorated with etchings of scarabs, giving the staircase texture, which helped prevent slipping. Once we were thirty feet down, the roar of the hurricane became a distant buzz. The air smelled of dirt after the rain, and I took a deep breath, enjoying the freshness of it.

Another thirty feet down and we reached the bottom. I took a moment to glance back at the staircase—I had never imagined the Grotto Labyrinth would be this deep.

Vethica withdrew the map from her satchel, her hands trembling. "This is it. We're so close now."

A single hallway sat before us. The walls had the appearance of natural caves, but glowstones were embedded in the ceilings and inside most of the cracks, keeping everything alight, though not completely. Dark shadows clung to the rocks.

Beads in the shape of scarabs hung from the ceiling on a silver string, sparkling in the natural light. They looked like stars, and whenever one twisted or moved, it twinkled. The entire area had a mystical presence, and I reveled in the beauty.

"This place is sacred," Adelgis said. "We should endeavor not to touch anything we shouldn't."

Fain, who had been staring at one of the scarabs, let out a forced huff. "Fine, Moonbeam. I won't take anything."

"I want to go first," Vethica said as she held the paper close to her chest. "I need to complete every room and puzzle without assistance."

"That'll slow us down," Adelgis said. "If we combine our knowledge and help each other through the maze, we'll have it done in half the time."

"*No.*"

Everyone stared at Vethica, obvious confusion written on each face. Her outburst seemed unwarranted. It took her a moment to calm herself.

"Those who want to bond with a khepera must complete the maze without anyone else's help," Vethica said. "You can all help each other, but *I* have to do this on my own."

Fain and Adelgis turned to me, as though waiting for my judgment. Karna, who hadn't spoken to me much over the last few weeks, didn't acknowledge my presence. She simply placed a hand on Vethica's shoulder. "We understand. Go ahead, but stay close enough that we can follow you through the maze."

"Thank you," Vethica said with a slight smile.

She ran ahead, traveling down the long, cave-like hall. Once she was twenty feet away, we started after her.

Were the traps of the Grotto Labyrinth deadly? I hoped not.

The long corridor went on for some distance, and a part of me wondered how this was a maze. As though the world could hear my thoughts, we entered a rocky chamber with several branching paths—*seven*, to be precise—and that shocked me.

How *large* was this maze?

Vethica stood at the mouth of the fifth pathway. She examined her map, double-checked it by counting the entrances, and then ran off down the hall. The grinding of gears hummed all around us, but it wasn't loud, just constant sound, like conversations in a tavern or crickets out in the woods. Was the maze moving right now?

I stopped and examined a wall, trying to find signs of machinery, but there was nothing. When I attempted to manipulate shadows into the cracks, I couldn't. My father had said the walls were made with nullstone, and now I understood. They didn't create an aura, like at the Thronehold castle—they just prevented magic from harming the labyrinth's structure.

"My arcanist," Luthair said. "You must hurry. The others are already on their way."

I nodded and followed after.

When I rejoined Karna, Fain, and Adelgis, they were waiting at the end of the hallway, standing in front of a large sandstone door. It was tall, at least eight feet, and plain— smooth from top to bottom except for the hand holds to push it aside. I took a position next to Adelgis as he smoothed his black hair.

"Vethica is inside," he said. "She's attempting to cross a pit."

"What kind of pit?" Fain asked.

"One with a jagged bottom. Falling would hurt, but it probably wouldn't kill her."

Fain rubbed at his nose. Then he crossed his arms. "You know what would be fun? If *we* attempted all the obstacles as non-arcanists would."

"Oh?" Karna asked, one eyebrow playfully raised. "You think you can overcome the Grotto Labyrinth? I find that unlikely."

"It'd be amusing to try. What say you, Volke?"

"I'm willing to attempt it," I said. What was the harm?

Adelgis lifted his hand, and the light around us coalesced into bits of solid form. His ethereal whelk came into existence, first the spiral shell, then the tentacles. The glow of her body, and iridescent sheen, seemed to match the décor of the Grotto Labyrinth.

"Yes, my arcanist?" Felicity asked as she waved her shimmery tentacles.

"I thought you might enjoy watching everyone attempt the puzzles and traps," Adelgis said. "Apparently, they're going to do it without their magic."

Felicity giggled. "Oh! I will like this. Thank you, my arcanist."

I didn't know if this was a bad sign or not, but if the Grotto Labyrinth was theoretically doable by a non-magical mortal, then why couldn't Fain or I complete it?

"Vethica has made it to the other side," Adelgis said. "We can enter now."

Fain pushed the stone door open, and we stepped

inside. Just as Adelgis had said, there was a pit in the room—a simple rectangular ditch that stretched from one wall to the other. It was about eight feet across, and the bottom was lined with jagged rocks and the points of crystal geodes. In the middle of the pit was a small rock pillar with a tiny foot-wide platform. From what I could tell, the point of the room was to jump from one side of the pit, land on the platform, and then jump to the other side.

Two four-foot jumps weren't impossible, but landing on a small platform and jumping again would be tricky.

Vethica stood on the other side of the room. "What're you all waiting for? Use your sorcery and get over here."

"They want to attempt it as though they were mortals," Adelgis said.

With a laugh, Vethica shrugged. "Go on, then."

"These mystical scarabs want people to jump well before bonding with them?" Fain asked as he glanced over the edge of the pit. "That's odd."

"Actually," Adelgis said in a matter-of-fact tone, "the khepera are mystical creatures of both the body and the soul. Most legends regarding their initial creation talk about the harmony they achieve between the physical and the emotional. It isn't surprising to see that some of the traps would require physical precision. On the other hand, I suspect the rooms in the labyrinth will have two ways to complete them, because—"

"I get it," Fain interjected. He motioned everyone anyway from him. "I'll go first, just to see if it's trapped."

Wraith dropped his invisibility and lifted his head, his ears perked straight up.

Felicity also hovered nearby, watching intently.

"You're going to hurt yourself," Karna said, rolling her

eyes. She stepped in front of Fain and swished her hand. "Watch a master."

Before Fain could protest, she took two powerful strides toward the pit, leapt at just the right moment, hit the platform with a single foot, and then continued with her momentum to jump again, clearing the last four feet of the pit with a graceful arc. She had the fluidity of an expert dancer, and I could've watched her leap over the pit all day.

When Karna landed, she barely made a sound, but the stone platform in the middle of the pit crumbled away a second later, the stones clattering against the jagged bottom.

"It broke?" Fain asked. "Of course it did..."

I stared at the pit, wondering if that had been intentional. Was that part of the trap? The platform would break after someone stepped on it?

But then, how had Vethica gotten across? How would the rest of us continue?

To my fascination, the stones of the pillar shook and trembled. A moment later, they rolled together, stacked themselves back into place, and once again created the platform. Any cracks in the rocks melded and sealed, like flesh knitting together after an injury. It only took a minute, and the platform was just as I remembered it.

"What happened?" I asked.

Adelgis motioned to the pit. "Khepera are creatures of renewal. Their magic can refresh anything, not just the body and soul. If their magic is on the traps and puzzles here, I assume they will all reset once activated or solved."

Clever. That would prevent the need for people to enter the maze to reset everything.

Fain rotated his shoulders. "Okay. I think I can handle this."

He backed up a few feet, giving himself room for a

running start. After two deep breaths, he sprinted for the edge. I held my breath when he jumped, and for a half second, I thought he was going to *overshoot* the pillar. Thankfully, he landed, and just like Karna, continued with his momentum for the second jump. He landed on the other side of the pit with a stumble and huff, far less graceful, but without much difficulty.

Again, the pillar and platform collapsed into the pit. Adelgis observed the reconstruction with narrowed focus, never blinking until the structure had refreshed itself.

"Beautiful," he said.

I didn't see much majesty in reforming rocks, but I nodded nonetheless. It was impressive, to say the least.

Karna glanced across the pit and met my gaze. "Well?" she asked. "Are you coming, Volke?"

With a short exhale, I backed up a few feet. I was afraid of falling, but I didn't want to be the odd man out—the pressure to succeed increased tenfold. Tense and ready, I ran toward the edge, leapt, hit the platform, and then jumped again, probably harder than I needed. I hit the other side with a foot leeway.

The pillar collapsed, reformed, and repaired itself.

Wraith whined, his tail slowly shifting from side to side.

Fain patted my upper arm. "Have your knightmare go get him, would you?"

I motioned to the shadows, and Luthair slipped across the pit, rose up as an empty suit of plate mail armor next to Wraith, and then took the wendigo into the shadows. In only a matter of seconds, Wraith was on the other side of the pit, though he seemed grumpy and panted when he emerged from the darkness.

"Moonbeam," Fain said. "Wait there. Volke can send his knightmare over again."

Adelgis shook his head. "We said we were attempting this as mortals, remember?"

Fain snorted back a laugh. "C'mon, man. Don't make this awkward. No one thinks less of you for needing help."

"I'll make it across on my own."

"Yeah, but in how many pieces?"

Felicity floated around her arcanist, her tentacles playing with his long hair. Adelgis waved to the pit. "Go to the other side and wait for me."

His ethereal whelk, untethered by gravity, floated over without a problem.

I knew, deep in my gut, Adelgis couldn't make this jump. He had spent too many days inside reading. He never moved with much energy or exertion, and for years he'd had an abyssal leech feeding on him from the inside. Then again, he could read my thoughts—and everyone else's—and I wondered if that doubt somehow pushed him to prove us wrong.

Adelgis examined the pit a second time, his focused gaze going over every inch. I thought he might give up, but then he smiled. "Oh," he muttered. "Here it is." He walked to the wall and then stepped off the edge of the pit.

"Hey!" Fain barked.

But Adelgis didn't fall. Instead, he stepped onto a stone ledge. It was small—too narrow to fit an entire foot—and it was so well blended with the stone that I couldn't see it until Adelgis was physically on top of it. The ledge extended from one side to the next, and Adelgis slowly inched his way across, taking careful steps and leaning his back against the rough wall whenever he needed extra balance.

Once across, he brushed off his coat and trousers.

"I knew you could do it, my arcanist," Felicity said as she "clapped" two of her tentacles together.

"How did you know there was a ledge?" Karna asked.

"Well, I was trying to tell you all about the khepera, but I got interrupted," Adelgis said. "You see, there was once an older wise man who took the khepera trial of worth. He entered the Grotto Labyrinth with nothing but his cane. The records say the people of New Norra thought him crazy and that he would surely die, but he managed to bond with a khepera and emerged from the labyrinth a day later. If a man like that can complete the maze, then the obstacles we'll face probably have a solution that doesn't require physical prowess."

That intrigued me. The khepera were creatures of body and soul, so why wouldn't they require physical prowess for their trial of worth? Perhaps the *body* portion was more than just strength. Physical perception—the ability to spot the ledge in the dim lighting of this underground maze—could be argued was part of the body.

Rumbling filled the maze, along with a series of clanks and metallic echoes. The cacophony came so sudden and from out of nowhere, I almost thought I was trapped in a nightmare. Luthair emerged from the darkness and merged with me, his shadows wrapping around my whole being and forming as black plate mail.

Scraping added to the awful noises.

"*The labyrinth is moving,*" Vethica shouted. "*We have to go!*"

She turned on her heel and ran out of the room. Everyone else chased after her, but I stayed in the back to make sure no one was left behind. Once I was in the hallway, the ground shuddered. I glanced back to see the room with the pit shift and move away—like it was on a circular tray that had been spun around.

A new room appeared in its place, one with mirrors and lights sparkling down from the ceiling.

Then the noises stopped, just as abruptly as they had begun, leaving the quiet hum of cogs behind the walls.

Everyone jogged to a stop and took a moment to breathe deep.

"You weren't kidding," Fain muttered. "It really *does* move. If we had still been in that room..."

"We'd have gone to a different portion of the maze," Vethica said. She held up her map. "That's okay. As long as we stick together, we'll make it out of here. Just... don't take so long in the next room. According to this, the maze moves every hour, so it shouldn't be a problem, but we also shouldn't risk it."

Everyone nodded in response.

"Let's keep going," Karna said. "Now that we know what to expect, it can't be too difficult, right?"

RIDDLES AND TRAPS

Vethica entered the next room—another cave chamber secured with a heavy door. The rest of us waited outside, hoping she'd be successful. I paced the hall, restless and anxious to finally meet one of these khepera.

"It's a riddle," Adelgis muttered. "Vethica is having a difficult time answering."

Fain sighed. "Ironic that *she's* the one wasting our time now."

Vethica had been in the room for close to ten minutes. How complicated was the riddle? Then again, I had never been that great with puzzles, and if Vethica was under pressure to succeed, the stress might have stripped away some of her problem-solving skills.

"She'll be fine," Karna said. She leaned against one of the rough walls and then grimaced. After moving away, she rubbed at her lower back. "We just need patience."

"Nice outfit, by the way," Fain said, his gaze moving up from her high boots to her tight breeches-like trousers, until finally lingering on the simple bandage wrap over her chest.

Karna flashed him a smirk. "You like it? This is what I wear when I don't know what forms I'll have to take."

He tilted his head. "Whaddya mean?"

Without warning, Karna shimmered and shifted, her doppelgänger magic taking full effect over the entirety of her body. Her hair grew shorter and darker, her body slightly taller, her fingers and the tips of her ears frostbitten...

In a matter of moments, she appeared to be Fain—though Karna kept her original outfit. All pieces of her clothing seemed to accommodate the slight change in size, each capable of stretching. That explained why she had opted not to wear a belt.

Fain looked away, his shoulders stiff. "You can change back. I understand now."

"What's wrong?" Karna-Fain asked, his voice a perfect match to Fain's. "You don't like your own look?" He ran his hand down his sides and then across his stomach, feeling every indent of muscle.

It seemed odd to watch Fain sensually caress himself, but also amusing in a surreal *is this really happening* kind of way. Karna had a distinct way of moving that made every-thing sexual. Did she do it intentionally? Or was this how she always conducted herself, even when alone?

"You're wiry," Karna-Fain said as he felt his own thighs. "I like that in a man."

Fain gritted his teeth and remained silent.

"Or perhaps you're worried I'll examine every inch of you and then report back to all the ladies on the airship?" Karna-Fain ran a hand down the front of his trousers.

"*Karna,*" I growled, my face hot.

Fain half-laughed and offered a smirk. "I'm not worried about that. I just didn't realize... how much I look like my brother. He died a while back, and I'd rather not have the reminder. Satisfied? Will you change back now?"

After a moment of reflection, Karna dropped her magic and returned to her previous form—an athletic dancing girl with long, blonde hair. After shrinking somewhat in size, she had to readjust the wraps around her chest, tightening them back into position.

"You're sentimental, for a pirate," she said, disappointment in her tone.

"*Renegade* pirate," Fain growled.

"Renegade just means you've left your crew. It doesn't mean you've given up on that way of life."

Adelgis chuckled, drawing everyone's attention. "Fain was a bad pirate. And by *bad*, I don't mean *wicked*. I mean he was an incompetent pirate."

"Thanks, *Moonbeam*," Fain forced out. He ran a hand down his face, his frostbitten fingers pinching at the bridge of his nose. "Way to have my back. Really appreciate it." The sarcasm was so thick he could choke on it.

"You were often held back by morals or sentimentalities," Adelgis continued. "And you weren't the best combatant. I doubt you'll return to a life of cutthroats and scallywags. Karna appreciates knowing that."

To my surprise, Karna laughed aloud. She sauntered around the group, mulling over the statements. "I wondered why someone like Volke would spend his time with you two, and I think I'm starting to understand."

Before the conversation could continue its levity, Adelgis snapped his attention to the door. "Vethica solved the puzzle. We can enter now."

I pushed open the stone door and stepped inside. Unlike the last room, which had been large enough to accommo-date an eight-foot-wide pit, this one was small, perhaps five feet by five feet. And it was cut in half by a wrought iron fence, no gate or door. Twisted into the metal were two simple sentences:

I'm only seen when your eyes are closed
I'm fun, frightening, never composed

Vethica stood on the other side of the iron fence, her arms crossed. "You need to speak the answer aloud," she said. "Then the path will open."

"The answer to what?" Fain asked.

"The riddle woven into the fence."

"*That's* the riddle? It's barely anything." Fain glared at it. "I don't even think those are complete sentences."

If I wanted, I could shadow-step through the fence without problem. However, despite the cryptic and short clues, a part of me knew the answer. It had clicked in my mind the moment I had read the riddle.

"A dream," I said, loud enough to echo in the room.

At first, nothing happened. Then, a few seconds after the last of my voice disappeared into the hallways of the labyrinth, the iron fence creaked and moved aside. It was pulled into the wall by machinery and magic, allowing a narrow opening for someone to walk through.

"You solved that quick," Adelgis said.

I nodded. "It's because of you. I don't usually think of dreams, but... I have a lot lately."

He tried to hide a smile by rubbing at his jaw.

Fain, Karna, Adelgis, Wraith, Felicity, and I managed to slip through the opening before the gate shut itself. I suppose we failed in our test to complete the maze as mortals, since I was the only one to solve the puzzle, but so far no one had violated the rules of our little game by using their magic.

We traveled down the next hall as a group, and when we were confronted with seven more pathways, each lit up with glowstones and scarab-carved jewels hanging from the ceiling, Vethica went straight for the first hallway. She checked her map several times while she hustled down the hall, and I trusted that she'd find us the way.

The next door we came across was just as plain as the rest. Vethica pushed it aside and went in.

I exhaled, ready for the long haul—perhaps another ten minutes of joking and bickering—but after a short sixty seconds, Adelgis motioned us inside.

"She solved it," he said.

Fain pushed the door open, and we stepped in.

The room was empty, except for the tiles that lined the floor. Some tiles were black, some white, and others were the natural tan of sandstone—all one foot by one foot. Vethica stood on the opposite side of the room, just beyond the tiles.

"I assume we have to step on the correct tiles?" Fain asked.

Vethica nodded.

"And what happens if we don't?"

She motioned to the floor, as though offering him to try.

Fain sighed. "For once, I'd love the fates to give me a *good* surprise," he muttered under his breath as he tapped the toe of his boot on a random tile. Nothing happened. Fain's eyebrows knit together. He slammed his whole boot back on the same tile.

A loud grinding of gears screeched from the walls.

Vethica stepped into the far hallway, shielding herself behind the rocks.

I placed my hand on my sword and waited. Three seconds and then a flurry of darts shot from the cracks in the wall, spraying across the room.

Without thinking, I stepped in front of Karna and blocked the darts with my forearm, as though I still had my shield. Three darts—thin and needle-sharp—pierced my coat and shirt and punctured my skin. They didn't go deep, perhaps an inch, and they didn't hurt much. I had suffered through worse.

To my surprise, Luthair had formed in the split second the darts had fired. He stood in front of Felicity and Wraith, his plate armor too hard for the darts to harm him. Ten of the projectiles were on the ground around Luthair's feet. They had tinked off his shadow-metal.

Fain and Adelgis stood close together, but neither had been hit by the darts.

"Curse the abyssal hells," I growled, ripping the three darts from my forearm. "Are these poisonous?"

"No," Vethica said. She held up her map. "The notes here say they're just meant to puncture."

Karna wrapped her arms around my waist and hugged me close. "And here I thought you didn't care about me," she whispered in a playful tone.

I used some of my wootz cotton to wrap the tiny puncture wounds. I couldn't allow even a single drop of tainted blood in the Grotto Labyrinth. I even took a moment to wipe the darts clean—just in case.

The darts on the ground shook and then rolled back to the wall, drawn by the renewal magic to reinsert themselves. I held my darts, fearful they could still contaminate someone. The magic wasn't strong enough to rip them from my grip, and while the rest went back into the cracks of the wall, mine remained.

Karna kept her hold on me the entire time, her chest pressed against my back, her warm breath on the base of my neck.

"It took a long while for the darts to shoot out," Fain said. "I think… if I ran and jumped, and then kept running, I could make it to the other side of the room before the darts came out again."

Adelgis nodded. "Oh, you would certainly make it. That was how Vethica completed the room, in fact. Do you mind if I try something first?"

Fain ushered him forward with a dramatic sweep of his arm. "By all means, Moonbeam."

Was there enough information to solve this puzzle? Was there even a solution? Or was running across the room the only way? If anyone could figure it out, it would be Adelgis, but I still feared it impossible.

Adelgis stepped on a black tile.

Nothing happened.

Then he stepped onto a tan sandstone tile.

Again, nothing happened.

Then he stepped onto another black tile, then a white tile, then a sandstone tile, then a white tile, then a black— all the way until he reached the other side of the room. No darts. Nothing.

"Is it broken?" Fain asked.

Adelgis shook his head. "I noticed that you touched the same tile twice before the trap triggered. I also noticed that all the tiles of the same color sank down when you slammed your foot, meaning they were connected underground, likely on the same trigger. That means the solution is one of two options: either you can only step once on each color, meaning you have to walk across the room in three steps, *or* you can't step on the same color twice in a row. I decided to test the latter. It seems I was correct."

Curious to see what Adelgis had noticed, I pressed my boot hard on a white tile. Sure enough, all the white tiles moved a tiny amount. They were connected.

Fain walked across the tiles using Adelgis's method. When he reached the other side, he sighed, as though irritated someone else had discovered the answer.

I was about to follow them, but Karna kept her grip on me. I rubbed at her arms, wondering why she clung so tightly.

Wraith walked across the tiles, though his trek was awkward, since he had four legs. Felicity floated—twirling in the air as she went—and kept Wraith's pace, as though helping him along. Luthair turned his empty helmet face to me. When I motioned to the other side, he decided to walk along the tiles as well, his armor clinking as he took each step.

It was almost comical to watch a full suit of plate armor jump from one tile to the next. I didn't comment, though. He made it to the other side and dramatically swished his cape, possibly in a display of pride.

"I don't understand you," Karna whispered. "I don't think I ever have. But I want to."

I sighed. "I'm not... *complicated.* I've always been open and honest with you. You're the one who wants to play games." I hadn't meant to sound confrontational, but it slipped out regardless. Why did she make things difficult between us? "It's almost like you never believe anything I say," I added.

When I told her what I liked and disliked, Karna disregarded everything and did her own thing. It seemed as though she *thought* she knew what I wanted more than I did —and that kind of misunderstanding always got in the way.

She let go of me and stepped away. "I've always been open and trusting with you as well, I'll have you know."

"What about when I brought up the Mother of Shapeshifters?"

Just mentioning that creature caused Karna to flinch. Obviously, there were things that bothered her—why wouldn't she admit it or at least stop pretending as though she were impervious? It was games such as this I didn't appreciate. And in that moment, I could sense that she understood.

"Are you two comin'?" Fain asked.

I stepped across the tiles, and Karna followed without another word.

Once reunited with the group, we all headed down the next hall. The labyrinth became darker as we progressed, but the air never thinned or became stagnant. I suspected there were vents to the surface, and I wondered how the architects had hidden them. As we hurried along our path, Vethica glanced over her shoulder at me—more than once. She never spoke, and before I could ask, we reached yet another set of seven paths.

"If I'm following this map correctly," Vethica said, "this next room will be our last."

"Only four?" Fain asked.

"This was the shortest route to the center."

She pointed to the sixth hallway. As a group, we jogged down the path until we came to another door. I would've said this door was identical to the others we had seen—and that was probably the point. The whole maze was constructed to look the same no matter where someone was.

Vethica pushed open the door and slid inside.

"What kind of room is this?" Fain asked Adelgis. "Something physical?"

"It's two riddles."

"Eh. The worst. Of course that would be the last room."

Adelgis furrowed his brow. "Oh my... It seems they need to be answered within a limited time frame."

A loud click and slam sounded from inside the room. I stepped forward, ready to bust in and help Vethica, but Karna held out an arm. "We can't help her," she said. "Remember? Vethica wanted to do this on her own so she could properly bond with a khepera."

"What if she dies?" I asked.

Adelgis shook his head. "She's not dead. It's just... if she doesn't answer soon, she will be."

Everyone exchanged nervous glances.

Would I sit back and allow her to die?

My chest twisted with agony, and I stepped away from the group. I hadn't thought about my time in Thronehold since I had joined the crew of the *Sun Chaser*, but now I couldn't stop myself. During the Sovereign Dragon Tournament, I *had* watched someone die.

Princess Lyvia...

I closed my eyes and shook my head. It hurt to think about—a painful memory—but this was *more*. The burning in my chest was different. I had never felt so unstable when it came to my emotions. Rage clawed at my thoughts, and for a brief moment, I thought the only thing that would cure my suffering would be breaking into the next room and pulling Vethica from whatever danger was in there.

"Are you okay, Volke?" Karna asked.

Adelgis shook his head. "He'll be fine. He just needs to take a deep breath." With telepathy, he added, "*I can feel*

*your agony as well. Please, calm down. This isn't like you. It may
be the work of the arcane plague."*

I rubbed at my chest as I took a deep breath. "I'll be
fine," I forced myself to say.

Luthair placed a cold gauntlet on my back. It was strange
having him nearby and not as a shadow, but I appreciated
his presence.

Lyvia...

I really didn't want to think of the late princess—or how
her brother had killed her—but how could I get the
thoughts to leave me?

It was just like Illia. Whenever I thought of her, whenever I thought about *anything* that pained me, it felt as
though I were caught in an undertow, pulling me deep into
waters of uncertainty and anger.

"Everything will be fine," Adelgis said, straight to my
thoughts. *"Vethica is almost finished. Within minutes, we'll have
a khepera. You just need to focus for a little while longer."*

I inhaled and exhaled. The smell of minerals sharpened
my connection with the area. I was in the Grotto Labyrinth,
and we needed to complete this last room.

"She's done," Adelgis said. "Let's go."

Fain pushed open the door.

We all stepped inside, but instead of a hallway on the
other end of the room, there was another door—this one
with a scarab etched into the face. Had Vethica gone
through? I didn't see her.

Another loud click and slam, and the floor under our
feet split in two, right along the center, and then both sides
slanted downward, creating a steep slope. We slid to the
center of the room, and right before we went into a central
pit, I grabbed Karna and shadow-stepped back to the top.
Without a non-slanted surface to stand on, I gripped the

jagged rocks of the wall and hung on, my palm hurting after just a few seconds.

Luthair went with the group into the center—it was just a pit with no obstacles or harm.

Clinging to me, Karna pointed with a single finger to writing on the floor. "There," she said. "The riddles."

I tried to read them, but Fain, Wraith, and Adelgis were picking themselves up and moving over the sentences.

"We should go down," Karna said.

I released the wall, and we slid down the slope and then fell into the pit with the others. Karna landed on her feet without a problem—she made it look like a dance. I also landed without tumbling, and I wondered how this room was meant to kill someone.

The labyrinth answered by opening up a large hole in the wall. Water gushed outward at a fierce rate, splashing into the pit. Where was this water coming from? No doubt from the Lion's Tail River above us—the same river powering the machinery.

We had to answer the riddles or else we would drown.

"I hate this maze," Fain said with a groan, staring at the ceiling.

Karna grabbed his upper arm. "Pay attention. We need to solve the puzzle."

The water rushed in at a frightening rate. If I had to guess, there was less than two minutes' worth of time left before the pit was flooded. *We* wouldn't die because we had arcanist magic, but I could imagine how this would feel to a normal mortal. The anxiety alone could kill someone.

The first riddle read:

A house for the useless

Forever prone
Many familiar faces
Yet always alone

Fain and Karna stared at the words. I wanted to answer, but Fain managed to blurt out, "A tomb."

Was that correct? It seemed to match. I almost cursed myself for not seeing it. I had worked in a graveyard most of my life. I should've known.

The letters glowed a soft golden. Everyone in the group, even Wraith and Felicity—who floated above us—let out a relieved sigh.

"Fantastic work, my arcanist," Wraith said. "Perhaps you are good at word games after all."

Fain shook his head. "A fluke. Nothing more."

The water rose to my ankles, and I smiled to myself. We would have this completed in no time. We only had one riddle left.

It read:

What has its strength measured in desire?
It provides light in moments most dire
An unfulfilled wish taking you higher

We all stared, but no one attempted an answer.

Really? No one? I gave Adelgis a sideways glance. He had listened to Vethica's thoughts—he *knew* the answer. Didn't he? Or had he been so distracted by my rage that he hadn't heard it? He didn't seem comfortable with the rising water. Did he even know how to swim?

"A candle," Fain said.

Karna shot him a sneer. "Seriously?"

"What? I thought maybe I was on a roll. I got the last one."

"*Candles* are an unfilled wish taking you higher?"

"Yeah, yeah. It's not right. What have you got?"

"*Well*," Karna dragged out the word. The rush of water made it difficult to hear, but we were so close that it didn't matter. "How about *a wish*?"

"*Wish* is in the wording of the riddle," Fain snapped. "Of course that's not right!"

The two stared at each other for a long moment. Then Karna shook her head, grabbed one of Fain's hands, and stared him deep in the eyes. "We won't get anywhere by fighting. We should focus. Put our minds together." She rubbed his knuckles as she stepped closer.

"This... isn't helping me focus," Fain said as he jerked his hand away. Slightly red in the face, he turned away. "Moon-beam, you know the answer, right?"

Wraith whined and then got on his back legs and propped himself up using the wall. "I hate to interject, but I need to remind you that some of us are shorter than others. And dislike water."

"Hope," I said. "The answer is *hope*."

Everyone waited with bated breath. The letters of the riddle glowed a soft golden under the water, and the hole in the wall shut off, saving us from drowning.

I wanted to celebrate, since we had completed the khepera trial of worth, even if we had done it as a group. The entire Grotto Labyrinth had been everything I had hoped. It was a thing of legend, and I couldn't wait to get home to tell everyone. Gravekeeper William and Illia would never believe it—in my mind's eye, I could already see their doubt. It would be mixed with mirth and laughter, and they would demand I tell them all the details.

I was certain Master Zelfree would believe me immediately, no need for explanation.

Zaxis would scoff and say it didn't matter.

Hexa would be jealous. This underground maze was practically built for her.

Atty...

I didn't want to think about Atty's reaction.

Adelgis whipped around on his heel, sloshing water around his feet from the sudden movement. "*Volke*," he said, panic in his voice. "Something's wrong. Vethica is being attacked by one of the khepera."

"What?" I asked. "I thought she was—"

"You need to help Vethica *right now*. The khepera is attempting to kill her."

SANDS OF LIFE AND SOUL

I stepped through the shadows and exited in front of the door marked with a scarab. Luthair shifted into the darkness and stepped out next to me.

"We can merge," he said.

I shook my head. "We shouldn't fight. We should just explain and protect Vethica."

"As you wish, my arcanist."

Together, we opened the door. I was prepared to run inside or even shadow-step as far as possible, but I hesitated once I caught sight of the room.

The Grotto Labyrinth ended in a gigantic circular chamber. The ceiling, a good thirty feet above us, twinkled with crystal lights. The floor, smooth and reflective, glistened underneath the wonders of the ceiling. Small waterfalls cascaded down the back wall, creating a constant splash and trickle that echoed throughout.

More intriguing were the contents. Six marble pillars, all four feet tall and a foot in diameter, stood in a semi-circle before us. Behind the six were hundreds of destroyed pillars, the marble debris piled separately, making it easy to count them, if I had the time.

Four fist-sized scarabs with iridescent exoskeletons sat atop the intact pillars, one per pillar. Their black eyes glittered with heightened intelligence, and they watched with pointed antenna. They each had six black legs, thin and delicate.

A single head-sized scarab stood on top of the fifth pillar, its brilliant, shimmering shell open, its four insect wings flared.

"I will not allow you to leave alive," the large scarab shouted. Its voice was regal and intimidating, despite its small stature. Its front legs were lined with barbs, each as sharp as a dagger, and were so numerous, it appeared as though its legs were sawblades.

The sixth pillar had no khepera. It was empty.

I glanced around, confused and unsure of what to do. Luthair pointed, and that was when I spotted her—Vethica on the floor, her coat, trousers, and satchel singed by fire. Parts of her arm had been burned, her skin blackened and curled at the edge of the wound. She shuddered and then looked up at me.

"The khepera attacked without warning," Vethica said, her voice shaky. She motioned to the large khepera. "It wouldn't listen to a word I said—"

"*Lies*," the adult khepera rasped. It buzzed its four wings. "I am Gamal, oldest of my kind. I will not be deceived!"

"Wait!" I stepped forward, both hands up. "We didn't come to harm you. Vethica completed your trial of worth."

Gamal's black eyes shimmered. Then it flew straight up, its wings flapping so fast, they became a blur. "You are tainted. Corrupted. A liar! I know you work for *him*. Our killer. The one orchestrating our genocide." His exoskeleton flared with intense heat, like molten metal. "I will cleanse your corruption from this world. Behold the purifying power of the sun!"

Luthair and I shadow-stepped away just in time. A blinding ray of heat burst from the khepera's body—so bright and vivid, it actually dispelled the shadows. I stumbled from the darkness a few feet from where I once had been, without the ability to shift away. Luthair had to wrap himself in his cape, the light searing his plate body.

I couldn't look at the beam of concentrated sunlight. It stung my eyes, even with my eyelids shut.

"*Stop,*" I said as I held up my hand and evoked terrors.

The khepera shuddered and then shrugged off my attack. "I will not be influenced!"

Gamal turned his whole body, thus turning the scorching ray of sunlight. I ran and ducked behind one of the pillars. When I tried to manipulate the shadows, they burned away, caught in the magic of the khepera's dazzling light. I cursed under my breath. The phoenix trinket I had made with my father made my shadow magic more resistant to fire, but obviously not pure, scorching light.

"Leave him alone," Vethica shouted.

She threw her zigzag dagger and struck the glowing khepera. When the edge hit Gamal's body, a bolt of lightning shocked him. His ray of light disappeared, but his exoskeleton remained radiant. With angry buzzing, Gamal flew around the chamber and then swooped for Vethica.

"Luthair," I said.

Now that the brilliant light beam was gone, Luthair shifted through the shadows. Gamal flew down with his sawblade-like legs, but Vethica disappeared into the darkness before the khepera could slice her, saved by Luthair's quick movements.

What was I going to do? Most of my knightmare magic didn't work against the beast, and he was obviously deranged. If I did nothing, it would kill us all.

With a shaky hand, I withdrew Equalizer from its holster and then grabbed one of my father's special bullets. I had only fired a flintlock pistol a handful of times. With a normal gun, I'd need to pour in grains of shot and then pack down the bullet. My father had said this pistol didn't need gunpowder, so I removed the ramrod from under the barrel and used it to stuff the ball-shaped bullet deep into the weapon.

Once I was sure the bullet was secured inside, I reinserted the ramrod into its holder. Would the pistol fire? Even if I had no priming powder? I supposed I was about to find out.

Gamal rushed for Luthair and Vethica whenever they exited the darkness. He created another beam of light, preventing their quick escape. Luthair followed my lead and dove for cover, keeping Vethica with him, draped in his inky cape.

"I will destroy you," Gamal said. "Nothing but ashes will remain!"

I stepped out from cover, determined to divert attention away from Luthair and Vethica no matter the cost. "Over here," I shouted. When Gamal ignored me, I ran close to one of the young khepera and got within arm's length. "Aren't you trying to protect the others?"

I had no intention of hurting the little khepera, but my proximity enraged Gamal. He whipped around in the air, his wings buzzing louder and his exoskeleton glowing hotter.

After a quick breath, I held up Equalizer, took aim—my eyes burning—and then fired. Fire flared around the hammer and barrel. The sound wasn't the usual *bang*, but a shriek, like a firework. I feared I had missed, but the light from Gamal's body flickered and faded. His wings gave out, and he crashed onto the smooth tile floor, screeching the entire way.

The manticore bullet prevented magic use, but only for a short period of time. Now was the time to act.

I holstered Equalizer and drew Retribution. The moment the ebony blade left its sheath, the young khepera, all four of them, collectively gasped. They scuttled off the top of their pillars and hid themselves from me. They hadn't moved before—not at any point in the fight, not even when I had been close to one. Were they afraid of the sword?

Gamal hissed and pushed himself up onto his six legs. "Fiend! You are an agent of destruction." His exoskeleton slowly heated as the bullet injury to his carapace—the part covering the thorax—began to heal. His black eyes shimmered again. With cold certainty in his voice, he said, "I will kill you where you stand."

His last statement sent me beyond the limits of self-control. I wouldn't let anyone hurt me or those I cared about. Not if I could do something about it. Not ever again. This *bug* would regret starting a fight he couldn't hope to win.

With icy rage that seemed to hone my focus on my one opponent, I gripped my blade and rushed forward. The khepera tried to fly away, but the lingering effects of the bullet injury slowed it just enough. When I swung my sword, I imagined clipping it on its injured thorax—enough to incapacitate, but not kill.

That wasn't what happened.

In the millisecond before I connected, I turned the blade to aim for something vital. With all my might, I slashed right through the khepera's body.

It felt like I had cut through air.

No resistance. No drag. No sensation of contact. The sword sliced the mystical creature into two parts. It surprised me so much that I continued the arc of my swing until the blade struck the floor, chipping the tile.

Gamal chittered something as the half with his head separated from the back end. Both parts hit the floor with a soft *clack*. The buzzing of his wings ceased, even though his six legs twitched. Guts spilled out across the floor like a mixture of pudding and beef stew, hot and crimson.

Shaken, I dropped Retribution. The sword hit the ground with a hard clatter.

I had killed in the past, but in each instance I had *intended* to take a life. I had never... done something like *this* before. It bothered me because it had felt like a secret desire —I had wanted to harm Gamal, to make him pay for attacking us—and even though I had rationally understood death was unnecessary, I had gone through with it anyway.

Luthair and Vethica emerged from behind one of the pillars. Neither spoke as they rushed over to my side. The slice through Gamal was so clean and perfect that it invoked horror in both of them—even if Luthair had no face, just an empty helmet, I knew.

"You killed him," Vethica whispered.

"It was an accident," I said, terse. "I'm sorry."

She shook her head. "It was probably for the best. He had lost his mind."

I took several shallow breaths. "But—"

"The khepera never really die, remember? He'll be reborn in this chamber as a young khepera. Perhaps then his mind will be calm."

That fact eased my guilt.

But still.

The way I had acted troubled me. Had it been a result of the arcane plague? Or something else? The uncertainty added a new layer of anxiety.

"You can come out now," Vethica said to the four young khepera. She used a part of her burnt coat to hide the injury on her arm. "I promise, we mean you no harm. I tried to tell that to Gamal, but he wouldn't listen. We had to fight him to stay alive, but I assure you we didn't want that."

The four smaller khepera scuttled to the tops of their pillars, each waving their antennae. They glanced between one another, and then all turned their attention to me.

"He is corrupted," one whispered, its voice feminine. "We can see it in his magic."

Vethica stepped between me and the mystical creatures. "He knows he's ill. He came to beg you to help him recover, not to hurt you."

"He carries a weapon made from the end of times. It is wicked. I do not think he can be trusted."

"His weapon?" Vethica turned around and stared at my sword.

While on the ground, it seemed harmless—as wicked as any other longsword—but I remembered how it had cut through Gamal without any problems. The exoskeleton should've offered some resistance, but there had been nothing.

The door to the center chamber opened again to reveal Adelgis, Fain, Karna, Wraith, and Felicity. They hurried into the room, wet from the waist down. While the others had to glance around to take in their surroundings, Adelgis shot straight for me as though he knew the area well.

"Are you okay?" he asked as he reached my side. With his telepathy he added, "*Your thoughts have been panicked since you killed Gamal. You really must keep calm. I fear these outbursts will only take you down a spiral of despair."*

Luthair turned his empty helmet to face me.

I ran a hand down my face and forced half a smile. "I'll be okay. I was just startled. That's all."

"He is a knightmare arcanist," another young khepera said, this one boyish in voice. "Knightmares only bond with individuals who are both valiant and filled with a sense of justice. If he is corrupted, it is a tragedy." The khepera spoke with no contractions, making their speech elegant and formal.

The feminine-sounding khepera buzzed her wings, but didn't leave her pillar. "We need an arcanist to help him."

"The woman completed the trial of worth."

"She is... also corrupted."

The four khepera whispered amongst each other, their little voices becoming too hushed to comprehend, even if the sounds echoed in the large chamber. Vethica looked away from Retribution and then returned her attention to the khepera.

"I've also come for your help," she said. "Please. I want to become a khepera arcanist so I can aid others in my situation."

For a long moment, no one said or did anything. Everyone waited, silent and with rapt attention, for the fallout of our actions. Would the young khepera trust us, even though we had killed Gamal? I hoped I hadn't ruined this opportunity.

The boyish khepera scuttled to the edge of his pillar, as close as he could get to Vethica. "My name is Akhet," he said, his black eyes shimmering. "I will bond with you."

"You will?" Vethica asked, hope and desperation mixed

into the breathlessness of her speech. "Th-Thank you. Thank you so much!"

She stepped close to the pillar and held out a trembling hand. Akhet stretched out one of his thin insect legs. The moment they touched, Akhet glowed a soft white, and Vethica's forehead was marked a second time. A star with the shape of a scarab etched itself into her flesh, signifying to the world she was, once again, an arcanist.

Once the light calmed, Akhet removed his leg and fluttered his wings. "My arcanist, it is a pleasure to finally meet you. I hope, together, we will grow ever wiser."

Vethica rubbed at her eyes. Unable to speak, she just nodded.

The relief of the situation helped my frayed nerves. At least the waiting and the trek hadn't been for nothing. Vethica was now a khepera arcanist, and we could return to the *Sun Chaser* victorious.

Gamal's severed body shook. I stepped back, startled. Everyone else turned their attention to the corpse as well, clearly confused by the movement. The scarab body twitched and then flaked apart, similar to ashes from a fire. The exoskeleton broke down, the wings disintegrated, and the glistening guts shriveled and rotted.

Within the span of sixty seconds, Gamal's body transformed from a fresh corpse to...

Sand.

Everything broke down until nothing but two piles of sand remained.

One pink. One tan.

I held my breath, realization dawning on me at a slow rate.

The sand moved on its own, controlled by magic and willed to one of the pillars. The piles rolled around the ground, swept up by an invisible force. When the sand reached the base of the pillar, it slid up the sides, moving in a line only three grains wide. Once atop the pillar, the sands collected themselves back into colored piles, neat and tidy.

"What is that?" I demanded, even though I knew the answer.

Akhet buzzed his wings. "That is Gamal. The tan sand is his body. The pink sand is the soul that he has collected throughout his many lives. Once he has recovered, he will form again."

"What happens if someone removes the sand?" Adelgis asked, his expression neutral, his words careful. "Let me clarify. What if someone uses the sand for some purpose? Healing or... some other purpose."

The young khepera exchanged another round of sad glances.

"That was why Gamal was upset," Akhet muttered. "Khepera do not die, but they can be permanently destroyed. For decades, the only person to reach our sacred chamber in the center of the Grotto Labyrinth has been an imposing man who does not reply to our questions. He takes our sands and uses them..."

Akhet pointed to the broken pillars—the hundreds of broken pillars.

"They will never come back," Akhet stated. "If the sands are used or consumed—that is the end of the khepera."

PLAGUE HUNTING

Adelgis brushed his hair back with a quick stroke of his hand. Then he turned away from the group and bit down on his index finger. He said nothing as he stared at the polished tile flooring.

I opened the pouch on my belt and withdrew the two vials of sand—one tan, one pink. These were a khepera? I hoped beyond reason they were something different, something similar but ultimately unrelated. I uncorked the vials and then poured them onto the floor. The others watched me with knit eyebrows and curious expressions. All except Luthair, of course. He stood next to me without even the slightest of movement, an intimidating decoration, though I knew he understood the gravity of the situation. He had been with me every step of this journey.

Once the sands were free from their confines, I stepped away.

My heart sank like a brick the moment the sands shuddered and moved. They traveled across the floor, just like the sands of Gamal, and went straight for an empty pillar.

They slid up to the platform at the top and reformed as piles.

Unlike Gamal, who had remained sand, the grains from the vials sparkled and shimmered. Glittering the entire time, they reformed into a tiny khepera, coalescing together like Luthair whenever he formed from the shadows. It only took a minute, and the glimmer of magic stopped—the khepera had been reborn right in front of our eyes.

From the sands I took from Theasin's lab.

And the real map—the one with the correct solution to the center chamber—had come from the same place.

"What's going on?" Fain asked. He crossed his arms, uncrossed his arms, and then motioned around, obviously restless. "You just had a bunch of khepera sand in your *pocket*?"

The other young khepera buzzed and trembled.

"Evil," one whispered.

"He must work with the vile man," another added.

"Those sands," I muttered, barely hearing the others over the chaos of my own thoughts, "I first saw them in Thronehold. Theasin—Adelgis's father—used the tan sand to heal Adelgis's physical injury after removing the abyssal leech. And then later... I used the pink sand to heal Adelgis's soul of the lingering damage. I didn't know... I didn't know they were khepera."

Vethica and Karna gave each other one quick look that had a conversation's worth of information in it. I didn't know what they thought of me, but I would understand if they thought me a monster. I just hadn't known what the sands were, and no matter whom I had asked, no one had given me an acceptable answer.

"How did you get these sands?" Fain asked.

"I found them in Theasin's labs. Right alongside the map."

Vethica picked up Akhet and then held her new eldrin close to her chest. "I understand now. Theasin Venrover was the one who tampered with the maze. He's the one who stole all the khepera and used their sands for his own purposes. He killed them and trapped their sand in vials, preventing them from returning to the Grotto Labyrinth. That's the only explanation."

I had known the moment Gamal had dissolved into two colored sands.

Theasin had done this.

He was the only one with the knowledge, the resources, and the dark ambition to think he could get away with something so over-the-top. He had even been the one to conclude that the khepera were gone. In reality, he was the "imposing man" who had visited the center chamber over the last couple of decades—he was the one killing the khepera. *Him.* This was all his doing.

Karna huffed. She placed a hand on her hip and leaned back on one leg. "Okay, so what're we going to do now? We can't remain shocked and aghast forever."

"We should take the rest of the khepera out of here," I said. "If we leave them, there's a chance Theasin might finish the rest of them off for their sands."

"What're we going to do with them afterward? Give them to the governor of New Norra?"

I gritted my teeth, hating every moment of this. That seemed like a logical course of action, but I didn't know anything about the governor of New Norra. What if the governor was in on this with Theasin? Or perhaps all city officials were? Giving the khepera away could put them all at risk. They were small and young, and without Gamal, they had no protection.

Who would I trust to look after the khepera? There weren't many people who I could say, with absolute certainty, were beyond suspicion.

"We should keep them," I said. "And when I go back to the Frith Guild, I can take them with me."

"You want to give them to one of the guilds?" Vethica asked with a frown.

Although I figured Karna would agree, she tightened her grip on her arms. "No, Volke's right. We should take the khepera far from here. To a place where Theasin can't get them."

The remaining khepera conferred amongst themselves, their antennae waving back and forth as they whispered. I ignored their conversation and placed a hand on Adelgis's tense shoulder. His eyes were scrunched shut, and he didn't move. Fain and Wraith joined us, but it was obvious that neither knew what to say.

Fain met my gaze and then motioned to Adelgis with a subtle jut of his shoulder. Did he want me to say something? What was I supposed to say at this moment? *Sorry your father was involved in something so heinous. It happens, I guess.*

I rubbed at the back of my neck.

Adelgis could hear my thoughts... He probably didn't appreciate the jokes...

While everyone dwelled on the situation, Karna picked up Retribution and handed it to me, hilt first. I wasn't sure I wanted to take it back, but I needed to have a weapon. I'd just have to exert better self-control in the future.

"What's your sword made out of?" Vethica asked.

I shook my head. "Steel. Knightmare magic. And bones that I found in Theasin's lab." What were they from? Some other innocent creature that Theasin had harvested so he could use the parts for his purposes and experiments? "I don't know where the bones came from, but they felt powerful. I thought they would be perfect for a weapon."

"I still don't feel it," Karna said. "The sword is just a sword to me. Nothing more."

"I can sense it," Akhet said, his little boyish scarab voice mixed with fear. "Something terrible."

Luthair, who hadn't shifted at all, chimed in with, "I can also sense it. I'm not sure what it is, but the power is there."

Could mystical creatures feel the power? But why couldn't any of the other arcanists? Why me? I held the hilt of the blade out to Fain. "Can you feel anything?"

He touched it, his movements hesitant, but once his blackened fingers grazed the top of the blade, he relaxed. "I feel nothing."

Vethica held out her hand. Although I didn't think it would make much of a difference, I allowed her to touch Retribution as well. Like Fain, she didn't seem enthusiastic to handle the sword. Once she touched it, she grimaced and jerked her hand away.

"Are you okay?" I asked.

"It's powerful," she whispered. "I can feel it, too."

So... only the two arcanists who had been corrupted with the arcane plague could feel the power. And the khepera claimed it was wicked. What were those bones? What creature had they come from? Perhaps a plague-ridden monster? Had Theasin been experimenting with the plague in his free time? Or perhaps he was testing out the abyssal leech's ability to manipulate magic? Was that how he was developing a cure? Or was something more sinister taking place?

If I had to bet, I'd say anything Theasin was involved in wasn't pleasant.

I sheathed Retribution, more uncertain than ever.

Perhaps it was best… if I rid myself of this weapon.

The khepera stopped their conversation and turned toward us in unison.

"We have decided," the feminine khepera said. "We will leave the Grotto Labyrinth. However, you must know that our sands will always return here. If we die, there is no other place we can resurrect."

"We'll protect you," I said.

The khepera buzzed their wings.

"Not you," the same khepera replied. "You cannot be trusted."

I didn't protest. If they didn't want a plague-ridden arcanist to guard them, I understood. I didn't want to hurt any of them on accident, not like I had hurt Gamal. I just hoped they would be able to cure me before it was too late.

"Let's go," Karna said. She jogged up to each pillar and scooped up the khepera. They were tiny, and they scuttled to her shoulders, one climbing on top of her head—hiding in her golden hair.

Vethica pointed to the door. "We only have another fifteen minutes before the maze shifts again. We don't want to be stuck in the central chamber."

Everyone headed for the door, except for Adelgis and his ethereal whelk. He didn't move, and Felicity floated over him, her gestures and movements slow.

"We'll catch up with you," I said to the others as I stood next to Adelgis. "Don't wait for us."

"Will you be able to find your way out?" Vethica asked.

"We won't take that long. Just go."

The group lingered around the door for a few seconds, obviously debating on whether to leave.

"*Go*," I commanded, harsher than I had spoken to any of them before.

That motivated them. They left the central chamber. Adelgis, Luthair, Felicity, the pile of Gamal's sand, and I were the only ones who remained. The small waterfalls in the back of the room trickled down the wall, creating a pleasant melody of nature, but it wasn't enough to remove the tension and anxiety.

Adelgis clenched his teeth down on his index finger, breaking skin and allowing the blood to run the length of his hand.

"Adelgis," I muttered. A part of me wanted to stop him, but...

He lowered his hand, wiped the blood off on the edge of his coat, and stared at the floor, unseeing. "My father did a lot more than just kill a majority of the khepera," he said, his tone dark and serious.

"Like what?" I asked.

"Volke."

Was he even listening to me? I stepped closer to him, until we were inches apart. "Yeah?"

"My father doesn't think mystical creatures are worthy of consideration." Adelgis smoothed his long hair. His ethereal whelk floated down and used her tentacles to help him. When Adelgis continued, it was with a steely, almost emotionless voice. "He's written books and papers about how their lack of a soul means they're no different than a rock or a tree or any other material that can be broken down and altered. I've read his thesis many times. The fact that he would destroy khepera to use their bodies for his own personal healing doesn't surprise me."

"You seem upset," I said, trying to pick my words carefully, even though it probably didn't matter when he could hear my thoughts. "More so than I've ever seen you. If you knew your father would do something like this, why're you so shaken?"

"It's difficult listening to so many unpleasant thoughts," he stated. "And my own uncertainties don't help. They're eating away at my composure."

"What're you uncertain about?"

"Whether we'll find you a cure."

The statement shook me—I didn't want to think about that right now. Nevertheless, Adelgis continued.

"My father's writing said the khepera's renewal powers were great." Adelgis rubbed at his forearms. "But a young khepera won't have the magic required to cure you. I thought... Well, I *hoped*... there would be an answer here. An answer to why the khepera weren't returning—some answer that would help us solve your problem at the same time. Instead, all I found were my father's atrocities."

"You mean, even though Vethica is a khepera arcanist, she won't have the power to cure me?" I asked.

"Don't you remember your first few months as an arcanist? How hard it was to evoke and manipulate basic things? It'll be years before she has the power to rid someone of the arcane plague."

"But you said a khepera arcanist could help," I said, my voice rising. "We waited here in the city for three weeks because *you said* it was the best course of action. Now you're telling me it won't work?"

"I had been hoping to find older khepera," Adelgis said, his voice also rising. "Or something we could use! What if there had been a way to locate khepera arcanists here? What if the source of the khepera renewal was a magical artifact or powerful natural resource? There were lots of possibilities, all plausible."

"Are you saying Gamal could've helped if I hadn't killed him?" I asked. Had I inadvertently destroyed my only hope? "Were you just hoping Vethica would second-bond to a khepera that was already capable of healing me?"

"Gamal's magic was stronger—perhaps he could've helped you—but I heard his thoughts. He never would've stopped until we were all dead. It was best you killed him when you did." Adelgis paced back and forth, only walking a few feet before turning around. Then he stopped. "There are other ways to cure you," he muttered. "But I don't know if you're going to like the options I present." Adelgis sighed. "Maybe Jozé can help me. He's quite skilled—more than I thought. I just... I can't fail you. I refuse. You're always helping everyone else. You're always helping me. I *need* to help you or else..."

"My arcanist," Felicity said with a pout. She used a tiny tentacle to grab a lock of his hair.

Anger slowly drained from my system. I exhaled and reminded myself I still had time. "Let's get back to the *Sun Chaser*. We can discuss it more then."

Adelgis and I had spoken so long that we needed to run through most of the Grotto Labyrinth to avoid the moving rooms and hallways. The others had already gone ahead— no doubt to avoid being trapped—and by the time Adelgis and I made it to the entrance, we were winded. The maze really was gigantic and the rooms were spaced so far apart.

We climbed the long staircase to the entrance, but at a

slow pace. My legs burned, and the terrible information had taken a toll on me. I needed to sleep.

To my surprise, a clear day greeted us as we exited the Grotto Labyrinth. Where had the hurricane gone? The plan was to use the last of it as cover as we returned to the *Sun Chaser*. If anyone saw us leaving the underground maze, they would surely report us. And while I understood why Vethica, Karna, and Fain had run ahead in the labyrinth, why wouldn't they wait for us at the entrance, where the maze didn't move at all?

The streets of New Norra remained abandoned. Sand covered everything and filled in the minor nooks and crannies between bricks. Anything not secured or tied down was strewn across the roads or collected in piles between buildings. Although it appeared messy, there was no major damage. A few days' worth of cleaning and everything would be back to normal.

Determined to make it back to the *Sun Chaser*, I glanced around—and once I made sure no one was watching out a window—I ran for the closest alleyway. Adelgis and I made it from the plaza to the next street over in a matter of moments.

Adelgis grabbed my arm, stopping me before we went any farther. "Volke. Hunters."

Before I could process what he had told me, a group of four individuals stepped around the side of a sandstone building. I didn't recognize three of them—they weren't even arcanists—but they held rifles and short swords. The last man I knew. It was the reaper arcanist, Jevel. His reaper eldrin, Ruin, floated alongside him as an ominous hood, cape, and scythe, its many chains rattling as it swayed through the air.

Jevel stroked his goatee and smiled. "Oh, I knew we'd

find plague-ridden arcanists behind all this. *I knew it.*" He held up his hand and flashed a crimson bracelet. It glowed slightly, the red hue shining across his skin. "But you can't hide from us anymore."

My mouth went dry, and I instantly regretted traveling anywhere with Adelgis. I didn't want him to get caught up in a fight.

Jevel stared at me for a prolonged moment. Then his expression switched from jovial to hardened. "Wait a minute—*you're* plague-ridden? No wonder you're not with Master Zelfree anymore. Everything makes sense now."

I pushed Adelgis away. "Go," I muttered.

"It's my lucky day," Jevel said, his mirth returning. "I still need Zelfree's name on my chains."

Adelgis spoke telepathically, "*Volke, you need to be careful. This man intends to incapacitate you and then use you as bait to lure Master Zelfree away from the Frith Guild.*"

A DIFFICULT CHOICE

Jevel intended to use me as bait?

I'd like to see him try.

I unsheathed Retribution, no longer concerned about whether or not it was wicked. It was a blade, wasn't it? And it'd cut this man down in a matter of seconds if he thought he was going to use me for anything.

"My arcanist," Luthair said from the shadows. "They're just hunters doing their jobs. Please reconsider this course of action."

Holding me as ransom to lure Master Zelfree was far from *doing their job*, but I supposed the four men with Jevel weren't privy to his personal plans. Killing them wasn't necessary. It worried me that my first thought had been to slice them all to pieces.

Jevel's reaper wrapped its cloak around him. In half a second, the two were merged, much like how Luthair and I combined our strength to become one living being. The hood of the cloak half-covered Jevel's face with shadow, the chains of his reaper hung as a belt, and he now held the scythe with both hands.

In response to Jevel merging with his reaper, Luthair formed up out of the shadows and wrapped around me. The darkness hardened into cold plate metal, giving me a renewed sense of strength. In addition, Luthair's logic and control helped me regain focus. If I had killed Jevel and his cohorts, I would've sent the city into a panic. I didn't want that to happen.

"You're nothing but an apprentice," Jevel said, his voice dark at the edges—an odd mix of his and his reaper's voice. "This won't take long."

He readied his scythe, a weapon with a pole at least five feet in length. The blade was chipped and the metal rusty, giving it a timeworn and neglected visage. Just looking at it could give someone an infection.

Jevel held up a hand and evoked terrors. Normally, a person would succumb to their greatest fears—becoming immobilized with visions only they could see—but my knightmare magic kept me immune. When Jevel lunged with his scythe, I was ready.

I shadow-stepped away, avoiding his slash. Instead of appearing behind him, which was what most enemies predicted, I emerged from the same spot in which I had gone into the darkness. Sure enough, Jevel had turned around, expecting an attack from the rear. While he was momentarily confused, I stabbed forward with Retribution.

A small part of me feared I would try to kill him, much like I had killed Gamal, but with Luthair's stalwart personality mingled with mine, I struck Jevel in the bicep of his dominant arm, just as I had wanted.

The black blade cut through Jevel without problem.

Again, no resistance. No drag. It didn't even feel like I had hit anything solid.

Jevel's blood splattered across the sandstone bricks of

the street. He leapt again, his teeth gritted, but a smirk at the edge of his lips. He used his left hand to grab at his own bloody wound. Then he arched his hand outward, throwing a smattering of blood out in front of him. I didn't know what reapers could manipulate, but it became apparent in that moment—the droplets of blood became tiny razors that sailed through the air like throwing daggers.

I leapt away. One blood-knife sliced through the edge of Luthair's cape. Another hit my shadow armor and failed to pierce through.

Careful, Luthair spoke straight in my mind. *Injuries from a reaper cannot be healed through magical means.*

Curse the abyssal hells! I couldn't afford to take an injury and bleed for days.

Jevel threw his blood knives again, but instead of aiming for me, he went for Adelgis. One sliced through Adelgis's upper leg, and another gouged a chunk of flesh from his shoulder.

The four hunters with Jevel all went for Adelgis—no doubt seeing him as the weaker combatant. When I turned to help, Jevel was on me in an instant. He swung with his scythe, which took my attention. I had to dodge, but I also had to come up with a plan. If I wasn't going to kill them, what should I do?

Two men lunged for Adelgis. He grazed both of them with a feather-light touch of his fingertips, his hand connecting with the skin of their necks for less than a second. In that moment, both men collapsed to the street, their bodies becoming limp. One snored loud as he hit the ground face-first, like a whole night's worth of sleep had been trapped in his gut and wanted to escape. Adelgis had forced both men into a magic-induced slumber.

Instead of attempting to grapple Adelgis, the last two men readied their flintlock pistols.

I slashed with my longsword and clipped the arm of the first gunman.

But it wasn't like with Jevel. I *felt* the blow to the man's arm. There was a connection—resistance—it almost startled me, considering there hadn't been anything before. My attack had been enough to rip open a wound from the man's elbow to his wrist, disarming him in a single blow.

Jevel swung wide with his scythe. It caught my side and sliced through the shadows of my armor, but it didn't break my skin. Panic gripped me—although I hadn't tested my theory, I was convinced that Luthair would become plague-ridden if I were injured while we were merged.

Desperate to control the battlefield, I manipulated the shadows of the alleyway. Tendrils lifted up from the blackness and grabbed the legs and arms of Jevel and his four hunters, even the ones who were asleep. The shadow tendrils acted like ropes, holding them in place.

Jevel slashed and cut and manipulated his blood to tear through my restraints. I didn't have much time to act, though it was enough to distract him.

The blood he had splattered on my armor continued to move. It burned—Jevel's magic had created an acidic blood —and it corroded Luthair's body. If it went all the way through, it would harm me as well. Not only that, but Adelgis had been hurt by the same attack... Could he hold up with so many injuries?

I unmerged with Luthair, wanting to keep him plague-free. He returned to his shadow-state around my feet to clear away the harmful blood.

Knowing I only had a few moments, I ran to Adelgis, grabbed him by the arm, and took us both into the darkness.

As a shadow, we slid up the side of the building, but if I took us to the roof, the full force of the desert sun would make using my magic difficult. Instead, I leapt out of the shadows, taking Adelgis with me, and smashed through the second-story window on the opposite side of the alley.

Glass scattered everywhere as we rolled across the wood flooring. People gasped, but I was too disoriented to see them clearly. My vision had blurred and my ears rang. I hadn't imagined that the impact would affect me as much as it had, and my second-bonded magic burned throughout my system. I had forgotten how costly it was to take another person through the darkness.

I clenched my jaw and withdrew Equalizer from its holster.

Master Zelfree had told me to think like my opponents. I knew Jevel wouldn't let us get away that easily. He had seen me in the Sovereign Dragon Tournament. He would use what little information he had about my fighting style in an attempt to corner me, which meant he probably knew I couldn't travel through the shadows very far. He'd assume I'd still be in the building, and once he came in, I'd have to be ready for him.

I used the pistol's ramrod to load another manticore bullet, my hands shaky after the collision with the window.

Adelgis rolled to his side, rubbed at his head, and then examined his many lacerations.

I didn't have many injuries due to my armor and the wootz cotton.

There were people in the room—dressed from head to toe in dark clothing—but they huddled away from us, keeping behind baskets and beds. It was for the best. I didn't want to get them involved. As an apology, I untied the pouch with the last of my coins and threw it to the nearest individual. Hopefully, it would be enough to repair a window and bedroom.

The door flew open, and I fired Equalizer.

It wasn't Jevel—it was one of his non-arcanist hunters. I hit the man in the arm, and he stumbled to the ground, crying out as he went.

Jevel had been so craven that he had sent one of his lackeys ahead of him? I should've known. Any man who was willing to hold someone hostage wasn't going to fight with any sort of honor.

"*My arcanist*," Luthair hissed.

I whipped around and found Jevel leaping in through the broken window. I hadn't expected him to get up this high—not to the second story—but perhaps he was more athletic than I had given him credit for.

Jevel swung with his scythe, aiming for Adelgis. I reacted by lashing out with shadows. I grabbed Jevel's blade with the darkness and forced the shadows to cling tight, but it wouldn't last forever. I grabbed Adelgis and stepped into the shadows, traveling under the door, into a hallway, and down a flight of stairs. Then I had to emerge. I gasped for air, and so did Adelgis.

Jevel crashed through the door and rushed down the hall. He would get down the stairs in a matter of seconds, and I didn't have much time.

I half-carried Adelgis out the front door of the building. We stumbled into the street, and I wondered if I'd be forced to kill Jevel just to escape him. If it came to it... I would.

People dressed in long robes rushed away from us.

I helped Adelgis across the street as Jevel emerged from the building, chuckling the entire way. "You can't escape me. I've hunted far more talented arcanists than the likes of *you*."

One robed individual—someone close to the door—walked toward Jevel while his attention was focused on me. Before Jevel could react, the person reached out and grazed Jevel's hand. Much like with Adelgis's magic, all it took was a single touch.

Jevel straightened his posture, his reaper cloak falling over his shoulders and concealing most of his body. He held his scythe close and then glanced around with jerked motions, almost as if he were fighting himself. After a short moment, his movements became natural.

"Go get the Watch Battalion," Jevel shouted to the people on the street. He waved his arm around. "We'll need this whole street cleaned once I'm done. *Quickly.*"

The citizens of New Norra nodded and fled the road, obviously overjoyed to comply with the command. Well, everyone except for the one who had touched Jevel. That individual raced across the street and met with Adelgis and me.

"Are you two okay?" the man under the robes asked. I didn't recognize his voice or appearance, but there was only one explanation.

"Karna?" I asked.

The man nodded. "Come. I have control of the plague hunter. He'll go that way; we'll go home."

Sure enough, Jevel took off in the opposite direction, chuckling to himself the whole way, a sociopath who enjoyed the hunt. Karna played his personality well—just as well as she had played Theasin. I was starting to notice a pattern...

We headed away from Jevel and followed the blue lines painted on the ground toward the docks. I knew we wouldn't go to the delta, but the lines would get us close to the sky dock, and then we could safely return to the *Sun Chaser*...

Although we were back on the *Sun Chaser*, and far from the reaper arcanist, my panic didn't leave me. We had stayed in the city to find a khepera, and now that we had one, it still didn't matter. It couldn't heal the arcane plague. Adelgis was right. Vethica's magic was too weak. So what had this all been for? Why had Adelgis insisted? Why hadn't we left New Norra immediately and headed for his father?

I hadn't voiced my questions. I didn't need to. Adelgis could hear—yet he hadn't answered.

Something was wrong.

"Everything will be fine," Luthair whispered from the darkness as I walked from my storeroom to my father's quarters.

I didn't bother answering. At this point, it was difficult to imagine everything turning out well in the end.

With an unsteady hand, I rubbed at my eyes. What would Illia say to me in a moment like this? She always knew what to say—always knew how to pull from the depths of misery. If Illia were here, I was certain she would tell me she would handle the matter. Maybe her eldrin, Nicholin, would crack a joke about how amazing he was and how this wouldn't be difficult for him to solve.

I wished, more than anything, that I'd be able to see her again.

I entered my father's quarters—the same officer's cabin I had grown familiar with. A table. A built-in bed attached to the bulkhead. Cabinets filled with his crafting materials. Tine, his phoenix, sat on her perch, her feathers fluffed. She lifted her head when I entered and said nothing as I shut the door and took a seat at the table.

Then she said, "Your father and Adelgis will be right back."

I exhaled, my whole body heavy. I had taken the time to bathe and change my clothes, and Adelgis had said to meet him here once I was done.

"Where did they go?" I asked.

"To the Norra Library. Your friend needed reference material, and your father wanted a few things as well."

I hadn't seen Vethica or Karna since arriving back on the *Sun Chaser*. They had gone off together to discuss something, leaving me alone with my thoughts.

"Why did the captain stop the hurricane early?" I asked, hating the silence.

"Bounty hunters were sent to the air dock." Tine puffed her feathers, revealing her flame body underneath. The white fire shone bright until her feathers relaxed down on her body. "One of the hunters could sense magic, including auras. Captain Devlin didn't want to risk the safety of the crew. He kept the aura up as long as possible."

"How did they sense magic?"

Tine shook her head. "Trinkets. One man even said he had a trinket for detecting plague-ridden arcanists. He searched the crew and found nothing."

With no more questions to ask, I leaned against the table and stared at the grains in the wood. A knock on the door drew my attention. Jozé wouldn't knock on his own door—who could it be?

"Come in," I said.

To my surprise, Fain stepped into the room, hesitation in each movement. He gave the phoenix a quick bow of his head and then took a seat at my father's table. He tapped his blackened fingers on the edge of the furniture.

"Moonbeam said I should meet everyone here," Fain said. "Where's everyone else?"

"At the library. I assume they'll be back soon."

A couple of minutes passed without conversation. Despite that, Fain seemed to relax, comforted by the stillness. His restless tapping went away, and he better positioned himself, sitting on the bench.

The door opened again, almost startling me. My father walked in, his limp worse than before. Adelgis followed, several books in his arms, including a book with a chain attached to the spine. Typically, the most valuable and rare books were kept in a restricted section—each book was then secured to the wall through the use of a chain, to prevent theft. The books were never meant to be taken away. Had they made an exception for Adelgis, because he was the son of Theasin? Or perhaps my father had used his ability to mold metal to break the chain?

I was about to ask when Adelgis slammed the heavy tomes on the table.

"We have a cure," Jozé said, unable to restrain a smile.

Fain and I both stood in an instant.

"You do?" I asked.

Jozé nodded. "Now that I had a chance to examine the khepera, I think I have something." My father hobbled around the table and took a seat. He rubbed at the top of his sore leg, but it didn't impact his smile. "Adelgis told me about the khepera when they die and how they become the two sands."

"Okay." I took my seat back on the wooden bench. "And?"

"I think, if we had enough rose-colored sand, we could have a caladrius arcanist imbue some of their magic into it.

Caladrius are the most powerful of healers—anything with their magic is potent."

I scratched at my neck. "So?"

Jozé reached across the table and smacked my upper arm. "Don't you get it, boy? That sand heals the soul. With caladrius magic, it'll cure *anything* to do with the soul. I know a caladrius arcanist not far from here. Captain Devlin can take us in less than an hour."

I held up a hand. "Wait. But we need to use the pink sand?"

Jozé nodded. "I think, given what Adelgis told me, we'll need about three kheperas' worth."

"But..." I looked directly into his dark eyes. His enthusiasm hadn't waned. Did he not know? "If I consume the sand—or use it for a trinket—the khepera will cease to exist."

"Well, we don't need to use the tan sand," Jozé said. He sat back, leaning away from me, his expression shifting to something conflicted. "I have a theory that the khepera might be able to reform with just that. Ya see, the khepera keep bits of soul from their previous arcanists after one dies. That must be what the rose-colored sand is. Which means the tan sand is the khepera's body—and the khepera might be able to live with just that."

I stood again, restless and on the verge of anger. "So you want to kill three khepera and take their sand?"

"I just said it might not kill them."

"This is ridiculous," I said, curt. "It's the same as saying, *let's cut off this man's arms to heal you—the surgery might not kill him, and he can live without arms, so it's perfectly acceptable.*"

No one said anything.

I motioned to the door. "Did you even ask the khepera?"

Jozé rubbed at the stubble on his jaw. "You realize that arcanists hunt mystical creatures for their parts all the time, don't you? Where do you think most of the trinket and artifact components come from, boy?"

"The khepera are almost extinct," I said, unable to hold back my incredulity. "They don't breed, and there is no fable that creates them. There are only six left—including the one bonded to Vethica. You want me to kill three of them for a one-time cure to the arcane plague?"

It hurt to even speak those words. I wanted a cure more than anything, but killing off a small race of mystical creatures in order to fulfill that desire seemed... wretched.

"Now isn't the time to be foolishly idealistic," Jozé stated. "Real life isn't like a heroic story written for children."

Was that what he thought? I could hardly believe my ears. It wasn't my desire to cling to old stories. This was different. More than that.

"I have an alternative," Adelgis muttered.

Everyone turned their attention to him. Somehow, deep in my gut, I knew I wasn't going to like this option, either. Everything about Adelgis—from the slumped posture to the averted gaze—told me he knew it, too.

"I know where my father is," Adelgis continued. "He's at a place he refers to as *the Excavation Site*. It's in all his letters and research notes. But there are a few problems, the first of which is getting there. The Excavation Site is beyond the Lightning Straits."

Jozé let out a forced huff. "We can't go through the Lightning Straits. It's filled with plague-ridden monsters, not to mention the continual thunderstorm. It's a death trap. No way Theasin made it through himself."

"He did." Adelgis said the words with a cold, almost callous, tone.

"There's nothing beyond the Lightning Straits anymore. All those towns and ports were destroyed. All boats sail around the ridge."

"Trust me. My father went through the straits, and he's there now." Adelgis then turned his focus to me. With telepathy he added, *"But you know my father. He's talented, intelligent, educated, powerful—and he has no regard for anyone but himself. At first, I wanted to reach him because I thought he could cure you, but after everything I've read from his labs... I fear this may be a terrible mistake."*

"What did you read in his labs?" I asked, my voice nearly a shout.

Adelgis refused to voice his end of the conversation aloud. *"I'm afraid..."* He turned his gaze away, unable to meet mine. *"Volke, I think he's capable of more than just altering a labyrinth to claim mystical creatures for himself. He's... dangerous. But given all that, I do think he has the cure to the arcane plague. Even now, as we speak. He's been working on it for years, apparently."*

Adelgis's dithering finally made sense. He had been determined to find his father until we had broken into the labs. After that, Adelgis had changed his mind and suggested we seek out the khepera, hoping to find a solution, even though he hadn't been certain there would be one.

It was because he realized his father couldn't be trusted.

If we sought out Theasin Venrover—if we somehow went through the Lightning Straits and found this *Excavation Site*—there was still a real possibility that Theasin would turn us away, not because he didn't have the cure, but because he wouldn't want to share it, for whatever reason.

There was no doubt in my mind that Theasin had little

regard for life. And whatever Adelgis had seen in the labs had frightened him—Theasin's own son.

Once upon a time, Adelgis had had nothing but good things to say about his father. That seemed like an eternity ago. Now Adelgis trembled just thinking about confronting his father.

Fain spoke up with, "Wait, so the options are *kill three khepera for a single use cure* or *travel through dangerous territory to reach Theasin Venrover*?"

"This is inane," Jozé stated. "We can't entertain the idea of traveling through the Lightning Straits. I know you've never seen them, but thunderstorms infest the area and—"

"I've seen them," I said. "I know how dangerous they can be."

Jozé opened his mouth to say something more, but stopped halfway through.

"Are those really the only options?" Fain asked. He glanced over at Adelgis. "That's it, Moonbeam?"

"Yes," Adelgis intoned.

It would be simple to kill the khepera and take their sand. I could be free of the plague in less than a day. But what if I became infected again? What if someone else became infected? This really was a *one-time fix* to a major problem. If Theasin had an actual cure, it didn't matter how unfeeling the man was.

What would Master Zelfree say? I could already hear his wisdom, and I agreed. If the khepera really could help heal the soul, then we needed as many khepera arcanists as we could get to fight this menace. I couldn't kill three of them for my own personal gain. Not when they could go on to great things.

Robbing from the future to deal with the problems of the present was a fool's tactic.

I had to see Theasin Venrover.

"*Please, reconsider,*" Adelgis spoke telepathically. "*Just cure yourself, return to the Frith Guild, and let me risk the perils of seeing my father.*"

I shook my head. "I won't harm the khepera. I just… can't. It would go against everything I believe in."

None of the swashbucklers and arcanists from the old stories would destroy baby mystical creatures for their own gain—not even if they were infested with the plague. I wouldn't do it.

Not now. Not ever.

SECURING PASSAGE

"We can't take the *Sun Chaser* through the Lightning Straits," Captain Devlin said, finality in his voice. "It's too dangerous."

The captain's sitting room was filled with people, but no one else spoke, creating an odd atmosphere. The long map table separated one half of the room from the other, and everyone either sat on the leftmost couch or the right. Captain Devlin, Jozé, and Vethica sat together, while Fain, Adelgis, and Karna sat opposite. Only I stood at the head of the table, too restless to relax.

"The storms subside at regular intervals," Adelgis said. "We could take the *Sun Chaser* through when the lightning wanes."

Captain Devlin slammed his hand on the edge of the table, shaking the map and the small wooden blocks used as markers. "That's not the only problem, dammit. Decades ago, that place became a death trap. Plague-ridden mystical creatures as far as the eye can see. *Especially thunderbirds.* Those beasts can follow the *Sun Chaser* no matter how far up we fly."

It was just as my father had said—the hazards were too great.

Yet Theasin had somehow managed to get through, so it wasn't impossible, just difficult. If Captain Devlin wasn't going to take me, I'd have to find another captain willing to make the trek. But who? And what would I pay them with? I basically rode for free with Devlin because of Karna's good graces. I knew no other ships, no other arcanists, who could help.

"It's not like you're defenseless," Karna stated. She scooted to the edge of the couch, just as riled as the captain. "I've seen you fight off plague-ridden creatures hundreds of times in the past. If you wanted, you could take the *Sun Chaser* through the Lightning Straits with little difficulty!"

Captain Devlin also scooted to the edge of his seat and half-leaned across the map table. "Are you sayin' you *want* me to risk the safety of the whole damn crew to get this kid to Theasin Venrover?"

"He helped us," Vethica interjected.

She kept her young khepera in her arms at all times. Even when Akhet squirmed as if trying to crawl onto the table, she held him close. His lustrous exoskeleton didn't sparkle in the low light of the ship's lanterns, but it still seemed mystical.

Vethica continued, "If it weren't for Volke, I would've died in the Grotto Labyrinth."

"And the entire crew owes him a debt now?" Captain Devlin snapped. "Do you think someone like Biyu would survive if we had to make a crash landing?"

"Now you're just being dramatic," Jozé said, waving his hand to dismiss the comment. "We could leave the majority of the crew in New Norra—safe in an inn until we return."

"Jozé, I know he's your son, but you can't possibility be

arguing we go through with this. Look at your damn leg. If we got into a scrape, you'd be one of the first we lost."

"The captain makes a good point," I said, drawing everyone's attention.

It was clear no one had expected me to say that. Well, Adelgis didn't seem surprised, I supposed.

The truth was: I didn't want to endanger the crew. I wouldn't be able to sleep at night if something happened to Biyu, or anyone else, while on this trip. And even if we did what my father said—leaving most of the crew behind—I'd be just as distraught if he died. I never wanted anyone to suffer because of the arcane plague running through my veins. No part of me had helped Vethica find the khepera because I'd thought I could compel her through guilt to return the favor.

"I'll have to find some other way through the Lightning Straits," I said. I turned for the door, my body stiff. "I'm sure there's someone in the city foolhardy enough to make the trek."

Mentally exhausted, I went straight for the storeroom and threw myself on my hammock.

Tomorrow, when the sun rose over the city, I would scour the docks for a captain willing to take me through the Lightning Straits. Until then, I needed rest. I closed my eyes, and despite being fully clothed and uncomfortable, fell asleep in a matter of moments.

And then I was dreaming. It happened so fast, it felt as though I had blinked and become another person. One moment I was on the *Sun Chaser*, in the darkness of a barely lit room, and the next I was on the deck of the *Red Falcon*, sailing the open ocean, the midmorning sun shining down with all its glory.

I was in the middle of a battle—or should I say, *Zelfree was in the middle of a battle*. Pirates littered the deck, their cutlasses at the ready. In the distance, out across a few hundred feet of waves, was another ship. It flew black flags that marked it as a vessel for pirates, and it seemed smaller than the *Red Falcon*, but lighter and quicker.

While Captain Eventide and her first mate, Gregory Ruma, fought off a handful of scallywags near the quarter-deck, I leapt from the ship's rigging and confronted a young scoundrel attempting to get below deck. I landed in front of him, blocking his way to the door leading to the confines of the ship.

When I pulled my sword, the man held up his cutlass—a curved blade with a sharp point. I held my weapon with confidence, but my opponent held his with a shaky grip, his lanky body devoid of hard muscle. This pirate wasn't an arcanist, and every time he glanced to my forehead and saw my mark, his trembling worsened.

I lifted the tip of my blade. "Ready?"

We clashed with blades, and the pirate staggered backward. I pressed the attack, but instead of attacking his undefended side, I just struck his blade. It would've been easy to strike at the pirate's ribs or legs—he was only wearing a thin tunic and soft leather pants, no armor—but Zelfree seemed content to keep his attention on the enemy's sword.

"You need to tighten your grip," I said, smiling. "A weak hold like that won't win you any fights."

The advice appeared to anger the younger pirate. He hardened his expression and lashed out with a powerful overhead swing. I stepped to the side, evading it with little difficulty. The cutlass slammed into the wood of the deck and got caught.

"Where's your strategy?" I asked as I stepped away, allowing the pirate time to pull his sword free of the wood. "Back me into a corner next time. Don't give me room to dodge a heavy swing."

With a frustrated grunt, the man swung wide. I moved away and then leapt in close, obviously startling him. He tried to defend himself, but he fumbled with his own cutlass and somehow dropped it in his attempt to put distance between us. The sword twirled across the deck and then slid away as we were rocked by the waves.

The pirate dove across the deck and scrambled for his weapon, but he was clumsy and uncoordinated. The splash of waves made the deck slick, and coupled with the pirate's panic, resulted in a scene that bordered on slapstick.

I exhaled and leaned against the mizzenmast, my sword held low, but still in my hand.

"Hey," I said, lax and unconcerned with the combat all around us. "While we have a break, I just want to say—I don't think you appreciate the fact that I'm fighting and giving you advice at the same time here."

Once the pirate retrieved his cutlass, he leapt to his feet and whirled around, his weapon at the ready.

Shaking my head, I pushed away from the mizzenmast. The pirate thrust his cutlass forward, no doubt hoping to skewer me, but I dodged in the opposite direction I had last time, clearly confusing my opponent. While the pirate tried to regain his composure, I slashed hard and struck his sword. The man stumbled backward. I did it again and again, forcing the man all the way to the railing of the ship.

Then, instead of running him through, I feigned another

heavy strike. The pirate brought his weapon up to defend himself, and while he had his arm up, I stepped close and tripped him. The man went over the railing, shouted some sort of surprised curse, and then hit the water with a belly flop *sploosh*.

If I'd had control over my actions, I would've laughed. *This* was the very definition of swashbuckling! It was just like the old tales and legends—everything I had ever hoped. Fighting pirates, sword duels, witty remarks—I loved every second. I wished I could have lived in this moment and reveled in the enjoyment. Why couldn't all adventures be this effortless?

Captain Eventide and Ruma also threw their opponents overboard, but before anyone could celebrate, the pirate ship sailed in close, lining up so that both ships ran parallel.

I knew the maneuver well. It was the first step to using a ship's artillery. Cannons were lined on the sides of ships, and once in position, the enemy would unload all their shots at once, hoping to devastate the opponent and sink them in one fell swoop. This *broadside* attack had been especially common decades ago, before longer-range artillery had become the standard.

Well, I supposed this memory was from the past. Even the cannons were straight from the pages of history. Both the *Red Falcon* and the pirate ship used bronze *culverins*— prototype cannons used to bombard targets from a relatively short distance. They were inferior to the iron and steel cannons I had seen on modern ships.

"Don't be a fool, Jennings," Eventide shouted across the waters. I didn't know if those on the enemy ship could hear her, but she stood on the edge of her ship's railing, holding on by just the rigging. "You'll kill your whole damn crew!"

I knew of the Dread Pirate Jennings. I had read about his

attacks on merchant vessels several times, especially late at night, after Gravekeeper William had gone to bed. He hadn't liked it when I'd read reports of successful pirate raids, but I had wanted every ounce of detail on the matters.

Captain Jennings wasn't someone to take lightly. He had killed hundreds. Why was Eventide warning him? And why hadn't she moved the *Red Falcon*? The pirate ship sailed closer and closer, matching our speed and positioning themselves to unload all their cannons.

Ruma and I just stood by and watched. Was no one concerned?

The pirates readied their artillery and then opened fire. The boom of the cannons rang out across the ocean waters like thunder in the middle of a raging storm. My ears rang, and my bones felt the vibration in the air.

Had the *Red Falcon* been damaged?

No.

Captain Eventide had her hand up, her fingers spread. She had evoked a powerful barrier that shimmered in front of the boat, completely blocking the attack. Her atlas turtle magic couldn't be beaten by the likes of simple cannon fire.

"What a damn idiot," Eventide said as she shook her head.

"If he made wise decisions, I doubt he would've become a pirate," Ruma replied with a chuckle.

"Now we have to destroy his ship. I wanted to avoid that."

"Should I command Decimus to rip a hole in the hull?"

Eventide sighed. "No. He'd likely kick up the wind and try to leave us behind. I'll handle it. Have Decimus ready to search the remains of the ship."

"Aye, aye, Captain."

To my fascination, Eventide leapt down from the railing and jogged over to the helm. She gripped the wooden wheel and turned it toward the pirate ship.

"All hands, brace for impact," Ruma shouted.

I returned to the mizzenmast and held on tightly, but I didn't take my gaze off of what was happening. Were we really planning on ramming the *Red Falcon* into the pirate vessel?

Sure enough, Captain Eventide swung the helm around in a tight turn. The pirates had been close for their cannon fire, and they didn't have the room to maneuver away in time. The bow of the *Red Falcon* collided with their ship right in the middle of their starboard side.

At first, I thought both ships would take major damage from such a tactic, but Eventide had evoked yet another powerful barrier. It protected the *Red Falcon*, even when we slammed into the target, like the barrier was a bubble that couldn't be pierced, no matter what. I had never considered Eventide's magic to be an offensive weapon, but clearly, I had been mistaken.

We tore through the enemy ship with little difficulty. Their hull broke apart, the deck caved in, and the crew leapt over the sides to avoid being crushed. The splintering and cracking of wood echoed out over the ocean just as loud as the cannon fire had, and although we had a barrier, the *Red Falcon* still shook after impact, as though our bubble of protection had been knocked back into us slightly.

Once we sailed over the wreckage of the pirate ship, Ruma's leviathan, Decimus, emerged from the ocean. His giant serpentine body was too massive for the waterlogged pirates to deal with. Decimus had to be over a hundred feet long and as a thick as a small boat himself. Using his massive tail and many fins, he scooped people from the water and brought them back to the *Red Falcon.*

"Search for any signs of a kirin," Captain Eventide commanded. "And make sure you capture Jennings. He can't be allowed to escape."

A kirin?

I released the mizzenmast and approached Eventide. "Captain," I said. "Their ship wasn't carrying a kirin."

"You're sure?" she asked.

I nodded. "I'm a mimic arcanist, remember? I told you I can sense nearby mystical creatures. When we sailed over their boat—which was both glorious and hilarious, by the way—I didn't feel any new presence. They weren't carrying a kirin or even any kirin parts."

Eventide pulled back her long, brown hair. Then she turned her gaze to the fat clouds dotting the blue skies overhead. "Damn. Where are they? I can't believe we haven't found the ringleader of this smuggling operation."

"We just have to keep searching," Ruma said. "Or maybe we can persuade Jennings to tell us something. These pirates are obviously all in cahoots."

Interesting.

Kirin were rare mystical creatures. They appeared like horses with majestic horns made of metal or gemstones—they were considered the dragons of unicorns, and capable of predicting the future to limited degrees. Unlike all other mystical creatures, who had a trial of worth to see who they would bond with, kirin knew who they would bond to the moment they were born.

And they would bond with no one else, even if their original arcanist died.

They called it their *sight of destiny.* Kirin bonded to

people they believed would change the world—whether for better or worse.

Pirates were smuggling kirin away from their homelands? Why? If the kirin only bonded with specific, preordained people, it meant just one thing. The pirates were using the kirin for parts—perhaps for trinket and artifact creation.

Again, I grew excited. Master Zelfree had once taken part in an epic quest to stop mystical creature smugglers? If only I weren't infected with the arcane plague. I wanted nothing more than to return to the Frith Guild and ask him all about it—or perhaps make my own such memories.

"We need to get to the heart of this," Eventide said. "If a gang of pirates can conceal their operations from us *for this long*, can you imagine what will happen when they turn their sights on other mystical creatures?"

Ruma nodded along with her words. "We've already gotten word from some of the other guilds that it's happening."

Decimus continued to collect pirates out in the water. Eventide turned her attention to the half-drowned men.

"Perhaps we need to try a different approach..."

The dream shimmered and faded. The colors melted away and then swirled together, becoming something black and unrecognizable. Then they untwisted and became colors again, but this time rearranged.

I had left the last dream-memory and entered another.

The images rearranged themselves into a tavern. Moonlight flowed through the dirty window, and the sounds of rowdy conversation filled the smoky room. I sat at a table in the far corner under a doused lamp, half-hidden in the shadows. Slow piano music played from the opposite side of the room, adding to the noise.

A man walked in, and a couple of patrons stood from their seat in order to clear the way.

I could tell—from the man's considerable height and impressive build—that it was none other than Lynus. He strode through the tavern without looking at anyone else and headed straight for my shadowy corner. When he took a seat, the rickety chair squeaked in protest.

How often had Zelfree and Lynus met in the past? It still bothered me that I didn't understand how they had become enemies.

Lynus's copper hair hung over most of his face, but this time he wasn't injured. He offered me a lopsided smile as he leaned forward on the table.

"Everett," he said, mirth in his voice. "Long time no see."

I also leaned forward. "I'm glad you could make it."

The other patrons returned to their chairs and continued their conversations, obviously satisfied that Lynus wasn't here to start a rumble.

"I have good news," Lynus said. He scooted his chair around the table until we were less than a foot apart. "I think you'll appreciate it most of all."

I scratched at the stubble on my chin, mulling over the comment. A small *meow* drifted up from one of my coat pockets. I dug Traces out of the depths of cloth and set her on the table. Her cute little kitten body was larger than before—time had passed, but not much.

Traces stretched and purred. "Thank you, my arcanist."

Then I turned my gaze to Lynus. "You've become an arcanist," I said. "I can... sense the magic around you."

Lynus smiled wider as he brushed back his hair. The mark on his forehead was just what I had expected—a manticore. Lynus was, without a doubt, Calisto. But what had happened?

"You said you liked cats, right?" Lynus asked with a chuckle. He ran a couple of fingers over the etching in his flesh, tracing the marks of the lion body all manticores had. "Manticores are probably the most deadly cats of all."

I laughed. "You somehow bonded with a manticore just to show me up, is that it? You want your cat to fight my cat? See which one has the bigger... claws?"

Lynus clicked his tongue. "Tsk. I don't wanna fight your kitten." He waved away the comment. "I thought you'd be impressed. I passed the trial of worth, and I've been an arcanist for months. I'm a lot stronger now. A lot more capable."

"Oh, yeah?" I furrowed my brow. "I'm happy for you—I really am—but I'm a little concerned about *how* you got your manticore. Don't those beasts require the eyes of children or something? It's a disturbing legend about how they're attracted out of their dens."

"Somethin' like that. Power requires a price. At least, that's what Captain Redbeard said."

The music played louder, and someone in the tavern suggested a round in celebration. I didn't know what they cheered for, and it didn't matter. I placed a hand on Lynus's arm, and he tensed.

"I'm glad you mentioned your *disgusting* captain," I said with a sneer. "I asked you here because I need to talk to you about him."

"What of 'im?"

"Didn't Captain Redbeard turn pirate after the revolution? He didn't get paid, right? Lots of mystic seekers turned to piracy then, and I've heard the reports of your ship. Captain Redbeard is one of the worst of all."

"That's right."

Lynus said each word as though they tasted bad. He had

been in such a good mood talking about his manticore—now it seemed like he couldn't wait to leave. He leaned away, his jaw tight.

But then Lynus smiled, though it was forced and cold. "Is this the part where you whisk me away from my life of misery? Now that I'm an arcanist, maybe the Frith Guild will take a sad sack like me?" Sarcasm filled his voice, and something else, too. I couldn't identify it. Anger?

"Actually," I whispered. "I had... a different idea."

Lynus lifted an eyebrow. "Oh? You only say shit like that when you have somethin' interesting up your sleeve, Everett."

"Tell me—do you respect your captain? Or even like the man?"

"No." Lynus didn't hesitate. He rubbed at his face, his hand unsteady for a fraction of a second. "The captain's a sadist. If I hadn't become an arcanist, I don't know if I'd even be here. Crewmates go missing in the night, and the dastard has the stones to say they fell overboard."

Although I hated Calisto, the moment he spoke those words, I felt some sympathy for Lynus. He wasn't like himself—not like in the other dream-memories. He seemed uncertain and fearful. Perhaps Zelfree sensed it, too, because he placed a hand on Lynus's knee and leaned in closer.

"What if I said I wanted to help you commit mutiny?" I asked.

Lynus stared at my hand and chortled. "Really? You'd help me kill Captain Redbeard? Why's that? The Frith Guild wants him dead?"

"No. I want *you* as the new captain."

"Me? Why? To turn it back into a mystic seeker vessel?"

I shook my head. "I need help dealing with the pirates. You're already a part of that world—more than me. If I help you become the captain of your own ship, I was hoping you'd help me uncover a mystic creature smuggling operation."

Lynus didn't reply, and the rowdiness of the tavern filled the emptiness between us. A lot of things made sense in that moment. I understood why Zelfree thought this was a cunning plan, and yet... A part of me wanted to intervene, but I knew that was impossible. These events had taken place decades ago. Everything had long been set in stone.

"I do want him dead," Lynus muttered. "I've had plenty of daydreams about it."

"If he's been hurting you or the crew, it's even more reason he should be ousted."

"And you'll... be there with me when this happens?"

I nodded. "*Of course*. I'll have Traces make me look like some other arcanist. I'll take a different name—no one will know I'm Everett of the Frith Guild. I'll stay with you after the bloodshed, all throughout my investigation. It'll be like old times. Just me and you."

Those last few words changed Lynus's demeanor. He relaxed—I hadn't realized how tense he had been until he had unwound—and let out a short exhale. "I'd like that. I never thought I'd miss life on the streets, like when we were younger. I didn't have so many damn problems then."

"There's nothing we can't handle when we're together," I said. "Trust me. It'll be fine, and you'll even help me save a lot of mystical creatures in the process."

Traces purred and rolled onto her side. "I like this plan. I approve."

"And I..." Lynus bit at the words, unable to say something. He shook his head. "I do want you to meet my eldrin. Maybe we *will* see whose cat's claws are larger."

<hr>

I awoke without warning, the dream-memory terminated at a jarring speed.

Someone knocked on the storeroom door, startling me out of my groggy state. I slid out of my hammock and massaged my temple as I stepped around the many barrels. When I opened the door, I hadn't been expecting to see Vethica and her new eldrin, Akhet.

"Volke," she whispered.

The dim lanterns informed me that it was evening. "Yes?"

"I wanted to tell you thank you for what you did. And that... Karna and I will make sure you get a ship that'll take you through the Lightning Straits."

"Thank you," I said. "But that might be impossible."

"Finding a way through the Grotto Labyrinth was impossible. Finding a ship will be nothing in comparison."

I couldn't help but smile. "Yeah, I guess finding a ship would be easier than solving a decades-old mystery. By the way, I never got a chance to tell you that I was impressed you made it through the maze without any assistance."

Akhet wiggled in Vethica's arms. "I was impressed, too. That is why I bonded with her, even though she carries a lingering illness."

"We're going to find a way to fix it," Vethica stated. "I promise. As soon as I can—as soon as I master even the slightest of healing—it'll be everything I focus on."

I nodded. "I believe you."

Vethica held her khepera close, her determination apparent. "The Marshall of the Southern Seas has everyone cooped up in the docks, so we'll have plenty of ships to ask for passage. Someone will take you. I promise."

Again, I smiled. "Thank you."

33

LEAVING NEW NORRA

I wanted to participate in the search for a ship, but with Jevel and other plague hunters wandering the streets of New Norra, I couldn't risk it. The crew of the *Sun Chaser*, along with Fain and Adelgis, had said they would handle the matter. In the meantime, I practiced aura manifestation.

A piece of me feared it would take weeks to convince a captain to help us—weeks of my limited time—but I tried to remain optimistic. What did Biyu say? Look forward, not behind?

"You've handled this well, my arcanist," Luthair said from the dark corner of the storeroom. "Mathis never handled unexpected changes with as much patience as you've displayed."

I wanted to ask about Luthair's first arcanist, but the door to the storeroom opened, breaking my chain of thoughts. Fain and Adelgis wandered into the room, neither looking too pleased. They gave me polite nods, just enough to acknowledge my presence. I nodded back.

"So, what's your father doing at this *Excavation Site*?" Fain asked Adelgis.

"His notes said he's overseeing the excavation."

"Of what?"

"Something large. Perhaps *massive* would be a better word. My father stopped in New Norra to hire more people for digging. According to his expense report, he hired twenty people."

"Twenty people?" I asked. "Is he digging up a city?"

Adelgis took a seat on his ratty hammock. It swung back and forth as he mulled over my question. Fain leaned against the bulkhead, his fidgety movements and intent gaze betraying his restlessness.

"I think it's a creature," Adelgis said. "One letter addressed to my father mentioned the condition of bones."

My thought immediately went to the black bones I had taken from his office. Perhaps Theasin had unearthed the corpse of a powerful mystical creature? Long ago, there had been thirteen god-creatures and arcanists, but they had all perished, and only their remains proved they had once existed. My shield was made from a scale of the mighty world serpent—what if Theasin had found the rest of the body? The power contained in the corpse of the world serpent would be tremendous, and I suspected Theasin didn't have noble intentions.

But were they evil intentions? I still wasn't sure.

"Well, the faster we get there, the faster we'll have the answer," Fain muttered.

I couldn't sleep.

For the entire night, I stared at the ceiling, trying to clear my thoughts and manifest an aura. For a short period, I thought I had it. So close. But then I'd think of Illia and mess up my own concentration. Where was she? What if she had already found the new world serpent?

I wondered...

A creak in the corridor beyond the storeroom door halted my musings. Tense, and slightly on edge, I slipped out of my hammock and crept to the door. The soft footfalls of someone on the other side got me curious. Instead of opening the door, I stepped into the shadows, slid under the door, and emerged on the other side, far enough away so that I exited the darkness behind the mystery individual.

Karna stood in the hallway, unaware of my presence. She hovered around the door, almost like she was caught in a silent debate.

Her outfit...

I had seen her in stunning garments before, but this seemed more elaborate. The two-piece dancer's outfit shimmered, even in the low light, and exposed her stomach, arms, and most of her legs. Her sandals laced up to her knees, but otherwise, she wore nothing else. Had she been out dancing?

Bells rang in the distance, signaling the approach of dawn.

"You look beautiful," I said.

Karna flinched and whirled around on her heel. Her expression held more anger than fear, but it softened the moment she recognized me.

"Oh, Volke. I came to see you." She straightened her blonde hair and forced a smile. "You're up early."

"Is something wrong?"

"No." She stepped close and placed a hand on my upper arm. "I have good news, actually."

"Really? Did you find a ship?" I hadn't meant to sound so eager, but it slipped out regardless.

Karna nodded. "I did." Her expression became distant and her voice low. "Vethica, Jozé, and I spent all of yesterday narrowing down our options. Only certain kinds of ships can make it through the Lightning Straits in the short time frame the storms aren't active."

I held my breath, absorbing every word.

"And there are only certain captains who have the capability to defend themselves from plague-ridden creatures," Karna said, but each word came out as if specially chosen. "*And* we need someone who will ignore the Marshall of the Southern Sea's commands. The ship we need requires all three things. You understand that, right?"

I understood her words, but not her hesitation. "Which captain said they would help us?"

For a long while, Karna said nothing.

Why was she afraid? Any captain willing to take us was a hero in my book.

"Does this captain want an exorbitant payment?" I asked. "I'll find a way to get the coin."

"It's not that. I arranged payment. It's…"

"What?" I shook my head. "Enough of the games. Just tell me."

"Well, I know how *upstanding* and *chivalrous* you can be," Karna said. She grabbed my arm and pulled me close, her gaze hardening into a glower. "But you have to let some of that go. The only captain who has a fast enough ship, and the crew to handle the plague, and the rebellious attitude to defy the marshall, is a dread pirate."

I gritted my teeth, unable to find any appropriate words. My gut twisted in fear as I imagined the worst possible outcome.

"Tell me it's not Calisto," I whispered.

Karna lifted a delicate eyebrow. "You know him?"

Curse the abyssal hells.

I pulled my arm from her grasp and stepped away, my heart hammering hard. Out of all the pirates—*out of all the ships*—it had to be the *Third Abyss*. Calisto's vile vessel was the last place I wanted to visit.

"Calisto is the man who cut out my sister's eye," I said.

"You have a sister?"

"My adopted sister. Illia's family's merchant ship was attacked by Calisto. He killed her parents and took her eye. And now you want me to sail with the man? I just... I can't do it."

Even knowing that Calisto had once been Lynus—once Master Zelfree's confidant—I still found it impossible. Boarding the *Third Abyss* would be a betrayal to Illia. I could already see her reaction to the situation. Her anger and pain would haunt me forever.

"I know Calisto as well," Karna said matter-of-factly. "And he's never gone back on his word to me. When I asked him for passage through the Lightning Straits, I made him agree it would be a simple trek. He won't attack any merchant vessels or harm anyone innocent. I knew you'd never be okay unless those terms were in place."

"I don't think you understand. I once *attacked* Calisto. My sister and I boarded his ship. We even wrecked it. I doubt he'll want me as a passenger."

"My arcanist," Luthair said. His shadows slipped around me. "You never faced Calisto by yourself. I was always armor covering you. He may not know."

I shook my head. "I'm a knightmare arcanist—there aren't that many of us. He'll figure it out. And then what?"

Karna grabbed my arm a second time, tighter than before. She held me close, almost like she didn't want to lose me. "I didn't know any of that. Let me speak to Calisto again.

Unlike you, I know *exactly* what he likes, and he's always happy to see me. It won't take much persuasion. He'll agree to take you."

"Fain was once a member of his crew," I said, searching for any possible reason to sour this deal. "There's no way Calisto will tolerate a renegade pirate."

Karna fluttered her eyelashes. "I assure you, that'll be the least of our problems. Calisto has taken back several renegades. He only has a problem with traitors. I can get him to overlook your frostbitten friend, so long as nothing horrible transpired between them."

It wasn't the answer I wanted.

Sailing with Calisto was out of the question. It had to be. He was a villain and the worst kind of pirate. Even being in close proximity to him would test my self-control. Calisto deserved to be cut down. Did I have the strength to do it? I didn't know, and I almost didn't care.

"Please," Karna said as she matched my gaze. "You don't have to do anything. You don't even need to speak to the man. I'll make all the arrangements, and once we disembark, he'll be on his way, far from us."

"Why are you so desperate to help me?" I whispered.

She narrowed her eyes and dug her fingers into my arm. "I think I've made my intentions pretty clear since we attended the Queen's Gala together. Not only that, but you helped Vethica—a person whom I care for. You're also Jozé's son—and I'm fond of him, too. And then there's Biyu. Do I really need to list all the reasons I'm concerned about you? Why won't you just let me help?"

"I..." It took a second to align my thoughts in a way that wouldn't be offensive. "I never know what you're really thinking, Karna. It makes it difficult. I have to guess what you genuinely want."

To my surprise, she slid her hand up the back of my neck into my hair. Slow, but confident, she stood on her tiptoes and guided my mouth closer to hers. I didn't stop her when she kissed me, not even when it lasted longer than expected. She smelled and tasted of the ocean, which brought with it a sense of comforting nostalgia.

Karna lowered herself, breaking off our kiss, and stood firm with her feet flat. "I genuinely want to help you," she whispered. "If there were any other way, I would take it. But this is it. Please let me make arrangements with the *Third Abyss.*"

"Okay," I muttered.

I hoped Illia would forgive me.

And Master Zelfree, for that matter.

She stepped away and brushed her long, golden hair over her shoulder. "Then you should get ready. We'll leave as soon as Calisto has gathered his crew."

"You're sure you can get him to agree to everything?"

Karna smiled, a mix of impish and coy. "Like I said, I know what motivates Calisto. Everything will be handled. I'll make sure you reach Theasin as fast as possible." She took off down the corridor, quick in step and filled with energy.

I wondered if—at any point I had known her—I had interacted with her doppelgänger instead of her. I touched my lips, the taste of sea salt lingering at the edge of my perceptions.

"I know this bothers you," Luthair said. "But think of it this way—if Calisto does attempt to harm someone, we will be there to stop him."

That thought hadn't occurred to me, but it was something to keep in mind. If this did go south, perhaps I could turn a bad situation around. Lost in thought, I opened the storeroom door to find a lantern had been lit.

Adelgis had perched himself on the edge of a wooden crate, and Fain paced the back wall like a caged animal.

"I think you're overreacting," Adelgis said as he crossed his legs.

Fain sarcastically stroked his chin. "*Hmm.* Nope. I think this is the appropriate amount of *reacting*. I might be *under*reacting, actually."

"Karna is sincere in her beliefs. She doesn't think Calisto will harm us."

"You two know already?" I asked.

Both of them snapped their attention to me, as though they hadn't realized I had come in. Adelgis relaxed after a deep breath and then offered me a slight smile.

"I overheard the conversation," he said. "And relayed it to Fain. The part about Calisto agitated him, but I'm trying to reassure him that everything will be fine."

Fain shoved his hands into his trouser pockets. "Nobody here knows Calisto like I do. He's ruthless—if he changes his mind, we won't survive."

"You can stay here, if you want," I said. "Either in New Norra or on the *Sun Chaser*. You don't have to go with me to the Excavation Site."

Those words seemed to irritate Fain more than the plan with Calisto. He met my gaze, a wounded expression across his face. Then he hardened up, his whole body tense. "I'm not abandoning you. I just... want you to be aware."

"Trust me—I'm plenty *aware*."

"Then I'll stick with you," Fain muttered. "Even if it means returning to the *Third Abyss*."

Adelgis joined in with a single nod. "Fain and I are committed no matter the troubles."

"You should stay," I said. "I'm already plague-ridden, and Fain is immune. You'll be in danger if you come with us."

"I'm always in danger no matter where I go, but you'll need me to get to my father. My company isn't up for debate."

Their reaffirmation helped to ease some of my anxiety. At least they would be by my side as we traveled through the Lightning Straits—a small piece of the Frith Guild, helping me along. I wanted the others, even Illia, though she would never agree to ride with Calisto.

What would they say about the *Third Abyss*? Zaxis would complain from here to the sun and back. Hexa would cause trouble. Atty would have a reasoned response and attitude —mature beyond her years.

Master Zelfree...

I still didn't know what had happened between him and Lynus. I couldn't imagine his response.

"We should gather anything we might need," Adelgis said as he slid off the crate. "It might be a while before we'll be able to find someone to take us *back* through the Lightning Straits."

34

PASSENGERS ABOARD THE THIRD ABYSS

Gathering my things didn't take long—I owned little at this point. But everyone on the ship seemed anxious when they heard I was leaving. Every few minutes, I had a new visitor. I didn't know most of their names, but they spoke as though we were friends.

"It's a shame you have to leave," one woman with a round face said as she handed me a pouch of fresh—and properly salted—jerky. "We're going to miss you."

Miss me?

"Uh, thank you," I said as I took the pouch.

Once I shut the door, I placed it on the pile of all the other things I had been gifted: a quality canteen, a leather jacket with several pockets, new laces for my boots, and a brass compass. Before I could decide on my next course of action, another knock sounded at the door. I opened it, shocked to see the ship's surgeon, Tammi, standing in the corridor.

"Am I interrupting?" she asked, her voice soft.

I shook my head.

Tammi half-smiled, which was probably the happiest I

had ever seen her. "Oh, good. I wanted to catch you before you left." She held up a satchel filled with wootz cotton and various other medical supplies. "These are for your trek. Just in case."

I took the satchel, almost at a loss for words. "Thank you very much."

"Everyone is hoping you'll be okay."

I stared at her, my eyebrows knitted. "Tammi... I don't understand. I mean, I almost hurt a crewmember when—"

"You'll have to forgive everyone," Tammi said, cutting me off. She broke eye contact, her cheeks flushed. "And please, uh, would you mind turning away? I'm sorry. I get flustered."

I did as she asked and glanced at a spot on the bulkhead over her shoulder.

Tammi smoothed her clothes and muttered, "Thank you. And, um, as I was trying to say... I don't know if you're aware, but everyone on this airship has come here from hard times. Thankfully, we have each other. And everyone talks to everyone. So, whenever you've done anything—even when you were just training with Fain and Moonbeam—the entire crew eventually heard every detail."

"Did you just call Adelgis *Moonbeam*?" I asked.

Tammi closed her eyes, her shoulders bunched at the base of her neck. "Everyone thought it was a fitting nick-name. He said some odd things to us from time to time." After a moment of silence, she continued, "What I'm trying to say is—at first everyone thought you were a plague-ridden killer, like those laughing mad beasts. But we realized you were just like us. Someone who came here from hard times."

"Well, I'm fortunate that I have good friends," I said.

Tammi nodded. "I'm sorry you never got to know the rest of the crew, but we all got to know you, and you'll be missed." Then she opened her eyes in surprise. "Oh, I almost forgot. Biyu wants you to have this." She withdrew a folded piece of paper from one of her many jacket pockets and handed it over.

"Where is Biyu? She's not going to give me this herself?"

"Biyu said she didn't want to say goodbye." Tammi frowned. "She told me she didn't want you to think she was throwing you away."

"I would never think that," I said.

"I know. But perhaps, once you're cured, you can come back and tell her yourself."

I liked the optimism in her statement. It was *once* I was cured, not *if* I was cured. I intended to take that kind of attitude with me. I would make it out of this gloom no matter what.

Curious about Biyu's paper, I unfolded it and stared. It wasn't a letter or message—just a drawing. Although she was young, her steady hand and skill were apparent. The drawing depicted Fain, Adelgis, and me on the deck of the *Sun Chaser*. I had shadows all around me, Fain had ice, and Adelgis was sitting on the railing, his ethereal whelk floating above his head. Most parts were childish, but it was a better drawing than anything I could do.

"Thank you, Tammi," I said as I pocketed the picture. "For everything."

Before we were to leave, my father summoned me to his quarters. Luthair and I headed straight there, and while I knew Jozé couldn't make the trek because of his bum leg, I also didn't want to say goodbye.

A part of me hated the fact that I was separated from the

Frith Guild, even if I had done it to protect them, and now another part of me hated leaving the *Sun Chaser*. Finding a cure would mean I could go home, so I held on to my feelings of hope. I'd see them all again.

I knocked on Jozé's door.

"Come in," he said from within. "We don't have much time."

I stepped into his quarters. His bright blue phoenix was the first thing I saw, but the black leather boots on the center table were the second. They were the type of high sailing boots that most ship captains and officers wore—high quality material meant to keep one's feet dry, even in difficult weather.

"Do you think you could imbue your knightmare magic into these boots?" Jozé asked. He limped around the table, a pouch of star shards in one hand. "You'd really help me out if you did."

I stepped close and nodded. "Of course."

"You're too good to me, boy."

I rubbed at the back of my neck, a little confused. "You know I'm leaving, right? Tomorrow morning the *Third Abyss* departs from port."

Jozé stopped once he was on the opposite side of the table. He met my gaze with a sarcastically raised eyebrow. "Oh, is that right? I had no idea. Next you'll be telling me you're plague-ridden."

"I'm serious."

He pushed the boots toward me. "I know the situation. That's why you need to imbue these boots before you leave." Then he rolled over six star shards.

Six? Seemed high for a simple trinket, but it also meant these weren't going to be an artifact. If the Second Ascension used their terrible item-destroying dust, these boots would never make it.

Regardless, I did as my father wanted. I took the shards, then the boots, and allowed my magic to pour into the items. At that moment, it made sense why we needed six—three for each boot. They were individual items that needed individual attention. It took me a moment to grasp that fact as I shunted knightmare magic into one and then the next.

"I fashioned these boots from the leather wings of the byakhee," my father said as he pointed to the phoenix imprint he had left on the side—his signature mark. "The byakhee are interesting creatures, to say the least. They travel supernaturally fast, have the ability to teleport, and don't need to breathe. Some say they come from the stars. Fortunately for us, the merchant selling the wings didn't know what they were."

Once the star shards had been used up, and my hands had stopped shaking from the transfer, I said, "So these boots will enable fast travel?"

"They'll allow their wearer to shadow-step like a knightmare arcanist—probably even a little faster, thanks to the magics of the byakhee."

"Interesting."

There was still a lot for me to learn about item crafting, but it was clear my father had a solid grasp. The combinations were infinite, and it impressed me that he could see opportunity in every little piece of magic. Even if he sometimes went too far—like with the khepera.

Jozé gathered up the boots and placed them on the ground. "That was it. All I needed." He limped around to the side of the table and then rapped his knuckles across the top. "We'll reunite soon enough. No need for long goodbyes. Just take care of yourself, you hear me?"

His phoenix lifted her head. "We'll both miss you."

I gave them each a nod, thankful neither wanted this to be an ordeal. "Well, then, I'll see you once I return."

The *Third Abyss* was just as I remembered—a nightmare vessel.

It was a man-o-war, a type of ship meant to carry heavy weapons. Swing guns lined the deck, the type of artillery meant to destroy smaller vessels. And if that weren't enough, the 100 cannons on the other decks would do the trick. The three masts were lined with sails, and I suspected the *Third Abyss* had run down many a ship that couldn't compare.

The worst part—the defining feature of the terrible ship—was its ghostwood. The entire thing was grayish and dead, built from the magical trees that surrounded Port Crown. Fog poured from the wood, even in its current state, surrounding the *Third Abyss* in a mist that stretched on for thousands of feet in all directions. It kept the ship hidden, even on the open ocean. That was how Calisto had avoided capture in the past. Once lost in the fog, it was difficult to deal with him or his cannons.

The *Third Abyss*, while stationed in the delta of the Lion's Tail River, blanketed most ships in its terrible fog. Most people would've considered this an irritation, but the mist damped the harsh rays of the sun. Most dockhands seemed pleased with the change, even if it limited their visibility.

I stood on the dock, gazing up at the many decks of the *Third Abyss*. It was a giant of a vessel, weighing over 1,000 tons. The thing could easily carry a crew of 700 to 800 sailors. Were there that many pirates aboard? It wouldn't surprise me.

Adelgis and Fain stood by me, both examining the ship as I did. Pirates loaded the ship with supplies, walking up and down the lengthy gangplank. Unlike Fain and me, who only had a satchel each, Adelgis carried two bags—one for books and one for clothing. His book bag strained his shoulder, and when I went to hold it for him, he clung tightly to the straps.

"It's okay," he said. "I have it."

Fain sighed. "I'm going to stay invisible."

Adelgis replied with a nod. "Probably for the best."

"And I think we should stay as far from the rest of the crew as possible. If we upset them, they'll get Calisto involved, and he hates looking weak in front of anyone. If it looks like there's a fight, just apologize and hope he doesn't follow through."

I placed my hand on the hilt of Retribution, mulling over my options. Part of me knew I wouldn't back down. I couldn't seem to keep control of that anymore.

"The arcane plague erodes a person's rationality and restraint," Adelgis said aloud, no doubt a response to my thoughts. "It just means we'll need to be careful for the entirety of the trip. No unnecessary provocation."

Once the dockhands and merchants were done sorting through crates and barrels, they whistled to the crew of the *Third Abyss*. Everything was loaded. Even Karna had boarded hours prior. There were no other reasons to delay.

"We should board," Adelgis said.

Fain shrouded himself with invisibility as we headed for the gangplank. Luthair shifted around my feet, no doubt to remind me he was present.

The last time I had been on the *Third Abyss*, Calisto had

almost killed me. I had to block those thoughts from my head, at least until we made it through the Lightning Straits.

I stepped onto the deck of the ship, disturbed by the grayish wood and lingering fog. The presence of mist made everything cold—a pleasant change from the Amber Dunes—but terrible nonetheless. The chill reminded me of a graveyard.

Standing on the deck, ready to greet us, were two arcanists, one of which I recognized.

Spider. Calisto's first mate. I had seen her in the *Waterside Notable* when Biyu had been taken. She wore fitted trousers, high boots, and a shirt that had one too many buttons undone. Her black hair had been secured back, showcasing her arcanist mark. A disgusting fish-man was wrapped around the star. A kappa.

Her eldrin sat at her feet. The kappa looked like a twelve-year-old child with pond-scum-green fish scales for skin. Its giant eyes, glowing yellow, stared at me with a malevolent glare. When I didn't glance away, it flashed its needle-thin teeth and hissed. It was a man-eater, immune to the arcane plague.

The other man... I didn't recognize him. It wasn't an arcanist who had served with Calisto over a year ago. This was someone new. His arcanist mark intrigued me. He was bonded to a *carcolh*, a half-snake, half-mollusk creature that grew to the size of a house and had a shell that couldn't be penetrated. According to legend, the carcolh swallowed people whole—another man-eating creature immune to the plague—and the tentacles around its face were covered in a slime that paralyzed its enemies.

I didn't see the carcolh around, but it could easily be in the water.

The carcolh arcanist himself was lanky and leathery,

similar to a piece of meat that had been left out in the sun for far too long. His dark hair clung to his face at odd places, like he had stolen it from another man's razor and glued it to his cheeks. And his ratty coat, belt, and tall boots didn't help his appearance much, either.

How did Calisto always find the creepiest arcanists to serve under him?

"You must be our *esteemed guests*," Spider said, her voice rich and confident. She crossed her arms as she gave me the once-over. "You're that same knightmare arcanist who snuck aboard our ship. And you—" she turned her gaze to Adelgis for a brief moment, "—are Artificer Theasin's son. Of course you'd have some bizarre mystical creature as your eldrin."

Adelgis and I said nothing. I wasn't even sure where to begin.

"Where's Fain?" she asked. "Or is the coward hiding from us?"

"That's none of your business," I growled, already losing the grip on my self-control.

Adelgis placed a hand on my shoulder. "*All is well,*" he said telepathically. "*Inquire about our quarters. That's what they expect.*"

I exhaled as I asked, "Where will we be staying?"

"You'll be confined to the officer's cabins near the bow." Spider pointed with a long finger, opposite the quarterdeck, where the captain's quarters were. "Malaki and I will be right next door." She tapped the chest of the carcolh arcanist—Malaki, apparently. "So we can keep a close eye on the lot of you."

Her kappa hissed again, its mouth open wide enough to fit a cantaloupe inside.

"Fain should know the way," Spider added.

I glanced around the deck, taking note of the heavy guns

and the crew members tending to them. Karna had said Calisto wouldn't attack anyone on this voyage, yet the crew was preparing for combat. Perhaps it was something I needed to discuss with her.

"Where's Karna?" I asked.

Spider's face pinched in a tight frown. "The doppelgänger whore? She's with Calisto, working on her payment for the ride."

My blood ran cold.

Although I knew Karna had no compunction with using her body like a currency, I hadn't expected her to offer such a deal to Calisto. The man wasn't worthy of her time or attention, and even the slightest thought that he was hurting her drove me to the edge of rage.

I must've shown it on my face, because Spider lifted both eyebrows.

"Oh, ya don't like that?" she asked. "You should go tell Calisto. This might be a short trip after all."

Malaki snorted, a slight smile at the corner of his sun-dried lips.

While I was tempted to put this to rest right here, right now, one of Calisto's pirates approached us with a stiff posture and bemused expression. Spider snapped her attention to the man and sneered.

"What is it?" she barked.

The crewman motioned to the gangplank. It hadn't yet been pulled up.

"What're you waiting for?" Spider asked.

"There's an arcanist here," the man said, his voice thick with saliva. "From the Huntsman Guild. He said he's after plague-ridden arcanists, and he wants to search the ship before we take off."

35

THE LAST GODS

Spider adjusted her bosom as though unconcerned with the new information. "It'll be handled," she said as she smoothed her half-buttoned shirt.

The pirate stammered as he pointed toward the gangplank. People strode up to the ship, including my new constant companion, Jevel, the reaper arcanist plague hunter. His trinket—some sort of blood bracelet—would detect my presence, even if I hid. Would Jevel force a fight on the *Third Abyss*? Probably. Especially if he thought I was about to escape his clutches.

I went to unsheathe Retribution, but someone placed a hand on my arm. I couldn't see them, but I felt the icy touch, even through the sleeve of my coat. Fain. He didn't want me to act. Instead, he touched the side of my neck and pointed me toward the quarterdeck.

Then I saw Calisto's manticore eldrin—Hellion.

The beast flew off the quarterdeck with leathery wings. He landed on the deck with a hard slam that betrayed his considerable weight. If I had to guess, Hellion was four or five tons of pure muscle. He had the body of a white lion, but instead of a brown or gold mane, he had a crimson mane that resembled curdled blood.

The worst aspect of Hellion's appearance—the one I'd remember until I was buried—was the mask covering the manticore's face, like it was a body part that had replaced the long muzzle. A plain, expressionless mask, oval in shape and designed for a human. The eyes were slits, and so was the straight line representing the mouth.

The mask matched Hellion's human-like hands, complete with thumbs. Claws jutted out of the "fingers," each clicking on the wood of the deck as Hellion made his way to the gangplank. He blocked the plague hunters from boarding, his massive body an impassable obstacle.

Jevel, the only arcanist in the group of ten, was pushed to the front. His reaper floated alongside him, unconcerned with gravity. It twirled its long scythe and said nothing. The other hunters stepped back, their frightened muttering audible, even from my distance some thirty feet away.

"I'm a p-plague hunter," Jevel forced himself to say.

Hellion swished his scorpion tail back and forth. It was seven feet long—black as the darkest shadows—and when it curled up and around, ready to attack, the non-arcanists rushed down the gangplank in such a hurry, I thought some would fall into the delta.

"I have the authority of the governor to hunt anyone carrying the arcane plague," Jevel continued, more confident than before. He held out a piece of paper. "An informant told me that a plague-ridden arcanist boarded your ship."

Hellion reached out his disgusting, human-like hand. It was massive—Hellion could fit all of Jevel's head in his palm—and retained the features of a cat, including the fur and padding. Careful not to scratch Jevel, Hellion took the piece of paper and brought it close to his emotionless mask.

He crumpled the paper and said, "The governor's jurisdiction doesn't extend to the *Third Abyss*." He spoke every word calm and cold, his voice emanating from behind the mask.

"If the ship is still tied to the dock, then that means I'm allowed to—"

Hellion lowered his hand, and Jevel flinched away, his arm up as if to defend his eyes. With a chuckle, Hellion offered the crinkled paperwork. "If you wish to force your way aboard, by all means. Try."

Jevel glanced to his reaper. Although his eldrin had no face, the two seemed to share a silent moment.

"Or you can run to the Watch Battalion," Hellion said. "But by the time you bring them here, we won't be tied to the dock. Seems to me there isn't much of a choice if you want to find this plague-ridden arcanist."

The mouth of Hellion's mask twisted into a small smile. The eyes curved upward, mimicking a happy expression. Every slight movement of the "mask" knotted my guts and made me want to vomit. It wasn't natural. Every part of the freakish manticore seemed designed to instill terror.

Jevel's oily face paled, and I didn't blame him. He distanced himself from the manticore one step at a time. "My informant... must've been mistaken."

A low rumbling growl issued from Hellion. It was the only warning Jevel needed. He hurried down the gangplank without a second glance back, his steps so hasty, he almost tripped.

The crewmen watching the exchange quickly resumed their work the moment Hellion turned around. Even Malaki and Spider seemed disturbed when the manticore gave them a prolonged stare. The manticore's face returned to its true neutral—no expression. Spider motioned to the officer's quarters and led us away from the beast.

I took note of the deck. Some pieces of ghostwood had been replaced—their gray different than the gray of the old wood. Were these the battle scars from when Illia and Calisto had fought? It amused me to think they were.

Hellion paced the ship, the harsh click of his claws lingering in my mind as we entered the drab corridor of the *Third Abyss*. The fog haunted the hallway, light and misty. It didn't obscure my vision, but it felt as though I had entered a dream.

Spider pointed to the room at the end of the narrow corridor. By giving us that room, we would have to pass every other room when we exited. Although I understood why they wouldn't trust us—and why they had made that their choice—I hated giving them any advantage.

Adelgis and I entered without further instruction.

To my surprise, it was a spacious room, obviously meant for four officers. The beds were built into each corner, and a large table had been secured in the center of the room, preventing it from moving should there be turbulence on the waves. Pillows and blankets were tied down inside the cabinet on the back wall, and a barrel of rum sat next to it.

The *Third Abyss* was three times the size of the *Sun Chaser*.

Adelgis shut the door. "Volke, Fain—I need to speak to both of you."

Fain allowed his invisibility to drop. Wraith also appeared by his side, his emaciated wolf figure a scary sight, though nothing in comparison to Hellion.

"What is it?" I asked as I threw my bag down on the nearest bed.

"I think now is a good time to share everything I know about my father."

Fain took a seat on the mattress in the far corner. He leaned against the bulkhead, his whole body tense.

"Go on," I said.

Without a moment to waste, Adelgis placed his book bag on the center table. He withdrew several items, including the book with the broken chain—something he had definitely taken from the Norra Library, even if he hadn't admitted it yet.

"I read all my father's notes," Adelgis said, his attention on the books, but his voice clear and unambiguous. "He planned this trip to the Excavation Site years ago. However, he refused to go until he had one of two things: an abyssal leech or a mimic arcanist."

Content to listen, I also sat on my bed. Restless energy caused me to stand a moment later. I couldn't relax, so I walked around the edge of the room, examining all the tiny details as Adelgis continued.

"I was the one who gave him both things." Adelgis opened two of the books, his gaze hard-set. "But his last letters in New Norra said he was no longer interested in the mimic. He wanted the Mother of Shapeshifters—he said it was unlike other creatures. He postulated it was the child of gods. And I think he's right."

"Gods?" Fain asked.

Adelgis pointed to a book. "Yes. I told you before, the Second Ascension is responsible for creating the new world serpent. Well, thousands of years ago, when the first round of god-creatures roamed this world, some of those arcanists tried to breed their eldrin together. I had never read anything about that until I found this tome in the Norra Library—the same one my father referenced in his letters."

I walked over to the table and stared down at the ancient book, taking note of the worn pages and faded ink. The letters were legible, and I read through the opening pages.

Thirteen god-creatures are born every turning of an age, during a time of great magical disturbance. They are meant to usher humanity through turbulent times. These creatures first appeared when the sky tore open and star shards rained to the ground.

"And you said the world serpent is the first god-creature to appear?" Fain asked. He seemed focused on the conversation, and I wondered if it was to distract him from our environment. He hadn't looked up since he'd taken a seat on the edge of his bed.

"The world serpent is the first of thirteen," Adelgis said. "And one of the strongest. The other twelve gods came later —one at a time. Like a clock counting down."

"Why do you say it like that?"

"Because the last god to spawn was the *apoch dragon.* Once it was born, it killed the other twelve. Its purpose was to wipe away godly beings, and once it did, it died."

Fain chortled. "Oh. Fun. Sounds like it would be the rage at all the parties. I bet everyone wanted to bond with it."

"Actually," Adelgis said, "according to all texts on the time period, the apoch dragon bonded to no one. It was a destroyer of magic—incapable of having an arcanist." He ran his hand over the tome. "But we should focus. The thing my father cared about most was the story of breeding. You see, the god-arcanists who bonded to the other twelve were very interesting. Especially the woman bonded to the *soul forge.* She was obsessed with learning how these god-creatures operated and tried to produce offspring at several occasions."

I pulled the tome toward me. "Do you mind if I read a bit more?" I asked.

Adelgis shook his head in response.

What were the thirteen creatures? I didn't know, but now seemed a prudent time to learn. I flipped the pages until I came to a diagram of the thirteen gods. Twelve were drawn in a circle with the world serpent at the top. The apoch dragon was in the center. Each creature was listed with a number to represent their order of appearance.

They were:

1—The World Serpent
2—The Soul Forge
3—The Fenris Wolf
4—The Sky Titan
5—The Garuda Bird
6—The Abyssal Kraken
7—The Typhon Beast
8—The Scylla Waters
9—The Tempest Coatl
10—The Progenitor Behemoth
11—The Corona Phoenix
12—The Endless Undead
13—The Apoch Dragon

"The woman who had bonded with the soul forge—they refer to her as *the scholar*—bred her eldrin with the progenitor behemoth arcanist's eldrin. Or at least... she tried.

Apparently, most things born of that union became twisted monsters they had to destroy."

Fain rubbed at his eyes. "Moonbeam, do you ever read anything normal? Something not so depressing or foreboding? A fluffy romance, perhaps? An instruction manual?"

Adelgis dwelled on the question. Then he continued, as though it were unimportant. "But some of this text implies one child wasn't a hideous monster."

"Plot twist of the year."

"Given the power of the Mother of Shapeshifters, and the fact that the soul forge could change its own shape, the possibility denotes a substantial connection. My father became fixated. He wrote to his associates at the Excavation Site to say he would need it captured. They wrote back, saying they would."

"I wish I had butlers capable of capturing god-babies at the drop of a hat."

"Fain," I said, shooting him a glare. "Please. Focus."

Scolding him wasn't necessary, but his running commentary had already gotten on my nerves.

He scoffed and then shrugged. "Look, I'm just trying to keep up. *The Frith Guild* is in a race against the Second Ascension to see who will bond with these god-creatures first. *Moonbeam* is concerned about his father's motives and moral compass. *And you* need to a find a cure for the arcane plague before you go insane. Everything is a problem, and if we don't solve some of it soon, we might as well put pistols to our temples and get this over with."

Wraith whined like only a dog could. He placed his skull-covered face on Fain's lap.

Fain sighed. "I was exaggerating. We just have a lot of problems. Why do we need to bring in things like the

Mother of Shapeshifters? She can handle her own damn troubles."

The rock of the ship, coupled with the shouting from beyond the door, told me the *Third Abyss* had left dock. Our trek to the Lightning Straits would take less than a week, and once we were through, it would take another week to reach the Excavation Site. Although these were short time-frames, every second counted.

"I wanted to tell you this because I'm certain we'll find my father at the Excavation Site," Adelgis said. "I doubt he's left yet. And... I think it's important you know everything I do. He's planning on creating powerful artifacts. He needs magic from the abyssal leech and the Mother of Shapeshifters to complete his goals. Most interestingly, he's amassed five hundred star shards."

I snapped my attention to Adelgis, taken aback. "*That many*? For what?"

"You can't use that many on a single item. It seems my father wants to mass produce several things, and he's gathering all the ingredients. Given what we saw in the Grotto Labyrinth, I suspect whatever he's doing will be questionable. I didn't want anyone else to deal with it... since I feel partially responsible after growing an abyssal leech for him... but there's no helping that now."

"And you're worried we might stumble into something we're not prepared for," I said.

Adelgis nodded. "To be honest, Fain's assessment of the situation is just the beginning. You see, there's something else I wanted to tell you. I couldn't hear my father's thoughts. They were blocked by some sort of magic—either a trinket or an artifact or some power, because relickeeper arcanists aren't capable of shielding their minds. And when we boarded the *Third Abyss*, I tried to hear Calisto's thoughts, to see if he was planning to betray us."

"And?" I asked, my heart locking up for a moment.

"And I can't hear his thoughts, either. I don't know if those facts are connected, but if they are, there could be several terrible explanations, and I don't want to think about those right now."

Fain scooted to the edge of his mattress, his expression a sardonic neutral. "Joining the Frith Guild was a calculated risk, but this just proves I'm bad at math."

I rubbed at the back of my neck, disliking my train of thought.

Could Theasin and Calisto have ties to one another? What would that mean? Theasin seemed adamant on finding a cure for the arcane plague—and Calisto was working for the Second Ascension, the people who had created it. It appeared as though their goals were the complete opposite.

What if...

I shook the notion away, hoping I was wrong. I still needed to remain optimistic. We weren't out of the worst of it yet.

But we were getting close.

OLD FRIENDS

I didn't leave my room the entire day. Once night fell, Adelgis had to use his magic to help me sleep, otherwise I would've continued pacing the length of our cabin.

Then I dreamt.

Again, I was Zelfree, watching his memories through his eyes, but unable to hear his thoughts. This time, however, the memory played out in an abstract manner. Events happened, one after another, too fast to experience the individual moments. It was like observing a deck of cards as they fluttered through a shuffle.

Lynus and I fought against Captain Redbeard—the sadist pirate that Lynus had served under. It was fierce and heated, but it flew by too quickly to grasp all the details.

Unfortunately, Redbeard escaped with his loyal sailors. Lynus didn't handle that well. In some memories he locked himself in his room. He didn't emerge for several days.

Regardless, Lynus was in charge of the ship. His first act as captain involved fighting in a pirate war over territory and waters. Port Crown served as the center stage. Bloody waters haunted most of those memories.

We made alliances. Lynus helped turn the tide of battle, gaining his ship recognition and allies. The entire time, I took on different personas. With my mimic—or should I say, *since Zelfree had a mimic?*—I pretended to be a great many pirates, sometimes even the captains of the fake merchant vessels, so I could "lose" in dramatic fashion to Lynus's attacks.

When everything ended, we took new names. Lynus had become Calisto, and I was referred to as *the Faceless*.

Soon after those wars on the waters, I returned to Frith Guild. Calisto continued making a name for himself and sending me information. Eventide and Ruma—and occasionally others—took advantage of my duplicity.

Each memory, including the ongoing fights with pirates, was tinted with a feeling of mischief and amusement. Zelfree had enjoyed his time amongst the scallywags of the high seas, not because he was one of them, but because he was one-upping them.

But Calisto...

Each time I returned to him, everything was colder and harsher than the time before. Seeing Zelfree's life in quick succession made the change noticeable, but nothing in the memories indicated anyone took note of it. The crew of Calisto's ship grew harsher and the tales of his exploits darker. I didn't stay with him for long, though. I always left, and when I returned, it was worse.

It made me wonder—if Zelfree had stayed, would things have gone differently?

Then my thoughts turned inward.

What if I had stayed with the Frith Guild? Would things be different for me now? Perhaps I should've kept Illia, Zaxis, Atty, Hexa, and Master Zelfree close by. Perhaps I shouldn't have allowed the darkness of my condition to seep in like it had.

Perhaps if I had seen these memories sooner, I would've changed my mind, but it was too late for that now. I didn't even know where they were.

The dream-memories took hold. I paid more attention to schemes and pirate attacks. No one seemed to know I was a mimic arcanist—er, *Zelfree* was a mimic arcanist. He changed his eldrin around so often, and hid Traces so thoroughly that the only hard detail anyone knew was that Calisto could always summon up a capable friend if ever in danger.

Until...

The dream-memories slowed, the details becoming more vivid.

I fell into a memory that took place in the empty back room of a tavern. It was a room with three empty card tables, each smoother and nicer than the walls around us. I sat on one side of the table, and Calisto sat opposite. He didn't yet wear his intimidating manticore mane coat, but he did have a menacing aura—the type of expression and tension that betrayed his willingness for violence.

A young Hellion, an adolescent manticore who hadn't yet developed a mane, stood next to his arcanist. He didn't wear a face mask. Hellion's head was that of an average lion. His whole body was that of an average lion except for the fact that his fur was white. That was unusual, and I admired the ivory pelt of the monster for a fleeting moment.

Traces was also a manticore, but with the standard golden coloration. Why didn't she copy the white fur of Hellion? I wished I could've asked.

I withdrew a letter from my coat pocket and glanced over the message.

. . .

Everett,

Thank you for the information. We intercepted the pirate vessel before it reached its destination.

As soon as you figure out who's allowing the smuggled kirin and mystical creatures through the Lightning Straits, we'll get support from several other guilds to shut down the operation. Send us a letter with the grifter crow arcanist at Port Veeyan.

Stay safe,
  Gregory Ruma

"Why do you keep lookin' at that thing?" Calisto asked, his tone softer than I personally knew it to be.

"It's been a while since I've sailed with Ruma and Eventide," I said as I tucked the letter away. "It's just... Never mind."

Calisto waved away the comment. "You know you don't need them, right? After everything we've done together, we could put everything behind us and do anything we wanted."

"Perhaps."

My curt tone didn't seem to sit well with Calisto.

He shot me a glower and rubbed at the copper stubble over most of his jaw. When he glanced away, his brow was furrowed, and I thought he might apologize, but the door to the back room swung open without any announcement.

A woman and three men stepped forward. The harsh

clunk after every other step was familiar. Those with peg legs often stepped harder on their artificial appendages. Sure enough, the woman had a stilted gait, and when she got close, I noticed her peg leg was a carved piece of ghostwood. A rose and twisted face had been ornately fashioned into the design.

She straightened her wide brim cap and buttoned up her long coat. Although she only had one leg left, the rest of her appeared capable. The arcanist mark on her forehead bore the picture of a hippogriff—a half-horse, half-eagle creature.

The three men flanking her had the air of thugs. Each carried a cutlass, but no pistols, and I wondered when, exactly, this meeting had taken place. It was difficult to keep track when time skipped so much through the dream-memories.

"Captain Liska, I presume?" I said.

The woman offered a tight smile. "Here I am."

Calisto stood from his chair. "You're late." His voice had shifted to something dark and gruff. "I hope you have the information you promised us. For your sake."

"Pipe down," Captain Liska said. She turned away from Calisto and gave me her full attention. "I don't want to deal with any lackeys."

"Lackeys?"

"You heard me. I've done my own share of investigating, and I know which of you gives the orders." She snapped her fingers and then motioned for her thugs. "I'm not gonna discuss anything until I'm alone with the Faceless. Everyone else, out."

My whole body tensed as I chanced a quick glance in Calisto's direction. He gripped the edge of his chair, his strength enough that he splintered the wood.

"He stays," I said, motioning to Calisto. "Consider him

more my right-hand man, than a lackey."

Captain Liska clenched her jaw as she shifted her weight from one foot to the other. Then she motioned her goons out of the room, never bothering to acknowledge my demand. She continued on as though it had never even been an issue.

Calisto retook his seat at the table. We exchanged glances, and it seemed to me that Calisto was grateful I hadn't sent him out like a dog. On the other hand, I knew he was a fighter—perhaps Zelfree kept him close for his own safety.

Once Liska's three men had left, she said, "I don't intend to stay here long." A no-nonsense attitude laced through her words.

"I got the information you wanted, but it came at a price. I'll need to leave the Shard Sea before daybreak."

"So you know who's responsible for helping the pirates get through the Lightning Straits?" I asked. "Is it a merchant or some arcanist with the ability to shroud objects in invisibility?"

She shook her head. "Worse than that. It's the Marshall of the Southern Seas. He and his typhoon dragon eldrin have been allowing the smuggling to occur."

"The marshall? Impossible."

"I assure you, it's him."

"He's a hero known through the area," I said, defiant. "A good man."

"It's him. There can be no mistake. He cooperates with pirates, shipping things to and fro from the straits. I have witnesses who're willing to back up the claim, if my word isn't good enough."

I sat back and rubbed at my chin. It was a shame I couldn't hear Zelfree's thoughts. I remained quiet and still for a prolonged moment, as though the information just wouldn't sink in.

"I believe it," Calisto stated.

I glanced over, an eyebrow raised. "Oh?"

"Think about it. The Marshall of the Southern Seas only answers to a handful of people in the world, and those people aren't out sailing the waves with him. He doesn't need to concern himself with anyone or anything. Why wouldn't he do whatever he wanted? The pirates offer him money and magic on the side—it makes sense to me."

A part of me wished I were there. Power didn't corrupt everyone—there were good people in this world that used their influence and magic for the better. Zelfree must've agreed with me because he immediately said, "You're wrong. I've been sailing with Ruma and Eventide and other arcanists from the Frith Guild. They *could* get away with what you're talking about, but they don't."

"Feh." Calisto waved away the comment. "It's only a matter of time, then. You'll see."

The dream-memory melted away a second later, cutting off the discussion and leaving me shocked. I knew Master Zelfree had killed the previous Marshall of the Southern Seas, but I had never heard the full story. Now it made more sense. He had been rooting out corruption.

But a typhoon dragon? All dragons had devastating magic, and their arcanists were counted among the strongest. Had Zelfree mimicked his and fought on the open waters? I almost couldn't wait for Adelgis to show me, but at the same time, I was confused. Zelfree had an *infamous* reputation for killing the marshall. Why hadn't it come to light that the marshall had been corrupt?

When the colors of the dream returned, they swirled and formed into a new environment—a new memory. I was back on a boat, this one much nicer than even the *Red Falcon*. Polished wood, lavish rugs—furniture that displayed both form and function. I sat inside an officer's lounge, the kind found on a ship-of-the-line, some of the largest and most battle-ready ships that ever sailed the ocean.

Again, I found myself with Calisto, Hellion, and Traces. The many chairs around the conference table were empty. Traces leapt from one to the next, giggling while Hellion playfully chased her, swiping in her general direction without ever connecting. Calisto stood next to the windows overlooking the sea. Waves splashed against the side of the ship, misting the glass with salt water.

I fidgeted with a letter in my hand, the message reading:

Dearest Everett,

I relayed your information to the Marshall of the Northern Seas, hoping to get official sanctions for activities. We were denied, and he demanded all investigations come to a halt. Arcanist guilds don't answer to a single authority, but to go against the marshall could anger other nations. Both marshalls are held in high regard. I fear there are people in the shadows who are trying to halt our efforts.

Guildmaster Gin and Guildmaster Anton have both withdrawn their offers of assistance in this matter.

When next we meet, I'll go over our latest plans.
Liet Eventide

. . .

No one had wanted to stop the mystical creature smuggling? The other guilds had turned their backs on the investigation? That was odd, but I understood that it was worthless to get worked up. Again, these memories had taken place decades ago—whatever had happened was long over.

It still irritated me, though.

I thought... the arcanists guilds were meant to handle matters that pertained to all arcanists. Like this one. Why would any nation impede Eventide's progress? Perhaps she was right. Perhaps people were working against her.

"What're you doing?" Calisto asked, jerking me from my thoughts.

I folded up the letter and then twirled it. "I need to return to the Frith Guild. We can stop at New Norra and I'll disembark there."

"Why don't we just handle the Marshall of the Southern Seas ourselves?" Calisto asked. He turned away from the window, his shirt open, revealing the unicorn horn trinket he wore around his neck. "That arrogant bastard doesn't think he's able to be touched. Your mimic is our element of surprise."

"He sails around on a *flagship* surrounded by navy vessels," I said, sardonic in all regards. "My mimic isn't going to stop the twenty arcanists who answer his command or even have an effect on their cannons. We need more of a plan than *power through everything*. What we need is solid evidence."

"Why isn't the Frith Guild riding in to stop this right now?" Calisto stormed away from the window. "They're so *noble* and *just*—what's stopping them?"

His manticore rushed to his side. When Calisto took a

seat on a nearby chair, he kicked one of his boots onto the table and leaned back. Hellion threw himself into his lap, despite being close to 300 pounds of muscle. Calisto groaned, but didn't push the beast off. Hellion flapped his leathery wings to stabilize himself. His scorpion tail swished from side to side. Somehow, even though he was a monstrous griffin, he offered his arcanist a rumbling purr.

"The Frith Guild needs to act within the boundaries of the law," I said, glancing down at the letter another time. "Eventide wants us to discuss our next course of action."

"The Marshall of the Southern Seas is allowing pirates through the Lightning Straits, right?"

I nodded.

"*We're* pirates. Why don't we work with the marshall and get in good with him? That's the fastest way to figure out what the old lout wants—and it's the fastest way to gut him when he's not looking. We can gather whatever evidence you need."

"It's not a bad plan," I said. "It just lacks finesse. I need more time to think of something else. Maybe Eventide will have a clever idea."

Calisto let his boot down, almost dropping Hellion onto the floor. Then he slammed his hand on the table, breaking it in his outburst. I flinched and jumped up from my chair. The shattered wood remained mostly intact, though splintered.

"What's your problem?" I growled. "You've been acting wild lately."

"I don't have the problem, Everett. *It's you.* Go on. Get out of here. Go to the Frith Guild and think of something. I'll stay and run things until you bring back orders."

"Things have gotten heated around here. You think you can handle the ship and crew on your own?"

That one question shifted the whole mood of the room.

Calisto stood from his chair, allowing Hellion down as he did so. The hackles of the manticore stood on end, its white fur shuddering with tensed muscles.

With a soft meow, Traces ran back to me. She was too large to fit into the pocket of my coat and instead transformed into a pair of bangles to hang around my wrist.

"Calm down," I said with a half-smile. "It was an honest question. You know I meant nothing by it."

Calisto didn't reply. His hard-set gaze didn't sit well with me.

Then he broke the silence with, "Haven't you heard what they're sayin' in ports? That I was Captain Redbeard's tool. That I'm your pawn. I'm gettin' tired of this, Everett. I don't need your help to run a marauder ship."

I walked around the table and approached Calisto. If I had been in charge of the situation, I definitely wouldn't have done that, but Zelfree didn't seem apprehensive. He patted Calisto on the shoulder. "Lynus. C'mon. Keep the big picture in mind. We won't need to run a petty ship full of corsairs once these seas are secured. We can move on. Together."

Zelfree sounded so assured and youthful—almost the opposite of how I knew him as a master arcanist. He had said the words, smooth and confident, no hesitation. Had he meant it? Was it a lie? Had he really intended to take Calisto away from the pirates? Why hadn't he?

Calisto's posture relaxed, but his expression never changed. It remained cold—callous.

"Aren't you excited?" I asked, lightening the moment with a chuckle. "We're going to prove you wrong, you and I."

"What?" Calisto snapped.

"We're arcanists. We have power, and answer to very few

people. Yet here we are, on the brink of stopping pirates and restoring peace to the area. I'd even go so far as to say we're on the side of good fighting villainy." My volume increased with my enthusiasm. "Not even *Liet Eventide* has dealt with a threat this serious in all her time as captain. We'll go down in history as heroes."

"I don't care about any of that," Calisto stated.

I opened my mouth to say something else, but Calisto continued before I could interject.

"People, places—the world is infested with darkness. The only reason it hasn't killed me yet is because I'm stronger."

"No need to be so dramatic," I said.

"Fine. Let me put it simpler, then. I'm not here to save *people*. It's *people* who I hate—and who have always hated me. The majority are black-hearted scum. I'm here to help the only person I think is worth my time."

Then...

The dream stopped.

I awoke a moment later, startled by the shift back into reality. Groggy and half-awake, I rolled to my side, confused by my surroundings. Where was I? A ship-of-the-line? The *Third Abyss*? The dream-memories were so lifelike that the transition blurred them together with reality.

Bells and shouting filled the hallway.

Adelgis sat at the center table in the middle of our cabin, one of the large tomes held in both hands. He stared at the far door, unmoving. The longer the yelling continued, the more agitated I became.

I stood and rubbed the side of my face. "How long was I asleep?"

"Fifteen hours," Adelgis stated.

"*Fifteen?*" I snapped my attention to him. "What's

going on?"

"Calisto is alerting the crew," Fain said from the shadows in the corner. He sat at the edge of his bed, unmoving. "I've heard those bells a million times. It means we need to get ready for ship-to-ship combat—he intends to attack someone."

BLOODSHED ON THE HIGH SEAS

Calisto planned to attack another ship? Karna had said this would be a one-way trip with no stops or distractions. If Calisto intended on harassing merchants or innocents while I was aboard, I would fight him every step of the way.

I stormed toward the door, all lingering ill effects of sleep long gone. Luthair kept at my feet, the agitation in his shadowy movements an indicator of his own anger. With barely contained rage, I exited into the misty corridor and made my way outside, onto the grayish deck of the *Third Abyss*. The late afternoon sun couldn't completely pierce the magical fog.

The deckhands scrabbled from one swing gun to the other, stuffing ammunition into the cannons. Most were loaded with cannonballs, meant to rip through the hull of opposing ships, but two of the guns were loaded with *chain shot*—two balls connected by an iron chain. The chain shot would tear through rigging and break masts, preventing opposing ships from fleeing once the damage was done.

I pushed through the pirates on deck, intent on finding

Calisto. They growled curses, but backed away once they eyed my arcanist mark. The smell of gunpowder filled the surrounding fog, adding to the atmosphere of violence. My pulse ran hot and fast.

The dense mist prevented me from seeing much beyond the ship. The deckhands all wore small glasses, each with dark-tinted lenses. They were trinkets imbued with kappa magic. Kappas could see through all darkness, fog, and miasma. The glasses allowed even non-arcanists to do the same. No doubt everyone on the ship could see beyond the ghostwood fog.

Calisto stood near the quarterdeck, his white glowing arcanist mark a dead giveaway. Karna stood on one side of him, Spider on the other. Calisto's ivory manticore, Hellion, waited on top of the elevated deck, his freakish face mask once again set to "happy."

"*Calisto*," I called out.

He turned to face me, his arms crossed, his posture stiff. For a split moment, it seemed as though he didn't recognize me, but that fleeting expression faded, replaced with irritation.

Karna leapt away from Calisto's side. "Volke—everything's under control."

"You said he wouldn't be attacking anyone," I shouted as I reached her. "I won't sit back while this blackheart harms innocent people." I didn't bother keeping my voice low or my anger hidden. There was no need to conceal my intentions.

"We said we wouldn't target merchant ships," Spider snapped. When she continued, her narrow face elongated with a sneer. "But we never said we'd avoid other *pirate* ships. Captain Redbeard and *The King's Revenge* are fair game."

The information stilled my actions, but the rage remained. Redbeard was the pirate captain from Zelfree's dream-memories. The madman who had harmed Lynus—Redbeard had always managed to get away, though.

It wasn't uncommon for pirates to attack their fellow cutthroats. These fiends didn't like sharing loot, and some pirate captains claimed vast territories of ocean as their personal domain. That didn't mean pirates sought each other out, though. There weren't many places pirates could go for ship repairs and medication. We were only half a day away from New Norra, so perhaps Calisto wasn't worried about those details, but if we had to turn around and wait for repairs...

"Get closer to *The King's Revenge*," Calisto shouted to his crew. "Draw them into the fog and prepare to broadside their vessel."

I had heard tales of Captain Redbeard and *The King's Revenge* even outside of Zelfree's memories. Redbeard's ship was famous for killing arcanists and using mortals as chum for man-eating mystical creatures that dwelled in the depths. Could Calisto handle the might of the other arcanist and his crew?

Spider glanced over to Calisto. "Redbeard got away the last two times we tried to corner him."

"Don't worry," Calisto said, smiling. "Hellion has his true form now. This time will be different."

Spider smiled. Then snapped her fingers at me and motioned to the stairs leading to the hold. "Clear off, cretin. Unless you're gonna fight, we don't need you gettin' in the way."

Hadn't Calisto claimed that Redbeard was the man who had harmed Biyu? Even if it wasn't true, the crew of *The King's Revenge* were still pirate dastards. There was no reason for me to hold back. Plus, if I helped protect the *Third Abyss*, it would be less likely that we would need to return to New Norra for repairs.

"I'll fight," I stated.

For the first time since I had stepped foot on deck, Calisto gave me his full attention. "Redbeard is *mine*. You can do what you want with the rest of his crew—I don't care what happens to them."

"Are there other arcanists aboard?" I forced myself to ask, hating the fact that I was conversing with the man.

"His first mate, a wendigo arcanist, and his navigator, a ghoul arcanist."

Thanks to my training with Fain, I knew quite a bit about the capabilities of a wendigo arcanist. Ghoul arcanists were also man-eaters, and their undead eldrin carried diseases. Neither frightened me.

Karna placed a hand on my shoulder. "You don't have to do this. You can wait below deck."

I shook my head. "It's fine."

Calisto smiled, showing off sharp teeth. "I hate knight-mare arcanists, but I've never seen a plague-ridden one before. Let's see what you bring to the table."

More bells rang out. The *Third Abyss* rocked from side to side, no doubt affected by the wakes of a nearby ship. *The King's Revenge* had to be close—perhaps a few hundred feet.

"In position!" a man in the crow's nest yelled.

With more exuberance than I had ever heard from him, Calisto shouted, "*Fire!* Taint the water with their blood."

Hellion roared, his battle cry a mix of a lion's and an abyssal beast's. He spread his black wings wide and took to the sky, disappearing into the fog a moment later.

The *Third Abyss* shook as the sound of cannon fire filled the mist. The booming explosions and splintering of wood created a cacophony of destruction that hurt my ears. It lasted a full ten seconds as dozens of cannons unloaded all at once.

Had *The King's Revenge* returned fire? Unlikely. The fog we hid in probably prevented the other pirates from knowing our exact location until it was too late. They would surely counterattack soon, but from the sounds of things, their vessel was already crippled.

A *slam* echoed into the sky a moment later, reminding me of a tree falling from a great height. One of the enemy's masts had been torn down.

"Luthair," I said.

Without the need for further instruction, Luthair merged with me. His cold shadows wrapped around my body, coalescing into hard plate armor. Power coursed through my veins, heightening my need to do something with it.

Spider ran to the railing and leapt off the boat, an impressive feat, considering the fall to the water was at least forty feet. As a kappa arcanist, I was certain she could handle it, but still.

Although Calisto had made a claim on Redbeard's life, he didn't attempt to leave his ship. On the contrary—he walked to the center of the deck and waited, his long coat, and the lion mane on the collar, fluttering in the wind that whipped across the ship.

I stepped through the shadows, exiting next to the railing. The faint outline of another ship swayed in the distance. Could I make it over if I used our ship's rigging? Or would I have to plunge into the water myself and then use the shadows to climb the side of *The King's Revenge*?

"Volke," Fain muttered from invisibility. "They're boarding."

Sure enough, members of Calisto's crew had long, wooden planks with chains and hooks. When the *Third Abyss* sailed close enough, the long boards were lowered with a slam and clank. The hooks dug into the wood of the enemy vessel, allowing the boards to stay stable. The chains were used to help the pirates balance themselves as they ran across.

"I'm going," I said to Fain, my voice a mix of mine and Luthair's. "Follow me."

Unlike water, which hindered my shadow-step, the planks were perfect. I slid into the darkness, slithered across the wood, and emerged on the deck of *The King's Revenge*. The ship was massive, but not as large as Calisto's. Perhaps it was a frigate or some other combat vessel.

The enemy pirates ran from one railing to the other, trying to arm the cannons and secure the ruined sails at the same time. When the fighting between crews broke out, it was difficult to tell who was who. These seadogs all dressed alike—dark coats, button shirts, loose pants with thick belts—and the general lack of hygiene brought the whole look together.

Pirate crews didn't have uniforms, but fortunately, thanks to the marks on everyone's neck, I could distinguish them. All of Calisto's crew had the three horizontal lines, $\equiv$, whereas Redbeard's crew had a cracked cutlass as their tattoo.

That made things easier.

I withdrew Retribution, the innate power of the black blade another comfort.

When the enemy pirates noticed my presence, they staggered to a halt and moved away, obviously taken aback by the appearance of a knightmare arcanist. Some of them withdrew pistols with unsteady hands. They used the ramrods to load their weapons with powder and bullets.

I lifted my hand and evoked terrors. With targeted precision, I affected only the enemy crew, leaving them crippled. I had no idea how effective this would be until I saw Calisto's crew take advantage of the situation. Each person I stunned with fear was cut down. In a few moments' time, I had devastated the enemy deckhands.

A gunner jumped off a large cannon and charged me with a cutlass. I stepped through the shadows, appeared behind him, and stabbed him through the back, just under the ribs. The hit had impact and weight, and I felt the man shudder as I withdrew the weapon from his flesh.

Ice appeared across the deck of the ship, frosting the planks and hindering the advance of Calisto's pirates. A man with a cutlass tattoo strode across the frost-coated deck. His wendigo ran to his side. Unlike Fain's wendigo, this one had massive antlers protruding from its skull face. The points of the antlers were crimson-soaked with blood, and when the beast opened its mouth, pink saliva spilled onto the deck. His wolf-like body was larger, meaning it had to be older than Wraith.

The man making the ice had to be the first mate of *The King's Revenge*—the arcanist mark on his forehead confirmed him to be bonded with the wendigo.

Whereas most people had white to their eyes, this man preferred the color of bloodshot. His nose was also black and blue, as though frostbitten—a disgusting blueberry of a snout. He glowered in my direction, his lip curled in disgust.

More pirates rushed up from the hold, each carrying weapons. The fighting intensified as another round of cannons was fired. It shook *The King's Revenge*, but the frigate wasn't done yet.

The wendigo arcanist moved closer to me. He attacked members of Calisto's crew, grabbing at their necks and then manipulating their flesh, closing the windpipe as though it were moldable clay. When he removed his blood-soaked hand, his victim could no longer breathe.

"When did Calisto start runnin' with a knightmare arcanist?" he asked, speech slightly slurred, still heading in my direction. "Who're you?"

"Your demise," I said.

I hefted my blade.

His wendigo disappeared in an instant, invisible.

"You'll regret comin' here," the first mate said. "Redbeard will grind your eldrin down to dust."

I leapt back into the shadows, avoiding the attack from the wendigo that I knew was coming. I emerged on top of the enemy quarterdeck. It overlooked the battle happening on the main deck, and now was my moment.

With Luthair, I felt more in control of myself. I cleared my thoughts and visualized the magic in the metaphorical cup overflowing.

My arcanist, Luthair said telepathically. *Manifesting an aura would be—*

"Don't worry," I said. "It'll work."

When I forced my magic, I sensed every pathway and movement through my body. If I pushed a bit further, I knew I could make my eclipse aura appear.

A few seconds in, I doubled over, pained from my stomach to my chest. Still, I pushed through, but a piece of me imagined both Illia and Biyu. They must've been terrified when their eyes had been cut out—beyond anything I could even imagine. These pirates had hurt them, and while I didn't fully understand why they had, it didn't matter. I probably shouldn't have thought of Illia or Biyu since my anger returned in full force, but that couldn't be helped.

I intended to rip this whole damn boat apart.

The pain flared in my spine and legs, threatening to steal my ability to stand, but I soldiered through the process.

And like waves breaking on a shore—it happened.

Magic poured from my being and affected the surrounding area. A ball of darkness moved in front of the midafternoon sun, blotting out the light with a false eclipse. Shadows blanketed everything from the bow of *The King's Revenge* to the stern of the *Third Abyss*. The supernatural dark attacked lights, snuffing lanterns or dimming glowstones.

The false night empowered me. I *had* been in pain, but when I took my next breath, the sting had vanished.

And yet...

My anger had amplified. Jozé had warned me about manifesting an aura improperly. He had said the effects would be unstable, and my aura immediately proved him correct.

The darkness around the sun bled a waterfall of ink into the water, creating a disturbing effect, as though the sky had been stabbed. The shadows on both ships moved with aggression, slithering and darting. While the effects created a nightmare realm, I still felt as though I had some control.

You need to calm yourself, Luthair telepathically said. *My arcanist, you can't maintain this long while you're agitated.*

I didn't need much time.

"What's going on?" the enemy wendigo arcanist shouted.

He became invisible, but every step he took agitated my shadows. His presence wasn't as hidden as he thought it was.

"Fain?" I asked aloud.

"Yes?" he replied, his voice coming from the other side of the quarterdeck.

"Come here."

He reached my side and dropped his own invisibility. The darkness prevented him from seeing, and he had to grope around the open air before he found my shoulder. I touched him, augmented his magic, and allowed him to see in the darkness for a brief time.

"Kill as many pirates as you can," I commanded. "I can't keep this aura up for much longer."

He nodded, his eyes now adjusted to the inky shadows.

Fain leapt off the quarterdeck, and I went to channeling my desires into my magic. With the control of a novice, I willed the shadows to strike out at the enemy pirates. The dark tendrils slashed at my enemies like knives. When I focused harder, I could create chains and hooks. They tore men apart with supernatural strength, sloppy and inaccurate, but with the speed to catch men off guard.

And although I loathed to think it, my false eclipse synergized well with Calisto's crew. The kappa glasses they wore allowed them to see through the dark. While our enemies were confused, Calisto's pirates attacked without hesitation, unhindered by the eclipse. Pistols were fired, cutlasses were run through hundreds of men, and the cannons were shot a third time.

The first mate of *The King's Revenge* dashed up the stairs onto the quarterdeck. I sensed his footfalls, but I refused to turn in his direction. With Retribution held in my hand, I waited.

His wendigo lunged forward.

If the monster managed to penetrate Luthair's armor and then my flesh, the debilitating disease on the wendigo's fangs would harm me for weeks to come. Not only that, but it would spread the arcane plague to Luthair himself, and I still couldn't stand the thought.

Instead, I pivoted and slashed with all my might, hoping to catch the beast by surprise.

It worked. My blade flew through the wendigo as though it were air, blood spurting across the deck. I had cut off the beast's front leg and slashed through most of its chest. The wolf-like creature dropped its invisibility and then hit the deck with a yowl.

Then the arcanist evoked ice across the deck. He created half an inch of thick rime, and if he continued to evoke the ice, he could create more and more, until I was trapped in place with thick frost. Instead of giving him the chance, I focused my shadows on the deck, tearing at the ice and breaking it away.

The wendigo arcanist ran for me.

I held up my hand and evoked terrors, surprised to see the darkness also leapt toward my enemy. The dark tendrils thrashed around, cutting the man and his injured wendigo as though fueled by my rage. The arcanist's invisibility broke.

He dashed away from the shadows and backed up to the ship's railing. Could the arcanist see me? He seemed able to locate my general direction, but when he reached for his pistol, his bloodshot eyes never fixated on me.

"Surrender, *wretch*," he growled as he readied his firearm, even going so far as to load a special blood-coated bullet. "Or I'll make sure you're plague-ridden if it's the last thing I do."

"I'm already plague-ridden," I whispered, my double-voice haunting enough to disturb the dead.

I slipped through the shadows, emerged in front of him, and plunged my sword into his sternum. Even through the bone, Retribution barely registered the contact, and now I understood why. The blade sliced through magical targets without resistance—mystical creatures and arcanist—but not with mortals.

The brutal attack had left the man momentarily paralyzed, either from dread or pain, I didn't know.

The realization that bloomed across his face made it appear as though he regretted every decision that had brought him here. He grabbed my arm, no doubt trying to manipulate my flesh, but he couldn't affect Luthair's shadow-armor.

I withdrew my sword from his chest and kicked him overboard. The rampaging shadows under the darkness of my eclipse aura attacked him as he fell. Another round of ice sprouted across the quarterdeck, this time binding my plate armor sabatons in place.

Behind you, Luthair said.

The three-legged wendigo charged with his antlers. I held up my arm, blocking the worst of the attack with my gauntlets. The wendigo snapped at me, his fangs clacking with each rapid miss. I backhanded the beast and then sliced through its head with a quick slash of Retribution. Its skull slid away into two pieces.

My breaths came in shallow bursts. I couldn't maintain my focus or my rage. The eclipse aura broke apart, giving way to the scarlet rays of dusk filtered by the fog. The surreal shift from darkness to orange-red felt more like a dream than reality, but all I could think about was Luthair.

I'm unharmed, he said telepathically. *Remember that I am armor, designed to defend against such attacks.*

"Right," I muttered. "I understand."

The King's Revenge slanted hard to one side. It was sinking.

Desperate to return to the *Third Abyss,* I broke free of the ice, slipped into the shadows, and then emerged a few feet later, my magic burning in my veins. Instead of pushing myself, I ran for the stairs and leapt down them three at a time.

The deck of *The King's Revenge...* It might as well have been a graveyard. Or perhaps a charnel house.

Corpses and blood covered everything from the barrels to the railing. Calisto's barbaric men hadn't hesitated, and the iced and flesh-torn corpses told me Fain had complied with my commands. Captain Redbeard's crew had been massacred—at least, all those who had dared to show their faces on the deck.

The planks between vessels were in the process of being pulled back. The crew of the *Third Abyss* didn't want their ship damaged once *The King's Revenge* slid beneath the waves. I stepped onto the rime-covered plank and almost slipped. An invisible hand grabbed my shoulder and kept me stable.

"Careful," Fain said.

I nodded and dashed across the rest of the plank. At the last moment, I shadow-stepped onto the deck of the *Third Abyss.* My breath caught when I emerged from the darkness.

Calisto and Hellion stood opposite a reaper merged with its arcanist—Captain Redbeard.

THE KING'S REVENGE

Sunset settled over the *Third Abyss*.

Calisto's crew stayed far from the center deck, even as they looted what they could from *The King's Revenge*. No one approached, no one readied their weapons—it was clear that Calisto and Redbeard would fight with no interference.

The only reaper arcanist I had ever known was Jevel, the master arcanist from the Huntsman Guild. I had assumed all reapers had rusted scythes and chains, but after seeing Redbeard, I realized that Jevel was a joke.

Redbeard's reaper was primarily a hooded robe of ebony. Gold-thread writing lined the hems—the names of all its victims stitched into the reaper, like a fabric tattoo—and the elegant way the robe fluttered made it seem eldritch and powerful. Despite the wind, the cloth of the reaper spread in all directions, dark and ominous, practically shadows itself.

And the scythe Redbeard carried wasn't worn or chipped. The blade shone with a supernatural edge, the metal glistening in the lowlight of dusk. When Redbeard swished it through the air, I swear I could hear the deadly slice of the weapon, as though it had severed the wind.

I couldn't see Captain Redbeard's face—the hood of his reaper hung low, obscuring his forehead, eyes, and nose. His beard, on the other hand, was plenty visible: a black mat of hair with a single red-orange streak from the side of the chin down to the frayed ends.

Calisto withdrew a cutlass from a sheath tied to his belt.

"You've always been recklessly treacherous," Redbeard said, his voice mature and clear, the very definition of authoritative—and somehow singular, even when merged, as though Redbeard had forced his own voice over his eldrin's. "But attacking a ship that's also sworn loyalty to the Autarch? This will be your final mistake."

It wasn't a conversation. Redbeard didn't wait for Calisto to reply or comment—Redbeard lifted a hand and evoked terrors so strong that the crew of the *Third Abyss* collapsed to its knees, most caught off guard and reduced to shrieking.

As a knightmare arcanist, I was immune. Fain, on the other hand, lost his invisibility as he crumpled to the deck. He took shallow breaths, his body trembling as unseen horrors played in his mind's eye.

Calisto grabbed at the side of his head and staggered backward, but he didn't fall victim like the others. Tense and fueled by indomitable willpower, he shook off the worst of the magic-induced nightmares.

"*Hellion*," Calisto growled through clenched teeth.

The disgusting manticore removed his face mask, revealing the face of an old man. The skin tone matched the unnatural white of his fur, and the wrinkles ran deep from the corners of his eyes. His mouth, large enough to fit three rows of teeth, reached the bottoms of his ears.

Looking at the face of a true form manticore caused the

individual to freeze, bound by powerful magics. I had made the mistake of looking—I hadn't remembered the danger until it was too late.

A tingling sensation ran down the length of my spine and continued, ending at my toes.

Redbeard must've known of the danger. He kept his gaze low, and as long as he didn't look directly at Hellion's face, he would be fine. But could he fight blind? If Hellion kept his mask off, Redbeard would always be at risk of paralysis.

Perhaps that was why Redbeard dashed for the manticore, his scythe ready.

Calisto lunged.

He was fast. Way faster than any normal man had a right to be.

Before Redbeard could reach Hellion, he had to pivot and swing his scythe in a wide arc. It caught Calisto across the chest, slicing through the shirt, right above the stomach. Blood splashed across the grayish ghostwood of the deck, but that wasn't enough to stop Calisto's assault.

Calisto thrust with his cutlass. It drove deep into Redbeard's gut, adding another pool of crimson blood to the *Third Abyss*.

I thought Redbeard might be finished, but I should've known better.

In the next instant, the blood on the ship *moved* as though sentient, spreading out as far as possible. Redbeard "fell" backward, seemingly disappearing into the blood like I would disappear into the shadows whenever I shadow-stepped. Redbeard reemerged from the splatters of blood on the opposite side of the ship. The scarlet didn't stain his clothes—it simply acted as a gateway for his movement.

Calisto and Hellion turned around.

With a quick motion of his hand, Redbeard willed the

blood on the deck to lift up like knives and slash everything in their path. He sliced the mainmast, the sails, some of Calisto's crewmates still cowering on the deck, and large portions of the rigging. The blood daggers tore deep gouges in the wood and shredded the sails. Anyone caught by the attack basically lost a limb—if they didn't die outright.

Hellion leapt out of the way, his weight enough to shake the ship with each paw landing on the deck. Calisto suffered minor lacerations, but that was only because he was closing the distance between himself and Redbeard. In half a second, Calisto was by Redbeard's side, the wound on his stomach still bleeding.

"No one gets away with attackin' my ship," Calisto growled.

Technically, manticore arcanists had accelerated healing —more so than average arcanists. But at the same time, injuries dealt by reaper arcanists prevented magical healing. Would those abilities cancel each other out? Could Calisto heal the wounds he had suffered so far? I didn't know. I wasn't an expert on mystical creatures. All I could do was watch.

Calisto attacked so fast that Redbeard didn't have time to block. Again, the cutlass drove deep into Redbeard, and this time I was close enough to hear the wet grunt of pain from the reaper arcanist.

In that moment, I wondered why Calisto didn't unleash a series of fervent attacks. He was stronger and faster—why did he hold back? It was as if he were trying to incapacitate, rather than kill. I couldn't fathom why.

Redbeard reached out with a callus-covered hand and touched Calisto's stomach injury. I couldn't see what happened, but Calisto leapt away with a scream, his injury weeping more blood than ever before. The crimson soaked his black shirt and pants and cascaded down his inky-black boots.

Free of Calisto's hold, Redbeard disappeared into the blood and emerged a hundred feet away. He willed the blood to attack again, practically sending dozens of knives flying around the deck of the ship. One cut through Luthair's cape, and my panic increased tenfold. I was paralyzed—unable to move or defend—and if Redbeard ever turned his attacks on me, I'd be done for.

Hellion ran for Redbeard and struck with his scorpion tail. He missed with his stinger, and the strength of his attack caused it to smash into the deck of the ship.

Redbeard blood-stepped away, emerging out of another crimson puddle, still capable of moving. He fought without looking the beast in the face, but his diverted attention cost him.

If I could've gasped, I would've. Calisto had *shadow-stepped* from one side of the deck to an area behind Redbeard. It was obvious from the way Redbeard turned his hooded head from side to side that he hadn't seen where Calisto had gone, and I didn't blame him. Manticore arcanists didn't have the capability to step into the shadows. As far as I knew, only knightmare arcanists could.

The boots my father had had me make...

Was Calisto wearing them?

With unrivaled speed, Calisto wrapped his arm around Redbeard's neck and torqued the man's head back. The hood fell off, and that was all it took. Redbeard locked up from paralysis, his eyes on Hellion's twisted, weathered face.

Redbeard, unable to move, was at the mercy of Calisto—the fight was over.

I figured Calisto would kill him, but instead, he threw

down his cutlass and grabbed the reaper by its robe-like body and pulled.

Luthair and I lived and died as a single being when we were merged, but Luthair wasn't an object, per se. He was shadows infused with magic and given physical form—but he could also return to darkness. When merged, it was as if the coldness of shadows seeped into my blood, linking us together.

Reapers, as I understood them, were always corporeal, which meant it probably didn't fuse into its arcanist's bloodstream. Could Calisto rip it off and force Redbeard to unmerge with his eldrin?

Apparently.

With all his strength, Calisto tore the reaper from Redbeard. Threads from the robes ripped out of Redbeard's body, as though they had been woven into the skin at certain locations. Redbeard didn't scream—he couldn't— and the scene played out more like a hunter skinning a dead animal than two arcanists concluding a duel.

Once Calisto had Redbeard held in one hand and the reaper held in the other, he exhaled. With a chuckle on his breath, he tossed the ebony-robed reaper onto the deck of the ship. Hellion pounced on the mystical creature, his massive paws pinning the frayed fabric and scythe. Although reapers couldn't bleed, it had still taken damage, and the tattered holes in its body were plain to see.

The reaper's terrors lifted.

Hellion refitted his mask over his face. The flesh attached to the edges of the accessory, fixing it in place in the most permanent of methods. Once his face was hidden, I—and the rest of the crew—regained control. The paralysis fled me, and I gulped down breaths.

Calisto slammed Redbeard's body onto the deck and

stood over him. With a demented smile, Calisto slid a finger along the edge of his cutlass, both cutting himself and coating his hand in Redbeard's blood. He licked the crimson off his finger, and I shuddered.

Still bleeding, Calisto wrapped an arm around his stomach, holding his gut.

"You'll... *you'll anger the Autarch*," Redbeard said, his voice still clear, even if pained and breathless. "You'll interfere with his plans!"

The gunpowder on the air, mixed with the copper tang of blood, permeated my nose and mouth. I hadn't even noticed until I saw the crew gathering close. *The King's Revenge* had half-disappeared beneath the waves, its hull cracked in half and the wood above water burning from the oil of its broken lanterns.

"The Autarch," Calisto said, strained. "He would be upset if you died."

Redbeard trembled, his body losing blood at a steady pace. "Let me go, and this reckless attempt on my life... can be forgiven." He took breaths at odd moments, ragged and tired.

"Only if you give me your word that you'll never sail your ships on my tides again."

"Of course. You'll never see my flags on these tides again."

To my surprise, Calisto took a hesitant step away from Redbeard.

Was the Autarch that intimidating? I figured nothing would stop Calisto from brutalizing the reaper arcanist, but perhaps this other mysterious man was just too much.

That's not what's happening, Luthair said, his telepathy drawing me back to the spectacle.

Calisto must have delighted in the false hope he had

given the other man because he laughed as he grabbed Redbeard by the back of the neck. He then proceeded to slam Redbeard's head into the deck, cracking the ghost-wood. Once the deck was coated with blood, bone, and teeth, Calisto picked up the pirate captain and continued his reckless pulverizing by smashing the man's face into the railing.

Redbeard's reaper screeched and flailed, but it was too injured—too frayed and worn and weak—to escape from Hellion's clutches. Even when it tried to manipulate blood, the crimson barely moved an inch.

I looked away, uncomfortable with the gore. I had to remind myself that Redbeard had harmed Biyu. Even then, the sound of flesh being ground down into a fine paste wasn't one I enjoyed.

A part of me thought back to Zelfree's dream-memories. Calisto had mentioned—on several occasions—how he had loathed his previous captain. He had said Redbeard was a sadist who had harmed his own crew. But Calisto had never given specifics, and I had never seen the torture for myself.

I glanced back up, and Calisto was still slamming Redbeard against the ship. That part of the deck was broken, splinters everywhere. Redbeard was dead, but it didn't seem to matter to Calisto. He continued his berserker assault, his manticore magic giving him stamina enough to continue, even when normal men would've grown tired.

I didn't need to witness Redbeard's heinous acts—Calisto's fury was enough to tell me that I never wanted to know the gruesome details.

"Calisto!"

Spider ran across the deck, her clothing soaked in sea-water. Unafraid of being a target of his rage, she ran straight to his side and grabbed his shoulder.

"He's dead," Spider stated. "And *The King's Revenge* is sinkin' to the bottom of the sea. You won."

Calisto took a deep breath and then released the corpse of Redbeard.

Calisto didn't look well. His skin had paled, his eyes had sunken in, and he staggered away from the bloodbath.

"We should be on our way," Spider said. "Just give the order."

"Let's go, then," Calisto growled, his voice low.

Two deckhands stepped forward. "Capt'n, that was amazin'," one said.

"What should we do with the men who surrendered?" the other asked.

Calisto gritted his teeth. "Slit their throats and then throw them to the waves."

I hadn't done anything when Calisto had pretended to give Redbeard mercy, but this seemed too much. I stepped forward, the clink of my shadow-plate drowned out by the evening winds.

"Wait," I said, my double-voice garnering attention from everyone on board.

Calisto turned around, his brow furrowed in visible confusion. Then he relaxed, and I suspected that he finally realized who I was.

"I've heard tales of Redbeard," I said, confident. "If men from his crew surrendered, they're probably looking for an escape, not to betray you."

I didn't owe a group of pirates anything. They probably didn't even deserve to live, not after the crimes they had likely committed. But I had seen enough death for ten lifetimes, and I didn't want the memory of bodies hurtling toward the waters added to the experience.

Calisto swayed on his feet, but he caught himself and

then stood tall. "Throw Redbeard's crew in the brig. I'll deal with them later." He gripped his stomach injury tighter, slowing the flow of blood. "Where did the ghoul arcanist get to?" he demanded.

"I gutted the arcanist, but his eldrin fled to the water," Spider said. "It got away."

"And what about the wendigo arcanist?"

"I killed them both," I said.

Again, the crew turned to me, no doubt fascinated by my odd double voice.

"Where's the wendigo?" Calisto asked.

For a moment, I didn't know why he cared. "I left it on *The King's Revenge.*"

"Tsk."

While the crew scrambled through the fog to get the *Third Abyss* ready for sailing, another figure joined us on deck. It was the lanky man I had seen with Spider earlier—Malaki, the carcolh arcanist. His eldrin, the carcolh, slithered out with him.

I had never seen a carcolh in person, and I wasn't impressed. It had the body of a snake and the spiral shell of a snail. Its mouth had tentacles, like an octopus, with a beak instead of fangs. The green and black coloration of its scales was menacing, but the carcolh was an adolescent—young and smaller, perhaps only a few hundred pounds and fifteen feet long.

Had Malaki hidden during the fight because he was a newer arcanist?

"Calisto," Malaki called out, his sun-cracked lips twitching into a sneer. "Where're my mystical creature parts? You said you'd have 'em after this fight."

Calisto said nothing. He rubbed at his temple, his breath rough.

"Well?" Malaki pushed past deckhands and strode over. His carcolh kept pace, its tentacle-face reminding me of Adelgis's whelk.

"We didn't get any mystical creatures," Calisto drawled, his tone a mix of sarcasm and cold anger.

"This is the third ship in a row *you didn't get any*. I think it's time you pay up."

"Tough luck," Spider growled. She stepped close to Malaki, her fingers hardening into claws. "You'll just have to wait, *louse*."

Malaki pointed to the reaper under Hellion's paws. "There's one right there, *wretch*. I deserve my payment! It's not my fault Calisto keeps letting all those mystical creatures get away. I could be makin' trinkets and artifacts, yet you—"

"We're letting the reaper go," Calisto said.

That shocked me.

Why?

But no one asked. No one said anything. Even the rest of the crew seemed stunned into silence as they watched from a good twenty feet away. Redbeard had done substantial damage to the ship, and it needed to be repaired, but the men moved as though they were avoiding drawing attention to themselves, slinking through the shadows.

"You can't let a reaper go," Malaki spat. "I've never even *seen* a reaper trinket before. They'll fetch good prices. I demand you give it to me. I deserve it."

His carcolh "hissed" as though coughing up water at the same time. It half-puked liquid onto the deck.

"It's not up for debate," Calisto said. "We're letting it go."

"Oh, yeah? Cheatin' me out of my payments, just like that? Why would you *ever* let this reaper go? Huh? Some sort of farewell for Redbeard? Don't want to hurt his image too much, that it?"

Malaki's petty taunting almost made me laugh. Even in his injured state, I was certain Calisto could kill this man. Why was Malaki provoking him?

Calisto stumbled a step, steadied himself, and then laughed once. "Fine. You want the reaper? Take it."

"My arcanist," Hellion said, turning his face to the side, his neutral mask twisting into a frown.

"Didn't you hear Malaki? He *deserves* it."

Hellion made no other protests. He stepped off the injured reaper and then bowed his head, allowing for Malaki to take his prize.

The ominous way they offered the reaper didn't sit right with me. Malaki didn't seem to care, however. He sauntered over to the downed reaper, withdrew his cutlass, and then stabbed into the robe. The reaper tried to attack with its scythe, but the carcolh used its serpentine body to grab the weapon and knock it away.

Malaki stabbed again, and the robe crumpled. Dead.

To my surprise, the robes of the reaper disappeared as though unraveling into nothing. The beast's scythe, on the other hand, remained on the deck.

Then, as though also stabbed, Malaki grabbed his shirt, shock in his eyes. His fingers twisted into the fabric as he fell backward. His carcolh jerked its head to face his arcanist's; its snake-eyes were wide with confusion.

Malaki hit the deck, twitching and kicking. Then nothing.

Dead.

Calisto smiled as he headed for Malaki's body. "Get the ship going," he called out to his crew. He picked up the scythe, hefted it over one shoulder, and then made his way for the quarterdeck.

The carcolh whipped around and coiled, on the verge of lunging. Hellion pounced before the carcolh could act. With claws as long as daggers, the manticore vivisected the young carcolh into ribbons of meat—no hesitation. Hellion couldn't tear up the shell, however, but that didn't matter. The carcolh was dead.

"What happened to Malaki?" I whispered.

"Reapers are frightening mystical creatures," Adelgis telepathically said, catching me by surprise. He wasn't on deck, but he still knew what was going on? *"They're monsters of death. Anyone who kills a reaper is killed in return. They call this magical defense the king's revenge."*

Like Redbeard's ship? Now I understood the name.

"No one else knows about this?" I asked. But then I shook my head. Obviously, Calisto had known. That was why he hadn't killed Redbeard straight away, and why he had unmerged them before dealing the final blow.

"Reapers are rare, and no one knows how they come into existence. Little information is known amongst pirates and thieves."

Would I have died if I had killed Jevel? According to Adelgis, that was the case.

Calisto walked past me, his injury worse up close.

Although I was curious about the reaper's revenge, this opportunity struck me. With Retribution, I might be able to kill Calisto right here and now. All it would take was one precise strike.

But if I missed...

Calisto stopped at the door to the quarterdeck and glanced over. "Next time, bring back the bodies of any mystical creatures you slay."

I gripped the hilt of my sword. "There won't ever be a *next time.*"

"Aren't you plague-ridden?"

I said nothing. He knew the answer.

"You'd make for the perfect pirate," Calisto said, chuckling. "Give it a thought once you realize what kind of monster you've become."

39

ADMIRATION

It took the crew several hours to fix the *Third Abyss*. Once the rigging and spare sails were secured, the ship resumed course. For an entire day, I was too restless and disturbed to either eat or sleep. Adelgis and Fain remained with me in the cabin, both consumed in their own thoughts. No one spoke as we sailed the waves of the Shard Sea.

Adelgis turned the page of his book, intent on reading. His ethereal whelk, Felicity, hovered around his shoulders, performing slow-motion acrobatics from time to time.

In an attempt to ease my anxiety, I circled the center table and took a seat across from him. "What're you reading, Adelgis?"

"I'm trying to find more information regarding the Mother of Shapeshifters. I want to know why my father is obsessed with it and why he originally wanted a mimic arcanist."

"And those books are about the previous god-creatures that spawned?" I asked.

Adelgis nodded, though he didn't take his eyes off the page. "You might find the text on the world serpent interesting." He pushed a smaller book in my direction—one that resembled a journal.

I pulled it close and flipped to the first page. The writing had faded. I couldn't make out the words. I went to the next page, then the third. At that point, the ink seemed preserved, and the writing was legible.

The warlord made alliances with the monarchs of the land. Those who continued their warring, or challenged the warlord, had their territories rearranged. The magic of the world serpent could move mountains, rivers, and valleys. Enemy nations once lush with grass became deserts. Allies of the warlord knew years of plentiful harvests, their weather perfect, no disasters to speak of.

"Who is *the warlord*?" I asked.

"All of the arcanists who bonded to god-creatures were referred to by their title," Adelgis said. He flipped another page. "The man who bonded to the world serpent was given the title of *warlord* due to his ability to crush entire armies."

"All of the god-arcanists were given titles?"

"Yes. The woman who bonded to the soul forge was known as *the scholar*, the man who bonded with the fenris wolf was known as *the hunter*, the woman who bonded with the sky titan was—"

I held up a hand. "It's okay. I was confused at first, but I understand now."

"The warlord became the one who ruled over the majority of nations," Adelgis continued. "The world serpent's magic is perfect for a ruler of territory. No wars and bountiful harvests make for safe and secure kingdoms.

All the books I've read said he was one of the most powerful and influential god-arcanists."

"I can see why the Second Ascension wanted the world serpent so badly."

Adelgis stopped reading. He glanced up at me, his eyebrows knitted. Why did he look so concerned? Was it because I had mentioned the Second Ascension?

"Whoever bonds with the new world serpent will change the course of history forever," Adelgis intoned. "If it's the Second Ascension, we'll have no choice but to capitulate."

"Surrender?" Fain asked.

I turned to him, surprised he was listening.

Fain stood from his bed and walked over to the table, his movements stiff. Wraith remained on the mattress, his ears raised.

"You think we'd need to surrender to the Second Ascension if one of them bonded to the world serpent?" he asked.

Adelgis nodded. The tension between us created a still silence.

My stomach growled with the force of a 100-foot waterfall.

I rubbed at my gut, hating that I needed to leave this cabin. I had avoided it as much as possible—only venturing out when absolutely necessary—and I had refused to search out the galley. Sure, I was hungry, but I didn't want to mingle with any of the pirates here, and I certainly didn't want to ask them for food.

"My arcanist," Luthair said from the shadows. "Do you want me to search out sustenance?"

I shook my head. "I can do it. I just... don't want to."

"We can go together," Adelgis said. "I'm rather famished,

and perhaps the crew will leave us alone if they consider us a gang of sorts."

Fain snorted and laughed at the same time. As he rubbed at his jaw, he said, "Moonbeam, the only gang you'd belong to would be a gang of librarians."

"I meant it would be more intimidating to harass us all as a group."

Fain was about to say something else when realization struck. "Wait, you want *me* to go with you? No. I don't want to see anyone in this crew. You can be a gang of two."

"You can stay invisible," I said. "But I'd prefer if you stayed close to us."

Although Fain had sounded adamant a moment before, he took a deep breath and then exhaled. "All right."

I stood, and so did Adelgis. Felicity disappeared with a flash of light, leaving a small hail of sparkles behind. Wraith stayed on the bed, not bothering to move. The rest of us left our cabin and headed down the long corridor. Spider's door remained firmly shut, and Malaki was no longer with us. It was an uneventful trip to the deck of the ship, and the evening greeted us with a blast of icy winds.

Fain became invisible. "The galley can be found down the port-side stairs."

I turned my attention in the direction indicated and continued. I had been on the ship before, but I hadn't taken note of the amenities, just the plague-ridden creature Calisto had kept locked up in the hold. Did he have a new one down there? I didn't want to find out.

Deckhands who noticed me stopped their work and stared. I didn't acknowledge them.

With Adelgis by my side and Luthair shifting around my feet, I walked down the steps and descended below the gun deck. I didn't require any further directions once I caught a whiff of cooked food. My stomach groaned and tightened, and I pushed through a door with a lit lantern hanging overhead.

The galley room wasn't gigantic, but it could easily accommodate a hundred men if they didn't mind close quarters. Several long tables with bench seating filled the space. In the far back, held in a brick firebox, was a large copper cauldron. A thin man tended the contents, stirring everything with a long ladle. The smell of fish, salt, and herbs told me the cook had prepared seafood soup. Hard biscuits were held in a sack near the cauldron, their tough texture as clear as day, even from across the room.

It was the start of evening, and most of the crew had gone to sleep. Twenty men sat around the tables, nursing their soup—some soaking their biscuits in broth before attempting to eat them.

I stepped into the room, and all twenty men snapped their attention to me.

Uncertain of what to say or do, I just continued forward, my steps slow and my guard up.

"It's that knightmare arcanist," one pirate whispered.

Another nodded. "Slaughtered half the other crew by himself, so I heard."

"A right beast of the seas, that one."

The cook at the cauldron stood straight when I drew near. His long face reminded me of a half-melted candle, but once he forced a smile, that image vanished.

"You're legendary, you are," he said as he scooped up a tin bowl and filled it with soup. "I've never seen a knight-mare until yesterday, and it was impressive. You're amazin'." He held out the bowl.

I ripped it from his hand, hating every compliment he

had offered. The pirate flinched away, startled by my aggression.

"I didn't mean no offense," he muttered. "I swear."

I snatched a biscuit from the nearby sack, refusing to engage the cutthroat in idle conversation.

"May I please have a bowl?" Adelgis asked.

The cook's face returned to the long, melted expression. He sneered as he grabbed a bowl and filled it with mostly broth. When I shot the man a glower, he grew fidgety and feigned spilling the soup back into the cauldron. Then he doled out another helping, this time filled with various types of fish. The cook handed Adelgis the bowl and a biscuit.

"We need one more bowl, please," Adelgis said.

At this point, the cook didn't even bother to say anything. He gave me a sheepish glance before filling another bowl, no protest. Adelgis bowed his head, thanked the pirate, and then took both bowls to the nearest empty table.

We sat down, and Adelgis slid the extra bowl over to the seat next to him. It disappeared a moment later, wrapped in Fain's invisibility.

I lifted the bowl with both hands and sipped from the side, impressed by the taste of the broth. It reminded me of the Isle of Ruma. Fish soup had always been my favorite. *Seafood* soup was just a mixture of fish, crustaceans, and other ocean creatures—similar to the single-fish ingredient soup that Gravekeeper William would make for Illia and me.

I found it amusing that a pirate dish could remind me of my childhood.

As I took another sip, I couldn't help but think of Hexa. She hadn't grown up on the islands, and she hated fish.

What would she have done in this situation? Eat only the teeth-cracking biscuits? I could imagine her forcing one down without even chewing. She'd probably choke, someone would have to help her, and after a long fit of coughing, she would probably attempt it a second time.

Atty, on the other hand, would probably eat this seafood soup as though it were a delicacy. I could picture her sitting straight, lifting the bowl with both hands, bringing it to her beautiful lips. Her sense of poise and etiquette never left her. If the soup wasn't to her liking, I suspected she wouldn't say anything. Atty would smile and thank the cook, polite and mature.

Atty...

"I miss them both, too," Adelgis said.

I raised an eyebrow as I set my bowl down. "Anyone you miss specifically?"

"My sister, Cinna," he replied without a second thought. "She's always been sickly, ever since we were children. I worry about her. I last heard from her right before the Sovereign Dragon Tournament."

Sickly? I wondered—sarcastically—what Theasin had done to her.

I hadn't voiced my thoughts, but I should've known by now.

Adelgis tightened his grip on his bowl. He glared at the contents as he lowered it to the table. "It has crossed my mind that, perhaps, my sister's weak constitution wasn't a random occurrence. Knowing what I do now, I would say there's some chance my father caused her ailment through some sort of... tampering."

"I'm sorry I thought about it," I said. "Let's discuss something else."

I wanted to eat in peace, but the fates had different

plans. The door to the galley room burst open with a slam. A few pirates leapt from their seats, knocking over their benches in the process. Some even drew pistols or cutlasses.

Everyone froze in place when the Dread Pirate Calisto sauntered into the room. On a normal ship, captains had their food brought into their private quarters, but I supposed this wasn't a *normal* ship.

Calisto wore a simple coat and trousers, nothing else. It showcased his muscled stomach—free of all injury. Perhaps he wanted everyone to know he was no longer injured. A petty show of his abilities so that his crew knew he was still a capable captain.

The pirates gave each other questioning glances.

"What're you all lookin' at?" Calisto asked, somewhat amused and annoyed at the same time.

"You've already recovered, Capt'n?" one man asked. "That was fast, even for you."

"A pathetic dullard like Redbeard can never harm me." He kicked a long table out of his way and continued through the room, his hard gaze set on me. "Now shove off. I need to speak with our newest arcanist about potential business."

Calisto didn't need to give the command twice. Everyone leapt from their tables and rushed for the door, leaving their half-eaten soup behind.

Fain moved away from our table—I could see it in the way the bench moved. His shallow breaths, laced with panic, eroded some of my self-control. Calisto thought he could talk *business* with me? I was closer to attempting to assassinate him in the middle of the night.

Calisto shot the cook a cold glare.

With shaky hands, the pirate dumped water over the brick firebox. Steam wafted around the room, carrying with it a smell of fish and coal. Then the man scurried away, keeping to the bulkhead as he went.

The second the door closed, I stood from my seat. "I'd rather throw you to the monsters in the abyssal hells than help you with anything," I stated.

Calisto lifted his leg and placed a single foot on the edge of our table. The wood creaked under his weight. He leaned forward, half-smiling. "You haven't even heard my proposition yet, boy."

"I already regret helping you fight the crew of *The King's Revenge*."

"Stubborn," he muttered. He scratched the stubble on his chin. "That's a shame. And here I was gonna invite you back to my quarters. I'm sure Spider and the doppelgänger would've been happy to keep us up all night."

All words failed me. It was like watching a ship sail straight into the side of a cliff and then explode. A part of me thought I had to be dreaming—or maybe this was a nightmare?—but there was no way it was reality.

Adelgis sipped his soup with a semi-prolonged slurp, watching as though this were an ordinary conversation between casual friends.

Then Fain dropped his invisibility, a look of sardonic irritation fixed into his hard brow. "Thank you for that mental image, Karna. I'll have to throw myself overboard now."

Karna?

A single laugh escaped me. *Of course* it was Karna. How hadn't I put it together?

Karna-Calisto smiled wide. "Oh, the look on your face. Priceless." Her magic shimmered and transformed her back into her usual dancer self. Calisto's short copper-red hair was replaced by Karna's long, blonde locks, and the muscles faded to reveal a lean, athletic body. She had to pull the coat closed in the front, but her hips kept the trousers on just fine. "I've never wanted to laugh so hard before." She snickered afterward, a genuine reaction.

"You knew?" I asked, giving Adelgis a quick glance.

He nodded. "Her thoughts as she entered were, *keep it together—don't laugh.*"

Fain stormed around one of the tables, pacing away the frustration. "It wasn't that funny."

To my surprise, Karna leapt to his side and hugged one of his arms. "Oh, come now. It wasn't that bad. Just a little harmless fun."

Fain stopped walking. He glanced down at Karna, his expression an odd mix of worried and forced neutral. "I take it... you're okay, then?"

I took a seat next to Adelgis, confused by Fain's wording.

Karna tilted her head. "What're you asking?"

"Calisto," Fain murmured. "He's not hurting you, is he?"

With a swish of her hair, Karna offered him a smile. "I'd never agree to this if I thought Calisto was going to get his jollies from harming me. It's sweet you're concerned, though." She squeezed his arm. "You're turning into quite a fascinating person, ya know."

"Lucky me," Fain drawled.

I placed a hand on Adelgis's shoulder. "Tell me," I whispered. "Is she lying?"

"*About?*" Adelgis telepathically asked.

"About Calisto. Is he hurting her?"

"*No. From what I can tell, Calisto treats her well. Karna's thoughts seem to revolve around his occasional tenderness, and his very specific requests. I don't think you want to hear the details, though.*"

While I was relieved to hear he wasn't hurting her, I still

loathed the situation. I finished the soup in the next couple of gulps and then slammed the bowl on the table. I wanted to retire to our cabin and sleep the rest of the week away, just to avoid interacting with the scallywags.

Karna let go of Fain when I stood from my seat.

"Volke," she said. "Wait. I came here to speak to you. Apparently, Malaki and his carcolh eldrin were using their sorcery to help navigate this large ship through tight spaces. Through water manipulation."

"Okay," I said.

"Well, he's dead now." Karna stood in front of me, her gaze fixed to mine. "It's riskier to go through the Lightning Straits with a ship of this size and no way to make fine corrections. Do you... still want to go through with it? We have time to turn around and head back to New Norra. Perhaps we could find someone and—"

"*No*," I said, curt. "No. I don't want that. If we go back to New Norra now, I might just get off this ship. We should... keep going. Calisto has gone through the Lightning Straits before. I'm sure he'll handle it."

"You know he's been through the straits?"

I nodded.

Adelgis finished his soup and then stood. "Most of the crew is confident that Calisto will make it through as well. I suspect we'll be fine."

There could be no turning back. My doubts and hesitations couldn't be allowed to consume me.

I stepped close to Karna. "I'm going to wait in our cabin, but if you ever need me, just say the word and I'll be there."

She half-smiled as she placed a hand on my chest. "Always the noble gentleman. I hope for everyone's sake we make it through the straits without trouble."

40

NAVIGATING THE LIGHTNING STRAITS

The week took a toll on my sanity.

Calisto's crew seemed to admire me. Whenever I emerged from my cabin for food or water, they went out of their way to ingratiate themselves. They ran to get me the "good rum" and told me war stories from their time on the waves. I found it ironic that, no matter what I did, the crew of the *Sun Chaser* distrusted me until the very end, but this pirate crew accepted me into their ranks the moment I proved useful.

The cook—the young man with the candle-wax face— served my food with great care, taking as long as possible to extend idle conversation. Apparently, he had joined Calisto's crew when he was fifteen, the day he had become a man. From what I had gathered, we were roughly the same age, seventeen, but after the young man had been singed by a salamander, Calisto had taken pity on him and taken him off the front lines, making him a cook instead.

The cook had told me his name, but I never remembered. Every word he uttered just irrationally deepened my hatred for him.

And on the sixth night aboard the *Third Abyss*, I had a dream that involved killing everyone on the ship.

I awoke in a panic, my heart out of control, sweat soaking my sheets. It hadn't been a nightmare—I had killed Calisto while he'd slept—and none of the non-arcanist pirates could put up much of a fight. It was just... an indiscriminate slaughter. Some of them had begged for their lives. No matter where they hid, I had hunted them down, going from room to room in methodical order, delighting in their fear.

I ran both my hands through my hair, my whole body shaking.

"My arcanist?" Luthair whispered, careful not to wake the others.

"Do you remember when I spared Fain's life?" I asked, my pulse still high.

"Yes."

"Do you... remember how you advised me to kill him, rather than allowing him a chance for redemption?"

"Indeed."

"Would you say that aspect of me—the willingness to forgive or allow someone to change—is a major part of my personality and demeanor?" I glanced at the corner of the room, to the darkest shadows. "I need an honest answer."

"Yes. You are much more forgiving than the average person. Sometimes I think your trust and idealism borders on foolish, but you've proven me wrong on enough occasions that it makes me question my own jaded views of the world." The darkness shuddered, and Luthair stepped out of the corner, fully formed as hollow plate armor. "Why do you ask?"

After a deep breath, I rested back on the bed, my gaze on the ceiling. It didn't calm me.

"Luthair," I said. I gripped the sheets. "I think if I had met Fain right now... I wouldn't have spared him."

"What do you mean, my arcanist?"

"I don't feel like myself. It's like *I'm slipping*. Adelgis said plague-ridden arcanists don't become laughing mad, they lose their rationality. He's right. But it's also more, like I want to act out my deepest desires, even if it would destroy everything around me. Like... a loosening of morals or conscience."

Despising pirates for their villainous actions wasn't irrational, but the growing intensity of my rage was. It didn't matter what the pirates did—they could save a drowning baby at great cost to themselves, and I'd still want to see them suffer. Just thinking about killing them brought me a bit of happiness, which was the most disturbing fact of all.

It just didn't feel like *me*. Like someone else was taking control, and that someone was the arcane plague.

Luthair stepped close to the bed, the clink of his armor comforting. "You should get some rest."

"I'm afraid," I said. "I'll keep changing. What if I reach a point where I can't even recognize that I'm different? What if I lose everything that makes me *me*? Am I... making sense?"

Luthair took a long while to mull over my questions. Finally, he said, "Despair won't help you. This will all be over soon. And even if it's not, I will be by your side. If you feel yourself slipping, tell me. I can lend you my strength."

On the seventh day, the air filled with static. Although I couldn't see through the fog surrounding the ship, I felt the presence of the surgestones that made up the Lightning Straits. We were close—nearly to Theasin Venrover.

Against my better judgment, I laced up my boots and headed for the door of our sleeping cabin. Both Adelgis and Fain followed me into the corridor, no need for words between us. Fain went invisible, and Wraith waited behind, content never to see the rest of the ship.

It didn't take us long to emerge on deck. The midmorning sun tried its damnedest to pierce through the fog of the *Third Abyss*, but its efforts only resulted in soft pillars of light filtering down around us.

My attention on the sails, I didn't notice the kappa that scuttled around my legs and hissed. I flinched away from it, disturbed by the fish-man body and bulbous head. The giant eyes—like a fish or perhaps a frog—glared at me as it rushed across the deck of the ship. It stopped at the base of the mainmast and flashed its needle-like teeth.

"What're you doing out of your quarters?" it asked with a hiss at the edge of its words.

The grate of its voice drove me straight to anger. "Adelgis —*you* speak to it. I won't be reasonable."

"We're here to see the Lightning Straits," Adelgis said.

The monster didn't answer. It arched its back and flared its dark green scales before hurrying across the rest of the deck. Its webbed feet and hands had long claws it couldn't retract, so the entire way it made a slight clicking noise as it ran.

Relieved the beast had gone, I returned my attention to the ship. Deckhands removed the largest sails and secured the smaller ones for slower speeds. Winds often traveled through the length of the straits, creating a hazard for larger ships. If we went too fast, we'd crash into the rock walls.

I went to the railing, disappointed by the fog. The dream-memory of Master Zelfree sailing the straits with Ruma and Eventide lingered on my thoughts. Would I recognize the sights? Or had that happened so long ago that the environment had shifted?

"Why haven't you shown me another one of Zelfree's adventures?" I asked.

Adelgis stood next to the railing and brushed back his lengthy hair. "I apologize. I've been distracted. I'll resume them once I've finished with the last tome. After I have all the information available to me, I'll try to draw conclusions."

I nodded, enjoying the saltwater mist that clung to the wind.

"Why not just ask your father what he wants with the Mother of Shapeshifters?" I asked. "Hopefully, we'll see him soon."

"He's never been one to share his private research or plans."

Cracks of thunder rumbled overhead. Adelgis flinched, his eyebrows knitting. Lightning sparked bright enough to show through the fog. When another round of thunder followed shortly after, he placed a hand on my arm, as though comforting himself with my close proximity.

"You saw Zelfree's memories," I said. "The straits aren't *that* bad."

"Oh, you don't understand," Adelgis said, his voice shaky. "There're plague-ridden creatures in the air. Thunderbirds. Their thoughts are quite erratic." Thunder rolled over the ship a third time, and Adelgis got closer than he ever had before. "The birds... aren't interested in someone else who's plague-ridden, and they don't seem to care about those who are immune. But Karna and I..."

"Don't worry, Moonbeam," Fain said, still cloaked in invisibility. "We won't let them get you."

"I don't know if there's anything you can do about their voices in my head, but I appreciate the sentiment."

The *Third Abyss* creaked and groaned as we sailed closer to the surgestone mountains. The crash of waves on rocks echoed in the distance. A loud scrape sounded off the starboard side, as though the ship had scratched along something. It stopped a moment later as we continued forward at a slow pace. The helmsman kept us steady, but I suspected Spider was using her kappa magic to help keep us on course.

When we entered the Lightning Straits, we were close enough to both mountains that I could see them through the fog. Cracks of electricity bounded from one rock face to the other.

"Have the storms subsided?" I asked, fearing the ship would be torn asunder by nature itself.

Adelgis nodded. "They subsided yesterday and won't start again for another three days. In theory, we should make it through long before then. The flashes of lightning you see are just from the rocks."

The dark speckle coloration of the rocks was familiar. Zelfree had touched one in the dream-memory, and it had shocked him with enough force to lay him on the ground. When the *Third Abyss* got close to one of the mountains, I stepped away from the railing. I had vicariously learned my lesson.

"Hey!"

I whipped around, tense and with my hand on the hilt of my blade.

Spider stormed across the deck, her long hair flowing behind her like a black curtain. She clenched her jaw as she approached, her gaze set on me.

"Get back to your cabin," she commanded, pointing to

the door for the officer's rooms. "We don't have the manpower to save you if a bird swoops down and plucks someone from the deck."

"Calisto isn't going to fight the creatures?" I asked.

That seemed to bother Spider. She stopped and crossed her arms, her fingers gripping her shirt sleeves tight. "Calisto is busy with your whore," she finally replied, saying it like a taunt. "He doesn't have time to coddle the likes of you."

"*Calisto is still recovering*," Adelgis said telepathically. "*Spider doesn't want us—or anyone in the crew—to know*."

That information got me smiling.

I offered Spider a shrug. "Old age finally catching up with Calisto? He doesn't heal like he used to?"

"Don't be a fool," Spider said. "Calisto has recovered. Didn't you see him walking around for the last few days?"

Had Karna duped Spider? Or was she in on the secret? Regardless, it amused me that Calisto had asked Karna to help him trick the crew into believing he wasn't injured.

"The captain would rather roll around in bed than protect his crew, huh?" I asked, sardonic. "Pathetic."

"You watch your mouth," Spider snapped. She stepped closer, her posture stiff and her muscles tense. "Calisto is *ten times* the man you'll ever be, you festering lout. One more comment and I'll force you to disembark right here."

I grabbed the collar of her shirt, twisting my fist into the fabric, more than willing to end this here. Anger flashed in her eyes as boney claws sprouted from the tips of her fingers. Spider hooked them into my coat and yanked me closer, daring me to follow up my physical threat. We had fought in the past, and I had been frightened then, but not now.

Adelgis placed a hand on my shoulder and then pointed above us.

A large *creature* descended through the fog, pushing it like a blanket of clouds. Although I couldn't see it, the swell of movement told me it was a bird the size of a roc. Was it *actually* a roc? Here?

I knew one thing for certain—it was infected with the plague. I could sense that much, like I had sensed the arcanist back in New Norra.

Spider released her hooks and shuddered. "Damn."

But the creature didn't land on deck. It flapped its massive wings and took off, sweeping the ship full of mist from the gust of its movement. I held up an arm to shield my eyes. The beast disappeared from my perceptions, flying high away from the ship.

"What was that?" I asked.

Adelgis smoothed his hair with a trembling hand. "A plague-ridden thunderbird."

"I didn't know they got that large."

"They usually don't," Spider said through gritted teeth. "These monsters get larger every time some idiot arcanist falls victim in the straits. They eat magic and gain more power—they don't normally get this close, but now that we have *guests*, they're being drawn to us."

Adelgis was right. The thunderbirds would come to take him or Karna, the only people on the ship who weren't immune or already plague-ridden. And Captain Devlin had been correct when he had said that the *Sun Chaser* would have a difficult time here in the straits.

I kept Adelgis close and motioned to the officer's quarters. "We should go."

"Thank you," Adelgis said.

"Don't come out again," Spider commanded. "Next time you might not be so lucky."

Thunder shook the ship as we made our way through the Lightning Straits.

I stared out the porthole for the entirety of the trip, watching as the *Third Abyss* neared the rocks every few minutes. Maintaining a ship this large was difficult, and I was impressed by the finesse the crew mustered.

The trek through the straits took a grand total of twelve hours. Each hour seemed to disturb Adelgis more than the last. He sat on his bed, rocking back and forth, muttering to himself. How many plague-ridden monsters were out there? How many voices in his head did he have to contend with?

Most importantly, what could I do to help him? I didn't think there was any way for me to affect the situation.

Once we sailed out the other side—free from the narrow pathway between mountains—the flashes of lightning and rumbling of thunder became a distant memory. Still, Adelgis didn't recover. He remained frightened, whispering things.

"Volke," Fain said from the corner opposite mine. "You look terrible. You should get some sleep."

I gave Adelgis one final look before taking a seat on the edge of my mattress. "Okay. But keep an eye on him?"

"Of course."

I rested back on my bed, thankful we were so close to Theasin.

Less than a week... and we'd be there.

Dreaming.

It wasn't the nightmares where I slaughtered everyone on the *Third Abyss*. I had returned to Master Zelfree's memories.

I wasn't in one of his favorite taverns, nor was I in the safety of the Frith Guild. Instead, I was standing in a room on a giant ship. Given the maps, books, imposing desk, and assortment of chairs, I assumed it was a captain's room. I sauntered around the desk, grazing the tips of my fingers over ivory paperweights and fine quills.

A younger Calisto sprawled out on an upholstered chair, one leg over the armrest, one arm over the backrest. He didn't sit on the side of the desk meant for the captain, and his beyond-bored expression told me that we had been waiting in this room for some time.

I returned my attention to the surroundings. The items on the desk were sharp and jagged. The paperweights were of sharks, the ink containers had been shaped to resemble skewered squid, and the captain's chair was draped with a griffin pelt, complete with feathers stitched together to resemble unfurled wings.

The dim lighting and dark coloration of the rug and walls only added to my growing unease. This place had all the welcoming warmth of a dungeon. Whom did the room belong to?

"For someone so high ranking and influential, it wasn't difficult to get a meeting with him," I said, eyeing the compass on the corner of the desk.

I recognized it. An Occult Compass. A special kind of trinket made from an eye of an all-seeing sphinx. In the future—in my time, not Zelfree's past—only one existed. The others had been lost or destroyed. The Occult

Compasses could find any mystical creature, so long as the compass was attuned with a piece of the beast.

"You're *the Faceless*," Calisto said, dismissively waving a hand. "Of course the Marshall of the Southern Seas would want to meet you. *Everyone* wants to meet you."

We were in the marshall's quarters? Was this the moment in history when Zelfree had killed him? I could only wait and watch from behind his eyes.

I picked up a quill made from the feather of a caladrius. Was it magical? Or was the snow-white coloration of the feather just decoration?

Calisto glanced over. "Hey. Where's your new pirate lackey? The one you've been bedding."

I shot the man a glare. "You know what happened. Why even ask?"

"I heard details from the first mate of the *Storm Eater*, not from you." Calisto laughed as he leaned back in his chair. "Or should I believe all the rumors now? They paint an *interesting* picture."

"It didn't work out between me and him," I stated. "That's the end of the story."

There had been flashes of Zelfree's personal life in the previous dream-memory. Apparently, Zelfree had tried many times to have lasting relationships, but the nature of being a secretive double-agent known as the *Faceless* had prevented him from ever having anything substantial. It was almost disheartening how often he'd seemed to lose the people he'd cared for.

"What about you?" I asked. "I heard you met a lady."

"Eh. It was good... until the witch tried to steal from me."

"Steal what?" I set the quill down.

"A pouch full of coins. I threw her in the brig."

"When?"

"A few months ago."

I finished my circle around the desk and stopped next to Calisto. "You're just going to leave her there, is that it? Over a few coins? How reasonable."

"Redbeard would've cut off her fingers to lure out skull scorpions from the Amber Dunes," Calisto growled. "Throwing her in the brig was a mercy."

"Yeah, I bet everyone looks like a saint when compared to one of the vilest men on the seas. Please, keep using Redbeard as a moral guidepost for your actions. I'm sure that'll work out well in the end."

"Who would you have me compare my actions to?" Calisto spoke each word as though they were formed with the last of his patience.

"Literally anyone else, but preferably someone you admire, not loathe." I sat next to Calisto, my whole body tense from the supposedly "casual" conversation.

The massive ship creaked and groaned from the waves. Silence stretched on between us until Calisto forced a short exhale.

"What would *you* do?" he asked.

"Let her go. I'm sure she'll never haunt your ship again, and she'll likely tell tales of how frightening and ruthless you are. That's what you want, isn't it?"

The anger in Calisto's voice vanished as he said, "I don't know what I want."

I settled into my chair, more relaxed than I had been a few seconds ago. "Let me do the talking with the Marshall of the Southern Seas. I want to figure out what drives an honorable man to do such questionable things."

"Power," Calisto stated, no hesitation. "It'll turn any man into a fiend. And once they get a taste, they can never go back."

"That's what I love about you—your never-ending opti-mism," I quipped.

"Heh. Well, let's assume I'm right. What're we going to do then? Tell him to stop aiding pirates, since now he's been caught? Kill him?"

"We won't do anything." I laced my fingers together. "I need to report back to the Frith Guild first. Eventide wants to form a plan."

Calisto rubbed at his temple. His arcanist mark—a star and a manticore—was etched into his forehead, but not glowing. He hadn't yet achieved his true form. I wondered when it would take place, since he had it in the future.

The door to the captain's quarters opened, and a gust of icy air rushed inside. I tightened my coat, but I didn't move from the chair. The door closed, and the echo of heavy boots filled the room. A mountain of a man walked around behind the desk, his shoulders teeming with so much muscle, he had lost his neck.

He wore all the decoration befitting the Marshall of the Southern Seas—a bright blue coat, white shirt and trousers, black gloves, and more than a dozen medals. Marshalls also wore silver torcs—a type of neck ornament that looked like a reverse necklace. The metal went behind the neck and hung down in front, resting over the collarbones.

The weirdest part was his cap. It was a tricorn, common on the seas, but he wore it with a bandana that covered his forehead. Arcanists never covered their mark. Well, some did, but the majority didn't. The mark was a sign of one's magical status. I supposed the marshall was so famous, everyone *knew* he was an arcanist.

When I looked closer, the bandana had a star and dragon stitched into the blue fabric. That was his mark, but why had he shown it on the clothing rather than displaying it openly?

"I'm sorry to keep you waiting," the marshall said, a rumble to his voice as he smiled. "I had to finish some matters before I could start new ones."

His clean-shaven face seemed larger than most and definitely more square. His dark brown hair poked out from the bandana, but not much.

"Thank you for agreeing to see me, Marshall," I said.

"You're not someone under my command. You'll address me as *Maddox*." He leaned forward, torturing the desk with his considerable bulk. "What I need to know is—how do I address a man of many faces?"

I forced half a smile. "You may call me Simon."

How many false names had Zelfree given out over the years?

"Simon? What an unimpressive name for a ruthless pirate, such as yourself." Maddox snorted and laughed. "Calisto, though—that's fitting. The same name as the infamous Death Lord, right?"

Calisto hadn't moved from his lackadaisical position on the chair. He regarded the Marshall of the Southern Seas as though thoroughly disinterested in his opinion. He didn't even answer the question.

Cutting straight to the chase, Maddox continued, "No matter what you call yourself, I'm pleased you reached out to me. I want someone of your talents in on my operations. Especially the next one."

"Is that so?" I asked.

"That's right. If your reputation is to be believed, you'll have no trouble helping me move things across the seas. Maybe even into the Argo Empire. Maybe even to the far northern islands."

"You want me to be one of your smugglers?" I chortled. "My talents would be wasted bringing things from point A to point B. Any ol' cutthroat can do that."

"The cargo is so important that I'd only trust a man of your talents to deliver it."

After the last statement, Calisto sat straight in his chair, clearly interested. I was as well. From what I remembered of the last dream-memory, the Marshall of the Southern Seas had been smuggling mystical creatures, specifically the legendary kirin. What could be more important than those?

"You're not very good at negotiations," I said. "Now that I know you *need* my services, the price has doubled."

Maddox opened a drawer in his desk and rummaged through the contents. "Oh, no, no. We won't deal in coins. This is beyond gold. I'll be paying you in magical power."

"Trinkets and artifacts have price values. We still need to talk numbers."

"What I'm offering is priceless. Beyond your imagining."

The words were spoken with a haunting kind of glee.

"You just have priceless magical power lying around, huh?" Calisto asked. Then he crossed his arms. "You sound like you've been day drinking, Maddox. Might want to sober up before you make agreements."

I shot Calisto a sideways glower. He responded with a sneer before leaning back in his chair. Despite Calisto's outburst, the marshall didn't seem upset. The opposite, in fact—like he was delighted to have a chance to prove Calisto wrong.

Maddox withdrew two glass vials from a drawer. He slid them across the desk, and they twirled twice before stopping right at the edge. The crimson contents almost seemed black in the dim lighting.

"Blood?" I asked.

Maddox tapped a thick finger on his desk. "Have you ever seen arcanists with glowing white marks? The ones who have achieved a true form of their eldrin?"

"Once or twice."

"Their eldrin are more powerful than normal, but the method of acquiring such a transformation is still baffling. Now there's a way to force it. That's what the blood is. A means to have your eldrin transcend into its perfect form." Maddox held up both hands as he said it, his fingers spread.

Calisto chuckled, but didn't offer commentary.

"I'm skeptical," I said as I picked up the vial and turned it over in my hand. "How do I know it works?"

Maddox removed his tricorn hat and then yanked off his blue bandana. His hair, slick with sweat, was stuck to one side and puffed on the other—but his arcanist mark demanded all my attention.

It glowed red. The star. The typhoon dragon.

A part of me had feared the vials of blood were the arcane plague, but I thought this was too far in the past for that to be the case. Now I knew they were. The Marshall of the Southern Seas had been infected, and the plague had gone on so long—he had consumed enough magic—that he now had a dread form dragon as an eldrin.

Why weren't Zelfree and Calisto running from the room? Was this really the first time they had ever encountered the arcane plague?

If I could have laughed, I would have. The marshall was tricking them into thinking the plague was a boon—and since Zelfree and Calisto had never encountered it before, they didn't know what they were getting in to. This snake oil salesman would sell them a product that would twist their minds and warp their eldrin.

When I really thought about it, the whole situation

disgusted me. Maybe that was how Maddox had been tricked. Perhaps before the plague had become a rampant problem on the high seas, it had been secretly given to powerful individuals as a way to "force their eldrin to transform." If that had been the case, they had gotten exactly what they'd wanted—only they hadn't realized the price of the change would be their sanity.

I stared at Maddox's mark then glanced back at the vial. "This blood did that?"

"That's right," Maddox said. "You take a swig of that, and you'll never be the same. Suddenly, everything will make sense. You'll have power and control. An amazing thing, that is."

Calisto took the other vial and uncorked it. He sniffed the contents. "This isn't human blood."

Maddox rested back in his impressive chair. "I wasn't involved in the creation. I'm just a middleman."

"You want us to deliver this?" I asked.

"That's right. I need you to deliver several other vials to specific individuals. But now you know they're precious—that's why I need someone like you to carry out this operation."

There wasn't much blood in the vial, but the arcane plague only needed a few drops to take hold. Was Master Zelfree really giving thought to drinking it? Would he really *deliver* it?

"You don't want us to smuggle kirin?" I asked. I kept the vial in hand, still twirling it about. "That's why I contacted you in the first place. I want one."

"Ah, well, I can secure one of those for you. I'm friends with the ruler of the kirin village. The Autarch owes me a few favors."

Wait, what?

But Zelfree didn't seem to care about the mention of an *Autarch*. He continued the conversation as though nothing interesting had been spoken.

"I want a kirin foal, then," I said. "And I'll deliver your blood."

"That's it?" Maddox chuckled. "You're cheaper than I thought you'd be, *Simon*. Perhaps you're not as skilled a negotiator as you thought you were."

"I also get to keep this," I said as I held up the vial.

"Most certainly. But only if you take it now." Maddox smiled, the red glowing mark on his forehead transforming his expression into a terrifying sight. "I want you both to admit you feel the power rushing through your veins."

"How do I know this isn't some poor attempt to poison us?" I asked.

"I'm bonded to a typhoon dragon. You're on my ship, with my crew, surrounded by my arcanists. Trust me, if I brought you here to kill you, there are faster and easier ways to do it. You just gave me such a skeptical reply earlier, and now I want to prove you wrong."

Calisto snorted and then gulped down the blood, no more questions. He tossed the empty vial onto the desk. "Happy?" he asked. "Because I don't feel a damn thing."

I knew—from years of experience—that the arcane plague didn't affect arcanists and mystical creatures who were immune to blood diseases. All man-eating creatures were—which included manticores. It didn't matter if Calisto drank the blood or not, he would never be infected.

But Zelfree...

I uncorked the vial and swirled the contents. Then I brought the container close to my lips and tilted my head back. Dread filled my thoughts, but that emotion vanished the moment I felt liquid trickle down my sleeve. Zelfree had the sleight-of-hand skills to make it appear as though he had consumed the blood, but instead, he had dumped the vial's contents into his coat. Thankfully, the dark leather of my clothing hid the small amount of crimson now sticking to my elbow and shoulder.

I placed the vial on the desk and smiled. "An interesting sanguine aftertaste. What year was that? '86? '87?"

Maddox sneered. "Don't you feel it?"

"A slight tingle. But that may just be my overwhelming disgust." I stood from my chair, careful to keep my tainted sleeve up, just in case any blood would trickle out. "If we've concluded with our arrangements, I have other matters to attend before I become a courier for your blood."

The Marshall of the Southern Seas motioned to the door. "The shipment will come in a week's time. You'll get all the details then. Make sure you're near the Lightning Straits."

Calisto and I left the marshall's quarters without another word. Once outside, on the deck of a ship I didn't recognize, and shivering from the cold sea winds, I shook my head.

"I can't believe you drank that," I muttered. "Are you insane? Or have *you* been day drinking?"

"He said it would give us a true form eldrin." Calisto shot me a glare. "Didn't you end up drinking it?"

"Of course not. That man can't be trusted."

"Even if that's true, *now what*? The marshall didn't admit to anything heinous. Redbeard is more of a monster than that man."

"Perhaps. First, I'm going to take this blood back to the Frith Guild," I said as I lifted the sleeve of my coat. "I have a feeling this is exactly what we were looking for."

41

ARRIVAL

I awoke with a million questions at the edge of my thoughts. The darkness of the cabin told me it was still night. In an attempt to organize my mental issues, I tried to connect everything together.

The Second Ascension were the ones who created the arcane plague. They had done so to spawn the legendary god-creatures. Somehow, and many years ago, they had infected the late Marshall of the Southern Seas. That man had helped them spread the plague by working with pirates.

He had also been smuggling kirin.

And the person who ruled over the kirin was someone named *the Autarch*.

I had heard the *Autarch* mentioned twice before—once from Redbeard, and once from the woman in Theasin's lab.

Theasin...

Were they all connected? Perhaps the late Marshall of the Southern Seas and Theasin himself were members of the Second Ascension. If that was the case, perhaps Theasin wanted the Mother of Shapeshifters because...

Because...

I didn't know. Even if everything was somehow connected, I didn't know why. What motive did everyone have to do this? I understood the marshall being tricked and driven to lunacy—the plague coursing through his body explained his shift to power-hungry tyrant—but I knew next to nothing about Theasin's personal goals, and I knew even less about what this *Autarch* person wanted.

But they were connected. I could feel it. All of it. Somehow.

Adelgis sat up from his bed. He glanced in my direction, even though he couldn't see in the dark. "Volke..."

"Yeah?" I whispered. Fain was still asleep.

"I had similar thoughts and concerns," Adelgis said. "That's why... I had hoped we could avoid speaking to my father. What if he's a member of the Second Ascension? What if he harmed the khepera for the Second Ascension's benefit? What will we do then? I promised you we would find a cure, and he's the only one I know to turn to."

My chest tightened as I took in shallow breaths.

I had no idea what we would do then. I supposed we'd have to fight Theasin, but then...

Adelgis shook his head and stood from his bed. He crossed the room with soft footsteps and stood next to me. "I'm sorry for bringing this up. I know it upsets you, but I think it's best not to worry about it until we can speak directly with my father. We'll get our answers then, I swear it."

How could I sleep at a time like this?

"Don't worry," Adelgis said. "I'll help."

He touched the side of my neck, and then a haze came over my mind.

I was forced back to sleep.

When I awoke again, it was to the gentle shaking of my shoulder. I rolled over, confused and half awake. Although the cabin was dark, my eyes had no trouble identifying Karna. She lay on the bed next to me, dressed only in a long tunic and trousers.

"Volke?" she whispered.

I grunted some sort of response as I positioned myself on my back. Karna curled into the spot under my armpit, and I rested my forearm over my eyes, tempted to fall back asleep.

"I need to speak with you," she said.

I tensed and sat up, my grogginess gone in an instant. "Are you okay? Did something happen?"

"Everything's fine." She sat up and shook her head. "I didn't mean to alarm you. I just wanted to speak to you about the Mother of Shapeshifters."

After a deep breath, I ran my hand through my disheveled hair. "Really? Why?"

"You wanted to know about her, didn't you?"

"Yes. But I thought you didn't want to speak about it."

Karna motioned to the bed, as though we should lie back down. I hesitated, only because my heart rate had doubled since first I had awoken, and I didn't feel like resting.

"I bathed before I came here," she said. "If that's what you're worried about."

"What? Uh, no, that's fine." I slowly returned my head to the pillow. "Please just tell me about the Mother of Shapeshifters." Ever since I had seen it in Zelfree's memories, I had been curious, but now that I knew it was the offspring of gods, I had to know more.

Plus, I didn't want to think about the present. My thoughts turned dark far too quickly.

Again, Karna curled up next to me, her touch soft. She wasn't her usual self—touching me needlessly or smiling any time I looked over. She kept her gaze low and her knees tucked close to her chest. In all regards, she appeared pensive.

"When I was younger, I ran away," Karna said. "When it got dark, I found myself lost in the woodlands east of Thronehold. I didn't know where I was going."

"You ran away from what?"

"I don't know. My life? I just wanted to get away, and I didn't know how. So I left, and I never intended to return."

Master Zelfree had also been in a wooded area when he had met the Mother of Shapeshifters. If the creature dwelled in a specific type of terrain, perhaps it wouldn't be difficult to find it, so long as the hunter knew the signs. That worried me. I didn't want Theasin to find the Mother of Shapeshifters, not after what he had done to the khepera. Clearly, he had no compunction about destroying mystical creatures if it served his means.

"A fog bank rolled in," Karna whispered. "It became difficult to see."

"And then you found it?"

"That's right. The Mother of Shapeshifters emerged from the fog. I... didn't know what to do. She was so alien, yet powerful, and I lost the ability to use my legs. It was like being trapped in a nightmare where a monster is chasing you, but you can't run."

I wrapped an arm around Karna, trying to comfort her, even though this experience had taken place years prior.

She continued, "She asked me what my deepest fear was. At the time, I didn't realize it was some sort of *trial of worth*. I just thought... Well, I wasn't sure. Part of me thought I had died."

"What did you answer?"

Karna closed her eyes. "I told her I feared loneliness—of having no one and nothing."

For a brief moment, it intrigued me that the only two acceptable answers for this trial involved drastically different fears. Then again, they resulted in bonding with completely different mystical creatures. I had never heard of a trial of worth with such nebulous terms and results, but it seemed fitting for a mystical creature unbound by the limitations of form.

"Was that really your fear?" I asked.

Karna gripped the blankets and pulled them close. "Yes. I figured no one would love me for *me*—not after those men in Thronehold abused me. I was *tarnished* after that, and... and not worthy of someone's affection. Those kinds of fears haunted me back then. When I told that to the Mother of Shapeshifters, that was when she gave me my doppelgänger. She said I'd never be alone again, but..."

"But what?"

"But she warned me that I would never achieve my doppelgänger's true form until I understood human nature. That was her final statement before she left me."

True forms... They were only achieved when an arcanist embodied the magics and telos of their eldrin. A doppelgänger arcanist needed to understand human nature? That made sense—they were creatures who looked and acted just like humans, and their magics involved manipulating and controlling them.

I held Karna closer. "Why tell me this now?"

"I thought about our interactions. About how you say what you mean and how you want people to do the same for you in return. I just realized... I wouldn't regret sharing this part of me. At least, not with you."

The rocking of the ship, coupled by the sounds of water breaking against the hull, lulled me back into a relaxed state. My eyelids grew heavier with each silent moment.

"Can I guess your greatest fear?" Karna asked, preventing me from sleeping.

I nodded.

"Is it death?"

"I'm sure everyone is afraid of dying, in some small part," I muttered. "But the thought of death doesn't keep me up at night. There's no point in fearing the inevitable."

Karna laughed into my side, her velvety mirth a surprise. She buried her face into my shirt, smiling enough I could feel it through the fabric. "I don't think I'll ever get a true form doppelgänger. I couldn't guess what you're afraid of—how would I ever understand all of human nature?"

"I think you understand some of it," I said. "I've seen the way you impersonate certain people. Theasin, Calisto—or when you were acting out the part of a desperate dancer in Thronehold—there are certain archetypes you feel comfortable with."

"And what archetypes are those?"

"Villains."

My answer struck a chord. Karna slowly sat up, her long hair spilling over her shoulder and covering my chest. "You honestly think so?"

"Any time you've tried to impersonate someone more honorable or decent, like Captain Devlin or Fain, you *act as though you're acting* when you're them, if that makes any sense. Almost like you can't believe anyone could be so genuine without hiding something deeper and darker. It's... hard to articulate."

"Everyone has dark urges," Karna said. "Why do some people pretend otherwise?"

"And the night sky might be black, but that doesn't mean you should ignore the stars."

"The *night sky*, huh? What're you trying to say?"

I sat up and scooted closer to her, trying to impart wisdom I had never voiced before. "I liked reading tales of swashbuckling arcanists when I was younger. Their stories of bravery and kindness are like the navigational stars, a guiding presence in the blackness of night. I might never be exactly like them, but as long as I want to be, then it's easier to overcome moments of darkness. I'm not *pretending*—I'm working toward a goal I haven't reached yet. I'm following the stars."

After a minute of silence, Karna placed a palm on my shoulder and guided me back down on the bed. I complied with her unspoken command, and she once again curled next to my side.

"I like your night sky analogy, Volke," she said. "You've given me a lot to think about."

I closed my eyes, the sleep too much to fight.

"I intend to help you in whatever way I can," Karna continued, her voice distant. "I won't stop until we find a way to rid you of this plague."

Two days until we would reach our destination.

Thunderstorms flashed in the clouds that blocked the majority of the sun. A light misting of rain followed us from the straits, never letting up. Although surrounded by chill and gloom, I steadied myself for the eventual confrontation with Theasin once we reached the Excavation Site.

What would he say when we mention the khepera? How would he justify his actions? Would I even ask? If he had a cure, but I upset him, he might not share it. Was that a concern I should even consider?

And then there was the question of the Second Ascension. Perhaps his actions with the khepera could be explained, but if he had helped the Second Ascension attack Thronehold, there was nothing he could say to exonerate himself.

In a moment of meditation, I decided that I was calm enough to risk gathering information from the one person I hated most on this vessel—Calisto.

He stood on the quarterdeck, overlooking the gray waves, his manticore at his side. When I started toward him, my shadow shifted with agitated movements.

"My arcanist," Luthair said. "You should stay far away from that man. Nothing good will come of this."

"I'm just going to ask some questions. It'll be okay." I walked over the shadow and took the stairs to the quarterdeck, my hands in my pockets.

As I approached, Hellion got to all four "feet." His front hands disturbed me since they looked so much like a human's, and I couldn't help but stare as I walked across the deck. With my eyes low, I took note of Calisto's boots. They were, in fact, the trinkets I had made for Jozé right before leaving the *Sun Chaser*. Had Karna asked my father to make them as part of Calisto's payment? That was the only explanation—and Jozé hadn't told me because I would've said *no* had I known.

Calisto turned around. He must've caught me staring because he half-smiled and said, "I should thank you for these. They worked perfectly." Then he returned his gaze to the distant waters, as though unconcerned with my proximity. Although he had been struck by Redbeard's reaper scythe, it seemed as though he had mostly recovered at this point—much faster than a normal arcanist.

Hellion kept his neutral mask-face on me.

With hesitant steps, I moved within ten feet of Calisto, my anger clawing its way up my chest. I had to remind myself to take even breaths. I only had a few questions. This would be over quickly.

"Do you have a moment?" I asked, though I didn't know why I was bothering to be polite.

"As part of the agreement to transport you, we were told not to engage you in conversation," Hellion said, his creepy voice partly muffled by the mask. He "smiled" as the edges of his mouth-hole curled upward. "You should stay locked away in your cabin before something happens."

"*I'm* the one engaging *you* in conversation," I said. "Not the other way around. You're not breaking your agreement."

Calisto tore his gaze from the sea and gave me his full attention. His copper hair, wet from the sprinkle of rain, clung in clumps over his glowing arcanist mark. "What do you want?" he asked, the words slow and deliberate.

"You work for the Second Ascension, right?"

"What of it?"

"Do you know if Theasin Venrover is also helping them?"

Calisto narrowed his eyes. His manticore swished his scorpion tail, his expression still set to "happy."

"You don't know much about them, do you?" Calisto finally asked.

"Will you answer my questions or not?" I growled.

"Oh, I'll tell you." Calisto shrugged and forced a laugh. "I'll tell you everything you want to know. Their leader, their organizational structure, their plans, the next step in their plans, the arcanists who make up their ranks—anything you want."

"You... you will?" I rubbed at the back of my neck, shocked by the sudden turn in the conversation. "You'd betray them?"

This time, Calisto responded with a genuine laugh. "What's it matter to you who I betray? It's your lucky day."

"Then tell me about Theasin."

"Hold on. I didn't say the information was *free*." Calisto took a single step forward. "But I will make an exchange."

My anger twisted into rage. I managed to quell it just as fast as it emerged. With gritted teeth, I asked, "What do you want?"

"You're one of Everett Zelfree's apprentices, right? You were here on my ship more than a year ago."

I held my breath as I replied with a nod.

"Then you know the rizzel arcanist—the girl missing an eye. Tell me about her, and I'll tell you everything you want to know about the Second Ascension."

His cold tone and twisted proposal sent me right back to the edge of self-control.

"What is your sick perversion with Illia?" I asked, my volume increasing with each word. "Why won't you just leave her alone? You took her family and her eye, and now you have to search for her at every port?"

"So her name is Illia?" Calisto wiped some of the rain from his face, half-concealing a smile. "I didn't know that."

"You're a disgusting bastard."

Calisto shrugged. "You're gonna have to use more creative insults than that, kid. I've heard that one plenty of times."

"Tell me. *Tell me why you hurt her.*"

"Heh. It wasn't personal, at first. I needed the eyes of

children for Hellion's true form, and her parents hadn't been willing to part with one."

I placed my hand on the hilt of Retribution. Before I could draw the blade, the shadows lifted up around me. Luthair merged with my being, and I allowed the process to happen—happy for his added strength—but the moment his cold power soaked into my veins, so did a stronger sense of self-control.

Please, calm yourself, Luthair said telepathically. *This isn't like you, my arcanist. Starting a fight here will help no one.*

Hellion's mask contorted into an angry face, complete with narrowed, V-shaped eyebrows and a drastic frown. It wasn't until that moment that I took note of Hellion's stature—seven feet at the shoulder, his crimson mane pouring over his muscular neck and shoulders. The claws of the beast put most daggers to shame.

Calisto drew his cutlass, though he didn't seem concerned—the opposite, in fact. He chuckled as he took a wide stance.

With Luthair's extra bit of sanity, I managed to take a deep breath.

"Go on," Calisto said. "This is the part where you get mad and try to avenge your friend. Tell me I'll never hurt Illia again and strike. It's what you want to do."

He was taunting me. Why? He wanted a fight? Here on the deck of his nightmare ship?

Instead, I turned on my heel. Luthair's cape swished around me as I headed for the stairs, my gait stiff.

Calisto didn't attack me, but he did call out, "Whenever you're ready to talk, I'll be here, waiting to exchange information."

"Land ho!" a pirate shouted from the crow's nest.

I hadn't expected to see so much smoke on the horizon, but the black pillars rising in the distance were all I could focus on.

The crew of the *Third Abyss* hustled to get everything prepared for landing. I stayed on the deck of the ship while we sailed closer and closer to a rickety port not far from our location. When we neared land, I took note of the broken buildings, devastated landscape, and shadows in the bay—sunken ships. Dozens of them.

Although the trees still stood, most of the area had become a wasteland. The drizzle of rain continued its gentle downpour, preventing the flocks of birds from taking flight. The ravens rested on the debris of the ruined city, their shiny eyes visible, even from the port.

The Lightning Straits was the easiest route into this bay, and it had been filled with thunder and plague-ridden creatures. It didn't surprise me that the port here would be abandoned, but what else had happened to it?

As the crew tied the *Third Abyss* to the dock, I figured out the answer to my own question. The arcane plague infested this area. In all directions, I could *feel* its hold. The ravens weren't normal birds, but plague-ridden mystical creatures. Mermaids filled the sunken ships beneath us, the shimmer of their vibrant tails visible whenever they chanced a swim out—plague-ridden, all of them.

This wasn't a safe location. It wasn't even really a location. No one had lived here for years, perhaps decades, given the plants growing over the destruction. It was a graveyard of a town and port, worn down by monsters.

Theasin had come here?

Here?

The smoke in the distance was our only indicator of civilization. It had to be the Excavation Site. What were they digging up there?

Spider sauntered over to the port side of the ship and ordered the pirates to lower the gangplank. Then she had them start fetching supplies and unloading. I watched with idle curiosity, surprised to see them preparing for a long stay.

Spider turned to me and fixed her half-open shirt. "You got a problem?"

"You're going to shore?" I asked.

"That's right."

"Why?"

"It's really none of your concern," she said with an edge to her words. "But you weren't the only reason we came out this way. We'll be picking someone up."

Odd. Then again, if pirates were the only ones capable of sailing the Lightning Straits, it made sense. They could make honest coin acting as a passenger vessel.

"You heading off, then?" Spider asked, motioning to the gangplank.

I pulled my coat tight. For the last few days, I had rarely been dry.

"We'll be leaving," I said. "Thank you for the ride."

Spider crossed her arms. "Just hurry and get off our ship, try-hard. I'm tired of seeing you and your whore friend around these parts."

That was what I got for being polite. I should've known.

I headed for the officer's quarters, intent on gathering Fain, Adelgis, and Karna for our short trek across land. We had to be careful—not because we were in grave danger, but because I couldn't allow Adelgis or Karna to also get infected with the plague during our journey to the Excavation Site.

THE EXCAVATION SITE

Karna, Fain, Adelgis, and I disembarked from the *Third Abyss*, what little belongings we had packed away into satchels. At first, I thought we needed to stay on high alert for the entire trip, but the plague-ridden beasts didn't approach us. We traveled through the desolate remains of a town, following a worn path made of cobblestone. The monsters watched from afar, some laughing or chuckling, some watching with bulging dead-fish eyes. It was as if they couldn't get near us—and I didn't understand why.

We arrived at the southern edge of the village and discovered a new path had been carved through the woods. The dirt road led straight to the dark smoke in the distance. I stopped once the cobblestone ended, my attention on the trees. They had white trunks and gray leaves—as though drained of color. I remembered them. They had been in the first dream-memory Adelgis had given me.

Were we close to Zelfree's hometown? Or was the rubble behind us what remained of it?

A gentle breeze rushed by. Karna grabbed at her long,

blonde hair and then tied it back into a ponytail. She had worn her loose trousers and cloth wrap over her chest—the same revealing outfit she had worn into the Grotto Labyrinth. Did she plan on changing her shape often?

Fain glanced over his shoulder and then flinched. He whirled on his heel and pulled out his dagger, his whole body tense. "Who're you?"

I looked around Fain, ready for a fight, if needed.

Standing behind us, holding a heavy satchel over one shoulder, was an eccentric man. He wore a top hat, and his thick belt could barely contain his gut. His purple shirt and black trousers reminded me of a circus troupe.

Wraith dropped his invisibility and snarled at the strange man, his long wolf fangs glistening with saliva.

The man forced a smile and held up both hands. "Hey, there. No need to get upset."

"Why're you following us?" Fain demanded.

Karna placed both hands on her hips. "That's the rudest thing I've heard you say." She leapt to the man's side and straightened his shirt. "This is my eldrin."

The odd man tipped his top hat. It calmed Wraith enough that the wendigo stopped growling and returned to his invisible state.

"Your eldrin?" Fain sheathed his dagger. "Why haven't we seen him before?"

Karna shook her head. "He's always been around. You just haven't been observant enough to spot him. But now that we're not surrounded by crowds of people, there's nowhere he can hide."

"Okay... What's his name?"

The man with the top hat exchanged a questioning look with Karna. After a long bout of silence, Karna shrugged.

"You may call him *Karr*."

The name struck me as amusing. Was it the male version of *Karna*? Did the doppelgänger take a new name for every form and that was why they had hesitated to answer? I glanced over at Adelgis, wondering if he had heard my thoughts and hoping he would have some sort of explanation for the name.

He didn't say anything, though. He kept his eyes down, practically drilling a hole into his boots with his gaze.

"Are you okay?" I asked.

"Yes," Adelgis replied. "But ever since we left the ship, I haven't been able to hear anyone's thoughts."

"Really?" I asked.

Karna, Fain, and *Karr*—if that was really his name?—turned their attention to us.

Adelgis continued, "Once we stepped off the gangplank, I couldn't hear any thoughts. I tried, but it failed. I suspect whatever is preventing me from hearing thoughts is also keeping the plague-ridden mystical creatures out of the nearby vicinity." He lifted his gaze and met my eyes with a serious expression. "I think this is a powerful aura. A master arcanist must be nearby."

"What kind of arcanist could create an aura like this?" I asked.

"I'm not sure..." Adelgis pointed to the road. "But we shouldn't stop here. Let's be on our way."

Although it bothered me that Adelgis hadn't said anything about his limited magical powers until now, I did agree that we needed to continue. I had too many questions and not enough answers. Now wasn't the time to dither.

We headed into the woods as a group, everyone walking within a few inches of each other. I suspected if I stopped, someone would collide into me, so I kept my pace brisk.

The color-drained trees of white and gray protected us

from the light misting of rain. Fat water droplets occasionally rolled off the leaves, but it was better than before and the more clement weather allowed most of my clothes to dry.

The road itself was made of packed dirt. Grooves from heavy carriages and wagons cut deep into the ground, and I suspected this was a straight trek with few deviations. No one turned off into the trees; no one took a different route.

The deeper into the woods we went, the more anxious I became.

"So, Moonbeam, you really can't hear anyone's thoughts right now?" Karna asked. Her playful tone helped ease my tension, and I suspected that might have been her goal.

"I cannot," Adelgis said. "It's quiet, but pleasant."

"Good. Because there's something I've wanted to ask you, but I've avoided you whenever I've thought about it because of... reasons."

Adelgis knitted his eyebrows. "Should I be worried?"

"No," Karna said as she brushed her hand over his shoulder. "I was just curious about your personal life. You keep to yourself, you never seem to seek out companionship, and unlike most men I know, your eyes never wander... Why is that?"

Fain walked between them, his expression set into an annoyed glower. "Leave him alone. He's had it rough."

"It's fine," Adelgis said. "I don't mind answering—it's quite simple. It's not that I don't want companionship. I do. However, for many years, I had a parasite in my body, and for the last several months, I haven't felt myself. At a certain point, I grew accustomed to avoiding people, and I think I'll maintain that until I'm *whole again*, if that makes any sense."

"I see," Karna replied. She held her hands behind her

back as she asked, "And if you had to describe your perfect companion, what would they look like?"

"Probably like my sister," Adelgis said.

Everyone snapped their attention to him, myself included.

Adelgis's eyebrows shot to his hairline, and for the first time in a long time, the color of his face shifted from honeyed to rosy pink. He flailed with his hands as he tried to speak. "Er, well, I didn't mean it like *that*. What I'm trying to say is someone who is opposite to me, but who's also understanding." He looked away, tapping the tips of his fingers together. "Cinna has always been socially astute and charismatic, and she's never had a problem with the way I... *conduct myself*. I didn't mean *her exactly*. Of course not. I meant someone *like* her."

The silence that followed only furthered Adelgis's embarrassment. He fidgeted with his long hair.

"Now I miss my ability to read minds," he muttered.

Karna let out a velvety chuckle. "You're cute when you're not playing the part of a *disturbed stranger*."

"I would've said *someone like Atty*," Adelgis continued, still preoccupied with his own thoughts. "But I didn't want to irritate Volke, so I went with the next best example, and my sister has been on my mind a lot lately, so that's why—"

Fain placed a hand on Adelgis's shoulder, cutting him off mid-thought. "We understand, Moonbeam."

"It was comforting to know when someone was speaking the truth." Adelgis smoothed his clothing. "Especially in these instances."

Although they continued talking, my mind wandered.

Atty...

If she were here, she'd be the quiet strength of the group, keeping calm, even when everyone else wasn't. I envisioned her walking alongside us, her gait smooth and regal, her conversation uplifting and pleasant.

Zaxis, on the other hand, probably would've rushed ahead, no plan in mind. He was always more impulsive than I was. Filled with bluster. His shouting would've carried through the woods; I could practically hear it. Despite that, I knew he would be handy in a fight. Some people hesitated, but not Zaxis.

If only they were here. I'd feel more confident about the situation.

Karna turned to me, no doubt intending to drag me back into the conversation, but before anything happened, the clop of hooves and the rattle of a cart echoed throughout the woods. I held my breath and moved off to the side of the road, curious to see who was heading our way.

To my surprise, a group of men and women, four in total, walked alongside a horse as they guided it down the road, toward the broken city. The cart carried wooden crates, each nailed shut and ready for sea travel. The individuals weren't arcanists, since they had no marks on their foreheads, and when they noticed us, they looked away and said nothing. They continued with the delivery, their shoulders slumped.

Fain watched until they had gone past us. Then he turned to me. "What's going on?"

I frowned and shook my head. "I don't know. Those people didn't seem surprised or concerned to see us."

"They didn't seem very friendly, either," Karna added. "It's a shame we don't have someone who can read minds anymore."

"I do still have functioning eyes," Adelgis muttered. He pointed to the trees. "Someone is approaching."

A creature flashed into view between the white trunks. It

had the shape of a horse, but it seemed more delicate and agile. It moved with the fluidity of water and at the speed of a powerful wind. The horse's coat shimmered with each movement, similar to scales, but the silver coloration gave it a mystical appearance.

The silver horse reached the road in a matter of seconds. It was then that I realized what it truly was.

A kirin.

It had all the markings from legend. Its "coat" was actually silver dragon-like scales. The kirin's cloven hooves—standard for a deer, and not a horse—had all the toughness and hard edge of real silver. Its tail resembled a lion's, and there was a horn on its forehead, much like a unicorn. A kirin's horn, however, grew in twisted and jagged. This kirin's horn glittered with an inner power and was semi-transparent crystal.

Everything about the kirin seemed magical. Even its eyes were tiny night skies—black and speckled with stars.

I fumbled with my words, unable to think of a greeting. Kirin were rare and precious, perhaps even more so than knightmares, and there were fewer than twelve of those left. I never thought I'd see one.

I didn't realize the kirin had a rider until a lady slid off its back.

The young woman had short, strawberry blonde hair, and she wore oversized clothing of white and silver, enough to cover her neck and the entirety of her arms. Her pants were tied snugly at her waist, but then they puffed out as they covered her legs all the way to the ground.

The most distracting piece of her outfit was the headband that covered her forehead. It reminded me of the Marshall of the Southern Seas. Why would this woman hide her mark? I was starting to distrust anyone who did such a thing.

Her emerald eyes had a vacant quality, even as she looked over us one at a time.

"You shouldn't be here," she said, her words slow and quiet. "This isn't right."

Adelgis stepped forward before I could respond. "I'm Adelgis Venrover, Theasin's son. I've come to see him."

The woman reached out and touched his jaw. Adelgis didn't flinch or move away. Her slender fingers traced the side of his face.

"You *are* Theasin's son," she said with a slight smile. "How curious that you've traveled all this way to see him. Theasin doesn't care for surprises."

For a prolonged—and awkward—length of time, the woman kept her hand on Adelgis's face. I assumed they were speaking telepathically or perhaps communicating in some other way. With a gentle motion, she grazed his ear and then the corner of his jaw. How long were we supposed to remain quiet and waiting?

"Your skin is so soft," the woman muttered. "Like... feathers."

Fain leaned in close to me. "By the abyssal hells—we've found Moonbeam number two."

"My name is Orwyn," the woman said, answering Fain. "And this is my first eldrin." She removed her hand from Adelgis and then placed it on the neck of the beautiful silver kirin. "You may call her Lith."

First eldrin? She didn't elaborate, and I almost asked what she meant, but I decided against it. The kirin regarded us with her twilight-eyes and then pointed to the road with her crystal horn.

"Lith wants us to hurry along," Orwyn said, her tone airy

and distant. "We mustn't keep Theasin waiting. He won't be here much longer."

"Wait," I said.

Orwyn stopped before climbing onto her kirin. She had no saddle, but that didn't seem to bother her. With unhurried and careful movements, she turned to face me. Her half-vacant gaze was difficult not to dwell on.

"Where are we?" I asked. "What is this place?"

"Don't be silly, you know where you are," Orwyn cryptically replied. "This is the Excavation Site, the heart of our operations. We're in control here." And then, with no further explanation, she climbed onto Lith's back and gestured for us to follow.

We continued on the straight road, and Orwyn went ahead, her kirin much faster than any of us. I could've shadow-stepped to keep her pace, but I decided against it. I didn't want to take my eyes off our surroundings, not even for a second. Although Orwyn and Lith seemed *pleasant*, I didn't trust them. My gut told me we were in danger, but nothing negative was actively happening to us.

We had to continue.

It didn't take us long to pass through the woods. The rest of the group grew equally as tense once we came upon the fires creating the black smoke.

Despite the drizzle, massive flames licked into the sky, spewing inky smoke with each flicker and wave. There were four bonfires, each with trees and dead creatures inside. The smell of burnt flesh filled the area, but another scent, similar to charcoal, lingered as well.

The trees in the surrounding area, perhaps half a mile in all directions, had been cut, the dirt had been leveled, and the grass burned away. Ash and scorch marks covered everything. I couldn't breathe deep without hurting my lungs.

Hundreds of people—*hundreds*—hustled around the man-made clearing. They carried tools, hauled away fresh dirt, or operated pulley systems with chains and cranks. A massive hole had been carved into the ground, the type of rectangular ditch used to craft graves—if the grave was for a mountain-sized person. The pulleys helped the workers clear the dirt from this giant hole, and they took it out by the wagonload.

No one acknowledged our arrival. Everyone was too busy, and too rushed, to do anything other than their work.

I slowed my steps as I approached the workers. A few dozen of them used a long pulley to extract bones from the hole. They weren't human bones. Nor were they horse bones. Or elephant bones. Or whale bones.

Those were all too small.

These were dragon bones. *Gigantic* dragon bones. The type of bones that could be hollowed out and lived inside.

And they weren't white.

No.

These were black bones—just like the bone fragments I had found in Theasin's lab—ebony and filled with powerful magic. The same bones that made up Retribution.

An excavation worker bumped into me. He spilled dirt across my boots, his hands shaking. I mumbled an apology and moved away, my gaze lingering on the bones. The man hurried to clean his mess.

Orwyn and Lith trotted in front of me. Orwyn pointed to a collection of buildings on the edge of the burned clearing. "This isn't for you. Speak with Theasin."

I managed to tear my eyes off the excavation and turn toward the buildings. Adelgis, Fain, and Karna joined me, but to my curiosity, I didn't spot Karr the doppelgänger anywhere. Had he transformed himself to look like a worker? Or had he disappeared into the woods?

The buildings were nothing more than hastily constructed warehouse-style structures, each made from the color-drained trees of the surrounding area. They were long, rectangular, and tall, but they didn't look comfortable or inviting. Orwyn pointed to a specific building, one with double doors made of white wood and iron. They were shut tight, but two workers leapt up from their tasks in order to open them for us.

Orwyn and Lith stopped twenty feet away from the entrance. Orwyn watched until we entered, her gaze haunting till the last moment.

Once inside, I realized we had entered a field lab.

Tables and containers filled the large space, and fragments of black bone covered most surfaces. Even indoors, non-arcanist workers ran to and fro, all seemingly in such a hurry that they didn't have time to acknowledge our presence. They carried bone fragments to meat-grinder-style tools and crushed them into a fine dust. The sound of crunching and gears turning echoed inside the building.

Thankfully, the walls kept most of the smoke outside. Now all I could smell was copper and sweat.

I shook my coat to clear it of water, grateful to be out of the rain.

"Father," Adelgis said, drawing the attention of everyone inside, including the busy workers.

Theasin Venrover stood at the far end of the lab, his tall stature and cold expression unique to him. His eyes filled with instant recognition, and I swear his emotions went through an entire spectrum before he finally settled on *disapproving*. He shoved two workers aside as he stormed between the many tables, his attention locked on Adelgis.

When Theasin reached his son's side, he grabbed Adelgis by the upper arm and held him close. "What're you doing here?" he demanded, his voice controlled, even if his mannerisms weren't.

Fain stepped forward as though he intended to give Theasin a piece of his mind, but I placed a hand on Fain's shoulder and held him back. I knew Adelgis enough to understand that *he* wanted to be the one to deal with his father. Everything we had to say—from the plague cure, to the crimes against the khepera—Adelgis needed the chance to address them first.

"You said you were working on a cure for the arcane plague," Adelgis replied. "We've come to see if you've created it—and if you haven't, we've come to help."

Theasin stared at his son, his eyebrows knitting together in slow confusion. It was obvious Theasin hadn't expected *that* as an answer. He ran a gloved hand over his clean-shaven face, but he wasn't as tidy as I remembered him from Thronehold. His black trousers and robes carried dirt smudges, and there were dark rings under his eyes.

Then Theasin hardened himself, hiding away any hint at emotion. He released Adelgis, turned on the heel of his shoe, and then snapped his fingers. The workers of the lab stopped their actions and gave Theasin their full attention.

"Everyone out," he commanded. "Assist the dockhands in filling crates and then return here at nightfall to finish your tasks."

No one needed to be told twice. They hurried for the door, falling into a neat and orderly line as they moved past Theasin.

The moment the last worker disappeared through the double door, silence descended.

In the far back corner of the room, behind crates and

tables, was a large pile of rubbish made up of glass, metal, nails, and broken magical items. If I hadn't seen that trash heap before, I never would've known it was Theasin's eldrin —a relickeeper. As a pile of trash, the relickeeper blended with its surroundings, but it could form into a dragon-like monster within a matter of seconds.

The blood relation between Theasin and Adelgis was undeniable, though there were definite differences. Theasin was just more... athletic and imposing. He kept his hair short, and although his clothing had been sullied by the excavation efforts, he kept everything smooth and in place.

"How did you get here?" Theasin asked, the ice in his words cutting.

He wasn't speaking to anyone else but Adelgis. Even so, both Karna and Fain shifted their weight, each of them ready to say something. I shook my head and gestured for them to stay out of it. Adelgis was handling the matter.

"I arrived aboard the *Third Abyss*," Adelgis said. "I chartered a ride with them once I figured out where you had gone."

"Who told you my location?"

"I pieced together your whereabouts from your personal letters. You spoke of specific locations, and I narrowed down the possibilities until this was the only logical explanation."

Although I figured all of this would upset Theasin, the information seemed to calm him. He smoothed his dark robe and then tugged at the edges of his gloves. "I see."

"Father," Adelgis said, his voice somewhat desperate. "Please tell me you have a cure for the arcane plague."

Theasin smirked. "Of course I do."

43

THE CURE TO THE ARCANE PLAGUE

I exhaled, relief flooding my system and easing my anxiety. Thank all the good stars in the sky. I almost couldn't believe it. Theasin Venrover had a cure for the plague, and now this terrible chapter of my life could come to an end.

Adelgis rubbed at his shoulder, his posture shifting from tense to fidgety. After a shaky breath, he asked, "Can you help Volke? He was infected with the plague some time ago. He needs treatment."

"Who?" Theasin snapped.

With a quick gesture of his hand, Adelgis identified me from the others. "You met Volke before. He was with me when I delivered you the abyssal leech."

Theasin stared at me with dark, unfeeling eyes. Then he returned his intense focus to his son. "Who is he? Your lover? Why would you go so far out of your way to bring him here?"

"After you extracted the leech, I began dying," Adelgis said matter-of-factly. "Volke searched tirelessly for a remedy. He saved me. It's important that I return the favor."

It was Theasin's fault that Adelgis had nearly died, but that new bit of information didn't seem to faze the man. If anything, Theasin returned to his disapproving tone and expression. "So, this was merely a fetch quest for your *friend*. I should've known it was mundane aspirations that brought you here, but this seems like extreme effort for a single arcanist. Tell me—who else knows you're here? Everett Zelfree? The rest of the Frith Guild?"

"No one," Adelgis said. "I separated from the Frith Guild when Volke was infected. We traveled here without their aid."

"I see."

Theasin turned away, his robe fluttering outward in his haste. He strode off, his gait stiff, until he reached a far back table covered in small glass vials. The glass *tinked* together as he rummaged through them, but he said nothing as he did so. Was Theasin gathering up the cure? Collecting his materials before we left? Why wouldn't he just tell us?

"Interesting," Karna said to Adelgis. "I don't think my impersonation of your father was accurate. I'm not capable of being *that* callous."

Adelgis didn't reply.

When Theasin returned, he held a single vial tightly in his gloved hand. "For a moment, you almost impressed me," he said. "I thought you had discovered the importance of my work and wanted to assist. I would've had a proud moment as a father if my son had gone through the effort of sleuthing through my personal materials to deduce my location, all to dedicate himself to my cause. *But instead,*"—Theasin regarded me with a glower—"you've wasted your considerable talents on an errand for some acquaintance. It's beyond disappointing."

I had heard Theasin's longwinded pontifications before,

so his statements didn't come as a shock. Fain and Karna, on the other hand, couldn't hide their visible seething.

Adelgis clenched his jaw and straightened his posture. In a move that mirrored his father, he hardened himself in icy condescension. "I'm sorry to upset you, but what I read of your work disgusts me. I had hoped it was untrue—or that I had made incorrect conclusions about what you were doing, but after seeing this place, I know I'm right."

Theasin held the vial close, his eyes narrowing. "Oh? And what do you know?"

"I know what you're digging up," Adelgis stated. "I didn't want to believe it, but there it is. The corpse of the *apoch dragon*—the god-creature who killed the rest. You found it, and now you're using its bones for your item creation."

"*Wait, what*?" I asked aloud, too shocked to form a more coherent response. I bit back all other words, my thoughts buzzing. Retribution had been crafted from the bones of the apoch dragon?

Theasin didn't glance in my direction. His focus remained solely on his son, his expression unchanged after the revelation. "And my efforts disturb you?"

"The apoch dragon's sole purpose for existing was to eliminate other powerful magical beings. It was a monster of destruction. The only things you could make with its bones are weapons." Adelgis took in a ragged breath, like he didn't want to continue with his accusations—but he had come too far now. "There was a ruinous substance used during the assassination in Thronehold. Our enemies called it *decay dust*, and part of it was made of nullstone... but the other part was this bone powder, wasn't it? That was how our enemies destroyed the trinkets of the guards and their queen. With the remains of the apoch dragon."

I didn't know what to say, and neither did Theasin.

Everyone remained quiet as Adelgis continued with his disturbing conclusions.

"And while I can understand using the remains of a dead mystical creature to craft trinkets and artifacts, I don't agree with decimating an entire species for your own personal use." Adelgis shook his head. "You altered the Grotto Labyrinth so that no one else could get to the center chamber. You killed those khepera to steal their sands. That was how you healed my injury."

Theasin lifted a calculated eyebrow, his lip twitching into half a smile. "You've done quite a bit of sleuthing. More than I thought you capable of."

He didn't even deny it. Despite being faced with someone who knew all his crimes, Theasin replied without a hint of remorse. I almost couldn't believe how callously he conducted himself.

And it pained me to think that Theasin Venrover—a scholar, an artificer, a professor—a man who had dedicated himself to mystical creature research, would use his vast amount of knowledge for this purpose.

Adelgis steadied himself with a deep breath. "You're a member of the Second Ascension, aren't you?"

"Of course," Theasin stated.

Of course. That was his response—*of course.*

I darkly chuckled to myself. Only someone like Theasin would claim membership to that organization as though it were the obvious choice.

Which meant the Excavation Site was probably the property of the Second Ascension. The workers, the arcanists—this was their operation. All of it.

"Why?" Adelgis asked.

"They're the only ones with the courage and innovation to usher us into a new future. The return of gods was inevitable, they're just controlling the process, and I intend to be there when the first of these all mighty beasts appear again."

Although I had wanted to give Adelgis the chance to confront his father, the last few statements threw me right back into a rage. I stepped forward, past Adelgis and into Theasin's line of sight. With gritted teeth, I said, "The Second Ascension is responsible for assassinating Queen Velleta, throwing the Argo Empire into turmoil, and—worst of all—spreading the arcane plague. You don't give a damn? About *any* of that?"

"It wasn't my hand that brought about those deeds," Theasin said.

"You helped create their decay dust! If it hadn't been for that, those people in Thronehold wouldn't have lost their lives."

"It must be difficult for you," Theasin drawled. "But you should understand that some of us are capable of seeing the bigger picture. Sometimes sacrifices must be made by the masses to better the world."

I didn't need to hear anymore.

In one forceful motion, I unsheathed Retribution and took a combat stance. Luthair lifted from the shadows and coalesced around me, forming into hard plate armor. His cold power added to mine—and so did his rage. He wasn't a calming presence this time. We both knew Theasin had to pay for his crimes.

The rubbish in the room stirred. It lifted up, one broken bit at a time, as though held with invisible strings. Glass clattered, metal rattled, and the form of a dragon took shape as the pieces fitted themselves together like a bizarre puzzle. Wispy magical threads bound the relickeeper's many broken fragments. Stained glass shards made up its fangs, and copper flakes made the scales of its "face." When the relickeeper lifted its tail, I caught sight of the jagged wrought-iron spikes—pointed ornaments that looked like they had been stolen from a fence.

With the addition of the *trash dragon*, Fain moved to my side, a subtle misting of frost coating the nearby tables. His frostbitten fingers were clenched so tight that blood dripped from his palms. Karna stepped away, inching closer to the doors.

Theasin's mouth curled in disgust. "You'd attack me? Your only hope for salvation? I suppose that fits the mentality of a plague-ridden arcanist."

His comment stilled my attack.

I hadn't yet been cured.

Adelgis placed a hand on the shadow-plate covering my shoulder. "Volke, please. Wait."

When the relickeeper moved, it created a cacophony of scratching and rattling. The beast stepped closer to Theasin, flashing its sharp "teeth." Fortunately, the warehouse-like building had a tall ceiling. The relickeeper stood at least thirteen feet at the shoulder, its patchwork body jagged and bulky.

Theasin motioned for his eldrin to move away. "Calm yourself, Essellian. These arcanists traveled quite a distance to get here. They're not going to do anything to risk losing the prize they came for. *Are you?*"

My arcanist, Luthair spoke telepathically. *He's the only one who can cure you.*

I didn't need to be reminded.

But still—I couldn't lower my weapon. I couldn't bring myself to attack, either.

Theasin must've sensed my dilemma, because he chortled and relaxed his tense shoulders. He twirled the vial in his hands. It was empty. I thought it had been the cure, but perhaps I had jumped to conclusions.

"Unmerge with your eldrin," Theasin commanded. "Or else we'll have to play out this skirmish."

Adelgis again turned to me. "Please, Volke. Just for now."

I hated doing anything for Theasin. A small piece of me wanted to run my blade through his chest and forsake the cure, all because he *thought* he could control me with a threat. In the end, it was Luthair who unmerged from me—had Luthair decided he wanted me cured more than he wanted to bring the villain into justice?

Losing his power shook me a bit, like I had lost his support in the matter.

Even Fain backed down, no longer angry enough to ice the surrounding area.

I lowered my blade.

Theasin forced a tight smile. "There's no need for unnecessary violence. I'm impressed enough with Adelgis that I'll cure you, but only on two conditions."

"Out with it," I growled. Rage twisted my insides. I knew I'd hate whatever *conditions* he named.

"First, I want a sample of your blood." He held up the empty vial. "For research purposes."

"*No.*"

"Come now. I can get plague-tainted blood whenever I want. What's the difference if I have a little more?"

With gritted teeth, I gestured for him to name the second condition.

"You'll need to be sedated," he said. "The man who will cure you is the abyssal leech arcanist, and I don't want him to know you dislike and distrust the Second Ascension. Once you're cured, I'll keep you here, asleep but alive, until the last of the apoch dragon has been excavated. Only then can I risk you returning to the Frith Guild."

I gritted my teeth.

Who knew how long that would take? I'd be helpless. Relickeeper arcanists could keep creatures in a suspended stasis for quite some time, paralyzed and unable to escape.

"I'll make this simple for you," Theasin said, sardonic. "Either comply with my conditions or suffer the fate of all plague-ridden arcanists. It really doesn't matter to me."

Adelgis moved closer, his cold demeanor returning. "Father—you can't expect us to stay here."

"Yes, I can. You've made your stance on the Second Ascension clear, and I can't have you running to the master arcanists in your guild. It's either this or conflict. And trust me, you aren't even aware of half the arcanists stationed at this site. You'll never leave here alive."

A war raged inside of me as I weighed all the options. I could have Theasin cure me at the cost of allowing the Second Ascension to continue with their dastardly plots. Or I could fight the man. Theasin was probably right— we'd all likely die. Could I do that to Fain, Adelgis, and Karna? The only reason they had come here was because of me.

I supposed the third option was attempting to escape. Perhaps we could make it back to the *Third Abyss* before it departed. But I would still be plague-ridden... and without another lead, it was only a matter of time before...

"You swear you'll cure Volke?" Adelgis asked.

I shot him a concerned look.

"You have my word," Theasin said.

"What're you thinking?" Fain said under his breath.

Adelgis ran an unsteady hand through his long, rain-soaked hair. "I... I told him I would get him a cure. If we don't get it from my father, we won't get it from anyone." He faced me, his brow furrowed. "I'm so sorry."

"None of this is your fault," I muttered.

"I wasn't apologizing for the situation, just my actions."

Adelgis reached out, and before I could move away, his fingertips grazed my neck. In the next instant, my mind fogged with his magic-inducing sleep. I staggered backward, both shocked by his betrayal and confused by the cobwebs muddling my thoughts.

How could he?

I hit a table with my hip and collapsed to the ground, losing consciousness a moment later.

No!

I tried—I struggled—but the magic kept me confined in a mental cage made of sleep. Why would Adelgis do this? No. I knew why. But I still couldn't forgive him. *Forcing* me to accept Theasin's aid, because he thought this was the best course of action drove me to a new height of frustration.

It was probably best that I was asleep. A small piece of me thought about running Adelgis through with Retribution. That was irrational—too over-the-top for what had happened—and I needed a chance to regain control.

Then I was dreaming.

I hated sinking into Zelfree's memory. Before this, the dreams had been a pleasant distraction. Now it was torture —reminding me that time was passing while I did nothing.

The arcanists in the Frith Guild needed to know what was going on. I had to inform them about the whereabouts of Theasin and the apoch dragon. I had so much to do, but without the ability to wake, I couldn't do any of it.

In Zelfree's memory, I carried a small mystical creature into a map room on a ship, probably the *Red Falcon*. The table had a paper map sprawled across the top. Little boats carved out of oak wood dotted the water.

With the utmost care, I placed the mystical creature on the edge of the map, knocking over some of the figurines.

It was a kirin foal—a little baby creature no bigger than a housecat. It trembled as it glanced around, its black-and-star eyes examining everything. The silver scales of its body practically glistened in the afternoon light streaming through the nearby porthole. The kirin was majestic and beautiful, even as it quavered and tucked its thin legs under its body.

Captain Eventide entered the room and shut the door behind her. The foal tucked its face into the knees of its front legs, hiding its eyes and crystal horn.

She hurried over and removed her coat, her long, brown hair getting tangled around the collar for a moment. Once freed, she draped the coat over the kirin foal and bundled it with gentle motions.

"Kirin are delicate creatures," she said as she smoothed the soft leather over the back of the foal. "They die easily from disease and harsh weather. Even minor injuries could cost them their lives. You must handle them with care."

"I thought I had," I said. "I didn't realize the foal was cold." I crossed my arms and shook my head. "No matter how many times I tried to speak to him, the kirin never answered. I would've happily given him my coat if he'd said he'd needed it."

"Kirin don't speak to anyone but their arcanists," Eventide stated.

"Is that right?"

"It's their *sight of destiny*. They're born knowing who they will bond to, and they refuse to acknowledge or interact with anyone else."

I snorted back a sarcastic laugh. "Wouldn't it be easier for them to tell someone who they want to bond to?"

"The people of the kirin village have long cared for them. It's their responsibility to protect and carry the kirin foals to their new masters."

"Well, this was payment from Maddox, the Marshall of the Southern Seas," I said. "Which means these kirin villagers aren't doing their job."

The trembling foal poked half its face out from the coat, staring up at us with one twinkling eye. Would it really refuse to speak to us? I reached out to pet the kirin, but he flinched away and buried himself deeper into the coat.

"Why are the kirin being taken from their homes and sold across the seas?" I asked. "What kind of trinkets and artifacts would you build from weak creatures who'll die if you sneeze on them?"

Captain Eventide gently caressed the foal through the leather of the coat. It didn't take long for the kirin to calm down and stop its quavering.

"Most people don't know this, but kirin have weak magics," Eventide said, her voice low. "However, kirin allow their arcanists to bond to a second mystical creature, and then the kirin empowers it and the arcanist."

I rubbed at my chin as Eventide spoke.

The information intrigued me, even if I was still frustrated with Adelgis.

Master Zelfree had told me that bonding with a second creature would result in death since mystical creatures technically grew older by feeding from a person's soul. That feeding process was like a small cut; a little blood loss wouldn't kill someone. Bonding with another creature was like stabbing one's neck—too much blood loss at once.

But the kirin ignored that? Kirin arcanists could have *two* eldrin?

"People think they can craft a trinket that will allow them to bond with multiple creatures," Eventide said. She glanced up, her bright brown eyes alight with intensity. "But they're wrong. No combination of magic from another creature can create a trinket like that. Despite the many warnings, they still try."

I slowly reached out and patted the kirin through the coat. It returned to its trembling state, somehow disturbed by my touch specifically. I pulled away, and it regained its tranquility.

"Who put this idea in their heads, then?" I asked. "Maddox?"

"No. I think it comes from the legend of the gold kirin. Supposedly, the gold kirin arcanist can grant people the ability to bond with another creature." Eventide shook her head. "But just like blue phoenixes, these are creatures so rare, most people will never see one—even if they travel the seas for five lifetimes." She sighed. "But there is no rationalizing with pirates who think they can get their hands on easy power. As far as I'm concerned, they're being tricked into helping Maddox."

"You mean because none of them know anything about kirin?"

Eventide snapped her fingers. "You got it. They hear about rare creatures, and they jump at bait, willing to do whatever it takes."

"What did you discover about that blood, by the way?" I backed away from the table, giving the kirin as much room as possible. "Does it really give people power?"

Eventide's expression hardened. "Actually... It's much worse than that. We'll need to have a guild meeting on the matter. I think... something quite sinister is at work here."

The dream-memory melted away, the colors bleeding into black until I saw nothing.

Had Adelgis specifically shown me that memory because Orwyn was a kirin arcanist? Did that mean... Orwyn had a second eldrin? She had introduced her kirin as her "first eldrin," so it would make sense, but... Where had it been?

When the colors of the dream-memory came back together and formed a coherent picture, I found myself in the shadowy confines of a ship's hold. Captain Eventide and her first mate, Gregory Ruma, were also present, but mostly shrouded in darkness, to the point it was difficult to discern their expressions. I always missed my dark-sight whenever I experienced these memories.

"I gave the reports to everyone who would take them," Ruma said, his tone serious enough that, despite my current problems, I wanted to hear what he had to say. "But the Marshall of the Northern Seas denies everything."

"Even the conclusion about the blood?" I asked, equally as intense.

"He said he would have other arcanists examine the issue. But that'll take time."

Captain Eventide pulled a hat over her long hair. "The marshall sent word to me—we're to move out of this area. I tried appealing to other guilds, and to some of the monarchs of the nearby nations, but they refuse to get involved."

"If we disobey the Marshall of the Northern Seas, the Frith Guild will have its status revoked, and we'll all be declared turncoats and pirates."

Although I wasn't really there, I wanted to nod along with the conversation. The guilds were meant to act as extra safety and authority over all things magical. Some guilds primarily provided healing, some created items, others—like the Frith Guild—handled matters of law and justice. Technically, all nations who had cosigned the guild treaties agreed that guilds would have authority to carry out certain tasks. However, if those nations disagreed with how a guild handled matters, the nation could request to handle their own internal affairs and block guild intervention.

If the Frith Guild violated that—if they attacked Maddox without the support of other guilds and nations, and against the direct command of the Marshall of the Northern Seas—then they could be labeled as outlaws.

On the other hand, Maddox was spreading the arcane plague, smuggling kirin, and aiding pirates. Those activities weren't just *internal affairs* to a single nation. They would affect the whole damn world.

"The Frith Guild can't officially involve itself," Eventide intoned. "But after what we learned of this blood plague, we better step in before it's too late."

"*I* can handle Maddox," I said, cockier than I had ever heard Zelfree. "It's his typhoon dragon I'm worried about it. That beast will lose all control once its arcanist dies."

Ruma placed a heavy hand on my shoulder. "Eventide and I can join the sea battle if we're arcanists on another ship, dragged into the conflict. And you've been studying up on your chimera aura, right? This might be the time to unleash that kind of power."

I gritted my teeth and nodded. "I understand. We'll stop this plague from spreading, no matter what."

44

WOLVES LIVE HARD LIVES

Unable to free myself from my dream prison, I paid attention to the details of the memory, my inner child curious to see the conclusion of this swashbuckling tale.

How long would Adelgis keep me trapped here? I tried not to think about it.

The colors swirled and coalesced back together, reforming into the cold and uninviting quarters of Maddox, the Marshall of the Southern Seas. The griffin pelt on the back of his desk chair was the only piece of decoration I needed to identify the room.

Calisto stood next to me, but not for long. He handed over a serrated dagger. "Here. Coated in manticore venom."

Just like the bullets I used with Equalizer, my pistol, the dagger would cause magic to shut down. Unlike my pistol, with which the effect was short, fresh venom would surely result in a longer period of magical disruption.

Calisto left, and I waited in the room, the weapon tucked in my sleeve. The portholes looked out on a sea wrecked by storms. The waves lifted ten feet into the sky, and black clouds overhead pelted everything with icy rain.

When the door to the marshall's quarters opened, I leapt for it. Before Maddox could comprehend what was happening, I sank my dagger into his gut. He lost the ability to use his magic, but unfortunately for me, he still retained the ability to use his bulging muscles. Maddox punched me across the face, his knuckles busting my nose and eyebrow, and I staggered backward. A stray chair got in my path, and I tumbled to the floor, my eyesight spinning.

I figured Zelfree wouldn't lose, since he hadn't died here, but a piece of me wondered if Maddox would make Zelfree regret every decision that had brought him here.

Maddox held the dagger in his belly as he lumbered toward me. I rolled out of the way, jumped to my feet, and then withdrew a second dagger, this one without manticore venom.

Maddox swung wide. I ducked under his fist and then sliced his arm, filling his sleeve with blood. When he swung again, I slashed his elbow. Even if I didn't land a finishing blow, death by a thousand cuts would still get the job done.

I never hesitated during the fight—and I could see why Zelfree always told me to do the same.

Even when my back hit the bulkhead, a certain sense of calm helped me avoid getting trapped. I waited for an attack, rolled to the side, and then pivoted around behind Maddox. The man had muscles, but I clearly had speed, and in this case, it made the difference.

I stabbed at his neck when he whirled around, the blade sinking deep into the fleshy veins. He fumbled, grabbing at his wound, and then collapsed to the ground.

That was the end of Maddox, the Marshall of the Southern Seas.

After a deep breath, I stepped away from the convulsing corpse. The storm outside picked up speed and power. The rain rattled the porthole, and a terrible rumble shook the whole ship. Typhoon dragons lived in the deepest depths of the ocean, or so I heard. Their body could withstand the pressure of the abyss, and their claws could rend a ship in two.

I ran out of the marshall's quarters and met Calisto on the main deck. Maddox's men were rushing around, trying to secure their cargo, but I knew that was all pointless.

Calisto motioned to his eldrin. Hellion had his wings outstretched, his lion-like face focused on the black, storm-infested sky.

A twenty-foot wave rose up on the port side of the ship, easily capable of capsizing a whole fleet. The slick, rain-coated deck made it difficult for me to run, and instead of allowing me to make my own way, Calisto picked me up and dashed to his eldrin's side. His superhuman speed and strength saved us from the sea's wrath—the moment we climbed onto Hellion, the manticore took to the sky, avoiding the wave with a couple beats of his wings.

Sleet and wind made flying difficult. Hellion's leathery wings hadn't been designed to fly through hurricanes, and while he was strong, it was obvious we'd never make it high enough to clear the cloud line.

Hellion used what stamina he had to fly toward a ship floating on the troubled sea. The waves didn't approach this ship, and I already knew why. Ruma was a leviathan arcanist —his eldrin altered the flow of water.

In a show of impressive determination, Hellion flapped his wings against the storm, carrying both Calisto and me all the way to the ship. He panted and took breaths the moment he landed on the deck.

Ruma and Eventide were waiting for us, both of them soaked from head to toe. Eventide held Traces in her arms, and the little cat-like mimic mewed in irritation. No matter how deep she tucked herself into Eventide's shirt, she couldn't escape the weather.

We didn't have time to exchange pleasantries—the winds prevented most verbal communication, anyway. Out in the distance, emerging from the depths like a monster from a nightmare, was Maddox's typhoon dragon.

"*Curse the abyssal hells,*" I said through gritted teeth, the fierce rain getting in my mouth the moment I spoke.

The typhoon dragon lifted its long neck into the sky, its mouth open and its many fangs visible whenever thunder flashed through the clouds. It had the weight of a blue whale and the muscle of a jungle cat. Fins jutted from its spine and cheeks, and everything from the corners of its mouth to the area between its claws was webbed. The coloration of its scales covered the entire range of *blue*, from sapphire to aquamarine.

Unlike normal typhoon dragons—who were described as regal guardians of the ocean—this monster appeared as though it had gone through a severe case of leprosy and never fully recovered. Scales fell from its body, blackish blood wept from the gills on its long neck, and one eye was missing, leaving a gaping wound in its socket.

And even more bizarre, and freakish, were the crab claws that protruded from its shoulders and ribs, four in total, none of them symmetrical or equal in size. The pincers clacked and sliced as the dragon swam through the deadly waves. One claw struck out—as though it had a mind of its own—and crushed Maddox's ship, cleaving it in half. Wood and steel splintered into the water, the crack of a destroyed hull enough to carry through the storm.

The beast laughed, exposing more of its mouth. Its skiff-sized tongue lashed about, ice coating the blackened tip. When it exhaled, the storm around us took on a frightening chill.

"What happened to it?" Ruma shouted over the winds.

Eventide shook her head. "I... I don't know! It must've been the blood!"

The typhoon dragon swished its arms and claws through the sea water, altering the current. With powerful motions of its webbed claws, the waters swirled around it, creating a whirlpool effect that drew everything in the nearby area toward it.

Ours wasn't the only ship. Maddox's destroyed vessel was pulled under in an instant, and two other ships—both flying pirate flags—were drawn in closer. I hadn't seen the pirates due to the storm, but once they were near, their black and red flags were unmistakable.

"We'll get dragged under," Ruma yelled. He held onto the ship's rigging, steadying himself in place as he manipulated the waves with a gesture of his hand. "My magic won't save us from the force of that beast!"

Eventide turned to me. She used a hand to shield her eyes from the battering rain. "Everett, can you handle this? If you can't, I'll—"

"I'll handle it," I shouted back.

Traces leapt from Eventide's arms and sailed over the railing of the ship. She disappeared from sight, lost to the turbulence of the storm.

My arcanist mark burned my forehead as Traces shifted from cat to typhoon dragon—the power of the dragon so intense it stung my veins. I grabbed at my arms, taken aback by the sensation.

Calisto held my shoulder. "You got this?"

"I'm fine."

I scrunched my eyes closed, and my arcanist mark changed again.

The rush of magic, and the odd sensation that followed —I thought I understood what was happening. Zelfree was trying to manifest his chimera aura, but he wasn't doing it right. When I had incorrectly created my eclipse aura, it had felt the same way, and my aura hadn't fully functioned. It had drained me for every moment I had maintained it, which wasn't the proper outcome. Auras were supposed to persist without concentration or active effort—a passive magical ability that added to the arcanist's capabilities.

If Zelfree kept this up, he would be spent in minutes.

Was his chimera aura so powerful that it justified the short usage?

Breathing deep, I forced my eyes open, despite the splash of cold rain. Rising out of the water like Maddox's typhoon dragon was a *chimera*—a beast made up of multiple mystical creatures. It had the shimmering blue body of the typhoon dragon, complete with gills, fins, and webbed claws.

It also had multiple heads.

The first head was the typhoon dragon. The second head was a lion, much like a manticore's—sized up to fit the massive body. The third head was a turtle, similar to the atlas turtle. And the fourth was the snake-like head of the leviathan.

Zelfree had told me about his chimera aura awhile back. He had said it allowed his mimic to copy the magic and abilities of all nearby creatures, instead of one at a time. That meant Traces, in her gigantic chimera form, possessed the capabilities of a typhoon dragon, a manticore, a leviathan, and an atlas turtle all at the same time.

And by extension, so did Zelfree.

But he was too busy forcing his aura—he couldn't do anything with his newfound powers. He knelt on the deck of the ship, struggling.

Traces moved through the waves with purpose. She wasn't disgusting like Maddox's dragon—she had no evidence of the arcane plague—which meant she had no crab claws or actively bleeding wounds.

The plague-ridden dragon turned its malevolent gaze on her and opened its mouth wide. An avalanche of ice and snow burst outward like a blast of winter.

Traces shrugged off the rime, unaffected by the cold. The snow continued past her, threatening to damage our ship. Before we were covered in a thick layer of ice, Eventide held up her hand and evoked a powerful barrier. The attack didn't touch the ship. The ice broke apart on the shield, leaving us unscathed.

With all the power of a typhoon dragon, Traces also altered the current. She interfered with the whirlpool effect, ceasing the pull. When she got close enough to the enemy dragon, she lashed out with all four heads, biting the beast on its neck, face, crab shoulder, and arm.

The two mystical creatures were so large and capable, when the typhoon dragon twisted, it sent waves crashing through the sea. It vomited black blood into the water, and with three of his crab pincers, it cut into Traces, including decapitating the leviathan head in one brutal pinch. The slice—and resulting crack of bone—was so loud, I swear I felt it from my position on the ship.

The pain of the aura kept me incapacitated, and it was getting worse. Despite that, I soldiered through, determined to have Traces win.

Even though she had lost a head, she evoked lightning

so powerful it crackled across the typhoon dragon. As it spasmed, she used her three remaining heads—especially the lion's—to take chunks of flesh from the plague-ridden monster.

At first, I feared she would become plague ridden, but then I remembered that the manticore was immune, and since she had the powers of the manticore, she wouldn't be affected.

When the monster attacked with pincers a second time, Traces created her own atlas turtle barrier to protect herself. Then, with the added strength that came from the manticore, she crunched her fangs into the enemy and then pulled back, taking the dragon's throat with her.

The gouge was too large to recover from. The monster tried to scream and laugh, but it choked on blood instead.

It used its crab claws to strike at Traces, but each attack was weaker than the last, none powerful enough to break the barriers. It collapsed into the water, its one eye rolled back into its twisted skull, an odd smile on its dragon face.

The storm raged on, and the waves lifted and fell around its body, dragging it to the depths of the Shard Sea.

My pain persisted. I couldn't move. Somehow, it was also affecting Traces. The remaining heads cried out in unison, their three-voiced scream disturbing to hear, especially echoed over violent waters.

Ruma ran to my side. He grabbed me and shook. "Stop," he said. "*You can stop.*"

But I couldn't. I gritted my teeth so hard, I thought I'd shatter my molars.

Eventide also hurried to my side, her brow furrowed. "Gods... This isn't supposed to happen. He manifested his aura incorrectly."

It seemed that no matter what they said, I couldn't stop

the spiral of agony. Each moment the chimera existed was another stab straight to my chest.

Traces turned her many heads toward us. Her severed neck gushed blood at a rapid rate, and when she swam, she did it at a slower pace. Was she coming to attack us? Or returning home because her mission was done? I wasn't certain.

"Everett," Ruma said. "*Please.*"

Calisto shoved both Ruma and Eventide away. "*Get off him.* I'll deal with this." He used two fingers to whistle. The harsh sound pierced the storm, and Hellion came running. All Calisto had to do was snap his fingers once and point to me, and Hellion seemed to understand.

He raised his scorpion tail and struck down, puncturing my side with the stinger.

I didn't know what hurt more—getting stabbed by that damn tail or falling into a pit of constant pain and overwhelming agony. In the moment, I almost wished I had just died to avoid it all.

The manticore venom worked within seconds. My magic shut down, which meant my aura couldn't manifest. Traces lost her chimera form and instead turned into a manticore herself so she could fly back to the boat.

Calisto held me close, half-smiling. "What'd I tell you? I got your back."

I had never been trapped in my dreams for so long.

How many days were passing? Would I wake to find I had lost months of my life? The anxiety tainted the dream-memories. I couldn't help but fret about my body in the waking world.

The images played in my head, some making sense, others not so much. Somehow, after the death of Maddox and his typhoon dragon, word had spread of Zelfree's hand in the matter. Many pirates said *the Faceless* had murdered the Marshall of the Southern Seas because he'd wanted the smuggled cargo for himself. Others said that Maddox had tried to kill the Faceless first, and a fight had broken out afterward.

Some said that the Faceless went to rescue Calisto, who had been captured on the ship.

The last rumor stuck with me—that was what Fain had claimed happened. But Fain had also said that Zelfree was a pirate through and through, with no loyalty to the Frith Guild. A piece of me wondered if Zelfree had planned it this way. He had said that misinformation was as powerful as the truth, if used in the proper way.

And no one claimed the Frith Guild had been involved, which was exactly what Eventide had wanted.

But no matter the details of the story, it all ended the same: in admiration. At least, among cutthroats. The bounty on the Faceless had reached an all-time high, and while Zelfree hadn't actually done all the terrible things attributed to his alias, the death of the marshall was enough to draw the ire of big names.

Although the memories flipped by so fast, I couldn't see all the detail, I could tell that Zelfree wanted to distance himself from a life of pirates.

To celebrate his accomplishments, I found myself on the deck of the *Third Abyss*, only it wasn't finished. The half-constructed vessel in the shipyard of Port Crown didn't make for the most ideal place to celebrate, but that didn't matter to pirates. With enough rum, meat, and mead, any place was a good place to rollick around and swap stories.

I didn't live through the dream-memory like the others. Probably because I was drunk. The fleeting images made for amusing snippets into Zelfree's life, considering *I* was fully sober, but watching from the eyes of someone who had a fragmented memory.

Apparently, to commemorate the death of the marshall, and our time together on the seas, Calisto and I had opted for matching tattoos. A dragon was inked onto my shoulder blade. Calisto got his in the same location. The process of getting tattooed hurt in the dream-memory, but only for a moment. The images, sensations, and colors faded.

When they reformed, I was again on the deck of the half-finished *Third Abyss*.

Days had gone by within these memories. My shoulder didn't hurt from the tattoo work, and I could thank being an arcanist for that. The rapid healing meant nothing ached for long.

The night air wafted across the bay, filling it with the scent of gulls and salt.

After a long drink from my flask, I leaned onto a portion of the ghostwood railing, the lingering fog all around me. I squinted, trying to see out to the bay. Although I couldn't hear his thoughts, Zelfree held himself with a pensive tension. Was he bothered by something?

"I wanted to speak with you."

Even without looking, I knew who it was. I had come to recognize Calisto's weighty and gruff voice.

"It's about Redbeard," Calisto said.

"What about him?" I asked, my tone curt, a further indication that Zelfree wasn't in the best of moods.

"I'm tired of waiting. I want him dead." Calisto stepped around me, his boots landing heavily on the deck. Then he leaned against the railing, only half a foot away. "And I want you to help me."

"I've got other matters to deal with." After another swig of rum from my flask, I said, "That blood plague is more serious than we thought. An apothecary friend of mine needs more samples to determine what it is and where it came from. I need to help with that."

Calisto pushed away from the railing, his movements tense. He walked around to the other side of me, each step harder than the last.

"I think Redbeard might be heading south soon." He spoke each word slow and careful, his voice strained. "I don't want him to go on another *mystical creature hunt*. The more coin he gets, the more difficult it'll be to kill him later."

"What're you suggesting?" I asked. I tucked my flask into my coat. "He doesn't wander off alone. Your best bet is to wait for your ship to be built and then meet him on the open ocean."

"That'll be years from now."

I ran a hand down my face and exhaled. "Let it go. It's been years since you sailed with the man. What does it matter? This blood plague is more important."

A piece of me wondered if Zelfree had understood Calisto's obsession. I'd *seen* Calisto go savage on Redbeard—he had obviously had some pent-up rage. Had that not been apparent to Zelfree? How could he tell Calisto to just *let it go*?

"Killing Redbeard is important to *me*," Calisto growled. "More than whatever this blood disease is."

"Look, I've got a lot on my mind."

Calisto shook his head. "The guildmaster of the Frith Guild was killed, wasn't he?"

"That's right," I replied. "Captain Eventide will be taking his place."

"A lot of turmoil in the guild, yeah?"

I shot him a sideways glance. "I suppose."

"Those Frith arcanists trust you." Calisto stepped close, his arms crossed, the grip on his sleeves tight. "Get one of them alone, and we could use them as bait for Redbeard. You know the bastard will come out if he thinks he can fell someone with an interesting eldrin."

"I won't do that," I said. "I've told you before—my loyalties are to the guild first. I'm not going to risk someone for your petty revenge."

Cold winds rushed between us. A shiver ran down my spine. The tension had become so thick, I feared I might choke on it.

"I've never asked you for anything, Everett."

I didn't know why, but I hated the sound in his voice. It was *different* than before. Not hateful or angry or disturbed. Genuine—perhaps even sad.

But it was gone when Calisto spoke again.

"I've done *everything* you've wanted and then some. I've been there for you—and what have you done in return?"

I pushed away from the railing and put distance between us by pacing the deck of the ship. "We'll talk about this in the morning when you're sober."

"I haven't been drinking."

"Still. We should talk about it later. I'm not in the mood to argue this with you."

"We'll talk about it now."

That was more like the Calisto I knew—something in that moment seemed to change him. Zelfree must have sensed it, too. I stopped walking and gave Calisto my undivided attention.

"I won't risk someone from the Frith Guild," I said. "Red-beard is a reaper arcanist. Accidently killing him, without a real plan, will result in someone's death. You know about the king's revenge."

"When you wanted to leave our hometown, I was the one who helped you do it," Calisto stated, his demeanor and words cold. "When you wanted to become an arcanist, I was the one who took you to the woods. When you wanted to fight alongside pirates and you needed an in—that was me, too." He walked around the main mast and then toward me. "Or have you forgotten all that?"

"And what?" I snapped. "You want to run off chasing everyone and everything that's ever wronged you? Let me clue you in on a secret—you'll always have someone doin' you wrong. That's life."

"I'm through letting you call the shots. You always have some reason to keep with your own plans and schemes. At this point, it's not life wronging me, it's you."

"If you'd stop obsessing about certain things, you'd see that we have it pretty good." I shook my head. "That's why you're so damn pessimistic, ya know. You never let things go."

"Enough." Calisto gritted his teeth and clenched his hands into fists. "All I want is this favor. Help me kill Redbeard. I don't need any more of your lectures."

"I'm not going to do that," I said, no hesitation.

Although I didn't know the exact time frame, it seemed as though Zelfree had traveled for years with the Frith Guild. Of course he wouldn't betray them now. This entire conversation almost felt like bad timing on Calisto's part—if only he had asked for something like this before the arcane plague had been discovered or before Zelfree had grown to enjoy his time with the guild arcanists.

"This is my ship," Calisto said. "And I'll be the one calling the shots from now on."

I scoffed.

"I'm done. *We're* done."

"Calm down."

Calisto motioned to the gangplank. "I won't be your *dog* anymore, Everett. Don't you know that old saying? *Wolves live hard lives, but they never have to beg on command.* You won't help me? Fine. I'm in control now. I'll take my ship, do whatever it takes to get strong enough to kill Redbeard, and I'll do it myself."

"And do what, exactly? Become an *actual* pirate?"

"I said, *whatever it takes.*"

"Just wait," I said. "Give me time."

"You're a smart man—why're you having such a hard time understanding what I'm saying?" He gestured with an aggressive wave of his arm. "Get off my ship. I don't need you anymore."

"*Dammit,*" I growled. "You don't get it. I'm self-aware enough to ask for help when I need it, but you act on impulse—if I weren't here guiding you along, you'd be another cutthroat floating in the bay, killed by his own men in a mutiny. I've helped you plenty."

Calisto stepped up close, grabbed the collar of my coat, and then shoved me away with enough force that I hit the deck winded. It took me a moment to gulp down air. My chest felt bruised from where he had slammed me.

"And now *you're* gonna talk down to me?" Calisto asked, darkly amused. "I don't think so."

I got to my feet, a powerful ache running through my body. "Curse the abyssal hells," I muttered through shallow breaths.

"You're the same as all the other blackhearts in the

world, even if you're a bit more cunning about it. *Get off my ship*. Or I'll run you through."

In all these dream-memories, Calisto had never threatened Zelfree. I almost couldn't believe it.

Perhaps neither could Zelfree, because he didn't get off the ship.

"Don't test me," Calisto whispered.

"Listen," I said. "We can talk through this."

Although there had been a good fifteen feet between us, Calisto cleared that distance in an instant. He withdrew a dagger and stabbed it straight into my side, slicing through my coat and shirt and sinking it deep into the soft flesh just below the ribs. The metal cutting through my insides stung, but the shock of the manticore venom afterward hurt more.

Calisto slammed me back on the deck, his whole body shaking, his breathing ragged.

I tried to stand, but he knelt over me, pinning one arm down as he reached for his pistol with the other. Without magic, my options for retaliation were limited. I tried to reach for my own firearm, but Calisto ripped it off my person a moment later.

Injured and prone, I didn't know if there was much more to do. "Are you going to kill me, Lynus?" I asked.

That question dulled Calisto's anger. He tensed afterward, as though he had suddenly awoken from a dream and realized what he was doing. Still, he didn't move, his visible dilemma apparent in the way he stared down at me, his dark eyes searching mine.

Calisto combed his copper hair back with an unsteady hand. Then he stood. "Don't ever call me that again." He holstered his pistol and turned his back to me. "We had a good run, but now it's over. Whenever we meet again, we'll be enemies."

The colors and images faded away.

Zelfree had once told me that he had fought with Calisto on several occasions, and I'd never forget rescuing Zelfree from the *Third Abyss* after Calisto had tortured him. A small part of me wanted to see that memory specifically.

Another part of me didn't want to know more about Calisto. It was easier to hate the man when all I knew about him were his pirate deeds. One day, Illia would kill him. That was all that mattered.

I awoke a moment later, someone shaking my shoulder.

How long had I been asleep? It had been several days, I knew that much, but I didn't have the exact time. I had slept for far too long.

Now that I was free of sleep-prison, relief overwhelmed me. I wanted to laugh and thank whoever it was for freeing me from the dream. Then I realized a few facts that brought my panic back in full force.

First off, I couldn't move. Although I had fluttered my eyelids open, the rest of my body remained unresponsive. No matter how I tried to lift my arm or leg, nothing happened.

Secondly, the person who had woken me wasn't from the Frith Guild or the *Sun Chaser* or even Theasin or Luthair.

It was the Dread Pirate Calisto.

THE LEADER OF THE SECOND ASCENSION

Where was I?

I was lying on a table near the nullstone cages, unable to turn my head. With some effort, I used my peripheral vision to take in my surroundings.

It was... a room. Not the warehouse on the edge of the Excavation Site, but a new location I was unfamiliar with. The color-drained wood of the walls told me I wasn't far from the excavation, though. Unlike the warehouse, this new room reeked like a butcher's shop. Nullstone cages filled one corner, and an assortment of carcasses hanging from hooks mounted to the ceiling filled another. I couldn't tell what kind of animals they were. They ranged in size from rabbit to horse, some with many legs, others with none. They had been skinned, which removed most identifying features.

Linen had been thrown across the floor, most of it stained crimson with blood.

"Looks like you're not dead," Calisto said.

I had almost forgotten he had been the one to wake me. Although I wanted to speak, I couldn't. Even my breathing seemed restricted. I took in breath, but I didn't control the rate. It just continued, despite me focusing on slowing or speeding the process.

Calisto straightened his coat and brushed the red lion's mane he had stitched around the collar. Then he grabbed my jaw and tilted my head to the side, allowing me to see the rest of the room. I hadn't realized how large it was. The area around me was more a nook, a storage space without a door. The vast center of the room had black bones, tables, and hundreds of glowing crystals scattered over every surface—star shards.

No windows, just lamplight. No air flow. This place had all the comfort of a coffin.

To my shock, Theasin worked at one of the tables, picking up hand-sized fragments of bone and placing them together as though solving a puzzle. He worked without resting, his focus intense, his lips pressed into a tight line.

The only other person in this massive room was Spider. She stood next to my table, one hand on her hip, most of her weight on the opposite foot. With narrowed eyes, she stared down at me.

"What's wrong with him?" Spider asked, keeping her voice low. Did she fear disturbing Theasin's work?

"Relickeeper magic," Calisto replied, his voice equally as low. "It'll keep him fresh for weeks."

Spider snorted and half-smiled. "*Fresh*? That's a funny way to put it." She ran a hand through my black hair, her nails scraping my scalp. "Was the sleeping part of it?"

"No. Relickeepers don't do that. I suspect it was the ethereal whelk."

"Is the kid gonna get ground up and put into one of Theasin's trinkets?" Spider asked with a cruel smile.

Calisto shrugged. "Probably."

His casual indifference fed into my panic. Was it possible to use arcanists in item creation? I hadn't thought so, but I honestly didn't know for sure. Theasin would probably know, which didn't help my ever-growing fears.

He had given Adelgis his word that he'd help me. Or had that all been a lie?

Spider moved her hand down my neck, over my shoulders, and onto my chest. I hadn't realized until then, but I wasn't wearing my shirt or wootz cotton, just a pair of trousers without a belt or boots.

"Where's his equipment?" Spider asked. "He had some interesting magical items crafted by Jozé."

Calisto walked away from my table. "I don't know."

"Think they're in here?"

"I said *I don't know.*"

He sauntered over to a giant *thing* wrapped in white linen cloth. Ropes—and nullstone chains—had been used to secure the rough cloth in place, giving the linen a lumpy and bizarre silhouette, like a disturbing birthday present. What was underneath the cloth? An elephant? Multiple creatures piled on top of one another? Or was it a mutilated beast missing parts of its body?

Calisto touched the side of the linen, and blood bloomed across the white fabric.

"What're you doing?" Theasin growled. He stopped his work and rushed around the table, his robes billowing out as he hurried across the room. "*Don't touch that.*"

Calisto moved away from the bizarrely wrapped creature, chuckling to himself as he went. "I thought I could take something from the room as payment."

"Not *this,*" Theasin snapped as he got close to the beast hidden underneath the rough cloth. With gentle motions, he patted the bloodied spot and examined it closely. "Look what you've done, you lummox."

Calisto crossed his arms and tilted his head. "What is it?"

"The Mother of Shapeshifters." Seemingly content with his findings, Theasin stepped away from it. "A rare and powerful creature that must remain *undisturbed*."

Horror replaced my dread. Theasin had somehow captured the Mother of Shapeshifters? What did he have planned for it? If this was anything like the khepera, I knew it wouldn't end well.

"Your relickeeper magic isn't fully working on it, is it?" Calisto asked. "You're afraid it's going to break free of your paralysis. It probably will if you just keep it here."

Theasin glowered. "Don't speak as though you have any idea what's happening. A dullard sea rat like you can't comprehend the magics involved in this situation."

The look Calisto gave Theasin could've killed. A small piece of me hoped Calisto would lose control, rip Theasin into bits, and then proceed to smash this whole dig site into oblivion.

Unfortunately for me, Calisto sneered and turned away, seemingly uninterested in the Mother of Shapeshifters.

Spider, on the other hand, moved closer to the bundled beast. "What're you gonna do with this *mother*?"

"I'll take it apart, piece by piece," Theasin replied. He pushed his robes to one side, fluttering them as he turned to face her. "A flake of this creature's skin is more valuable than your life. Keep that in mind when you traipse around here."

"I doubt that," Spider growled under her breath. Then she turned and reached for something beyond my sight. "And what's this?"

Theasin stormed over to her and snatched the object

away—something so tiny, it fit into his fist, hiding it from my view. "*Refrain from moving anything*," Theasin said. "You can't comprehend what you're dealing with."

Without warning, Calisto grabbed Theasin by the shoulder and jerked him away from Spider. With his grip tight on Theasin's robes, Calisto hefted him close. "Touch her again, and I'll feed you to Hellion." It wasn't a loud threat, but the ice of his words stung.

Theasin didn't bother trying to free himself, no doubt aware manticore arcanists were incredibly strong. Instead, he forced a tight smile. "Of course. Where are my manners? In the meantime, why don't you both demonstrate the ability to follow directions by kindly keeping your hands to yourself? Or should I use smaller words and shorter sentences to get my demands across? Pirates have such limited vocabularies."

With the charismatic prowess of a cockroach, Theasin had made enemies of both Calisto *and* Spider. The two of them didn't lash out, though.

Instead, Calisto released Theasin and smoothed the robes over his shoulder. Then Calisto resumed his meandering, glancing at the carcasses hanging from the ceiling and then turning his attention to the nullstone cages—tiny prisons that no doubt held smaller mystical creatures, though I couldn't move my head enough to see the contents.

"Take something useful," Theasin said, curt. "I know the Autarch thinks you deserve a reward for bringing him a piece of the world serpent, but I'm still waiting for the Occult Compass. Perhaps, if you thought more than *five seconds* into the future, you would realize that there are many things here that could help you retrieve that compass."

Calisto rubbed at the stubble on his jaw. He didn't reply as he walked back over to my table.

"*Quickly*," Theasin stated. "I have work to finish before the Autarch arrives."

Calisto placed a hand on my shoulder. "I'll take this."

Me? Why? Because I had connections to Illia and Master Zelfree? It had to be. What other reason was there?

"You can't have *that one*," Theasin said. "He's under my protection until the plague is purged from his body. Once that happens, I don't care what his fate is."

A small piece of me thanked the lucky stars that Theasin planned on keeping his word. Even if I couldn't escape the situation, at least I would be rid of the plague by the end of it.

"Where's his knightmare?" Calisto asked.

"His eldrin is with my son and also not an option."

Calisto tightened his grip on my shoulder. "A pity."

A door opened and closed, but I couldn't see where. Everyone went quiet, their attention immediately on whoever had entered.

A short moment after, a series of popping sounds echoed throughout the room. Puffs of white glittering light appeared in my line of vision, and I recognized the effects of rizzel teleportation. More than a dozen individuals appeared within the room, each with an arcanist mark on their forehead, each with their eldrin. Before they had appeared, there had been plenty of space, but now it was a crowded room of arcanists with creatures ranging in size.

I didn't recognize most of them, but there were two familiar faces.

Akiva—the king basilisk arcanist. He had been the assassin who had killed Queen Velleta in Thronehold and who had nearly killed me as well. He wore a full suit of gray scale armor and stood like only a soldier could, stiff and prepared for combat.

And Orwyn—the kirin arcanist with the vacant gaze. She stood near the table where Theasin had been working, her strawberry blonde hair more orange in the lamplight than I remembered.

Most of the arcanists in the room had red glowing marks, clear indicators they were plague-ridden and insane. Their eldrin had all been twisted by the corruption. One unicorn had worms wriggling around in its bloated gut—so full it was on the edge of bursting. Another arcanist had a cerberus dog, and each of the beast's three heads had horns protruding from the skull. Other types of bones poked through the dog's back, jutting out at random angles, as though a second skeleton were trying to grow out of the creature.

A man in a long, black robe walked into my line of sight. He was thin—scrawny in a malnourished way—and walked with a jittery gait, like he wasn't fully in control of his motions. His black hair was cut short and neat, but his eyes were set so far apart, it was as though they were trying to escape his face. The man glanced around the room, searching for something, though I didn't know what. He licked his lips more often than I could count, and once he had finished his hasty investigation, he turned to Theasin.

"There you are," he said, his voice high-pitched and bordering on whiny. "Is it ready? Will the Autarch be pleased?"

Theasin rushed back to his table and arranged the black bones into place. "Almost. I need a moment longer."

"The Autarch doesn't want to wait. We're behind on our plans as it is."

Theasin didn't dignify the statement with a response. He

went to work on his project, ignoring the dozens of eyes that were now honing in on him. Each one of the plague-ridden arcanists and their eldrin seemed restless, and they moved closer to Theasin with small steps and hushed whispers.

Some mystical creatures laughed uncontrollably, their insane jovial attitude a permanent black mark on my memory. Those laughing-mad eldrin would forever haunt my nightmares.

No one paid attention to me, though, and for that, I was grateful. Even Spider and Calisto had turned their backs to me, more concerned with the gathering than the payment they were owed.

I felt like... a vial on a shelf. Or a book in a library. *An object they could ignore.*

That was what everything in this nook was—something Theasin had horded away, perhaps to be used later.

"It's ready," Theasin said with a sigh. "You may inform the Autarch, Rhys."

The jittery man, Rhys, nodded after the words, his quick head movements odd and giving him a sense of enthusiasm. He waved his hand through the air and another round of *popping* filled the room. Was Rhys a rizzel arcanist? I was too far away to see the detail in his glowing-red arcanist mark, but I assumed so.

Two more figures appeared in the room. The moment they emerged from the flash of white, everyone backed away, including Theasin.

The first was a man in simple, but tailored, clothing. He wore a sleek tunic of fine cloth, one without sleeves, revealing his arms from the shoulders down. His trousers were the same material, and neatly folded, though the man wore no boots.

I would've said the man looked half-dressed, but it

quickly became obvious why he had left certain parts of his body exposed. His forehead carried an arcanist mark, but so did both of his shoulders. The star and symbol of his eldrin were clear, even if he was too far away for me to make out what creatures he had bonded to.

His short, black hair, shiny in the lowlight, had been cut in such a way as to accentuate his lithe and muscled neck. Even his clothes seemed to make his toned body more prominent—nothing about him was out of place.

Standing behind the immaculate man, radiating inner magic, was a gold kirin.

Unlike the silver kirin, which shimmered when they moved, this gold kirin seemed to glow with a soft amber power. Its scales resembled a dragon, its cloven hooves glittered with each step, and its eyes appeared as molten amber. Instead of a single twisted horn, it had a set of antlers, both of which shone like they were made of star shards.

Everything about the kirin screamed of magic and power—and I would've been able to identify this man and his eldrin even if Rhys hadn't.

The Autarch.

Although I hadn't known it before, I knew now—the Autarch was the man in charge of the Second Ascension. Just the way everyone had reacted when he had appeared confirmed my suspicions.

I searched my memories, trying to remember every instance I had heard of the Autarch. When I pieced together what little information I had, everything fell into place.

Gold kirin were so rare and so powerful that it was no wonder this man would've been made the ruler of the kirin village after his bonding. Kirin only became the eldrin of people who would influence history as powerful rulers, regardless of whether it was a positive impact or a negative one, so why wouldn't the village be excited?

Then the Autarch must've taken the kirin foals and used them as payment for his plan—he gave them away to greedy pirates and to men like Maddox, so they could spread the arcane plague. The Autarch did this not because he wanted to see the world collapse, but because he wanted to make a fundamental change in magic, one that would cause the thirteen god-creatures to return.

Why?

I knew why. *It was obvious.*

The Autarch wanted to bond with one. Or perhaps more than one, if the number of arcanist marks on his body indicated anything. He had *three* marks. He could have two more eldrin beyond his first, all thanks to the gold kirin's innate ability. Even *one* god-creature would be powerful, but having *two* and then *empowering them*? The Autarch would have no equal—he would stand alone as a titan among even god-arcanists.

With that much power, could he defeat the second apoch dragon? Perhaps. I didn't know, but I could see it being calculated into the Autarch's plotting.

This had all been his plan from the beginning. The Autarch had probably even paid Theasin with a kirin foal—something that Theasin would happily throw straight into a meat grinder, just to harvest its organs.

What about the other arcanists? Were they paid in mystical creatures, trinkets, and artifacts, like Calisto? Or were they insane to the point they followed him with fanatic devotion? I could see both being the answer, depending on their eldrin.

And somehow along the way, though I didn't know how, the Autarch had discovered the apoch dragon's remains and decided to use its bones to make weapons for his vile arcanist underlings. The *decay dust* and others were powerful tools for sowing chaos and discord. With the world in turmoil, and everyone fearing the plague, *of course* this man had never been discovered. He had used the pandemonium as a smokescreen.

The jittery rizzel arcanist, Rhys, stepped forward, his hands shaking. "Ah, Great Autarch. Everything is ready."

The Autarch was the exact opposite of Rhys. He moved with purpose and precision—had muscle and a straight stance—and wielded his commanding presence like a weapon. Rhys bunched his shoulders close to his neck, his whole body shaking at this point.

Theasin motioned to the worktable, specifically to the black bones interlaced together. "I've finished with your suit of armor. It's made completely from pieces of the petrous—the hardest bone found in the apoch dragon's body. It will protect you from blades and bullets, like any armor, and it'll weigh half as much. The most impressive ability is that this armor will destroy magic that attempts to harm you—even from the likes of dragons." Theasin placed a hand on his creation, smirking. "It's better than nullstone because it won't impact your own magic use, nor will it need to be attuned. The apoch dragon's magic-killer properties are soaked into its very bones. *Nothing* magical will seep through."

"You never disappoint," the Autarch said, smooth and confident.

Orwyn stepped forward, her fingers combing through her strawberry hair, her gaze half on the ceiling and half on the Autarch. "You'll be pleased to hear that almost everything has gone according to plan. The rulers of six nations —including the Argo Empire—have been assassinated. The new rulers are the ones we helped to seize power. All of these nations have sworn loyalty to the Second Ascension and will openly declare fealty for the new world serpent arcanist as soon as one emerges. Once you bond with that god-creature, my Autarch, those nations will be yours to command. You'll have power over more territory than any other arcanist in history."

Orwyn gave her speech in a pleasant singsong manner. If I could laugh, I would've—it was such a harsh juxtaposition from the dark content of the report.

I had been present when the Second Ascension had assassinated Queen Velleta, and I had even witnessed them prep Prince Rishan to take the throne afterward.

"Do we have the world serpent runestone?" the Autarch asked as he lifted a perfect eyebrow.

Orwyn took a step away, her gaze more vacant than it had been a moment before.

No one seemed eager to offer up the information. I could understand—they *needed* the world serpent runestone in order to get to the creature. They had attempted to steal it from the castle in Thronehold, but I had beaten them to it. Before I left the Frith Guild, I had given the runestone to my sister, Illia. Hopefully, the Frith Guild had already arrived at the lair of the world serpent. If someone from the guild bonded with that god-creature, the Autarch would never get his hands on it.

Rhys sucked in a breath between his teeth and shuffled forward. "It's unfortunate, but we... *lost*... the runestone, my Autarch."

46

ENEMY OF THE FRITH GUILD

"W-we have others!" Rhys continued, fidgeting with his hands. "Six others! But not the jade runestone meant for the world serpent. D-don't fret. We will retrieve it soon."

The gold kirin stepped to the other side of the Autarch, its glowing antlers flaring for a moment with inner magics.

The Autarch placed his hand on the beast's muzzle. "Who has the runestone?"

"It's in the possession of the Frith Guild."

The mere mention of the guild seemed to agitate most of the plague-ridden arcanists in the room. For the first time since arriving, the Autarch hardened his expression, his smooth facial features marred by lines of hate.

"I thought I told you to handle them," he said.

Although she had stepped back into the group, Orwyn pushed through two other arcanists in order to step forward once again. She half-stared at the floor as she said, "Almost all your greatest enemies have been dealt with, my Autarch. We've eliminated the Grandmaster Inquisitor, the Steel Thorn Inquisitor's Guild, Master Arcanist Gregory Ruma,

Knight Captain Winton Rendell, Artificer Gayle Forner, Guildmaster Eva Stone, Guildmaster Ventis Durall, and the Marshall of the Eastern Seas."

Orwyn rattled off the death list with a casualness that bordered on the cruel. So many talented arcanists had been murdered to further their plan, yet there wasn't an ounce of remorse between them.

"The Frith Guild has been a problem since the first days of the Second Ascension," the Autarch said.

Then he motioned to the unicorn arcanist, and the man hurried forward. Without a word spoken between them, the unicorn arcanist picked up the armor and began fastening it over the Autarch, one piece at a time, starting with the shoulder pauldron.

"Liet Eventide, specifically, has attempted to stop me at every turn," the Autarch continued. He lifted his arms for the unicorn arcanist, allowing the man to secure the black bone armor in place. "Even though I've pressured monarchs and governors to have the guild removed from our territories of operation, Eventide finds a way to get involved and to kill my agents—even Maddox fell to her plots. And now she has the audacity to take my runestone? I want her dead."

Orwyn slowly nodded. "We've tried, my Autarch, but Eventide has evaded all our attempts to assassinate her."

"Infect her with the arcane plague."

Theasin picked up a piece of the armor set and handed it to the unicorn arcanist. Then he stepped forward. "Unfortunately, it's impossible to infect Guildmaster Eventide. Arcanists who have achieved true form with their eldrin become immune to the plague."

"She has a true form atlas turtle?" the Autarch asked.

"Eventide obtained her true form when some of your agents eliminated the last guildmaster. Apparently, despite fatal injuries, Eventide had defended several journeymen arcanists, and then killed our assassins. Since atlas turtles are known for their protectiveness, I assume her actions were what triggered this transformation, but I'm still not certain how each individual arcanist gains a true form. This is all speculation."

The Autarch narrowed his eyes. "Liet Eventide is responsible for a great many setbacks. I don't care what powers she has or how she got them. Bring me my runestone."

Although I didn't know much about true forms, it occurred to me that the requirement for obtaining one was like a secret *second* trial of worth. There was still *something* that needed to be completed before the mystical creature could obtain its telos—that much I knew—but I had never thought of it in terms of a task. I had read that the true forms embodied the creatures in question—true form wendigo came from arcanists who had turned cannibal, and true form sovereign dragons were formed from power-hungry authoritarians.

And I also knew that true form manticores needed the eyes of children—more than the few needed for a manticore's initial trial of worth.

As long as the arcanist displayed these capabilities, or met the requirements, their eldrin would transform, and their magic would increase beyond normal.

If only *all* arcanists could achieve that... Then the arcane plague would no longer be a threat, and the Second Ascension would lose one of its most powerful tools.

Once the Autarch had his bone armor chest piece in place, he turned his attention to Akiva, the assassin. "Find Liet Eventide. Kill her *and* her atlas turtle."

The image of Akiva murdering Queen Velleta stained my memories with the permanence of a tattoo. King basilisk poison killed on contact, and Akiva hadn't hesitated to put her in an early grave. Not only that, but his eldrin had killed the queen's sovereign dragon. Could Guildmaster Eventide escape his deadly magics? I didn't know, but I knew she had to be told of this meeting, and the plot against her and the Frith Guild.

Akiva replied to the Autarch with a quick bow of his head. Then he headed for the exit, his movements quick, precise, and quiet. No words—Akiva had his orders, and he left to carry them out.

The panting of the plague-ridden creatures increased, their breath putrid and filling the room with the musty odor of rot and decay. The Autarch donned the last of his armor when he fitted the helmet over his head. The outfit was a mix of full plate and scale mail, creating a hybrid of smaller pieces and larger bone fragments for protection. He moved with ease, showcasing his new toy. Theasin had crafted a masterpiece. It reminded me of Luthair.

"After I have the runestone," the Autarch said, "I'll bond with the world serpent and we can finally see the first of our ambitions come to pass."

The door to the room opened again, and I feared Akiva had returned. Instead, someone small and covered from head to toe in a black robe, shuffled close to the Autarch, their shoulders slumped and their head hung low.

"Pardon the intrusion," the newcomer said, her voice soft.

The dozen other arcanists in the room gave this woman their attention, though some of them had grown restless. They paced along the walls, their intense eyes darting around the area, taking everything in.

"What is it?" the Autarch asked. "Have you discovered something?"

"I have," she replied.

"Out with it."

"Word was sent from the Dread Pirate Kreel—he's found the birthplace of the *soul forge*, the second of the god-creatures to awaken."

"*What*?" Calisto growled under his breath.

The agitation in the room built like a hive of bees that had been disturbed. The arcanists and their eldrin hissed words between one another, most of which I couldn't fully hear.

From what I understood, the thirteen god-creatures spawned in order—first the world serpent, then the soul forge. I had assumed the second wouldn't spawn until the first had been bonded, and I suspected that was what the rest of these blackhearts had thought as well.

"We've taken too long with the world serpent," the Autarch said. "But the soul forge doesn't have magics of war —it's a beast of magical creation and manipulation."

"What shall I send back to Captain Kreel?" the robed woman asked.

"You tell him to guard the beast with his life." The Autarch focused his attention on Rhys. "You have the runestone for the soul forge, don't you?"

The jittery man nodded. Then he held up a hand, and a puff of sparkles filled his palm. He had teleported a pink quartz runestone into his grasp. "This is the key to the soul forge," Rhys said. He bowed deeply as he handed it over. "Everything is ready."

The Autarch took the runestone and then held it out to Theasin. "As per our agreement, and as reward for your loyalty and contributions to our cause, you may take this and head to the soul forge's lair."

Although I couldn't move, the adrenaline in my veins

kept me hyper-focused on what was happening. *Theasin* was to get one of these god-creatures? I supposed the Autarch couldn't take them *all*, but I hadn't expected someone like *Theasin* to get his hands on one of these legendary world-altering beasts.

Theasin was too cold, calculating, and unfeeling to wield the might of a god. How could anyone think he deserved such power?

"I will dedicate my magical research to your cause," Theasin said as he held the runestone delicately in his hands.

"Once you've bonded, return to me," the Autarch said. "Your status as a god-arcanist shouldn't be revealed until I have the world serpent. We must have the backing of nations if we want to have total control over the situation."

"Of course."

Theasin tucked the pink quartz runestone into his robes.

The hooded woman handed over a letter. I suspected it had the location of Kreel's ship.

"You should go now, Artificer Venrover," Rhys said. "The Frith Guild has technically been strengthening its numbers by recruiting arcanists across the Argo Empire. If they discover the soul forge has spawned, they'll attempt to hinder our plans with it, too."

"I'll leave immediately on the *Third Abyss*," Theasin said. "But before I go, can you move the Mother of Shapeshifters to our storeroom? It needs to go out with the next shipment of bones. I can't afford to lose it."

Rhys nodded. "It shall be done."

What did Theasin have planned? He had said he would take the Mother of Shapeshifters apart, but I knew it wasn't that simple. He had a *plan* for it. And whatever that was, it would end in tragedy.

With a quick turn on his heel, Theasin faced Calisto. "Come. We must meet Kreel." Then he shifted his attention to me. "Oh, and one last thing. No one is to disturb *that*,"—Theasin pointed to me—"I'll deal with him when I return."

Again, Rhys nodded.

Calisto and Spider exchanged heated looks, but neither said anything as they walked away from my table and joined the other arcanists in the center of the room. They strode out with Theasin in tow.

No one fought Theasin for the runestone. No one argued for the privilege of being chosen to be the soul forge.

Whatever the Autarch decided was law, and he would determine who bonded with what.

Still fitted in his eldritch suit of bone armor, the Autarch motioned to Rhys. "We should continue on our way." Then he faced the cerberus arcanist. "You will answer to Tamoi. He's clearing the forest and will finish excavating the bones of the apoch dragon. It's halfway done now—all you need to do is aid him. The moment it's done, complete our shipments and meet back with Rhys."

"As you wish," the man said.

I couldn't see the arcanist as well, but his three-headed dog barked in chorus, pink saliva running down all its mouths.

With the orders given, the room filled with pops and sparkles. Most of the arcanists vanished through rizzel teleportation—all except for the Autarch, his gold kirin, the cerberus arcanist, and Rhys. The three-headed dog lumbered out of the room along with his arcanist, their mission to guard this location. I suspected the Autarch's new armor couldn't be teleported, which prevented him from going with the others.

Rhys walked over to the Mother of Shapeshifters

wrapped in white linen. He placed his hand on the side of the beast—another bloom of blood appeared under his palm—and he made the creature vanish with a forceful burst of his teleportation, nullstone chains and all. Rhys gulped down air afterward, his whole body shaking. Then he glanced over, his far-set eyes examining me for a quick moment before he returned to the Autarch.

"We should join the others," Rhys said as he walked with the Autarch and the gold kirin toward the door. "And you should see the new territory boundaries that have been proposed. Once you're the world serpent arcanist, you can shape the way trading is done for the whole region."

They exited the room together, the Autarch's new armor clinking as he walked.

The instant the door shut, a stillness settled over the room. I was alone, and soon the lamps would run out of oil, leaving me in the dark, forgotten until Theasin made his way back to this location.

I understood then why Adelgis had trapped me in the dreams. It had been a mercy. At least with the memories, I had something to preoccupy my thoughts. Instead, now I would drown in the knowledge that everyone I loved was in danger—and I could do nothing about it.

The lamps hadn't yet gone out, but I suspected they only had an hour left. How would I tell time once they were gone?

Why couldn't I break free of this magic?

Was it because Theasin's eldrin was stronger than mine? Or was it because he had better mastery of his sorcery?

Although Theasin hadn't yet cured me, I desperately

wanted to escape, but nothing I did managed to change my circumstances.

The only things I had control over were my eyelids. I blinked several times, frustrated to the point that my whole body ached with a dull pain.

A door opened and closed.

Someone hurried from the far side of the room to my nook in the back. I had never seen this man before—he dressed in plain clothing, a simple white shirt and dirty trousers. When he neared, he smiled, his teeth not dark, but not white, either. And his facial features—plain in all regards. Mud-brown hair and eyes. Unremarkable, yet somehow familiar.

"I found you," the man said. "It's me, Karr. You remember? Karna's doppelgänger." He exhaled in relief. "I've come to get you out of here. The others are being held in some sort of makeshift barracks. You need to help me get them."

47

THE FINAL DECISION

Karr placed his hand on my bare chest, and magic gripped at my spine, sending a shiver through my body. Although a doppelgänger's ability to manipulate people had disturbed me in the past, now I was forever grateful. Karr's magic seemed to dispel the relickeeper's hold.

With the finesse of a puppet master, Karr forced me to sit up, kick my legs off the side of the table, and then stand. After I balanced myself, the claws of magic on my spine loosened, and I regained control.

"Thank you," I said with a shaky voice, weak from days of sleeping and dreaming.

"Take this." Karr withdrew an extra shirt he had tucked into the belt of his pants.

With unsteady movements, I threw the shirt over my head and allowed it to fall into place. I still had no boots or belt of my own, but at least I didn't look conspicuous.

Karr motioned to the far door. "We should hurry. There are enemy arcanists everywhere."

I nodded and followed him through the room, stepping

around the crafting tables covered in star shards. My legs threatened to buckle, but I gritted my teeth and forced myself to walk, no matter what. Phantom pin-pricks spread throughout my limbs, like everything had been asleep until I had stood up.

Karr opened the door and ushered me through. We exited out into the Excavation Site, the smell of dirt, ash, and blood thick in the air. I half-gagged and shook my head. Nothing felt right.

"Where are the others?" I asked.

"This way." Karr hooked his hand on my elbow and guided me away from the strange building.

"How did you escape?"

"They never caught me." Karr flashed a smile. "I'm a master at blending into a crowd."

The hundreds of site workers didn't bother looking our way. They remained focused on their duties, each hustling to get their assignments completed. The gigantic bones needed to be unearthed, secured to the pulleys, and then lifted out of the ground with care. No doubt they were on a strict timeline, and my gut told me there would likely be punishments for those who didn't follow through with the schedule.

The rain had stopped, but the sky remained dreary and overcast, blocking out the moon and stars. The bonfires raged in the distance, raining bits of ash down around us, like a sickening type of snow.

Karr pointed across the work site. "There. Do you see him? That's Master Arcanist Tamoi. The workers here say he's *the Autarch's personal enforcer* and the one in charge of the dig site."

I glanced over, but at first, I didn't see an arcanist—all I saw was his gargantuan eldrin, an atlas turtle. Not like Eventide's—hers dwelled in the water. This was an atlas *tortoise*, a creature that lived on land. It had to weigh 100 tons and was half the size of a blue whale, its shell large enough to carry a house. Its legs were boulder-thick, its claws sharp enough to rend steel, and the edges of the shell were jagged and sharp enough to resemble broken glass.

To my fascination, things grew on the shell, just like with Eventide's atlas turtle. This atlas tortoise, however, had tombstones jutting out of the dirt on its back, along with a variety of strange plants. Some were thorn-covered vines that moved like the tentacles of an octopus. Others resembled flytraps, complete with fangs and bright red "mouths."

The atlas tortoise's eyes bulged out of its sockets, jiggling slightly as it lumbered around the work site. They were glazed over and devoid of color, like a dead fish.

Its arcanist, Tamoi, the Autarch's enforcer, traveled beside it, holding a flintlock rifle in his hands as he observed the workers. His brimmed hat kept the falling ash out of his beady eyes.

"And look there," Karr said, pointing to another.

It was the plague-ridden cerberus and his arcanist. The three-headed dog, standing as tall as a draft horse, barked at workers who slowed or dropped anything, and the man laughed whenever someone cowered away. His arcanist mark glowed bright red, enough to spot it from anywhere in the clearing around the bone pit.

"There are three others," Karr whispered as he guided me along the edge of the massive clearing. We walked by warehouse after warehouse, each with the sound of grinding inside. "Two unicorns and one pegasus arcanist. They're patrolling the area, making sure no one leaves with anything they shouldn't."

I rubbed my face as my strength returned at a snail's

pace. Now wasn't the time for weakness, not when we were surrounded by the vilest of enemies.

Karr stopped at the edge of a smaller building. "Karna and the others are inside." He glanced around. "I don't believe anyone else is in there. It's a place for arcanists." Karr pointed to a much larger building across the muddy road. "That's where the workers go."

"Thank you," I said again, this time with confidence.

"I'll stand watch and let you know if anyone comes this way."

I stepped into the shadows, slid through the darkness under the door, and entered the arcanist barracks. When I emerged, my head spun for a moment, and I needed to take a deep breath. There wasn't much to my surroundings—some tugboats had more furnishings—but there were six cots, a simple table, and a lamp.

My breath caught when I realized Karna, Fain, Wraith, and Luthair were lying on the cots. It took a moment to process the image of Luthair "sleeping." Knightmares didn't need to rest like that. He had to be under the power of the relickeeper—stuck in a stasis-like state, like I had been. The others, including the wendigo, had their eyes shut, which meant they were probably locked in a dream world of Adelgis's design.

Sitting one cot over, stiff and straight, was Adelgis. He turned when he noticed me enter, his eyes widening.

"*Volke*," he said as he stood.

In one swift motion, I manipulated the shadows in the corner of the room to snuff out the lamplight. Adelgis flinched, and that was when I used the darkness as a net, snaring him and slamming him to the floor. The tendrils of shadows held him down, keeping him from getting back to his feet.

A bright burst of light heralded the arrival of Felicity, his ethereal whelk. Shards of iridescent shell linked together to form her body. Her snail form and tentacles shone with an inner light, illuminating the room.

"Let my arcanist go," she said, flashing bright.

The rays of her magic burned my shadows, but I refused to give in. I held up my hand and evoked terrors, forcing fears onto both Felicity and Adelgis. She cried out and floated to the floor, her inner light dimming.

Adelgis... didn't seem to have much of a reaction to my terrors. He closed his eyes and stopped struggling.

Anger fueling my magic, I covered Felicity in shadows and held her down. Even if she burst light from her body again, it wouldn't be enough to free herself.

I walked to Adelgis's side, confident he wouldn't put me to sleep a second time.

He opened his eyes, but they didn't focus on anything. He couldn't see in the dark.

"Volke," he whispered.

I loomed over him, still uncertain of what I should do. "Where are my things?"

"Try to calm down."

"I intend to leave this place, and I need my weapons to do that. *Tell me where they are.*"

Adelgis turned his head slightly to the side—the only part of him that wasn't actively tied with my shadows. "They're under my cot. But please reconsider. You're obviously not well."

I used the shadows to grope around under the cot. The tendrils dragged out my sword, gun, boots, and blue phoenix feather—the first trinket I had made with my father. Seeing it eased some of my rage. I knelt down and collected my things, thankful to have Retribution and Equalizer. I suspected I would need to make use of them.

"*You're* the one who isn't well," I said to Adelgis as I laced my boots. "You put me to sleep and then handed me to the Second Ascension. What were you thinking?" I shook my head and stood. "Unbelievable."

Adelgis frowned. "I want to help you, and I fear you're too far gone to see what's happening. That's why I put you to sleep."

"What aren't I seeing?" I asked, sardonic. "I just summed up the situation pretty concisely."

"The Volke I know never would've attacked me."

His statement further chilled my anger. I hadn't thought of the situation like that, but at the same time, Adelgis had never betrayed me so thoroughly, either. How would I have reacted a year ago? Would I have harmed him?

"I don't think you would've," Adelgis said, answering my unspoken question.

"You can hear thoughts again?" I snapped.

Adelgis nodded. "The arcanist who warded away the plague-ridden creatures left this area. It was a master ethereal whelk arcanist—the same one who shielded Calisto's and my father's thoughts. They seem to be a powerful member of the Second Ascension."

"I see." After a long inhale and exhale, I said, "I'm sorry I attacked you, but you have no right to force anything on me."

"Even if it was to help you?" Adelgis asked, a genuine tone to his voice that made it difficult to hate him. "Even if I thought your judgments were impaired?"

"There are some things more important than my safety," I said. "We can't allow the Second Ascension to control us just because they have something we want."

"My father wasn't trying to control our actions. He simply asked that we do nothing. Isn't that an acceptable price to pay for your life? If you die—or if you're driven mad—you'll never be able to stop the Second Ascension. But if you wait now, you can fight later. There's nothing wrong with taking the time to heal."

I opened my mouth to protest, but closed it a moment later, the words stuck in my throat. There wasn't anything wrong with taking the time to heal, true, but this wasn't the same. At least... I didn't think so. Doubt crept into my thoughts, adding to my hesitation.

"Please, Volke," Adelgis said. "You have the option to lie back and allow yourself to be saved. There's no need to fight this. We can return to the Frith Guild once you're better."

He was right.

If I did nothing—if I went back to the other building and slept on that table until Theasin returned—I would be cured of the arcane plague. But I knew things now... Things the Frith Guild needed to know, like the Mother of Shapeshifters and the appearance of the soul forge.

If I *did nothing*, I'd tacitly be helping the Second Ascension.

"Then please reconsider using the khepera," Adelgis said, desperation creeping into his speech. "We have time. You can return to the *Sun Chaser* and use their healing sands to help you. That's still an option."

"Why're you so determined to see me cured?" I asked. His fervor bordered on the obsessive, and it worried me.

"*I don't want to fail you*," Adelgis stated. "My father said I'd fail at most things in my life, and while he's been correct on some issues... I just don't want *this time* to be correct. You've done a lot for me, and now I've found two viable ways to save you—please pick one. Everyone will understand. No one will think you're a coward or that you took the easy way out. *Look at how much you've given up to get here.* Just take one of the solutions!"

Kill the khepera or allow the Second Ascension's plans to continue without opposition.

Those were my options.

How could I justify picking either?

"Think of what you're doing to your sister, Illia," Adelgis said.

I glared down at him. "Don't you dare bring her into this."

"You know there isn't enough time to find another solution. If you don't take one now, what will I tell Illia? You *chose* not to be saved? Can't you imagine how that'll upset her?"

Dammit! He was just trying to pick at me any way he could, and somehow, he had touched upon one spot that I didn't want to consider.

I ran both my hands through my hair and glanced over at the others sleeping on their cots. Adelgis's magic kept them quiet and tranquil. If I went back to Theasin's table, no one would ever know I had been up except Adelgis, Felicity, and Karr.

I shook my head.

How could I return to Illia and tell her that I selfishly chose myself? How could I tell her I killed the khepera? Or that I didn't try to warn the Frith Guild when I had the chance? All for my own personal gains?

I knew—in my core—that Illia wouldn't hold those choices against me. She'd say something comforting and tell me anyone would've done what I did.

But...

I hadn't spent my childhood on the Isle of Ruma reading

tales of *average people overcoming their own personal dilemmas.* I had read stories of great heroes who had dedicated themselves to honor and justice—men and women who had braved active volcanos, drank poison, and rode into the arms of death—all because they had believed they could make a difference in the world.

None of them would take either of my current solutions.

"Adelgis," I muttered, my anger gone. "You've more than helped me." I released my shadows on him and his eldrin. "You stayed by my side, even at the risk to yourself, and you did exactly what you said you would—you found me viable cures. You aren't a failure if I decide to squander your aid. That's on me."

Adelgis pushed himself to his feet, his eyes still unfocused. He said nothing, his breathing shallow.

I inhaled and then exhaled. "Wake the others."

"What're you planning?" he asked.

"I want you all to leave. You should head back to the Frith Guild however you can and then warn Guildmaster Eventide that Akiva, the assassin from Thronehold, is after her. Then you should tell her that the leader of the Second Ascension is a man bonded to a gold kirin—and that your father is working for the enemy."

"And what about you?"

"I'm going to free the Mother of Shapeshifters." I gripped at my shirt, my fingers twisting into the fabric as I clenched my jaw. "And I'm going to destroy this dig site."

"There are plague-ridden arcanists guarding this whole area."

"I know," I said, my voice strained. "But I'll distract them so you all can get away."

Adelgis moved closer. "And you think we can escape?"

"Pirates come here to off load supplies. I'm sure with Karna's abilities, you'll manage to find something."

"But you won't be with us," he said, his tone accusing.

I didn't reply.

Could I handle five plague-ridden arcanists on my own? Maybe. I had the element of surprise on my side, and even if I didn't manifest it correctly, I still had the option of using my eclipse aura to control the battle. But in all reality, I would probably only get a few of them, and then I'd eventually succumb to their attacks. It would be a *big* distraction. Enough for a handful of arcanists to escape the Excavation Site without notice.

And hopefully enough to free the Mother of Shapeshifters.

"You don't have to do this," Adelgis said. "You can escape with us. We can do it without a distraction—perhaps your eclipse aura will be enough."

"I'd still be carrying the plague."

"We can search for another solution."

I forced a sarcastic chuckle. "You said yourself, we don't have enough time. And most people never find *one* cure— I've spit in destiny's face by turning down two. She won't provide me a third."

Perhaps Adelgis knew it was futile to fight me—or perhaps he understood now that he wasn't a failure by allowing me to choose my own destiny. Either way, he walked over to Karna, Fain, Wraith, and Luthair and then released them from their sleep-prisons.

Luthair melted into the darkness and reformed a moment later, standing upright. He turned his empty helmet from me to Adelgis and back again to me, no indication he suffered from lingering side effects.

"Everything is fine now," I said.

"It's good to see you, my arcanist."

Karna, Wraith, and Fain slid off their cots with less gusto. They staggered, as though hungover. Even Wraith, with all four of his wolf-like feet, almost toppled to one side. How long had they been sleeping? If it had been a few days, like me, then I suspected they'd be groggy for a little while longer.

I placed a hand on everyone in the room, including Adelgis. Through the use of my augmentation, I gave everyone the ability to see in the dark. It would help with their escape, and if I managed to use my aura, then they wouldn't be affected.

"Adelgis," I said. "You help them recover and then fill them in on the plan. I'm going to search around the dig site and find the Mother of Shapeshifters. Once you all are ready, I'll..." I rubbed my sweaty palms on my shirt. "I'll make sure the patrolling arcanists are distracted."

Fain pinched the bridge of his nose. "We're escaping?" He groaned. "If it's not one problem, it's another..."

"I can help," Karna said as she tried to straighten her posture.

"Adelgis will fill you in on the details," I said. "But I have to do this alone. Just make sure you're ready to go."

Before anyone could say anything else, I stepped into the shadows and slid out of the arcanist barracks, and then moved around the side of the building. I emerged and gulped down air, my body shaking.

Although I had articulated my plan to Adelgis without trouble, the reality of the situation now sank into my chest and tightened my throat.

Luthair emerged from the shadows next to me. "My arcanist."

"You should go with the others," I said.

"You know I won't do that."

I took in a ragged breath. "Luthair, I don't know if…"

"Whatever darkness you face, you won't do it alone. I'll be there until the end. Perhaps it'll be my strength that makes the difference."

I rubbed at my neck and then hardened my determination. "Okay. First we need to locate the Mother of Shapeshifters."

48

ATLAS TORTOISE

The Excavation Site wasn't a complicated place. There were less than twenty buildings in total. Theasin had commanded the Mother of Shapeshifters be placed into the storehouse, and by process of elimination, I figured out which building it had to be. It was the only one with a watchman, and occasionally bones were removed from the larger piles and brought straight to it. Mostly fangs or fragments of claws—pieces of the apoch dragon that would make for deadly trinkets and artifacts.

I knelt down around the side of the storehouse, hidden from the watchman, and observed the workers going about their business. Even at night, with only lamplight to work by, they carried on.

What was my plan?

I wanted the Mother of Shapeshifters to escape without notice, but I feared that might be impossible. She was huge in Zelfree's memories, even when she changed shape, and if the linen covering her body was any indication of her health, she was wounded.

"My arcanist?" Luthair whispered from the darkness.

"We'll go in and free her," I said. "Hopefully we can piece together more of a plan afterward."

"As you wish."

I heard the crunch of dirt and ash. In one fluid motion, I stood, whirled around, and drew my blade. To my surprise, I saw nothing, but I had dealt with invisibility long enough to know I wasn't alone.

"Volke," Fain said, his disembodied voice quiet. "It's me."

"What're you doing here?" I asked.

"I want to help."

"Wait with the others."

"I'm immune to the plague," Fain said, his tone firm. "And I've done this all before."

"What're you talking about?"

"My brother left me—he said he would make everything right and then just took off. I get it. You're being noble. You're making a sacrifice. Well, let me be noble with you. This time, I don't want to be left behind."

We didn't have time to argue. I nodded and held out my hand. "We're going inside."

"Wraith, wait here. Warn us if anyone nears."

Fain, still invisible, placed his hand on mine. In the next instant, I dragged us into the shadows, traveling with the darkness and slipping under the door of the storehouse, completely undetected by the watchman. When we emerged, my veins burned with the magic use, and my head spun from the drain of taking a second person.

The inside of the building reminded me of a library. Shelves upon shelves had been constructed to house bone fragments and other disturbing "items." Dead mystical creatures sat beside the fragments of the apoch dragon, most of the corpses still fresh. A few were still in cages, and I wondered if they had been brought here alive and then allowed to slowly starve, forgotten by the workers of the dig site.

I didn't need to search the room—the Mother of Shapeshifters was too large to miss. She waited in the back, still wrapped tight in the white linen cloth. I jogged over to her and unsheathed Retribution. With a few quick strokes, I cut the ropes away, but my blade couldn't break the null-stone chains.

Fain's invisibly dropped as he grabbed a couple and yanked them to the side. The harder he pulled, the more blood sprouted from under the linen. Although it concerned me, I knew we needed to remove the chains as quickly as possible. Perhaps the Mother of Shapeshifters could heal once we had removed her restraints.

I sheathed my blade and grabbed the chains on the other side, working as quickly as possible. The nullstone clattered to the floor once removed, and I cringed, hoping beyond hope that if the watchman had heard, he thought it was nothing.

With shaky hands, I grabbed the linen cloth and removed it.

Fain grimaced, his eyes wide and his face paling.

I staggered back, my breath held.

In Zelfree's memories, I hadn't gotten a good look at the Mother of Shapeshifters, and at the time, I had been disappointed. Now I wished I could purge the image from my mind.

She was a mass of flesh, shiny and jiggly. It was as if... a small whale had been turned inside out, and all its bones had been removed. Everything writhed and moved, and I couldn't distinguish one organ from the next—they blended together like a plate of flesh-colored noodles.

Goosebumps ran the length of my arms.

Fain turned to me, his movements stiff. "*This* is what you wanted to save? You're a better man than me..."

I replied with a single forced chuckle.

Why wasn't she getting up?

Although I loathed examining her further, I spotted the problem. Several obsidian thorns had been stabbed into her undulating body. Those thorns were torture tools with hollow interiors. People would fill the inside with poison, venom, or other types of liquid meant to slowly drip out into the injury of their victim. I had seen one before—Calisto had used one on Master Zelfree. He had filled it with manticore venom, which prevented Zelfree from healing.

Had Calisto gotten his obsidian thorn from the Second Ascension? A piece of me wondered if he had been ordered to "bring in the Faceless."

I shook the thought from my head.

Not wanting to climb over the Mother of Shapeshifters, I manipulated the shadows to grab the five thorns protruding from her body. I didn't know what they were filled with, but I suspected they had to be the reason she wasn't moving.

A growl and bark caught my attention.

Fain turned to me. "That was Wraith. Someone's here." A moment later, he vanished.

Without needing to be told, Luthair merged with me, his shadows wrapping around my body and providing me a cold sense of vigor.

Sure enough, the door to the storehouse flew open. A unicorn arcanist strode inside, his arcanist mark glowing red. He wore a mix of metal and heavy leather armor, and when he moved, he seemed restricted in some ways, the bulk of his clothing almost too much. His unicorn entered afterward, its white coat patchy and disgusting, its horn broken, its eyes red, and its stomach so distended it looked as though it would burst at any moment.

When the unicorn arcanist caught sight of me, he withdrew a pistol.

If he fired it, I was certain everyone would come running. I used my terrors, and while the man and his eldrin flinched from the forced fears, I manipulated the shadows to grab the weapon from the man's hand.

My terrors didn't last as long as I would've liked, however. The unicorn arcanist shook away his dread and then evoked a powerful light. I squinted and stumbled back. The man withdrew a dagger from his belt and lunged for me, but as he rushed between shelves, an invisible Fain attacked. Fain had swung for his neck, but the blade of his dagger caught on the man's armor. He sliced a small part of the shoulder, between metal plates. The unicorn arcanist jumped back and hit the shelf.

The furniture toppled over, hitting the shelf next to it, which then fell and hit the next. Glass and bone fragments went everywhere. The hastily constructed shelves shattered upon impact with the floor, throwing wood splinters into the mix. The echoing crash and smash of metal on metal hurt my ears. There would be no hiding our current location.

The unicorn grunted and titled back its head. Its bloated gut ripped open along the underbelly, spilling out hundreds of tiny worms. To my horror, the worms flipped and writhed and splattered everywhere—but they didn't remain stationary. They wiggled and slithered with a frightening speed, rushing across the floor and heading straight for Fain.

Wrapping himself in invisibility, Fain tried to hide from the worms, but they found him regardless. They jumped and clung to everything, seemingly sticking by using their blood-coated bodies. Then they tried to burrow their way into Fain's flesh. He had to stop everything and swat them from his legs as he danced backward.

Wraith leapt into the storeroom and bit the unicorn. His frost appeared over the monster's legs and backside, hindering its movement.

Shouting from outside the storehouse drew my attention. We had run out of time.

I hadn't paid attention to the Mother of Shapeshifters the entire fight, and when a skeletal claw the size of a person reached over me, I almost attacked it with Retribution, not realizing what it belonged to. The claw extended out of the blob of flesh—being created as it went, the bone and tendons woven from the shapeshifter's body. Its reach was long and its arm gangly. With sword-like claws, the Mother of Shapeshifters swiped at the unicorn arcanist as the man was trying to free himself from the wreckage of the broken shelves.

The claws tore through the arcanist in a single swipe, slicing his armor and bones without difficulty.

"*Wait,*" I shouted, my double-voice haunting. "He's plague ridden!"

The unicorn arcanist—or what was left of him—splattered across the ruined shelves, his tainted blood mixing with everything here.

Fain evoked ice and frosted the many worms, killing them in one swift burst of magic. Then, before the Mother of Shapeshifters could intervene, he and Wraith attacked the plague-ridden unicorn. The beast tried to kick and gore, but Fain and Wraith went invisible and tore at it with claws, fangs, and daggers. The monster attempted to scream, but a slash to its neck had severed its windpipe. It collapsed to the ground, unable to breathe.

Both the unicorn and its arcanist were dead.

There was still another unicorn and its arcanist somewhere around the dig site, however. I had to stay alert.

The Mother of Shapeshifters pulled back her clawed hand, and before it was reabsorbed by the flesh, the blood-tainted claws fell off and melted across the floor.

Three eyes on the blob of flesh flew open, their gold irises locked on me.

"You're a friend of many shapeshifters," she said, her voice garbled, as though weak and waking from a long dream. "I can... smell them on you. My children."

"There isn't much time," I said. "You must escape now, while you still can."

The Mother of Shapeshifters closed her eyes and then shifted and lumped together. "Seek me out in the future, ally of shapeshifters. I will repay you."

Another clawed hand jutted out of her body, this one swiping at the ceiling. She tore a hole to the sky before pulling the clawed hand back into her nebulous shape.

Then her body exploded.

Not into fleshy chunks or blood, but into birds. Hundreds of crows, some with scarlet feathers on their underbelly, each with gold eyes and ebony wings. They flocked at terrifying speed, flapping their wings and swirling around before shooting for the hole. They poured out into the night, heading straight for the clouds, too fast to see properly.

Once the last of the birds disappeared out of the storeroom, my mind returned to the present. The other plague-ridden arcanists hadn't entered yet. Why? Were they waiting for us outside?

"*Volke*," Fain shouted while invisible, his voice near the door. "Look out!"

A torrent of red flames rushed into the storehouse through the door. I shadow-stepped away, but just barely, the heat from the attack causing me to sweat. When I emerged, I had to gulp down breath. My heart hammered against my ribs as another wave of fire forced its way indoors. The ferocity of the fire threatened to burn down the whole building in a matter of minutes.

Fain and Wraith got caught in the second wave, the flames licking across them and dispelling their invisibility. The front door was the only way in or out—but not for me.

I slipped through the shadows, grabbed both Fain and Wraith, and then dove back into the darkness. As a shadow, I slithered up the wall and out the hole in the ceiling, my speed much faster than I had ever gone before. I exited on the roof, not because it was the best place, but because the pain of my magic became too unbearable.

I crumpled onto the roof, my arms wrapped tightly around my gut, every inch of me hurting.

My arcanist, Luthair spoke telepathically. *Above us!*

I could sense it. Something plague-ridden.

Wind blasted across the roof of the storehouse, the pressure enough that the damaged building began to wobble. It wouldn't last.

The crack of gunfire echoed into the night. A bullet slammed into the wood next to me. I wasn't afraid of the gunshot, per se, but I feared the enemy's bullets could be coated in something.

Fain and Wraith couldn't withstand the wind and balance on the roof at the same time. They leapt off.

Although I still ached from my overuse of magic, I slipped into the shadows and emerged on the ground. With all my willpower, I brought Equalizer out of my shadow and turned my attention to the beast breathing flames into the storehouse.

It was the three-headed dog—the plague-ridden cerberus. The creature creating the gale-force winds was an equally plagued pegasus. The winged horse circled overhead while the heads of the cerberus puked fire into the building.

Fain lifted his hand and coated the ground in ice. The heads of the massive dog turned to us, its mouths dripping embers and pink saliva.

I stuffed my pistol with a bullet and then fired, no need for gunpowder. It hit the cerberus, ending its use of magic for a short bit.

Wraith and Fain ran forward. They both used their flesh manipulation to gouge out chunks of muscle from the dog's shoulder. Ice coated the monster afterward, and the beast bit at them with furious energy, missing with its many mouths as though it couldn't see them well enough.

More flames rushed into the area, covering the cerberus and both Fain and Wraith. I hadn't noticed the cerberus arcanist approach, but there he was—holding up his hand and evoking the fire with a smile on his twisted face.

Both Wraith and Fain had taken the brunt of their attack, their burnt flesh blackened and twisted. I manipulated the shadows to grab them and yank them away from our enemies.

More wind. It combined with the fire, spreading it everywhere.

I moved Fain and Wraith farther away, my shadows resistant to the fire thanks to my father's blue phoenix feather trinket.

"*Go,*" I commanded, my double-voice authoritative. "Tell the others it's time to leave."

I evoked my terrors, hoping to slow our enemies, but a barrier shimmered around them, protecting them from even my mental assaults. I recognized the shielding magic—it had come from the atlas tortoise.

The ground rumbled and quaked, and a moment later, the monster emerged from the dirt in a burst of impressive strength and movement. It clawed out of the ground and dragged its massive body over the rocks and mud, the plants on its shell acting as little arms that helped pull it up.

Half in the ground, and half above, the atlas tortoise laughed as it emerged, its shrill joy a torture to listen to.

"Look what we have here," it said, its voice much deeper than its laugh, each word rumbling over me. "*He's one of us. But he's... turned on his own kind. You know what that means...*" Its odd voice and cadence betrayed its plague-ridden state, even if the visual cues weren't there.

Another plague-ridden unicorn and its arcanist rode onto the scene, this one with an equally bloated belly that squirmed with inner worms.

"There're too many of them," Fain said. "You can't—"

I stood between him and the enemy arcanists. "This is all the guards. Now's your chance."

I hoped he understood—this was the best opportunity for them to escape. All the plague arcanists had their attention on me. And now that the Mother of Shapeshifters had been freed, my only goals were to kill as many of them as possible and wreck this dig site.

"Help Moonbeam," I said, the last of my mirth in those words. Karna could take care of herself, but I worried about Adelgis.

That seemed to resonate with Fain. He nodded before draping himself in invisibility. Wraith disappeared as well, leaving me alone with the four monster arcanists and their twisted eldrin.

"We'll track them down once we're done with you," the cerberus arcanist called out. He rubbed at the red glowing mark on his forehead, a devious smirk on his face. "My eldrin can hunt anything. You're as good as dead. Isn't that right, Tamoi?"

A lanky man climbed up onto the plague-ridden atlas tortoise, his armor accented with bits of jagged tortoise shell. "Don't tell him it's hopeless. I'd rather he figure that out for himself—slowly and painfully."

His giant eldrin chortled, its mirth rumbling the ground.

"*Brimstone*," the cerberus arcanist said to his eldrin. "Run down the others. We'll kill the knightmare arcanist in the meantime."

The three-headed dog barked and then attempted to run around me. I manipulated the shadows, intending to grab the monster's legs and stop him, but another flash of barriers sprang up, protecting the cerberus from my magic.

No!

I moved to step into the shadows—to get in front of the cerberus and physically block it—but the ground beneath my feet grabbed me. The atlas tortoise manipulated the dirt and rock, sinking me to my ankles, preventing me from escaping into the shadows.

Then the unicorn burst open its gut, spilling blood-coated worms across the area like a freakish birth of nightmares. The worms shot for me, and I struggled to move. They leapt onto my shadow-plate armor, attempting to burrow in. Some of them squirmed through the plates, getting to my flesh underneath.

The cerberus arcanist evoked flames, avoiding the ground with the worms. I lifted my cape, trying to block the attack, but I knew this wouldn't last. The heat washed over me for a brief moment. It felt like an eternity that my shadows and flesh burned, my thoughts focusing on every millisecond.

The pegasus flew around behind me, and a woman jumped off its back. The unicorn arcanist moved to block my escape on the side.

Tamoi, the atlas tortoise arcanist, laughed and snapped his fingers. "Gut him slow. We gotta pay him back for all the trouble he's caused."

"Let me... *eat him*," the tortoise said, its tongue crusty and long as it lulled out of its mouth. "One limb... at a time."

The pegasus arcanist fired her gun. The bullet slammed into my shadow armor, right in the middle of my back. The sting of the bullet affected me, even if it didn't pierce my skin.

Rage flooded my system. No matter how much it hurt or how much it would cost, I controlled all the shadows in the area, creating claws and hooks and knives—I ripped up the ground, freeing my ankles, and lashed out at everyone in the nearby vicinity. The barriers of the atlas tortoise protected them, but I freed myself in the meantime and slipped into the shadows, ridding myself of the blood worms and exiting out between warehouses.

"*Find him*," Tamoi shouted.

The plague-ridden monsters searched as I gulped down air, my body sore, my arm singed, and my spine pulsing. Their search was short-lived, however.

"We don't need to comb through the darkness," the cerberus arcanist said. "Just drag those other arcanists back here and get them screaming. The knightmare arcanist will crawl out of whatever hole he's in—trust me."

I scrunched my eyes shut. I had to do something or else

the entire group of those cutthroats would hunt down the others. But what? I found myself struggling to even think straight.

Luthair spoke in my mind, his voice comforting. *My arcanist, we must act. Escape or fight—any decision is better than indecision.*

I shook my head. A part of me already knew what needed to be done. Although I couldn't control it—although I manifested it incorrectly—I needed the added power from my eclipse aura.

It'll take too much from you, Luthair said. *If you fight these arcanists, you'll certainly die.*

I wasn't afraid of dying. I was afraid of monsters like these running free.

Without regret, I forced the magic to spill outward. It was night, and the moon was already covered by clouds, but the moment my false eclipse blanketed the area, even the lamps couldn't remain lit. The shadows moved of their own accord, snuffing out lights, darkening every corner, helping to ease my pain.

I turned my attention to the bonfires.

49

FOLLOWING STARS

Empowered by my eclipse aura, I slipped through the shadows and arrived at the edge of the dig site. The workers there were confused—stunned and frightened by my blanketing darkness. They murmured questions and pointed, all unable to see.

"Leave this area," I commanded, my double-voice booming over the excavation pit. "This will be your only warning."

Groping through the darkness, the workers fled from their equipment, dropping everything in their haste to escape.

The bonfires raged against the shadows, refusing to be snuffed. I suspected it was because they were fueled by magic, and that was perfect for my plans. With more power than I had ever put into the shadows, I willed them to grab at the side of the bonfire's pit, a wall made of latticed clay. My blue phoenix feather trinket helped keep my shadows solid, even when dealing with the flames. I ripped apart the massive sides, allowing the burning wood, bodies, and other materials to go spilling out.

Then I grabbed a nearby pulley system and flew it into the pit, smashing some of the bones in the process. Embers from the escaping bonfire fell onto the wooden pulley, and within a matter of moments, the blaze grew in size.

"There he is!" someone shouted.

I grabbed the clay siding of the second bonfire and broke it open as well, spilling the contents enough that embers floated to the trees on the edge of the clearing.

When I went to attack the third and final bonfire, a barrier formed around the outside, preventing me from destroying it.

The ground trembled with the movement of the atlas tortoise as it walked over to the dig site. The unicorn, pegasus, and cerberus arcanist joined Tamoi, all with their eldrins, except for the three-headed dog. The cerberus arcanist used his flame to illuminate the nearby area, but it wasn't nearly enough to fully see.

I tried using my terrors, enhanced by the false eclipse.

The barriers prevented them from taking hold.

When I manipulated the shadows, I tore apart half the dig site, ripping up dirt, equipment, and smashing crates— but nothing landed on the enemy arcanists due to the shields. Before I could shadow-step away, the atlas tortoise caught me again with the ground, this time sinking me down to my knees and causing the rocks to crush one of my ankles.

"*Kill him*," Tamoi shouted.

The cerberus arcanist flooded the area in flame. The pegasus whipped wind around, trapping the heat in an area and creating a mini firestorm.

The atlas tortoise had to be eliminated first if I had any chance of winning.

I threw Retribution and used the shadows to grab and wield it.

With a wide strike—that lacked all finesse, but had some power—I slashed at Tamoi. His barrier shimmered, but it couldn't block the black blade made from the apoch dragon. Retribution cut clean through his arm and chest, startling him enough that his eyes went wide. I had almost severed his arm. It remained attached only through threads of muscle and ligament.

The atlas tortoise laughed aloud, rumbling the ground. "He's made a weapon *from our best friend*. How ironic..."

"Wretch," Tamoi hissed.

He threw a pouch onto the ground, and it exploded into a fine mist of black and blue. I instantly recognized the decay dust, but I couldn't move to avoid it. The powder washed over me, and it ate away at my trinkets, destroying Equalizer and my blue phoenix feather.

The dust couldn't destroy Retribution, though. It was too powerful.

I used the shadows to strike again, this time at the cerberus arcanist. A barrier shimmered, but it was useless against my sword. The man clearly hadn't expected to be harmed—he didn't even attempt to dodge—and the deep slice to his upper leg caused him to scream.

He collapsed to one knee, his breathing heavy.

The pegasus and unicorn arcanist backed away, as though trying to predict my next actions. Instead, I willed the shadows to attack the atlas tortoise with Retribution. It was such a large target, I didn't need to focus as much to hit it, and instead, I clawed at the dirt, trying to free myself.

The worms rushed in, each trying to burrow into my flesh. My shadows grabbed and crushed them, the blood in their tiny bodies popping outward like fat zits.

Grunting a curse, the cerberus arcanist forced himself to stand. He unsheathed a sword and lunged for me. I tried my terrors, but the atlas tortoise still maintained its barriers. Unable to move, I attempted to trip the man with shadows, but it wasn't enough. Fortunately, the darkness affected his aim. He slashed down, cleaving into my shoulder with enhanced strength. The blade cut through Luthair and straight to my bone.

Which meant that Luthair was now infected with the plague. And unlike arcanists, who had months to attempt to cure themselves, mystical creatures had just a few short days before succumbing to madness.

I focused everything I had and forced Retribution to turn around in a wide arc. The cerberus arcanist's vision was impaired—and I sliced straight through his neck, removing his head. The red glow of his arcanist mark died as he did.

Enraged, I tore open the ground and freed myself. One of my ankles had been mangled, and I couldn't stand correctly, but I still managed to slip into the shadows and emerge near the unicorn. It hadn't seen me move, which meant I had a second to catch my breath.

I felt my magic slipping.

My eclipse aura would end soon, and then I'd have nothing.

I had only managed to deal with one of the enemy arcanists, but he wasn't the most important. The Autarch's enforcer and atlas tortoise had to die. But could I handle that? Luthair was plague-ridden, and my own rationality was fleeting. Everything hurt, and if I somehow managed to kill the rest of the arcanists, I suspected I'd still die. Could I even lift my injured shoulder? My pain continued to grow— the bullet had done something to me.

My arcanist... We could flee.

No.

It was more important that I finish this. A part of me wanted Luthair to escape, if only so I could protect one more person.

I would rather die than watch another arcanist fall.

His determination fueled my own.

Swallowing air, I shadow-stepped closer to the dig site and used Retribution to continue my work. Tamoi couldn't use his barriers to stop me, and I sliced the pulleys and collapsed the supporting structures. With as much magic as I had left, I spread the bonfire, catching more trees on fire. Although it hurt—I could feel the burning through the shadows now that my phoenix feather was gone—I made sure the buildings got caught in the devastation as well.

I wouldn't allow the Second Ascension to have any more of their weapons.

The atlas tortoise grabbed me with the ground, crushing my already broken ankle. Thorn-covered vines reached out of the ground this time, wrapping around my legs. I knew it hurt, but I didn't care. I couldn't really feel anything.

My unstable eclipse aura faded, allowing the light from the fires to return in full force. The illumination stung.

"You're a fool," Tamoi said. "I'll just rebuild, ya know. My magic *created* this dig site. I can do it again."

His atlas tortoise took a few steps closer, enough that the ground quaked and I felt it through my trapped feet. Its vines dragged me down, the rocks slowly twisting around my thighs.

"We'll rebuild on top *of your corpse*," the tortoise added, a snicker in its words.

This wasn't a matter of rebuilding—it was an issue of time.

The Autarch had made it clear. He needed the world

serpent to fulfill his promises and to gain control of far-off kingdoms. The Frith Guild was already aware of the world serpent, and they were poised to get it. As long as I slowed the Second Ascension here, I would help the Frith Guild snatch the god-creatures away from our enemies.

That was the most important thing. I had to weaken them. I had to cull their numbers and wreck their operations. I had to protect Fain, Adelgis, and Karna.

And when I feared I couldn't summon the strength to do so, I thought of the stars.

It didn't matter how black the night became—the stars would always be there, a flicker of light in a sea of darkness. They maintained their course through the sky, stalwart and unyielding, even if they were never recognized for their efforts. Like all great heroes.

I just needed a fraction of that dedication. Because it didn't matter what happened to me. It didn't matter if they fed me to their monster eldrin or used my bones to repair this site. It was too important that the Second Ascension fail to obtain the world serpent and too important that the people I cared for were safe.

I had come here knowing I would die, and now I finally felt okay with it.

I would be stalwart and unyielding until the bitter end.

Without warning, my forehead burned, and my vision blurred white. For a sliver of a second, it felt as though I were connected to something *infinite*—something so grand and powerful, it could only be described as *endless possibility*. But just as fast as I had experienced it, the feeling was gone, leaving me with a fraction of that potential.

I breathed deep and felt better than I had in months.

Power, and a sense of tranquility, overcame me. What

had once been overwhelming a moment ago no longer seemed impossible.

"What the?" Tamoi barked.

"Curse the abyssal hells," the unicorn arcanist muttered. "It's a true form knightmare."

I had never been so calm, and with my sudden flood of strength, I focused on recreating my eclipse aura. It happened almost without effort—the darkness returned, this time without flaw. Further fueled by my own aura, I manipulated the shadows to help me out of the ground. Claws and hooks ripped the rocks and vines away, freeing me from my earthly prison. I shadow-stepped out of the ditch, my ankle still broken, but the pain masked by my newfound wellspring of strength.

Tamoi struck his atlas tortoise on the side of its massive head. "I don't care what it takes—*destroy him before he does anything!*"

The atlas tortoise gleefully laughed, the bubbles of its voice a harsh juxtaposition when compared to its dead, jiggling eyes. The monster slammed its legs on the ground, manifesting an earthquake. The ground broke and shattered, boulders forced from the dirt, jutting upward. Holes opened up and then twisted shut, creating pits that would surely crush someone if they fell.

The thorn-covered vines lashed out, acting of their own accord and indiscriminately grabbing everything in the nearby area to drag into the crushing holes. Three latched onto the plague-ridden unicorn. Five others grabbed its vile arcanist. Both were dragged into a crag and then crunched to death a moment later, the splatter of weak flesh a harrowing sound.

When the vines came for me, I willed Retribution back into my hand and sliced them with little effort. More vines came, but my shadows sliced those as well, even without my active participation. None of the plants could get near me.

We can't stay on the ground, Luthair said, his voice as calm as I felt. *The atlas tortoise can sense our movements through tremors, even in the dark.*

I hadn't realized until then, but my armor was no longer the standard plate mail. It resembled heavy armor, covering me completely from head to toe, but the shadows themselves were shifting and flowing, like a waterfall of ink washing over me. And when I needed to avoid the ground, a skeletal set of wings ripped out of my back, formed by darkness and hardened by my magic. My cape ripped in half down the middle and then laced itself over the bat-like wings, becoming the leather webbing between "bones."

The darkness of the eclipse aura made it feel as if even the sky was part of the shadows, like I was underwater and everything was something I could shift across. When I flapped my wings, it took me higher than I expected, every shadow aiding in my ascent.

My sollerets—the plate armor boots knights wore— were tipped with hooked claws, which would make it easier to grip upon landing. My new armor shaped itself to the moment, crafting the perfect accessories.

Although in awe of what was happening, I didn't lose sight of my objective.

I dove for Tamoi.

His barriers were still up, but they just couldn't stop Retribution. I stabbed him through the gut, the force of my blow much more than I had been expecting. Tamoi stumbled off his eldrin's head, shock clear on his contorted face.

The atlas tortoise snapped its giant mouth up at me. It clipped my injured leg, but my liquid shadow armor reacted in a fraction of a second, hardening over my shin, creating thicker plates of metal, protecting me as best it could. Then, when the tortoise pulled back, spikes of darkness shot out from my armor, punishing the monster for daring to get close to me.

I thrust down with my sword, plunging it through the skull of the plague-ridden atlas tortoise, burying the blade to the hilt. The beast thrashed its head away, taking my weapon with it, but it was clear it had no sense of what was happening anymore.

The earthquake stopped, but the crash of its feet kept everything rumbling long after.

I used the moment to manipulate the shadows around the entire dig site. I ripped down the last of the pulleys and caught fire to everything made of wood. My eclipse snuffed out the smallest embers, but the magic-fueled fire refused to quit. Soon it would consume everything here.

The atlas tortoise stumbled to its side.

Tamoi picked himself off the ground, his footing unsteady due to the jagged rocks jutting out of the dirt. I flew low and lunged for him, my sense of flight similar to swimming. Although I didn't have my sword, my armor hardened at the tips of my gauntlet, forming claws as if the shadows knew ahead of time what I needed.

I slashed at the man, cutting into the injuries I had already given him. The darkness around him lashed out as well, every shadow cutting and clawing. It was too much for him, and Tamoi collapsed to the ground, his many injures gushing tainted blood.

"You're finished," I said, my voice mixed with Luthair's both confident and smooth.

The pegasus created a gale force wind, but without the atlas tortoise protection, she wasn't immune to my terrors anymore.

I held up a hand and forced her greatest fears into her head. She and her pegasus fell from the sky, hitting the rocks below. The moment she hit dirt, my shadows clawed at her broken bones.

And that was the end of her.

The atlas tortoise struggled—it refused to die so easily—and I used the shadows to rip my blade from its skull and stab again. Only then did it laugh and collapse, its body heavy enough that it shook everything a second time.

The tombstones fell off its shell and shattered on the ground. It was only then that I noticed there was another creature on its back—a silver kirin. It glowed, even in my eclipse aura, its crystal unicorn-like horn glittering.

I lifted a hand to evoke my terrors and kill it, but I stopped before I summoned the magic.

Eventide had said they were weak in personal combat and that they'd only ever bond with one arcanist. This creature was no longer a threat. It wouldn't even talk to anyone else but the dead Tamoi.

I lowered my hand, satisfied by the flames all around me.

The dig site had been destroyed and the Autarch's arcanists slain.

There was still the issue of a single cerberus, but a part of me knew that Adelgis, Fain, and Karna could handle one eldrin, even if plague-ridden. And if not, I would hopefully find them soon.

My aura faded, returning the area to a normal night.

My cape stitched itself back together, and the skeleton of the wings melted back into my armor. I caught my breath the moment I saw the inner lining of my cape. It had once been crimson red, but now...

It was the night sky, marked with hundreds of tiny stars.

50

A DYING WISH

Flames danced all around me, and black smoke billowed into the sky.

Despite the danger, I stood and watched, all my weight on one foot. My hazy thoughts cleared for a moment as I glanced around. What else was there to do? I gathered up Retribution and the sheath my father had crafted, but that was it. The bodies of my enemies could burn, and the remaining kirin could do what it wanted, I no longer cared.

I fled the Excavation Site, avoiding the fire as best as I could as I hobbled toward the woods. Most of the trees were ablaze in red and orange, and I had to shadow-step through the worst of it before I managed to find any place clear.

The farther I went, the more I realized I wasn't okay.

My whole body ached.

Despite the fact that I had somehow managed to gain a true form of my eldrin, it hadn't cured my injuries. The pegasus arcanist had shot me with *something*, and the sting of that bullet radiated from my spine, all the way down my good leg. My broken ankle throbbed, the agony growing with each moment. My shoulder pain spread to my neck, which meant even a slight turn of my head reminded me of my mortality.

I couldn't slow, though. I hurried through the woods, slipping through the shadows whenever I could.

At least my magic no longer hurt. The opposite, in fact. When I entered the darkness, I felt more at home than outside of it. The cold presence of night reassured me and gave me the strength to keep going.

But where was I going?

I rushed through the woods, hobbling and diving through shadows, passing tree after tree. I never found the road, just more thickets and shrubs.

My arcanist, Luthair said. *We're bleeding.*

I stopped and leaned against the color-drained trunk of a tree, my heart rate high. Sure enough, blood wept from my injured leg and shoulder, leaving a trail of crimson in my wake.

My armor, however, didn't look broken or busted. It still flowed like an ever-living metal, fixing itself and moving as needed. I took a moment to touch my breastplate, surprised by the hardness. My cape was now a cloak, capable of wrapping around my shoulders and shielding me from the winds of the night.

When I brought my hand over my helmet, I noticed horns that circled around the side, similar to a half-crown or set of laurels. And the face... There wasn't a visor or opening for my eyes. It was just a mask, shielding me completely. I could see through the shadow plate, though. My vision had never been better.

"Is our blood still tainted?" I asked aloud, my double-voice a comfort.

Theasin claimed that true form arcanists were immune. I assume that means we are as well.

I nodded and pushed away from the tree. With each dive into the shadows, I made my way farther and farther from the Excavation Site, but the moment the sun crested the horizon, I knew I had gone the wrong way. Nothing looked familiar, and when the rays of a new day pierced through the clouds, my magic weakened.

My breath came in ragged bursts.

The pain of my injuries prevented me from focusing enough to even shadow-step. I stumbled between one tree and the next, unable to put any weight on my broken ankle. Luthair never unmerged, which helped keep me up, but I almost wished he would.

"I think... we're dying," I said.

That would be ironic. Right after getting cured of the plague—right after gaining my true form with Luthair—I would still die anyway. I actually chuckled aloud.

I always said I had bad luck.

You mustn't give up.

I shook my head. "I won't. Not now, not ever. But..." I laughed again as I pushed away from one tree and went to the other. "We're in the middle of nowhere. I suspect the others think I'm dead. And weren't there plague creatures in these woods?"

They're weak grifter crows.

"I don't know if I could fight them off in my current state."

The morning sun filtered down through the grey leaves. My vision blurred, and the hue of light made it seem as though everything were silhouetted in a halo-glow. Perhaps the bullet had been poisoned? Even though it hadn't broken through the armor, perhaps all it had needed was contact.

When the trees thinned, I slipped off one trunk and

collapsed onto my good knee. I knelt there, in the woods, uncertain if I could stand again.

Even my lungs hurt. With each shallow breath, a part of me wanted to stop.

Despite that, I couldn't bring myself to be upset. The Excavation Site was ablaze, but I had gone far enough away that this portion of the woods seemed peaceful. My magic no longer hurt, and I didn't have the arcane plague—if I weren't taking my last few breaths, everything would be perfect.

No.

Not perfect.

A new kind of pain stabbed at my heart.

I wished the others were here. Everyone from the Frith Guild—Illia, Hexa, Atty, Zaxis, Adelgis, Zelfree, Fain, Gillie —and everyone from the *Sun Chaser*—Captain Devlin, my father, Vethica, Karna, Biyu—plus all their eldrin, from Akhet to Nicholin. I barely knew people like Guildmaster Eventide or Tammi, but I wanted them here, too. Seeing them would make this moment perfect.

"Volke?"

I lifted my head, my vision still blurry.

Illia stepped between two trees, her one eye wide.

She didn't look like I remembered. She seemed taller. Or perhaps it was because I was kneeling—it was hard to tell, and I suspected I was becoming delirious. I knew she couldn't be here. It was impossible. This was a figment of my imagination, brought about by the slow hands of death.

But even if that were the case, I had to hand it to death. This was a pretty spectacular delusion.

Illia hesitantly stepped forward.

She wore a sailing outfit, complete with loose trousers, a thick belt, and a long coat. An eyepatch—specially made by

Gravekeeper William, with the design of a ferret-like rizzel —covered her missing right eye. Her wavy hair had been pulled back into a tight ponytail, showing off her slender neck and sharp jaw. She always hated it when I told her that she was beautiful, but that was the only description I could think of in that moment.

"What happened to you?" Illia asked as she knelt beside me.

Luthair melted away from me, unmerging and returning to the shadows. His loss of power left me weaker than before, but at least there was nothing between Illia and me.

She stared at my forehead, her mouth falling open.

I half fell forward, and Illia caught me.

She felt real. At least, from what I remembered. Perhaps a bit sturdier than before.

I wrapped my arms around her and exhaled, agony still coursing through my body, but my optimism never dying. She smelled of salt and wind, just like the ocean. I tightened my grip, burying my face in her shoulder, unwilling to let go.

With a smile, I muttered, "I'm sorry I didn't say this before I left, but... I love you. I always have."

"Volke," Illia said, her voice shaky. She returned my embrace, her grip just as tight. "I love you, too," she whispered. "I want to say it all the time, but..."

"I'm sorry. I should've done a lot of things differently. Now I'll never get the chance."

"What's wrong?" she asked, her fingers twisting into the fabric of my bloody shirt.

"I'm dying."

"*What?*"

"It's okay," I said, with a single chuckle. "I've come to terms with it. I did what I had to do."

Illia broke our embrace and pushed away from me,

her expression hardening into determination. "Oh, no you're not. I didn't search half the world just so you could die in my arms, dammit." She stood and rubbed at her eye. "I'll be right back." Without another word, she disappeared from the clearing in a flash of sparkles, her rizzel teleportation better than I remembered.

"I don't think that was a delusion," Luthair said from the darkness.

Before I had gained a true form, I could always spot Luthair among the normal shadows. Now I couldn't. Luthair might as well have been invisible.

"How did she find us?" I asked, shaking my head. "This just... it can't be real."

A part of me wanted to tell delusion-Illia all about the world serpent and the Autarch's plans, but that would be a waste of my breath. Wouldn't it?

Another flash and Illia reappeared, this time accompanied by her eldrin, Nicholin, along with Zaxis and his phoenix eldrin, Forsythe.

Nicholin sat perched on Illia's shoulder, his white fur and silver stripes shimmering in the morning light. He stared at me with bright blue eyes, his tail swishing.

"Volke?" he asked. "Is it really you?" He rubbed his tiny hands over his ferret face. "Your arcanist mark!"

Zaxis stepped forward and then knelt beside me, his expression just as shocked and bewildered. "Why do you always do this to me?" he finally said, his voice low and his tone accusing.

He wore an outfit I had never seen before. It looked like scaled leather armor, fitted tight over his torso and then loose over his legs. The scales were a dark red, similar to bricks, and they shone as though wet, even though they were dry. His armor didn't have sleeves, but he wore steel bracers over his forearms.

Zaxis grabbed me, and I was instantly reminded of his strength. I never should've forgotten—I could see his large shoulders and biceps as clear as day—I had just been more impressed with his new armor.

His phoenix magic washed over me, healing injuries and giving me strength.

Forsythe hopped close and stared with gold eyes. Like all phoenixes, he had the body of a heron and the curved and lustrous tail of a peacock. He was red and orange and scarlet, and flames flared beneath his feathers. Soot fell whenever he moved, even when he tilted his head as he examined me.

"You've grown," Forsythe said, his voice regal. "I'm so happy we found you."

My injured shoulder and broken ankle no longer ached, but the pain in my spine remained.

"I think I'm poisoned," I said.

Zaxis stared at me, his red hair longer than I remembered, the dark green of his eyes alight with amusement. "You don't sound like you're dying."

"I feel better, thanks to you." My vision had returned to normal. "But I still think I'm poisoned."

Zaxis grabbed my upper arm and pulled me into a standing position as he got to his feet. I was a little taller than him—perhaps an inch or two—but he was definitely bulkier with muscle.

To my surprise, he yanked me into a tight hug, his hands grazing the injury on my back. I sucked in air through my teeth, but tentatively returned the gesture regardless.

Nicholin teleported from Illia's shoulder to mine. Then he snuggled against my neck, hugging me with little arms, emitting an odd purring noise. Forsythe hopped over to my legs and nuzzled against the side of my shin, the warmth of his flame body almost too much to bear.

After a long moment, Zaxis released me and then stepped back. "Okay, enough of this. You aren't *dying*. Get ahold of yourself. And even if you are, Master Zelfree brought medicine from the Grand Apothecary. It's back on the airship. We don't need to sit around crying over you."

"You were crying?" I quipped.

"*Of course not.*" His face reddened as he frowned. "Dammit, Volke—you made Illia worry. Now isn't the time for jokes."

I motioned to the darkness around the trees. "You should heal Luthair. He was just as injured as I was."

Luthair emerged from the darkness, forming up as a complete set of plate armor, along with a cloak and cowl. I admired his appearance more than when I was wearing him. The living armor, running like water, gave him a beyond mystical appearance. The horns of the helmet seemed more imposing when looking on from the front— and they reminded me of the sovereign dragon. The stars inside the cloak twinkled, just at the edge of my perception.

Zaxis's eyes went wide, and his eyebrows shot for his hairline.

Silence reigned for a few moments, and then Zaxis stepped forward and healed Luthair with his magic. The armor didn't seem to change, but I knew it helped.

Nicholin smacked the side of my face with his tail. "How dare you."

I glanced over to the shoulder he sat on, uncertain of what to say.

"You made us run all over the place! That wasn't easy,

mind you. And I'm a creature that teleports. You know you've messed up when I say you shift around too much."

Now that I felt better, and my vision was crisp, I couldn't claim this was a delusion. I turned my attention to Illia, my eyebrows knitted. "How did you find me? I'm literally in the middle of nowhere."

She reached into her coat pocket and withdrew the Occult Compass. The eye of the all-seeing sphinx was under the needle. "I used this to search for knightmares," she said. "Since there are so few in the world, we managed to track your movement once we got far enough away from Thronehold and the last of the Steel Thorn Inquisitors Guild."

I smiled to myself, almost in disbelief. This was probably real, then. I had forgotten that Illia kept the Occult Compass—she could find any mystical creature, especially those that were rare, like knightmares.

"I thought you needed a piece of the mystical creature you were searching for?" I asked, still a little confused about how she managed to find me.

"We have a knightmare," Illia said as she rubbed her eyepatch. Before I could ask questions, she motioned for me to move closer. "Perhaps we should return to everyone. They're worried about you."

As a group, we gathered around Illia, even Luthair in his new form.

When last I saw Illia, she had struggled to take more than herself through teleportation, but now it seemed she was more confident. She placed a hand on Zaxis and me, and Nicholin jumped to Luthair's feet and reached out to Forsythe.

Illia's magic took hold of me, and for a brief moment, I had the ability to reject her. I allowed her teleportation to work, and we were whisked away from the woods. We didn't go far, though, before reappearing. Illia had to take a breath and do it again. And then two more times. It reminded me of my shadow-stepping ability. I could only go so far before I had to reemerge. Teleporting was probably a bit faster, though, and the sensation of popping in and out of existence was interesting.

I just... couldn't stop grinning.

When we finally arrived at our destination, I only had a moment to take in my surroundings before a person-sized hydra with four heads came charging at me. The combat-hardened part of me wanted to pull my blade, but I knew who it was—Raisen, Hexa's eldrin.

He had gotten big.

And then he collided with me, his alligator-shaped body and long necks an awkward mass of muscle and scales. I fell back onto grass as Raisen climbed on top of me with stumpy legs, his 250 pounds making it harder to breathe. His scales were curved at the tips, which meant his whole body was pokey. I didn't reach up to hug him. Instead, all four of Raisen's heads forked out their tongues across my face. Last I had seen him, he only had *two* heads.

Raisen hissed.

"There you are," one head said.

"We've missed you," said the second.

The third licked into my ear. "I'm the oldest. I've missed you the most."

"*I'm* the oldest," snapped the last head.

All his voices were raspy and somewhat angry, but his affections couldn't be denied.

A moment later, I was swarmed with more mystical creatures. Titania the phoenix, Traces the mimic, Akhet the khepera, and even Tine the blue phoenix. They pushed and shoved and snuggled close, each trying to pile on top of me.

Then Mesos the roc drew near, her huge bird-like body casting a shadow over us. She fell forward, covering everyone in her golden feathers, to the point I found it difficult to breathe. Was this how a roc chick felt?

"I-I'm happy to see you all, too," I said, trying not to get roc feathers in my mouth as I spoke. "I need to get up, though!"

One at a time, they shuffled off, allowing me to stand.

It was only then that I spotted Atty. She stood nearby, a vial in her hands, her blue eyes wide. I brushed off the feathers and dirt, but she didn't wait until I had finished—Atty stepped forward and hugged me tight, a sigh of relief escaping her for just a moment.

"Everyone was so worried," she said. "*I* was worried."

I had missed the sound of her voice. I returned her hug, almost in disbelief that I was here with her and not dead in a ditch from the arcane plague. "I'm so happy to see you," I said. "I thought I never would, and... Well, I'm just so happy I get another chance. Things will be different this time."

Atty broke off the hug, her face pink. She placed the vial into the palm of my hand. "This is medicine from the Grand Apothecary. Illia rushed in and said you were dying, so I grabbed this, and—"

I uncorked the vial and drank the contents. Gillie, the Grand Apothecary, had never done me wrong, and I didn't want to discuss my illness any longer.

Atty smoothed her white shirt and trousers. Somehow, she always seemed pure and bright. Her gold hair fell around her face in slight curls, and she stood with a feminine poise. I had been too busy admiring her to notice the other person rushing up on me.

Hexa slammed into my side and then squeezed me tight. Her cinnamon hair, curly to the point it bounced, had been poorly restrained with a hair tie. Bits of it poked out everywhere, including a strand that hit me in the eye when I tried to turn and face her.

"You're the worst," Hexa said. "I don't care if you're carrying the plague. You shouldn't leave us. Do you know what you did to Illia?"

"I'm not plague-ridden anymore," I said.

Hexa instantly released me and took a step back. Like Zaxis, she wore armor without any sleeves. Unlike Zaxis, she had scars from her shoulders down to her wrists, some clean and straight, some gnarly.

"Your arcanist mark is glowing," Hexa muttered, unable to take her eyes off of it.

I glanced past her and held my breath. There it was. The *Sun Chaser* in all its glory. Winds swept around underneath it, disturbing the nearby trees and grass. Captain Devlin waited near the rope ladder, his arms crossed.

Master Zelfree stood next to him, his expression a lot more jovial than I had ever seen from him.

"Volke!" someone shouted. "It's really you!"

A girl ran toward me, her long white hair fluttering behind her. She never slowed her pace, and when she finally reached me, she collided with my chest, embracing me as though she couldn't believe I was real. Fortunately, she weighed much less than the others. She impacted on me like a leaf on a brick wall.

I held her, half confused.

She was Princess Evianna, from the Argo Empire.

Her shadow swirled around her feet. "My arcanist," the darkness said. "You should give him time to recover."

Evianna's knightmare! Of course. Now I understood how Illia had used her Occult Compass to find me. It all came together, and again, I couldn't help but smile.

"It's okay, Layshl," Evianna muttered as she pressed her face against my chest. "I know Volke missed me, too. And now that he's back, he can start training me."

I patted Evianna's back, my confusion returning. Before I had left to find the cure to the arcane plague, my relationship with Evianna hadn't been the greatest. She blamed me for a great many things and seemingly hated my presence. Now she was elated to see me? When did this change happen?

I suspected this was better than before. Perhaps I shouldn't remind her of her past feelings.

Illia walked up behind me and placed her hands on my shoulders. Then she guided me toward the rope hanging from the *Sun Chaser*, her steps quick and her touch light. I suspected she could've teleported us to the deck, but this seemed more about approaching Captain Devlin and Zelfree.

Evianna held onto one of my arms, never letting go.

And on top of that, the mystical creatures swarmed around us, Forsythe and Nicholin adding to the mix. They turned their attention to Luthair, all of them chatting amongst themselves as they touched his cloak and liquid-like armor. Everywhere I turned, there was someone or something crowding close.

When I neared Devlin, I gave him a nod. "I thought you couldn't take the *Sun Chaser* through the Lightning Straits?"

He scratched at his chin-strap beard. "Well, that was before some crazy arcanist from the Frith Guild came demanding I take him to you." He jutted a thumb at Zelfree. "And apparently he knows his way through those thunderstorms. We made it through, even if we had to avoid some plague-ridden thunderbirds in the process."

Zelfree stepped forward. He didn't say anything—he just

glanced at my forehead and then to Luthair. I could see in his eyes that he understood what had happened. When he returned his gaze to me, he shoved his hands into his coat pockets. "Illia said you were dying."

"I think I was poisoned," I said, though my high spirts made it difficult to feel anything other than joy. "I'm better now."

"Atty give you the medicine?"

I turned and found Atty at my side. I nodded and laughed and returned my attention to Zelfree. "That's right." But I shook my head, dispelling my good mood. Seeing Zelfree reminded me that I wasn't out of the woods yet. I stepped closer to him, my panic returning. "Master Zelfree, I have important news to tell you. The Second Ascension *needs* the world serpent for their plans. And, worst of all, Guildmaster Eventide is in trouble. The Autarch sent an assassin, and—"

Zelfree pointed up to the airship.

Adelgis, Fain, Vethica, and Karna stared down at us.

"Adelgis contacted me via telepathy," Zelfree stated. "He told me about the Second Ascension."

"No, I don't think you understand. The man who murdered Queen Velleta is going after Eventide. It's the king basilisk arcanist."

Zelfree nodded along with my words, his expression grim. "Well, then, let's get you on the ship. If we fly, perhaps we can beat the Second Ascension to wherever they're going."

"There's more," I said. "They found a second god-creature. And if they get their hands on the world serpent, they'll can take control of six nations, and—"

Zelfree placed a hand on my shoulder. "One step at a time," he said, firm and confident. "Eventide is searching for someone to bond with the world serpent right now. We're going to meet up with her and use that Occult Compass to get to the world serpent first, okay? Now take a deep breath and get on the damn airship."

"But the assassin—"

"Don't worry. Eventide has handled things worse than a king basilisk arcanist."

I inhaled and then exhaled. "Right. Thank you. Let's go."

Zelfree motioned to the rope ladder. "I'm glad you're okay."

When I approached the ladder, he grabbed my upper arm, his grip tight.

"And we're also going to have a talk about how none of my apprentices listen to a damn word I have to say." He gave me a sardonic glower. "*You're* supposed to be the good one."

While I wanted nothing more than to joke with him, there was one final thing that bothered me. I held the rope tight as I returned his stare.

"Above all else, we need to beat the Second Ascension to the world serpent. All their plans hinge on it."

ABOUT THE AUTHOR

Shami Stovall is a multi-award-winning author of fantasy and science fiction, with several best-selling novels under her belt. Before that, she taught history and criminal law at the college level, and loved every second. When she's not reading fascinating articles and books about ancient China or the Byzantine Empire, Stovall can be found playing way too many video games, especially RPGs and tactics simulators.

If you want to contact her, you can do so at the following locations:

Website: https://sastovallauthor.com
Twitter: @GameOverStation
Facebook: www.facebook.com/SAStovall
Email: s.adelle.s@gmail.com